# ALSO BY MEGAN BOWEN

Like Home

# Ghosted

# GHOSTED

---

THE RAVENWOOD SERIES
BOOK 1

MEGAN BOWEN

E-Book ISBN: 979-8-9918777-2-5

Paperback ISBN: 979-8-9918777-3-2

Book Cover design by Sam Palencia

Copy/Line Editing by Megan Carver

*For anyone who has ever hidden the most interesting part of themselves to fit in.*

# AUTHOR'S NOTE

Hello, dear reader. Welcome to the small town of Ravenwood where the hot chocolate is always delicious and ghosts are most definitely real.

*Ghosted* is a story about finding love, even when the circumstances seem impossible. It's also about finding yourself and embracing your own brand of weird. It's a story that combines some of my favorite things: ghosts and love stories.

This story is for anyone who has ever felt like they didn't fit in. Who felt like they had to make themselves smaller to fit in the box others gave them. This story is *also* for anyone who has ever thought that having a ghost boyfriend would be kind of hot (me too).

While *Ghosted* has a guaranteed happily ever after, there is some content that some readers may find upsetting. Here's a list of what to look out for if you have any sensitivities: death, mentions of suicide, mentions of drugging, explicit sexual content, explicit language, brief mention of abuse, and off-page murder. If you're someone who prefers to skip spice, be sure to check out my website for a list of pages to avoid.

Despite all of the listed triggers, *Ghosted* is first and foremost a love story with a lot of humor sprinkled in. Death is one of the inevitabilities we all live with, so I decided to make it fun. Otherwise, I'd spiral down into an existential crisis, and no one wants that. So here, in Ravenwood, the ghosts are hot and funny (for the most part), and things work out for the better.

As always, please take care of yourself first. Otherwise, may your blanket by cozy and your drink be as hot as Dean. Happy reading!

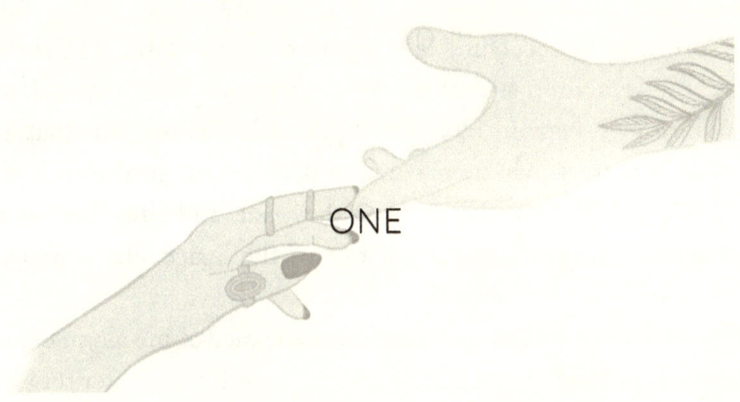


SCRATCH, *scratch*. I huff out a breath and roll over in bed, desperately clinging to the dream I'm having. Something about a hot pirate and shivering his timbers.

*Creeeaaaaak*. My eyes snap open against my will. Without moving my head, my gaze slowly roves around the darkened corners of my bedroom. A chill rolls down my spine in an infuriatingly wakeful wave. I defiantly close my eyes again and try to summon thoughts of Jack Sparrow.

"I know you're awake," an elderly man's voice half-whispers. I screw my eyes shut even tighter. Sometimes, if I ignore them, they'll leave me the hell alone. "Hey, I'm talking to you. Do you know how long I've been waiting to find someone who can help me?"

At that, I heave a sigh. Being helpful is my drug of choice. I have a downright Pavlovian response to the phrase, "I need help." Even if the recipient of said help is, well... dead. However, I usually prefer to be helpful in the light of day and not while I'm having a sexy pirate dream in the middle of the night.

I sit up in bed, clutching the covers a little closer. The room really does drop a few degrees when the dead make their appearance known. Hollywood gets a lot wrong, but that at least is correct. My mom's theory is that they need to pull as much energy from the room as they can, and since heat is a form of energy, they suck it out of the space like a phone plugged into its charger.

"Okay, okay. I'm up." I squint at the face of my alarm clock on my nightstand and grimace when I see it's just after four in the morning. "Couldn't you have waited until like, seven? That's when I have to be up for work, anyway." I shoot a glare at the older man standing at the foot of my bed.

He looks like any other octogenarian. Pressed slacks, tucked-in green polo shirt, and a wrinkled face topped with thick wire eyeglasses. Despite what TV wants you to think, not all ghosts are from the Victorian era. Most of them are indistinguishable from the people around us.

It's only if you pay very close attention that you'll see the odd things about them. Only then would you guess that something wasn't quite right. For one thing, the environment never affects them. Their hair doesn't blow in the breeze, and they aren't bothered by the temperature. They also have a slightly *not-there* quality that's hard to notice unless you know where to look. They're a bit hazy around the edges, but only if you concentrate a little too hard on them.

I have what I like to think of as extra cones in my eyes, letting me see a frequency that others can't. Like a spider seeing ultraviolet light. Just because others can't see it doesn't mean it's not there.

"I've been waiting forever to find someone who can help me. Excuse me if I didn't want to wait for you to get your beauty rest." He crosses his arms over his pudgy middle and scowls at me. Men. Always inconsiderate, even in death.

I scrub a hand over my face, chug the half-full glass of stagnant water on my nightstand, and click on the bedside light. "Okay. I'm awake. I'm listening. What do you need?"

He shifts his weight a little when my full attention is on him. I raise an eyebrow, and he says, "Sorry, you can't imagine how strange it is to have a two-way conversation with the living. It's been so long... I'm used to talking to people who can't hear me." I nod my understanding and relax a little. Being a medium means I've had some iteration of this conversation more than a few times.

Even though it's inconvenient for me, I can't imagine being on the other side. Being unable to move on, and then finally finding someone who can see and hear you. That's why I help as many as I can. I don't know what comes after, but it has to be better than being stuck in limbo.

He looks off somewhere behind me, and his face crumples before he says, "I just—I need you to tell my son that I buried..." His eyes narrow at me as he trails off. "Wait, you aren't going to con me, are you? Is there some code you sort live by?"

I scowl, annoyed at being awoken and accused of criminal activity in the span of less than five minutes. "No. Just my own personal code of ethics. There's not exactly a rule book for these kinds of things. I promise I won't scam you, though. It's not my style." I watch him take in my space and me. From the fraying wallpaper of my old studio apartment above my aunt's mystical occult shop, The Veil, to my numerous visible tattoos and my "boo-nana" sleep shirt featuring a cartoon banana wearing a sheet.

Judging from the face he's making, he's reached a conclusion about me, and it isn't favorable. I grumble under my breath and say, "Look, you said I'm the first person you've come across who can help you out. I'm offering. Take it or leave it. If you aren't interested, fine. Let me go back to sleep." I reach my hand toward the lamp to turn it off, and suddenly he's in my face, watery brown eyes only inches from my own.

"No! Please," he begs, and I can feel the cool phantom breeze of his breath puffing against my face. Sometimes, when a spirit gets really agitated, they can affect the environment around them.

"Okay, just back up." I make a shooing motion with my hand, and in a fraction of a second, he's at the end of my bed again.

"Sorry. I didn't mean to scare you," he says. I swallow to avoid laughing. My tolerance for all things scary is very high after being me for almost thirty years. I gesture for him to get on with it and pull my covers up over my shoulders.

"I just need you to tell my son that I buried gold bars in the backyard under the old oak tree. He can use the money however he wants, but I would love it if he spent it on my grandbaby," he finishes softly.

My own brows draw together sympathetically. "Okay. I can do that. We'll figure out a plan after I finish my shift at work."

"Thank you..." he says, trailing off.

"Rae," I offer with a tired smile.

"Thank you, Rae. I'm Leonard. I'll wait here until you're ready. Abraham's home is just a short walk from here," Leonard says, gesturing vaguely towards the window.

*So much for getting another couple of hours of sleep.*

It's one thing to know you *might* be watched in your sleep by the dead. It's another to see a member of the deceased puttering around in your bedroom, making themselves at home.

"Okay. I'm... just going to get ready for the day, I guess. Don't follow me, please," I ask, not wanting an audience while I relieve myself and take a shower. He nods and with a shimmer, disappears into the ether. If I concentrate, I can still sense him. It's like a vague impression. That feeling you get when you know someone is watching you. A shiver rolls down my unwilling spine as I shuffle out of the room.

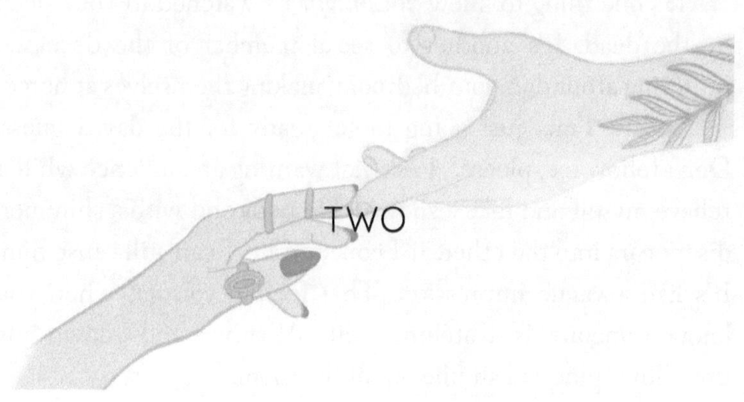

# TWO

"ONYX, LABRADORITE, AMETHYST, CLEAR QUARTZ..." I mumble to myself as I stock the various crystals my aunt likes to have on hand at The Veil. After arranging each type into artful piles, I tick off the corresponding box on my stock sheet. Believe it or not, Wednesday afternoons are not particularly busy for an oddities and occult shop, so I get through the rest of my restocking list without a single customer interruption.

My Aunt Clarissa wasn't born with the Gift, as my family likes to call it, but even so, she is obsessed with all things mystical. When she was in her twenties, she opened The Veil and began selling various oddities and items for the modern witch or spiritualist. Everything from herbal tinctures and full-moon water to tarot card decks and divining rods. Despite not having the Gift, she's a pretty good tarot reader, which boosted her business as well.

Ever since my aunt decided to take a step back from

running things, she's left the shop (mostly) in my hands. She's the owner, but I do most of the managing. She still offers tarot readings by appointment only—and when she's in the mood. We do surprisingly okay, considering how much of a niche interest our shop is. I started up the online section of our store years ago, and it's really improved our profit margin. You'd be surprised how many people want a "witchy mystery box" and will pay to watch you pull the items live. It also helps that I'm the only employee for most of the year. We're not rolling in the dough by any means, but we have yet to borrow money in the decade I've worked here.

I'm going through our online orders when the door opens with a melodic chime to announce the presence of a new customer. Or in this case, my best friend and little sister, Wren. Her shift just ended after the afternoon rush at Brewed Awakening, the coffee shop across the street.

Her pin-straight, chestnut hair is pulled back in a thick braid, showing off her high cheekbones and electric blue eyes. She looks like Rory Gilmore, if the youngest Gilmore decided to have an alternative rebellion and get a nose piercing and tattoos. She and I are a study in opposites. Where she's willowy and delicate, I am curvaceous and soft. Besides our hair color, the one thing we share is our intense-blue eyes.

She crosses the store with practiced ease, avoiding the upturned corner of the antique rug and ducking under the massive black chandelier that hangs just a little too low for anyone over five-foot-eight.

She plops down on the antique fainting couch in the library corner of the shop and groans, closing her eyes.

"So you came to rest and bitch, but you didn't even bring me a latte?" I ask, tossing a paperclip at her.

She glares at me and snarks, "I've pulled enough espresso for the day, thank you very much."

"Ah, so you just came to loiter?" I ask, shutting down the computer. One of the perks of being the manager is that I can close the store whenever I want. On a Wednesday afternoon, when the last customer came through four hours ago, I think it's safe to shut down for the day. I'll go live later tonight to do "potion pulls," where I draw mystery items for the boxes customers buy.

"Yes. And to see if you want to have dinner together," she says, eyes still closed. I wander closer, and the rich scent of coffee wafts off her. "Stop sniffing me," she gripes. While Wren doesn't have the same Gift as me, she is incredibly perceptive and has an uncanny ability to sense the world around her. Many women in our family line have had extrasensory gifts, ranging from seeing ghosts and auras, to communicating with animals and seeing the future. There's even an old family story about a necromancer, but I have my doubts about that one.

I pick her legs up, sit down, and lay her feet over my lap on the end of the couch. "Sure. I have a thing to do first."

"A ghost thing?" she asks, cracking one eye open to peer at me.

I look around furtively, even though I know no one else is in the store. The whole seeing ghosts schtick isn't one I like to advertise. Which is why when I help spirits, I try to do it as anonymously as possible. I'd rather not be known as the local ghost girl. Working in The Veil is already plenty strange for most in the small town of Ravenwood.

"Yes. Unfortunately, I'm going to have to do this one in person. I think I'm going to forge a letter from the guy because he wants me to tell his son where he has some gold buried."

"Is he a pirate or something?" Wren asks with a raised eyebrow.

"I wish," I say morosely, remembering my dream pirate and the unfortunate ghostly interruption. "But no. He's just a regular old guy who invested in gold and died before he told anyone where he hid it."

"Want some company?" Wren asks. She likes to go with me on my so-called "cold calls" because she has a better sense of the vibes and can spot danger a mile away.

"Please." I'm grateful for her offered company. She's always been much more at ease with herself, embracing the way people view her. She has no problem being the odd, spooky duck. I, on the other hand, try my absolute best to blend in. To be fair, reading auras and the general vibe of a room is much more socially acceptable. Plenty of people claim to be extra perceptive.

Seeing ghosts and communicating with them though? That's way too much for most to accept. So, as often as I can, I come up with elaborate ways to help spirits that don't oust me as the local medium. I don't do the whole "grab people by the arm and tell them their grandma loves them" thing. No, I'd much rather forge a letter from said grandma (with her blessing), rough it up a bit to make it look like it got lost in postal purgatory, and then send it off. If ghost-grandma leaves me alone after that, I've done my job successfully.

Since Leonard's son lives a couple of minutes down the road, I'm just going to hand-deliver the letter and claim I happened upon it while at an estate sale. Most people accept the stories I spin because it's easier to digest than believing their dead loved one has made contact from beyond the grave.

Wren watches me as I pull out some aged-looking

stationery from behind the counter and a pen. I close my eyes and extend my senses, casting a net that slowly unspools until I feel his distinctive signature. I give a gentle tug and feel Leonard slip closer to me. The sensation is a little like touching an old TV after turning it off. As soon as he enters the room, there's a distinctive *pop!* along my skin, raising the hairs on the back of my neck.

"Hey, Leonard. You and I are going to write a letter to your son together, okay? I'm going to have you step into me and take control of my arm and hand so we can write it in your handwriting."

"Are you nuts!? I can't do that," he states, backing away from me and into the counter, leaving the upper half of him exposed like a magician's assistant who's been magically cut in half.

Wren rubs her arms and says, "Okay, I'm going to let you two do your thing. I'll be over there." Her boot-clad feet take off in the direction of the apothecary section of the shop. She's never been the biggest fan of being in the direct presence of a spirit because it sends her extra-sensory abilities haywire.

"I know it sounds wild, but so is talking to me, right? So, you just have to step close to me, cover my hand with your own, and then write as if you are the one holding the pen. It's easier than it seems, I promise."

"Isn't that like possession?" he asks hesitantly.

I tilt my head side to side and reply, "Sort of, but you aren't taking over my mind, just a specific part of my body. As soon as you're done, you'll step away from me and the connection will be broken. The trick is to truly visualize my hand as your own." I shake said hand out, grip the pen, and try to relax into it. Having a part of your body snatched is a bizarre feeling.

"If you're sure," Leonard says, stepping towards me with trepidation. I nod once to confirm, and feel his presence slip into me. I fight against the instinct to push him out, allowing him to take control of my arm. Within a few minutes, we have a letter scrawled out.

> Abe,
>
> Before I die, I have to tell you where I have hidden a sizable amount of gold bars. You know that I haven't been doing well physically for the last few months, and I want you to know where they are. I'm not sure how much time I have left to tell you.
>
> I know you always thought I was a batty old man for investing in gold rather than putting my money in the stock market, but it is now yours to do with as you wish. However, I would be very pleased indeed if it went to baby Rose. For whatever it is she ends up enjoying in her life, or whatever academic plans she might have in the future.
>
> The gold is buried in my old work briefcase on the north side of the oak tree in my backyard. It is approximately four-feet down. Hopefully, you receive this letter before you decide to do anything with the property.
>
> I love you very much, son, and I could not be more proud of you. You have been the light of my life, and my only regret is not getting to spend enough time with you or Rose. Be well and take care of yourself.
>
> Love,
> Leo (Dad/Grandpa)

I work to school my expression as I feel Leonard peel away from me. The sensation is not unlike removing a sticker from your skin. I shudder a bit and nod to him, not wanting him to notice my teary expression. Fathers who love their kids will always get to me. My own dad is one of those, but I've come across too many that aren't.

"Okay, let's head out. Did you by any chance have a desk or bureau that got sold off when you passed?" I ask Leonard while folding the letter and crinkling it a bit. I swipe it through the dust under the desk for good measure and sneeze at the resulting dust bunny tornado.

He scrunches up his face in thought, his form flickering in and out as his concentration shifts from staying corporeal to flitting through his memories. Finally, he snaps his fingers. "Yes! My son got rid of our old bookcase that had some cabinets built into the bottom. When I get out of here and see his mother, she's gonna be pissed he got rid of it. He should feel lucky it's me haunting him. She would have brained him as soon as the sale went through. Especially since he used the money to buy an even bigger TV." He snorts and follows me out of the store.

"Great. I'll say I came across it at an estate sale and found the letter," I say, beckoning Wren to follow us out.

"Can you please inform Mr. Gold Standard to stay as far away from me as he can?" Wren asks testily. Despite the slight chill of the approaching Massachusetts autumn, I know the goosebumps along her exposed arms are from the ghost at my side rather than the air. She always overheats when she's working, so she tends to wear short sleeves, even in the fall and winter. All the better to display her various tattoos.

"What's her problem?" Leonard grouses, moving to the

other side of me and into the street. Cars can't hit him anyway, I guess.

I tilt my head towards Wren even though I'm addressing him, "She doesn't love the feel of ghosts. Sorry," I say apologetically, as we make our way up the street and toward the historic housing district of Ravenwood. Leonard nods and follows along quietly. I clear my throat and say, "So, listen. I don't like to advertise that I can see and speak to the dead, so please don't talk to me and expect an answer when we get to your son's house."

"Got it," he says, completely unbothered by the cars running through him. Yeah, this guy has definitely been a ghost for a while. New ghosts tend to operate with the same instincts they did when they were alive. Especially jumping out of the way of moving vehicles.

I link my arm through Wren's and we trudge onwards.

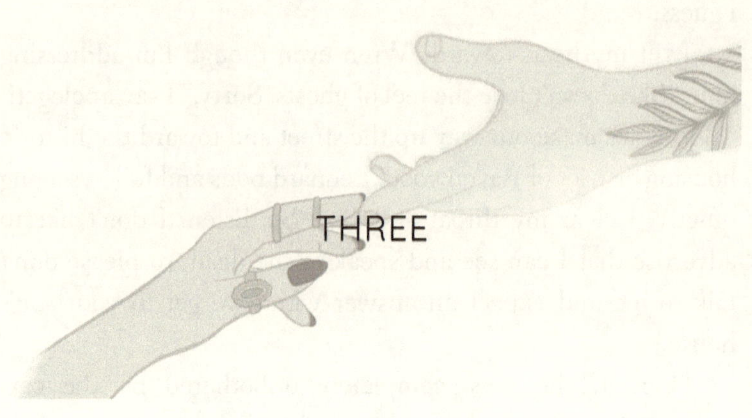

# THREE

"WELL, THAT COULD HAVE GONE BETTER," Wren says, barely suppressing her snicker behind her glass of red wine.

I scowl at her over the top of my own glass, then swipe the last bit of sharp cheddar off the charcuterie board between us before she can grab it. She gives me the finger as I chew, not caring at all that we're in a semi-fancy wine bar.

I can't even be upset at her because she's right. Meeting with Leonard's son had been a disaster. First, his wife, Holly, almost closed the door on us because she took one look at Wren and me and thought we were satanists or something. I should mention she was clutching her large, diamond-studded cross necklace as she proclaimed that, "This is a house that follows the church, not... whatever you're selling."

*Sigh.*

Eventually, once I showed his wife the letter, we got Abraham outside. Thankfully, she recognized Leonard's handwriting. The entire—and I mean the entire—time, Leonard would not shut up. And listen, I get it; he wanted to talk to his son in some way. But judging from Holy Holly glaring daggers at us through the window, I didn't think facilitating a conversation between the dead and the living would have gone over well.

The only good thing that came out of today is that Leonard is gone. He got his wish, thankfully, because Abraham didn't sell the house and instead has rented it out to a cousin. When we left, he was right behind us carrying a shovel over his broad shoulder, intent on seeing if he'd be thousands richer by the end of the day. Judging by the fact that Leonard is no longer in my ear, yammering about his son's poor choice of lawnmowers, Abraham must have found his gold.

I drain the last sip of my wine and ask, "So, how's it going in the land of MatchStik, home of the finest assholes dating apps have to offer?" Now it's her turn to scowl. She and I both have struck out more times than worth mentioning in terms of dating. The only difference is that she hasn't given up yet. I did after the last guy I briefly dated wanted me to get in contact with his dead ex-girlfriend. Talk about a mood killer.

"You're only asking to distract me from bullying you about today," she says, miming the way my eyes had bounced back and forth between Leonard and Abraham. I'm sure my eyes zinging back and forth from Holly's husband to a seemingly empty spot next to him didn't help our case.

"That's true, but I'm also curious how your last date went. What was his name again? Devon?" I ask.

"Damien," she hisses like the feral cat she is.

"So, I'm guessing things didn't go great," I sing-song.

"Hold. I need another glass of wine before I tell you this," she states, standing and swiping both of our glasses off the high-top table. She stalks to the mirrored bar, sliding her petite form between two couples.

I take a second to sweep my gaze over the interior of Barrel and Vine, making sure no wine enthusiast spirits are about to accost me while I'm alone.

I've always been terrified of someone seeing me talk to a person who isn't there. Truly, I was so thankful that Bluetooth headphones were invented. All you have to do is put an earbud in your ear, and most people will assume you're on the phone. No wonder so many people with the Gift were hung back in the day. Not many convenient excuses for talking to yourself in the 1690s.

Wren comes back with two very full glasses of merlot and a scowl for the crowd. "What are all these people doing here on a Wednesday?" I don't mention that *we're* here on a Wednesday, because arguing with Wren is futile.

"Thank you for the wine," I say, taking my glass out of her hand.

"Thank yourself. You bought it." She slides my credit card across the table to me and sits down. I don't even want to know how she got my card. I work to clamp my mouth shut against the retort that I've paid for dinner the last three times we've gone out, and she promised to pay this time. After all, I want to know about Damien, and she won't tell me if I force the subject.

I shove my credit card in my bra to prevent her sticky fingers from finding it again and ask, "What happened with Damien?"

She chews on a leftover basil cracker, takes a sip of wine,

and reaches for a piece of cheese when I yank the whole charcuterie board towards me and glare at her.

She sighs and sits back against her chair. "Okay. Fine." She takes a moment to glower at me, and I am, once again, thankful that her Gift doesn't extend to actual magic because I'm sure I'd have been incinerated on the spot a million times over by now. "The date was going fine at first. He was nice, he paid for my drinks, and when we got back to my apartment, he didn't push me into anything. We watched a movie, and just when things started to get interesting..." she trails off.

I squint at her, waiting for her to continue. When she still doesn't say anything, the older sister in me opens her eyes like an ancient beast. "What did he do?" I ask, already planning the ways I can track him down and relieve him of his favorite appendage.

Her eyes widen, and she says quickly, "No, Rae. Seriously, nothing like that. It's just... He started crying."

I shake my head in confusion. My sister can be mean, but not usually mean to the point of causing tears. "Crying?"

"Crying," she confirms with a curt nod. "I literally had my ankles up by my ears, and his tears started splattering on my chest." I clap my hand over my mouth to conceal the giggle bubbling out of my mouth. Her scowl twitches into a smile for a nanosecond before she continues, "Obviously, I asked him what was wrong, and—*while still inside me*—he proceeds to tell me that this is the first time he's been with anyone since his girlfriend broke up with him a few months ago."

"Oh. My. God." I cover my mouth with my hand.

"Yeah."

After a beat, I can't help but ask behind my hand, "Did you guys keep going?"

"No! Are you insane? I politely asked him to get off me and leave. He agreed, still sobbing, and got all his stuff together. Before he left, he kept apologizing and saying that he had a great time, but maybe it was too soon for him to move on. I had to physically lead him out of my apartment." She drains the rest of her glass and sets it down with a loud *clink*.

I suck my lips in a futile attempt to prevent my smile. Wren isn't fooled, though, judging from the thunderous look on her face. "So glad you find my misery amusing," she spits.

I raise my hands in surrender. "I'm sorry, but you know if the roles were reversed, you'd be cackling loud enough to get us kicked out of here."

She tilts her head to the side, making her hair fall over her shoulder. "Okay, true. Still, how humiliating. I love the idea of making men cry, but in such a compromising position?" She grimaces as though the mere memory left a foul taste in her mouth.

As much as I want to laugh because this is the type of shit that only happens to us, I feel for Wren. She may put up a front of being a prickly little cactus, but her heart is marshmallow soft. She just wants to find someone who likes her brand of weird, and apparently, someone who doesn't cry during sex. God, the bar is *truly* in hell.

She brushes off these failed dates, but I know they bother her. She's always been a romantic at heart, even if she does hide it behind a heavy armor of standoffishness and scowling.

"What can I do to cheer you up?" I ask.

When her mouth curves in a chilling impression of Jim Carrey's *Grinch* smile, I immediately regret asking. "Well, you *could* revive your dating profile again. Maybe finding you a date would help get my mind off it."

"What, so I can have my own sobbing sex story? No, thank you." I shake my head emphatically.

"Come on, Rae. It's been almost a year since you went on a date. You're approaching spinsterhood."

"Hey!" I exclaim. "I thought it was cool to be a spinster. Imagine all the cats I could have. Besides, I'm only twenty-nine," I sniff.

"You're allergic to cats," Wren replies with exasperation. "And your thirtieth birthday is only a few months away."

"Kill joy."

"Hag."

I glare at her for a minute and then sigh. "Fine." Her moody expression immediately transforms into something girlish and twinkling.

She extends her hand, fingers armed with deadly stiletto nails. I tap my own long ruby nail on the table a few times before relinquishing my phone. Despite how much we bicker, I trust her with my life. While we love to laugh at each other, neither of us would ever do something truly hurtful. We've always been inseparable; our mom jokes that we're twins at heart.

"You don't even have the app downloaded on your phone?" Wren asks, shaking her head in disapproval. After a few minutes, she says, "Oh, good. It saved all your data. Let's just take a new profile photo, because your last one is from when you chopped your hair off."

"Right now? No, Leonard woke me up at an ungodly hour. I probably look like the Grudge." I hold a hand up to shield my face, and I swear she growls.

"You're being dumb. You always look hot. Now shut up and let me take the picture." She proceeds to manhandle me into position, even going so far as to dab my lips with her blood-red lip gloss. "Now smile like I said something funny, but not too hilarious."

"Oh, so smile like I do any time you attempt humor?" I ask. At her pout, I can't help but laugh, and that's when she snaps the picture.

She checks it over and nods her approval. "Damn, I'm good. I should charge for this."

"You already did by making me pay for dinner," I respond flatly, making "gimme" hands at my phone. I have to admit, it is a really good picture of me. The way she positioned my arms made my boobs look extra perky, and the way I'm looking over my shoulder accentuates my cheekbones and heart shaped face. And, wow. That lip gloss makes my teeth look *white.* I make a mental note to ask her what it is and/or steal it from her later. Most importantly, I look happy. The warm glow of the low lighting makes my blue eyes softer. I don't look like a freak of nature at all.

The time at the top of my phone makes me groan. "Hey, I have to get home to do the potion pulls right now. I'm running a sale, and I'm expecting a lot of people to be watching."

"How convenient," Wren replies.

"Well, if I want to pay my rent, I have to make some money," I say defensively.

"Aunt Clarissa doesn't charge you rent," she retorts.

"Ah, but you're the one running up my credit card bill. Come on, do you want to watch?" I ask, standing and gathering my coat.

"Nah, I'd better get home. I have to be at Brewed early tomorrow," Wren says, stifling a yawn. She stands with me and grabs her black, vegan-leather purse off the table.

"See you tomorrow. I'll stop in for a coffee," I say, leaning in to kiss her on the cheek, which she grudgingly accepts.

"Okay, I'd better see that you've at least looked at a few guys," she says with a surprisingly scary glare. I roll my eyes and nod. She smiles toothily, then leads me through the bar and into the misty night.

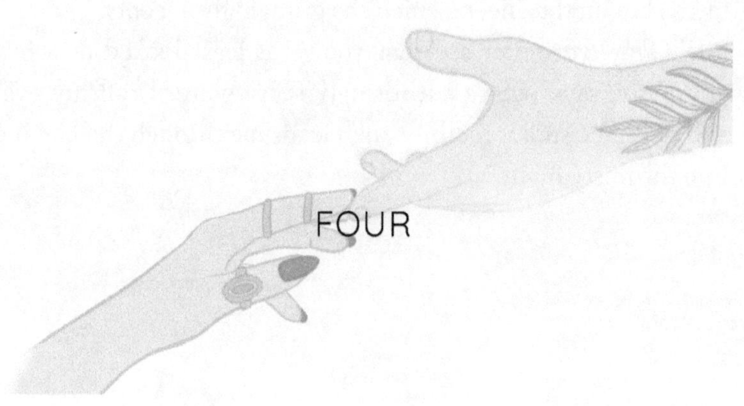

# FOUR

I VICIOUSLY FROG the last two rows of the maroon sweater I'm attempting to knit before I finally release a scream of frustration. Well, scream is a stretch; what ends up coming out of my throat is a weird mix of a strangled bird and a dying cat. I'm glad I live alone and don't have to explain that one.

I toss the whole project off my lap and stand from my couch in a huff. I've been trying to learn to knit for weeks because I thought it would be a nice, calming hobby to pick up.

Wrong.

Knitting *must* involve some type of witchcraft that I'm not privy to. No matter how hard I try or how many tutorials I watch, everything I make looks like a half-blind toddler was playing with yarn. Even that might be too generous a description.

I go to my small kitchen and gulp a glass of water to calm down. Just as I'm contemplating lighting every skein of yarn I've bought on fire, my phone *dings!* with a notification sound

I'm unfamiliar with. I frown down at it to see a MatchStik notification.

*I totally forgot I redownloaded this godforsaken app.*

I click on the notification and see that someone has "liked me," even though I haven't done anything with it since reinstating my profile with Wren last night. I scowl at my phone, unsure how to feel. On the one hand, it's nice that someone finds me attractive (at least enough to swipe right instead of left), but on the other hand, I don't know if I'm ready to dive back into the dating pool. A girl can only take so many men running and screaming (literally) when they get to know the real her before she decides that she'd rather be alone.

I think about my sister and how brave she always is. How unapologetically herself. How she keeps trying because she has hope that one day someone will love all of her.

I tap on the notification:

**Dean likes you!**

I tap on his photo icon and have to tamp down my immediate excitement. The man is gorgeous. Dark hair that curls just a bit over his starched white collar. Sun-kissed skin that makes his golden brown eyes glow. A bright smile, eyes crinkling at the corners, unapologetic in its brilliance. Muscular forearms peek out of rolled sleeves, and a botanical tattoo wraps around his right arm.

*Damn.*

I scroll through his profile and find that he's a lawyer, thirty-two years old, and a Gemini. I scroll to the prompts he chose to answer and appreciate that we have a very similar sense of humor. He comes across warm and intelligent, and I want to know more.

In response to the prompt "My Weird But True Story," he

said, "My weird but true story is that one time, in college, I brought a stray cat into my dorm room because it was freezing out and I felt bad for it. I fed her some of my canned tuna and named her Fish. Well, lucky for Fish and unlucky for me, she had her kittens on my favorite sweatshirt under my bed. I woke up in the middle of the night to the sound of meowing and realized I was now harboring five contraband cats instead of one. Fish and her four kittens, Trout, Bass, Salmon, and Tuna, were taken to a fantastic foster home and now 'work' at a local cat cafe."

I can't help but laugh, hoping that the story is true and not something he made up to seem sympathetic.

I go back to his pictures and quickly flip through them—the extra pictures tell a lot about a person. No gym-bro photos and/or man holding dead animal photos, so things are looking promising. With the sensation of jumping off a cliff, I swipe right on him too. Then, I immediately exit out of the app, silence notifications, and toss my phone across my small apartment so it lands with a bounce on my well-loved sofa.

I resolve *not* to look at my phone for the rest of the night. I wind up my knitting project and stuff it back into the storage basket next to my couch. I braid my hair into a long fishtail and then undo it. I pick up the book I was reading and plop on my armchair situated at the furthest point from my couch in the living room. I read for what feels like forever. I check the time on the antique clock mounted on the wall. Only five minutes have passed.

*Okay, I'll check one time to see if he messaged me, but that's it.*

I stride across the room, book forgotten over the arm of my chair. Unlocking my phone, my gaze is immediately drawn to the **"New Message!"** banner from MatchStik. I sink onto the couch and close my eyes, savoring the sense of anticipation and hoping he doesn't kill it with a "u up?" message.

I tap the link and am instantly relieved.

DEAN:

> Hey, Rae. I also like wine and cheese (whine and cheesy are acceptable variations) :)
> Would you be down to meet for a drink tomorrow night to get to know each other better?

Straight to the point and willing to make himself look a little silly. I bite my lip and reply.

RAE:

> Hmm idk, I usually like to make sure there's no murder-vibes before I agree to meet anyone in person. Although, the promise of wine and charcuterie does tend to override my instincts.

> I knew offering wine and cheese would be the perfect trap.

> Trap?

> Did I say trap? I meant that wine and cheese offer the perfect backdrop for a first date.
> Even if it goes terribly, at least you have wine.

> And cheese.

> Of course, and cheese. How could I forget our fermented friend?

> You forgetting cheese is at least one strike.
> Usually two, but I'm feeling generous.

> Your kindness knows no bounds. Sonnets will be composed in your honor.

I snort a laugh. Alright, he's smooth and quick-witted. So what? I click back on his profile and bite my lip.

*Dammit, he's hot.*

I sigh. As much as I tell Wren I'm over relationships and dating, a small part of me wants to try again. Like she said, I *am* allergic to cats. Let's hope Dean hasn't gotten any after Fish and her kittens.

> Okay, you've charmed me. I'll meet you there tomorrow. 7 PM at Barrel and Vine?

> Ha! My trap, I mean date idea, is a success! Seven sounds great.

> Ya know, if you're trying to squash the murder vibes, you should stop mentioning that this is a trap.

> Who said anything about a trap?

> I'll never turn down wine and cheese, but I'm bringing my pepper spray. A girl needs to be prepared.

> Fair enough. I'll be the one in the dark gray suit.

> Perfect. I've always wanted to know what it would be like to date a man who looks like he's on the way to a funeral.

> Hey! We can't all wear jeans to work.

> Except on casual Fridays?

I'm fully convinced that casual Friday is a myth created by corporate America to give a false sense of hope and camaraderie.

Lol. I look forward to hearing more of your conspiracy theories tomorrow.

Can't wait. Goodnight, Rae.

I press my phone to my chest and smile, glad no one is around to see the dreamy upturn of my lips. How embarrassing to hold out hope for something that will probably crash and burn.

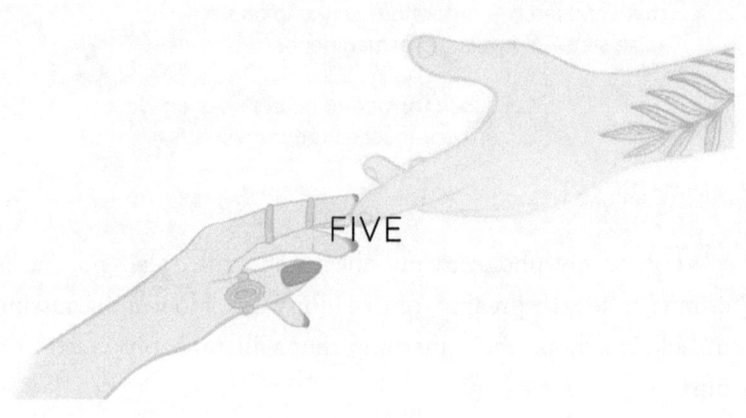

# FIVE

"WHAT ARE YOU SO NERVOUS ABOUT?" Wren asks from her spot sprawled out on my bed. Like a good sister, she came over early to help weigh in on hair decisions (down, but artfully curled, obviously) and makeup decisions (just a little, so I still feel like me). Like a *bad* sister, she's been giving me shit all afternoon about how nervous I am.

From the bowels of my closet I yell back, "Um, I don't know, the whole thing? What if he's a murderer? What if we don't get along? What if we *do*?" I aggressively yank my third top choice from the hanger. Wren has already vetoed the last two. One was too librarian, and the other was too oversized. We've already settled on a black, hip-hugging miniskirt with slightly transparent black tights and boots, but the top is about to end our sisterly relationship.

She picks her head up off my pillow and peers over her phone at me. "Yes, that's the one."

"You don't think it's too on-theme?" I ask, evaluating the merlot-colored sweater.

"If you spill any wine, it'll blend in. Also it makes your eyes pop. That's the one." She nods sagely and goes back to scrolling on her phone.

I toss the sweater over my head, trying to be careful of the curls and makeup. When I tug it down into place and assess my reflection in my full-body mirror, I have to admit that Wren is right. She usually is when it comes to fashion choices, but it irks me all the same. Can't she be wrong just once? The top hangs in a way that shows off my figure, and with it tucked artfully into the skirt, it accentuates my generous curves. The bold red color compliments my pasty skin and dark hair, making my complexion look warmer.

"Told you," she says without looking up from her phone. Damned aura reader. Her ability to parse out emotions has only improved with age, and it means she can clock how I'm feeling without even putting in the effort.

She continues without pausing her social media scrolling. "As far as him being a murderer, you're going to a public place. If it works out and you like each other, great. If it doesn't, at least you get some free wine. It doesn't have to be so complicated if you let yourself enjoy it."

I pluck the phone out of her hands and toss it to the other side of the bed just to be annoying. "I know you're right. I hate how vulnerable the whole thing makes me, though. Like, I'm presenting myself to some dude who swiped right on my picture. It feels dystopian."

She sits up and replies, "Yeah, well, it doesn't have to be that deep. Just don't bring up the ghost thing."

I grimace. "It makes me feel like I'm lying. Especially if the date goes well. It's this integral part of who I am, and I can't control it. If we end up being into each other, it feels wrong to omit." This desire to be ultra-upfront on the first date has ruined many of them in the past. I guess you could argue that the potential relationships wouldn't have gone anywhere anyway, but it still stings that something so intrinsic to who I am is the reason I get dumped before anything can even get started. Which is why I primarily stick to out-of-towners. I don't shit where I eat.

"Rein it in, Rae. You've spent a grand total of thirty minutes messaging the guy. Just see how the night goes and go from there, okay? Before you share your deep dark secret, why don't you just like, figure out what his favorite color is first or something?" I rub my lips together in the mirror and put my lip gloss in my bag. I nod at her, annoyed that she is, once again, correct.

---

"SO, WHAT'S YOUR FAVORITE COLOR?" I blurt, staring at Dean's intensely handsome face. The date is going well. Like, really well. And I'm having to work overtime to stop myself from hashing out the whole ghost thing. It's sort of twisted, because for those outside my inner circle, I have no problem lying or omitting the truth about myself. But for anyone who is close to me—or who I want to be close to me—I can't hold it back.

His lips quirk up in a grin, and he says, "Why? Is my favorite color supposed to reveal something about me?"

I smirk to cover up how nervous I am. In my attempt not to word vomit "I see dead people," I asked Wren's hypothetical question instead. Dates don't usually go this well for me, but he's been kind and flirty. He literally showed up with two matching keychain-sized cans of mace, joking that he wanted me to be prepared in case I forgot mine.

I feel itchy with my secret sitting just under the skin. It's made worse because there is, in fact, a dead twenty-something sitting in the corner booth across from us. She has her hands folded primly in her lap, and her hair is pulled back in a severe-looking braid. Her deep complexion makes her stand out against the cream-colored bench she's sitting on. Luckily, I'm great at not making eye contact with the dead in public, so hopefully she takes the hint.

"Well, I mean kind of. Imagine if you said your favorite color was gray or something," I say with a mock shiver. I am a color fanatic. My entire apartment is covered in antiques and jeweled tones, and all of my tattoos have bright color work. Gray is more lifeless than white or black, so if his favorite color actually is gray, I might have to end this date early.

*Kidding. Sort of.*

"I guess I'd better pay the tab and leave then. If someone can't appreciate Payne's gray, they clearly have no taste," he replies with a mock sniffle and makes to stand up.

I reach out and put my hand on his warm wrist to stop him with a laugh, "No! Okay, I promise not to judge," I say diplomatically, not missing his little smirk. "Any color is a good color in my book. Here, see?"

Dean resituates himself as I pull the neckline of my sweater aside so he can see the colorful collarbone tattoo that adorns my left shoulder. It is a simple fine-line vine of bright pink carnations and small blue forget-me-nots. It's not my most colorful tattoo (that one is the multicolored moth on my thigh), but it's the most readily available.

"It's beautiful," he says, studying the tattoo in detail like he's committing it to memory. He reaches across the small table as if to touch it, but then hesitates just before making contact. I lean in a bit so his fingertips brush the sensitive skin. He allows them to trail along the flowers once before retracting his hand.

I release my sweater and take a sip of my own wine, finding that my mouth is suddenly very dry. "Thank you," I say, hoping he doesn't ask about the meaning. It's too close to the "Hi, I'm a medium" conversation for comfort.

"It's red, by the way. Like the exact color of your sweater," he says, nodding down to my deep wine-colored top.

I raise my eyebrow and ask, "Is that a line?"

Dean laughs, "No, I swear! Look." He pulls out his phone and swipes around for a bit before turning the screen to show me a photo. In it, he's sitting on the floor in jeans and a worn-looking t-shirt, smiling a big, goofy smile, surrounded by opened birthday presents—all of them a dark red color. He's holding a wine-colored coffee mug and fancy pen to pose for the picture, but he's surrounded by various other gifts of the same color.

I can't help but laugh and say, "Okay, I believe you. I have to know though, was that planned?" I gesture to his phone.

"No, I'm just predictable. I've loved red for as long as I can remember, but my tastes have evolved from fire truck to merlot. My entire house has dark red all throughout. It's cozy."

"Some might say that amount of red leans toward vampir-ic," I tease.

He sticks his canines out and thrusts his arm in front of his face like a cartoon vampire and says, "I vant to suck your blaaaaaad," in a terribly done Transylvanian accent. I snort a laugh and cover it, not able to believe I'm enjoying myself this much on a *first date*.

"Calm down, Edward. No need to take your shirt off. I'll believe you if you say you sparkle in the sunlight."

"Damn, there goes my next wooing technique." He snaps his fingers.

"It's alright, I heard somewhere that Meyer's version of vampires kissing sounds like rubbing marble together, and that's probably the least sexy thing I've ever heard," I reply with a shrug.

Dean looks puzzled for a moment and then says, "Why would you make that the lore? Of all the other reasons to not go in the sun, and that's what stuck."

"Hey, leave Stephanie alone. Her books are cultural icons," I say, reaching the toe of my boot to playfully nudge his shin. The expensive material of his suit pants rubs up against the outside of my leg before he taps the side of it with his dress shoe. Butterflies explode in my stomach, but I check myself because we're basically playing footsie, and that's about as elementary as it gets.

"Okay, sorry," he says, holding his hands up in mock surrender before leaning in. "I've just never really been into the whole paranormal thing. Sure, I love a good horror movie or book as much as the next guy, but only really around Halloween."

*Well, shit.*

I lean back and take a sip of wine to hide how much that smarts. My whole existence is a paranormal movie come to life. And here I was thinking this was going to amount to at least a second date. Dean must sense the shift in my mood because he says, "Sorry, did I unknowingly put my foot in my mouth? Are you like, super into horror movies or something?"

I have to laugh a bit at that and feel my shoulders relax a little. "No, I'm not one for horror movies. I find most of them to be too unrealistic and don't even get me started on how they portray women."

"Fair enough." He searches my gaze and leans closer, placing a warm hand over my forearm. "Hey, I don't know what I said to upset you, but I promise I didn't mean to. I want to know more about you, so if I messed up somewhere, tell me. Please?"

When he sees me wavering, he gives me an encouraging look and a light squeeze to my forearm that has me wanting to give in. "Okay. I just figured now would be the time to mention that I run an occult and oddities shop called The Veil. It's technically my aunt's, but I'm the manager now." I decide to stop short of revealing my abilities because if this turns him off, I can't imagine what knowing *that* would do.

Speaking of which, I inspect the spirit sitting at the back table. Thankfully, she's one of the ones who either doesn't know she's dead or has enough self-awareness not to come up to me when I'm with someone else. She's staring around the crowd, a mild expression of disgust marring her otherwise beautiful face.

When Dean speaks again, I bring my eyes back to his. "Like I said, I'm not one for judgment. If you're into all that stuff for fun or for some sort of spiritual practice, that's cool. I may not want to join you for a seance or something—" he breaks off when I chuckle, eyebrows raising in surprise. "But, I fully support you in doing what makes you happy." He takes a sip of his wine and peers at me.

What he's saying should be reassuring, but spirituality isn't just a hobby for me. It's sort of my whole life, whether I want it to be or not. I look him over, noting the five o'clock shadow that stands out against his strong jaw, the slightly crooked nose that looks like it might have been broken once or twice, and my gaze snags on his warm brown eyes, crinkled in the corners like he's holding back a smile. Maybe my Gift is something I can sort of ease him into. Maybe he'll see that I'm more than just a freak who can speak with the dead.

I bite my lip and nod, "Okay." I smile at him and can't help but add, "But just for the record, I am *very* judgmental."

He laughs and says, "Yeah, I thought so"

I gasp in mock outrage and nudge his shin again. He gives me a light kick back and says, "Come on, let's get out of here."

"Where to?" I ask.

"I figured we could go walk around some of the shops here and maybe grab dessert?" he asks, standing and shrugging into his jacket.

I nearly squeal because I love window shopping and say, "Let's do it."

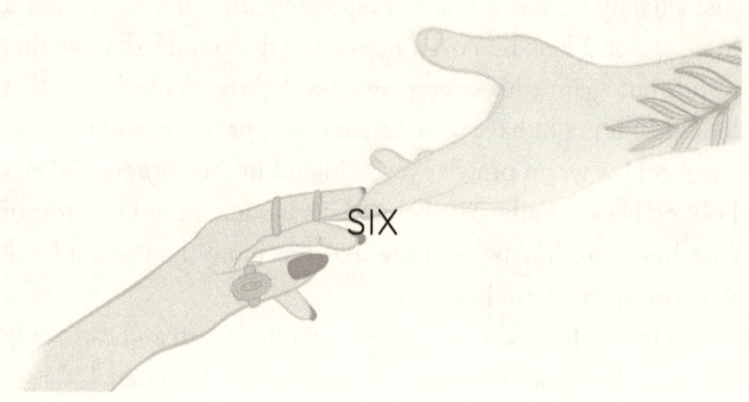

# SIX

"BE HONEST, does this beanie make my head look too round?" Dean asks me, squinting at himself in the too-low and too-small mirror hung on the wall.

I assess his reflection and say, "I mean, maybe a little." I grab him by the shoulders and turn him to face me. He smiles down at me, and I have to squint to keep the answering grin off my face. "Yup, definitely round. Were you a c-section baby?"

His head cocks to the side as he asks incredulously, "How did you know that?"

Rather than answer, I just tap my temple and wink at him. He shakes his head at me and pulls the beanie off his head to deposit it safely back on the display.

"Oh, well. There's a reason I don't wear those things, even when it feels like my ears are freezing off," he states, grabbing my hand with his own and leading me toward a different section of the store. Considering it's been what feels like a century since I've had casual physical contact with anyone outside of family, this should feel foreign to me. But it doesn't; I can't help but bite my lip at how easy it feels to hold his hand.

We walk around the small apparel store hand-in-hand for another few minutes, and then I lead him out the front door. "Come on, let's go get some hot chocolate. I know a great place just around the corner," I say, tugging him through the unseasonably brisk night. A few people are out and about, but most are inside to avoid the cold.

"I can always go for hot chocolate. You should know that I have a massive sweet tooth. It was a huge problem in childhood because I always came home from the dentist with at least one cavity. I had an issue with sneaking candy after bedtime," he says, cheeks coloring as he realizes he may have shared something embarrassing. "So anyway, if you're ever in need of gift ideas for me, something sweet is the answer."

"Wow, we're already at the gift-giving stage?" I ask, raising my eyebrow teasingly at him.

"Well, I wasn't expecting one right now, obviously. I'm thinking anniversaries," he says sincerely.

"Anniversaries?" I all but shout.

He takes one look at my face and snorts a laugh. He tugs me into his side, wrapping a long arm around my shoulders. "I'm kidding, but you should really see your face right now. You look like you've seen a ghost." I can't help but laugh and shake my head.

*If only you knew, dude.*

"Sorry. I was deciding if it was time to cut and run. It's creepy to talk about anniversaries a couple of hours into the first date, you know," I say, plucking his arm off my shoulder and continuing to walk down the street. Even if he was joking, the spike of anxiety at his words felt very real. My fear of commitment runs deep, apparently.

He ups his pace to keep stride with me and says, "I know, I'm sorry. You make me nervous." He looks at me sheepishly, that pretty blush reddening his cheeks again.

I stop at that and turn to look at him. "I make you nervous?"

He rolls his eyes and replies, "Yeah. Have you looked in the mirror lately? You're beautiful. Not to mention funny and easy to talk to. Our chemistry is off the charts, if you ask me," at my expression, he stops himself. "Okay, sorry. See? Nervous. Anyway, what I meant is that this date is going well, and it's been a minute since I've had a first date go well."

"Really?" I ask skeptically. He's truthfully one of the sexiest men I've ever seen in person, and when he isn't freaking me out, he's pretty funny.

"Yeah. I've had a few girlfriends over the years, but nothing that stuck for longer than a year or so. My last rela-tionship ended about two years ago, and every date I've been on since has either ended badly or we just didn't hit it off. I'm not sure why. Just bad luck, I guess," he finishes, looking down at his polished shoes. "So, yeah. When I noticed how well the date was going, I got overly excited. Sorry. Can we take back the last few minutes of embarrassing myself?" He smiles at me hopefully; his damned dimple looks adorably pokable.

I roll my lips and reach out to grab his hand, leading him down the street again. "We can. I get it," I say with a shrug. "I haven't had a serious relationship, well... ever. And clearly, very few of my dates go well, so I'm not one to judge on that front."

"You've never had a serious relationship?" he asks.

He doesn't sound judgy, more curious, so I feel comfortable

answering, "Not really. I've dated a handful of guys here and there, but it never moved past the first few dates."

Before he can reply, we're in front of Brewed Awakening. I pull open the doors and make my way inside, Dean following close behind. I watch him take in the funky decor, from the deep green damask wallpaper on the back wall to the various antique dining tables and chairs scattered in groups. The entire place has a vaguely Victorian feel with the added charm of thrifted pieces.

"Hey, Rae," Misha, the barista, greets. He waves, his mouthwatering, tanned arm flexing with the motion.

"Mish. How's it going?" I ask, leaning against the counter. He's been working here for years, and we've developed a casual friendship between placing orders and brewing coffees. Unfortunately, he's well off the market. He and his husband are very happy. I learned that the hard way when I hit on him years ago. I got a friend out of it, so I can't complain too much.

"I get off in an hour, so pretty good. Want a hot chocolate?" he asks, already turning towards the bar to make me one.

"Make that two, please," Dean says, stepping up next to me and wrapping his arm around me again. I shake my head at his obvious posturing.

"You got it, big guy," Misha says, lowering his voice flirtatiously.

I see Dean instantly relax, and he sends Misha a wink before pulling out his wallet. Misha pauses his work to swipe the card and then turns back to making the most delicious hot chocolate ever. I don't know what he puts in it because he won't tell me, but it's truly the best. Even Wren doesn't know his secret recipe, only that he adds extra spices to the mix they use.

"Come on," I show Dean to my favorite little alcove. I sit on the low couch, placing my bag on the antique walnut coffee table.

"I really like this place. It's very cozy," Dean says, sitting next to me. We both turn slightly to face each other, and the low lighting makes him look like a dream come to life.

"Yeah, it's my favorite in town. My sister, Wren, works here. She's been a barista for the last five years."

"Is she your only sibling?"

"Yeah, we're fairly close in age, so she feels almost more like a twin than a run-of-the-mill sibling. What about you?" I ask.

"I have three older brothers and one younger sister," he says.

I feel my eyes bug out. "You're one of *five?*"

Dean laughs and replies, "Yep. My parents were both from small families, so they wanted a big one. They definitely got their wish."

"Are you close with them?" I wonder.

He rubs his chin, long fingers rasping against the five o'clock shadow. "Yeah, for the most part. My eldest brother Adam is... overbearing sometimes. He's older than the rest of us by quite a bit, so I think he ended up taking on a parental role by default.

Unfortunately, he never stopped mother-henning us. It makes it hard to be close to him because it always feels like he's judging or parenting. The rest of us, Grant, Luke, myself, and Clara, are varying degrees of closeness. I would say I'm the closest to Grant and Clara. Grant, because we are very similar in personality and in the same business, and Clara, because we're total opposites, but we get each other on a fundamental level."

I try to imagine what it must have been like to grow up with seven people constantly around and just...can't. My little family of four already felt constrained in some ways. I can't imagine adding an extra three people to that dynamic. "Wow. That must have been a really interesting way to grow up," I say.

He shrugs. "I guess. It's just something you get used to. I can't fathom only having one sibling. What happens if you're mad at each other? Then you don't have another sibling to talk shit with. You just have to"—he shudders—"deal with it."

I can't help but laugh. "Yeah, when Wren and I get genuinely angry at each other, it's cataclysmic. It's only happened two or three times that I can remember, but those were dark days."

"You guys never fight?" Now it's his turn to look bug-eyed.

"Of course we do! But it's always over stupid things that don't really matter. Minor annoyances. Despite our very different personalities, we just get each other. Similar to you and Clara, I guess."

"Rae, I've got two hot chocolates for you!" Misha calls from the counter.

"I got it," Dean says, springing to his feet before I can even think about standing.

When he gets back, I ask, "So what made you want to be a lawyer?" It's something I've been wondering about because I couldn't imagine willingly going into a profession where you have to read thousands of bland legal documents. Especially because Dean seems like the least stuffy person I've ever met.

He laughs low in his throat, and the sound gives me instant goosebumps. "That is a long story. One for a different day."

"Ah, this is your way of trying to get a second date, isn't it? You're hoping the mystery will keep me coming back," I tease.

"Is it working?" he asks slyly.

"Maybe a little. Can I get the short answer?" I take a sip of my hot chocolate and sigh. All is right with the world. If it wouldn't rot my teeth from my skull, I'd drink Misha's hot chocolate all the time. It's sweet, but not overly so, and has a complexity of flavors that is hard to pin down. Not to mention it's the perfect thickness. Divine.

"Well, since my charm is working, I guess I can do that." He pauses to think it over, taking a sip from his own to-go cup of hot chocolate. "Holy shit. This is the best thing I've ever put in my mouth," he says, staring down at the cup like it just solved all of his problems.

"I know, right?" I nod and tap my cup against his.

"Okay, the short answer is that my great-grandpa was a lawyer. And ever since, every man in my family became a lawyer. Other than Adam and Luke, anyway. I'm in the same practice as my dad, actually. He and my grandpa founded it. Some went into different sectors, but being a lawyer was non-negotiable."

"Until Adam," I clarify.

"Right. Until him. When he decided he didn't want to do it, and then encouraged Luke to follow in his footsteps... Well, it was impossible for me to ignore the pressure. I'm a chronic people pleaser," he says with a rueful smile.

"I have a chronic desire to be helpful, if it's any consolation," I offer. I don't want him to feel like he's the only one opening up. We can probably relate more than he thinks. While my Gift isn't exactly a choice, I'm following in the footsteps of more ancestors than I can even conceive of.

"Two peas in a pod," Dean says, placing his arm along the back of the couch. It's barely skimming my shoulders, but the intent is clear. While the move is very high school, I have to say it's working for me.

"Smooth," I say, gesturing to his arm. He grins in a way that shows off the slight dimple in his left cheek again, and brings his arm fully around my shoulders. He looks at me with his brows raised in question, but rather than answer, I lean my head against the crook of his shoulder. I bask in his warm, clean scent and the feel of his expensive jacket against my cheek. His hand brushes softly up and down my shoulder, and I feel content for the first time in a while.

We sit there like that for a while in companionable silence, sipping our hot chocolate. I'm amazed by the fact that I'm not feeling the desire to fill the quiet. I'm not nervous at all anymore. The urge to tell him my biggest secret has also faded. It's like my brain knows the time will come when it's necessary. I'm allowed to just enjoy this date. Wren is right again, dammit.

"As much as I'm not ready for the night to end, I have to get going," Dean says quietly after we polish off our hot chocolates. He doesn't move his arm, but loosens it a bit so I can look at him. "I have to get into the office kind of early tomorrow."

"On a Sunday?" I ask.

He rolls his eyes. "I know. I hate it. One of my firm's biggest cases to date is set to go to trial mid-week next week, and we're sort of all-hands-on-deck. There's a rumor that whoever provides the most useful evidence could be in line for a promotion to partner." It sounds like a good thing, but the way he says it is less than enthusiastic.

"Is that something you want?" I ask.

I feel more than hear his sigh. "Isn't a promotion what everyone wants?"

I decide not to pry into his non-answer. We don't know each other well enough yet for me to figure out if he's the type to enjoy someone prodding for more information. I also don't want to seem like I'm upset that he has to work tomorrow. For all my talk of being freaked out by the mention of anniversaries, I definitely can't pull the "don't go to work, stay with me" card on the first date.

"Okay, I totally understand," I say, gently disentangling myself from his side. We both stand and stretch, a bit stiff from sitting in the same position for a long time.

"Where'd you park? I'd like to walk you to your car," he says, grabbing my cup from me so he can throw it away.

We head outside after waving to Misha, instantly chilled thanks to the cool night air. "I didn't," I say, "I live just across the street." I point to The Veil.

"You live in your aunt's store?" he asks.

"On top of it, actually. There's a studio apartment. I've lived there since I moved out of my parents. Rent is free, so I can't complain."

"Man, talk about an easy commute," Dean says with a laugh.

"I know, it's pretty sweet." We cross the street and walk down the small alley, slowing as we come to the stairs leading up to my place. We stop beneath a streetlight, and I say unnecessarily, "Well, this is me." I gesture lamely to the rickety staircase.

"I had a great time, Rae. Thank you for going out with me and not using the mace at your earliest opportunity," he jokes.

"Thought about it," I say primly.

He smirks in response and reaches out to tuck an errant strand of hair behind my ear. His hands are a little cold, but that's not what makes me shiver. "When can I see you again?" he asks, stepping closer so we're almost toe to toe.

I look down before flicking my eyes up to meet his. I worry my lip between my teeth, watching him track the motion. How do I respond in a way that doesn't seem desperate but still enthusiastic?

*Ugh, why is this stuff so hard for me?*

Finally, I settle on, "Soon. Let me know when you're free. I work most days, but we can figure something out."

"I'm pretty busy with this case through the end of the week, but I think that by next weekend things will settle a bit. Even if they don't, I'm happy to meet you for dinner. I don't want my stupid schedule to be the reason I don't see you again." My heart thuds irregularly at that. I knew it was going well, but to have him confirm so plainly is reassuring.

"Next weekend then," I say with a smile.

He holds out his arms for a hug, and I step into them without hesitation. I squeeze his middle and rest my cheek against his chest. We stay there for a breath or two, and then we both start to pull away. Before he fully lets me go, he presses a gentle kiss to my forehead that I feel all the way to my toes.

I snake my hands up behind his neck and impulsively pull him in until our lips meet. The plush feel of them moving against my own is intoxicating. He drags me closer and angles his head to give me more. He licks at my lower lip playfully, and I open with a gasp. His taste floods me, and it's like I'm drinking the world's best cup of hot chocolate again. Only this time, there's a hint of Dean—even more delicious. After a few of possibly the best seconds of my life go by, I pull away slowly. He chases my mouth down for one final kiss, making me laugh.

"I'm definitely seeing you next weekend," he says. "Or even

sooner if I can swing it." He presses his forehead to mine for a beat and then pulls back to peck my nose, the warmth of his kiss-swollen mouth a shock against my icy skin.

I smile at him and step back, knowing if I don't leave now, I'll invite him up and he'll probably say yes. I don't want to be the reason he doesn't get this promotion, even if his feelings on the matter seem complicated at best.

"Text me," I say, walking backwards up the first few steps.

"I will, sweetheart," he says. I can feel his attention on me like a hand on the small of my back the whole way up the steps. When I get to the landing, I unlock my door and wave one last time. I catch sight of his dimple before ducking inside. My phone buzzes inside my purse, and I pull it out, curious if Wren is badgering me for details already.

DEAN:

I'm so glad we got to go out.

I have to laugh because wow, that was quick. The man knows how to follow directions. I type out a reply right away, so he'll walk to his car. I don't want him freezing out there waiting for a response.

RAE:

Me too. See you soon. Goodnight, Dean.

Goodnight, sweetheart.

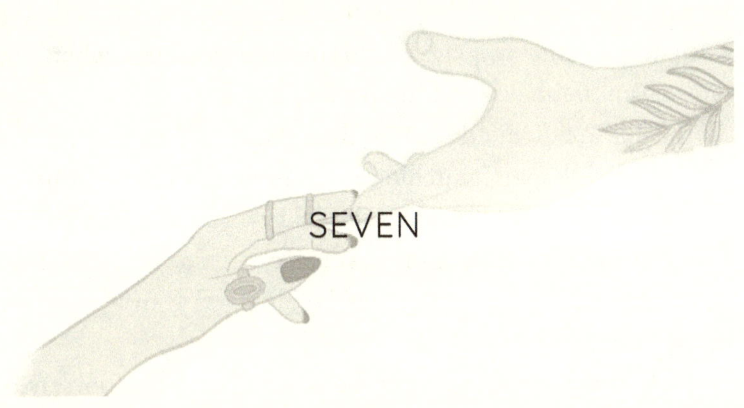

# SEVEN

"DO YOU GUYS HAVE ANY, like, potions?" I work hard not to roll my eyes at the teenage girl. She's spent the last ten minutes touching everything in my shop and moving it slightly off-center. I try not to think about all the time I spent earlier putting up new displays that she messed up within a few minutes. She's one of those people who don't pay attention to where they got something from and just sets things down all willy-nilly.

*What am I, eighty? Who says "willy-nilly" before they have a senior discount?*

"No, sorry," I say, trying to smile to soften my tone. She bobs her head, long blonde hair swishing with the motion. She bounces up and down on the toes of her worn Converse, and I can sense she wants to ask something more, but doesn't know how. "What's up? Anything I can help you with? Maybe some fun bath products or tarot cards?"

She shakes her head and goes back to rifling through the

clothing display near the front of the store. I decide to leave her be and start reorganizing all the things she misplaced. I'm straightening the display of artisan-made journals when she taps me on the shoulder. I jump about a mile.

People are definitely scarier than ghosts.

"What?" I snap, clutching my thundering heart. I turn to see her off-put expression and say, "Sorry, you just startled me. I was in my own little world. What can I do for you?" I set down the leather journals I was holding and lean against the display hutch.

"Do you have anything to help someone fall in love with you?" she blurts, quickly reddening from the tips of her ears all the way down her neck.

"Um—" I start.

"Never mind," she mumbles, before trying to rush past me.

"Hey, wait," I say, grabbing her arm before she can dart out. "There's no need to be embarrassed. I have at least one or two people a week coming in looking for the same thing."

"Really?" she hedges, looking optimistic.

"Yeah, really. I don't want to get your hopes up, though. I don't have anything that can manufacture something as strong as love."

"Oh," she whispers, looking down at her scuffed shoes.

"Sorry. Trust me, if I could brew up a love potion, I would. It's just not something that can be done, and anyone who says it can is swindling you. But to be honest, would you really want someone to love you because you tricked them into thinking they did?"

"I guess not," she grumbles.

"If you want, I can point you to some of our books on manifestation. That's more about calling out to the universe and letting it know what you're looking for. What comes to you may not be exactly what you expect, but the universe always delivers." She nods, and I lead her over to our book section, making sure she's mindful of the low-hanging chandelier.

Once she has a book on manifestation, a new journal, and some tarot cards, she's out the door. I don't have Wren's Gift, but even I can see that she's lighter than when she first came in. Now, to finish rearranging everything she touched.

Despite my best efforts, I check my phone for the thousandth time today. I tell myself I'm definitely *not* waiting for a text from Dean, but I know deep down that's a lie. I haven't heard from him since our date a few nights ago. I'm trying not to let it bruise my ego, but I can't help but wonder why he hasn't reached out. I know he said he would be busy with work. He just seemed really into me. And *that kiss*. I mean, come on. It was a pretty good kiss. Good enough to warrant a follow-up in my opinion.

I know it's childish, but I didn't want to be the first to reach out. For one, he told me his week was going to be intense with work, so I didn't want to bug him. But also, it's been a while since I've been chased, and it feels nice to play coy. Even if it isn't getting me anywhere. I make a growling sound in my throat that scarily reminds me of Wren and shoot off a text.

RAE:

> Hey! I know you said you'd have a busy week, so I just wanted to check in and say that I hope it goes well for you. I'm excited to hear all about it.

*There.*

I gave him a gentle nudge toward figuring out our next date

without sounding too desperate. I hope. After a minute or two of no reply, I grudgingly go about my tasks and try to put my phone—and its lack of buzzing—out of my mind.

---

"CAN you *please* put your stupid phone away?" Wren hisses at me across her kitchen table.

I scoff and stow it under my leg. "That's rich coming from you," I say, before popping a bite of chicken in my mouth. I chew for a full three seconds before surreptitiously lifting my leg to see if I've miraculously gotten a new notification and haven't felt it.

"I know I can be attached to my phone, but you're getting straight up diagnosable. Put. It. Away," she snarks.

"Okay, alright. Sorry," I say. I stand up, walk a few paces to her counter, and deposit my phone there. If it's not directly next to me, I can't check it.

When I sit back down and take a sip of my water, I notice Wren squinting at me. "What?" I ask, looking down to see if I spilled anything on myself.

"Your anxiety is off the charts. You're practically glowing orange." Wren reads most emotions as a color. My parents first realized she had the Gift when she started saying that they turned pink when they looked at her or me. Pink is the color she reads as love and adoration. Damned cute if you ask me.

Of course, my whole "Mommy, there's a man I don't know who comes into my room at night and stares at me" thing was much less cute.

Yeah. It's a wonder she's the one who turned out to be the grumpy little weirdo and not me.

I grunt because I knew I couldn't hide it from her. She knows my date with Dean went amazingly well, but if she knows I'm pining this bad already, she won't let me live it down. "It's nothing. Just a long day at the store," I hedge, stuffing my mouth with chicken so I can't be expected to answer any follow-up questions.

She narrows her eyes so much, they look closed. "You're lying," she says. I just tilt my head, chewing on my giant bite of chicken. She cuts into her own slice of tofu (she went vegetarian as a child as soon as she realized she could read animal's auras) and eats a bite. After she swallows, she sighs and says, "Oh, just spit it out. You know it'll make you feel better."

"Okay, fine. You can't make fun of me for it though—" I pause at her scoff. "At least not much, alright? I'm vulnerable here."

She holds up her hands, the stiletto points of her nails looking more menacing than surrendering, but I decide to tell her all the same. It's not like I have a host of best friends to pull from. She's kind of it for me as far as close relationships go, other than our parents.

"Remember Dean?" When she nods, I continue, "Well, he seemed excited about going on a second date, but he hasn't even texted me. It's been almost a week since we went out. We had planned to meet up again this weekend, and I haven't heard a peep from him. I've texted him, but now I'm feeling like if he isn't going to respond, I should just leave it alone. I'm so confused. Why tell me multiple times how much you enjoyed yourself if you're just going to fall off the face of the earth?"

"Hmm. That is weird." To my surprise, there's no ribbing about how needy I am. "Are you sure he wasn't giving off fuck-boy vibes?"

"No, he really wasn't. He seemed very sincere. I know I can't read people as well as you can, but he was a genuinely sweet guy. We both had a good time. And he was the one to initiate making more plans. He did say he'd be busy at work, but too busy to text me back at least once in the last week?" I push the rest of my plate away. It's not appetizing anymore.

What if he saw something fundamentally wrong with me and just doesn't have the heart to tell me? What if the tiny peek behind my creepy curtain was enough to scare him away after he thought about it a little longer? He did say he wasn't into the paranormal. Maybe he looked up the shop online and decided it was all too much. There *is* an About Us page that goes into detail about how my aunt is a tarot reader from a line of Gifted women. It doesn't mention me by name, other than to say that I manage the shop, but still. Maybe it revealed enough to scare him off.

"Maybe work was just really, really busy?" Wren's voice brings me back down to reality.

"I guess. Seems kind of unlikely though. Honestly, at this point, I'm not really expecting a response," I say, internally cringing at how mopey I sound.

"Have you looked up his socials to see if he's posted anything?"

I nod. "I tried, but I didn't know his last name, or even really where he was from. I looked up his number, and nothing came up. He agreed to Barrel and Vine for our date, but that doesn't mean he was from this town. He could be from anywhere in a fifty-mile radius. I tried looking up 'Dean, lawyer' but couldn't find anything. I even tried reverse image searching the photos on his MatchStik profile, but he's one of the only men I know who doesn't use the same picture for every social media platform. Or hell, maybe he doesn't have one. Who knows?"

"Wow, you've really deep dived this, haven't you?" she asks. I nod despondently, and she sighs. "Look, maybe he's just super busy, or maybe he lost his phone and has no way of contacting you. Maybe he's scared of how amazing you are. No matter what, his actions say more about him than they do about you. If he did ghost you, that's a shitty thing to do and you don't need someone like that in your life anyway, no matter how hot he is."

I nod again, knowing she's right, but still wishing I had closure.

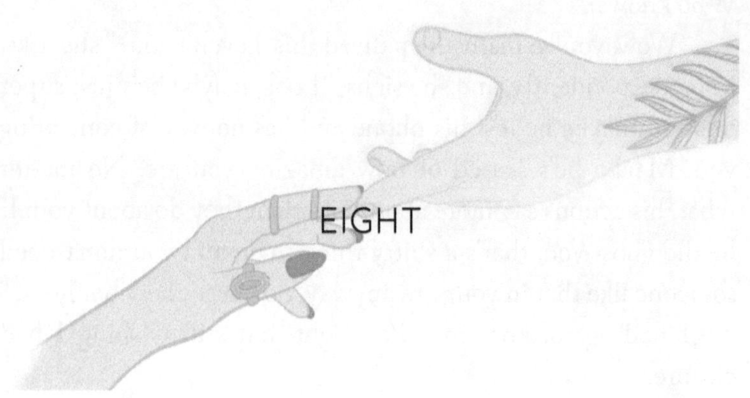

# EIGHT

BY WEDNESDAY of the following week, I have to accept it: I've been ghosted. Despite the fact that my date with Dean was the best date I've been on in years. Despite the fact that he made me feel like we had a chance. Despite that *kiss*. I have to move on and stop pining over a guy I knew for less than forty-eight hours.

I tell myself all of this while also trying to convince my body to get out of bed. I need to head downstairs soon so I can open the store, but lying in bed is much more appealing. I finally sigh and sit up, righting my tatty, old Salem sweatshirt. It's time to get back to who I was before I met Dean, no matter how monotonous my days were. I just have to get over the sting of putting myself out there and getting rejected. Again.

I shuffle out from behind the small partition that separates my bed from the rest of the living space and rub my eyes against the buttery morning sunlight streaming in from the windows. "Hello," says a voice I don't recognize.

I suck in a breath, ready to scream. When I open my eyes, the scream turns into a grunt. I realize it's the ghost woman I saw when I was on my date with He Who Shall Not Be Thought Of. She's wearing the same jeans and light pink sweater that complement her deep skin tone, and her black hair is perfectly slicked back into a high bun, showcasing her delicate bone structure and narrow eyes. She's sitting on my couch and observing her surroundings with a blatant look of distaste. I try to leash my annoyance, happy I'm wearing pants for this ghostly encounter.

Sweats are *technically* pants, right?

I give her a small wave and shuffle to the kitchen so I can get my coffee going, rubbing my arms to stave off the cold. Thanks to Wren, I'm a total coffee snob now and will only drink homemade if it's done through a French press. I get the water boiling and lean on my island, which acts as a divider for the kitchen and living area.

"Hey. I recognize you from the other night. Thanks for not trying to talk to me while I was with someone," I say, genuinely.

You'd be surprised how many dead people forget how to be polite, let alone to put themselves in someone else's shoes and see how talking to "no one" can give you a one-way ticket to a place where you aren't allowed anything sharper than a plastic spoon.

"I didn't want you to look like a raving lunatic and be taken away before you can help me," she says primly.

"Noted," I say shortly and go about doctoring my coffee the way I like it. I cross the room so I can sit on the opposite side of the couch from her. "What's your name?" I ask before taking a sip.

"Rebecca," she says, eyeing my chipped cup. It's technically a teacup, but I use it for coffee. I love the hand-painted flowers that bloom across it. It was a gift of sorts from one of the first dead people I helped. Constance was the sweetest woman I had ever met, and helping her and her husband find closure meant everything to me. Right before Constance passed on, she directed her husband, Ralph, to give me the cup. She had hand-painted it herself a few months before she passed. I use it all the time to remind me why I help these people, even if they can be annoying. I run my hands over the textured surface and think of her, hoping that by now, she and Ralph have found each other again.

"Nice to meet you, Rebecca. I'm Rae. Sorry that there's not a more delicate way to ask this, but do you know why you're still here?" I ask. I want to jump right in because she doesn't seem like the type to waste time on pleasantries.

"Hold on. Before I start answering your questions, I have some of my own. How can you see me, and why can't anyone else? Why am I able to move things sometimes, but not others? And where the *fuck* am I?" she finishes, chest heaving.

It's sort of odd that even after death, the body's reaction to stress is the same. She doesn't need to breathe, but she does anyway. I guess there are some things the mind doesn't want to give up, even if the lungs no longer require air.

I take one more sip before setting it down on my coffee table. "Okay, let me try to answer those for you." When I raise my brows at her, she nods and settles further into the couch. "First, I can see you because I have a Gift. Not everyone does. I don't have the numbers on it, but it's safe to say that I'm the only one around here. You can occasionally move things, but only when you get super worked up. My guess is you've been able to interact with objects when you've been in a high emotional state. Is that right?"

She nods her head in agreement, so I explain, "If you were to hang around longer and practice more, you'd get better at it, but since you're lucky enough to have found me, I'm hoping I can help you move on before that's necessary. As for where you are... well, that depends. If you mean in a metaphysical sense, you're on another plane of existence. If you mean geographically, you're in Ravenwood, Massachusetts. Are you from here?" I ask.

"No, I'm from Ohio. How the hell did I end up in Massachusetts?" she asks, looking around my apartment with new eyes. I can't even imagine how she views the thrifted pieces and riot of color. She seems like a white walls, white couch kind of gal.

"You were probably drawn to me without even realizing it. Unfortunately for me, I act as a sort of beacon for the dead. I don't know where you all go when you aren't 'here' with me, but it seems like you can travel vast distances without a conscious thought. At least, that's what I've gathered over the years." I don't know why some come to me when others don't. I have to assume it's because they don't want to be helped.

"Oh, no. I don't want to be stuck *here*," she says, putting her face in her hands.

I take in a breath and count to ten before letting it out again. "Perfect! That's what I can help you with," I say with forced cheerfulness.

"How can you help me?" she asks, quirking a dark brow.

"Well, I can sort of help you move on. We'll figure out why you stuck around, because most people don't, and then we'll try to resolve whatever issue you're having. After that, you should be able to go on," I say, gesturing vaguely out the window.

"Go on, *where?*" she cries, looking at me with suddenly teary eyes.

I don't think she's going to like my answer, but... "I don't know. I'm sorry, I wish I did, but I can't see beyond where you are now. I've never been there. It's better than here, though, wherever it is," I say gently.

"This was *not* supposed to happen to me. Not yet. I just graduated from college, my boyfriend just proposed, and I was supposed to start med school next semester. I had a five, ten, and twenty-year plan! Dying at the age of twenty-three wasn't on it." She caves in on herself, shoulders drooping forward as she grips her elbows.

My heart cracks for her. "I'm sorry," I say, hoping she can hear how much I mean it. Even if she has been abrasive, no one deserves to die so early.

After a while, she sniffs and looks at me to explain, "I used to bike everywhere. Heart health, you know? One day, I went to the grocery store to pick up a few essentials, and when I was on my way home ... I got hit by a car. They didn't see me, I guess. I was wearing a helmet, but it wasn't enough. Apparently, I died on impact. I figured it out after I attended my own funeral and heard everyone talking about it. Just my luck that the thing that was supposed to make me live longer is what killed me." She looks more furious than sad, like she'd avenge herself if she could.

"Just please tell me you didn't die over kale," I say, trying to lighten the mood. Death isn't something you can really dance around when someone has already died. I've found that it helps sometimes to joke about it. It's just too horrible otherwise.

She chuckles seemingly against her will and says, "No. But I may or may not have had sprouts on my grocery list." She groans, "Ugh, what an awful thing to die for. I should have eaten more ice cream." I laugh a little at that, wishing I could comfort her more.

"So, do you know why you're still here?" I ask eventually. I want to help her, but I also really need to get to work.

She shrugs. "I'm not sure. I mean, like I said, I had my life all planned out, and now that's not going to happen. So maybe that's why?"

"Maybe, but it's not like you can go to med school like this, so it must be something else. There's usually some sort of unfinished business, and in my twenty-nine years, I've never seen someone stick around for a degree."

"You can't tell me why I'm here?" she asks.

"No, sorry. Believe it or not, it's rare for a spirit to remain here. Sometimes it takes a while for them to fully understand why they're stuck, and I'm no fortune teller."

"No offense, but what do you even do? If I have to figure out why I'm here, why do I need you?" she questions with a snotty uptilt of her chin.

"You're right. I can't automatically see what has you stuck here. All I can do is try to help you figure it out. Sometimes, I can contact family members or friends and help in that way. Or I'll pass along physical objects or messages. But a lot of it is just talking and trying to think through the problem. And honestly, if you'd rather try to figure it out on your own, that's fine. It's no skin off my nose. I actually need to get ready for work, so if you could just... Go somewhere else for a bit, that'd be nice. If you want my help, come back whenever, but preferably during waking hours. If you don't show up, I can assume that you've got it handled." I'm trying to be patient, but I am over her rudeness and in desperate need of some me time.

"Fine," she agrees. In a blink, I'm alone again.

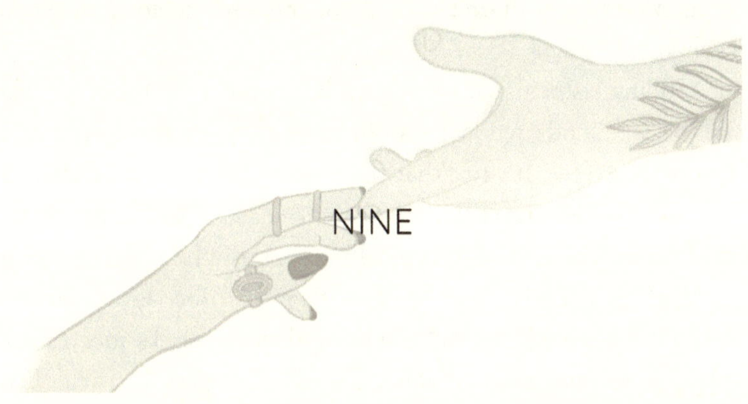

# NINE

AFTER CALLING Wren and getting her voicemail, I fear I'm on my own for the night. I know most people would probably think it was pathetic that my sister is my only friend, but it's just easier that way. Growing up, I had friends here and there, but I found out most of them were using me to get to my cool aunt, who had already become something of a local legend by the time I was in high school. Teenage girls *really* want their tarot cards read.

Wren has never had that same problem. Don't get me wrong, she's not exactly a social butterfly, but the confidence she carries herself with is magnetic. People are drawn to her, even if they are a little afraid of her. Sure, she had the same issue with people trying to get to know Aunt Clarissa growing up, but she usually got rid of those "friendships" before they even truly began. Maybe watching me get hurt over and over was enough to prevent her from attempting connections with those types. She saw how I often made myself smaller, trying to keep friends who didn't care about me, and decided never to shrink.

So, my sister usually ends up being out with other people on the weekends while I stay in to work or grab a coffee solo across the street. It's not that she doesn't invite me; she does. I just usually decline. I don't want her to feel like she has to be my buffer, which is what typically happens when I go out with her and her friends. I can be friendly on a surface level, like the way I am with Misha, but anything deeper spooks me. That's why I'm so disappointed about Dean. It felt easy in a way I've never experienced before. It sucks to learn that feeling didn't go both ways.

I shake my head, reminding myself that I am *not* supposed to be thinking about him because I've given him too much of my bandwidth already. I look around my living room and sigh, resigned to spend another Friday night alone. I perk up at the sight of the box of goods on my desk for the witchy mystery boxes and decide, like the rest of my generation, that the company of strangers on the internet is preferable to being alone. Even if they never see my face.

---

"RAE BABY! How is my favorite niece?" Aunt Clarissa billows into The Veil, bangles jangling on her wrists and dripping in a multitude of gems.

I can't help but chuckle from my place behind the counter. "You say that to both me and Wren. How am I supposed to believe you?"

"Well, you're the one carrying on my legacy," she says, sweeping her arms in a grand gesture around the store, making the bell sleeves of her shirt flap like butterfly wings. "That must mean I like you at least a little more," she argues.

"Ah, or it means that Wren couldn't be bothered to run an entire store," I say with a raised brow.

Aunt Clarissa scowls. "That girl never did care about our legacy."

"Oh come on, she doesn't hide her Gift nearly as much as I do," I say, always ready to go to battle for my little sister, even if Aunt Clarissa means nothing by it.

She turns her glare on me, those blue eyes just like mine and my sisters' burning bright. "True. Both of you need to realize what a privilege you are blessed with. Do you know how few people have the Gift?"

I raise my hands in defeat, not wanting to get into this lecture again. "Okay, alright. Super cool that I see dead people. Now, what's up?" She sniffs at my sardonic tone and begins straightening the display of teas at the register. She hardly comes into the shop anymore, especially unannounced. So her sudden appearance makes me nervous.

When she looks up from her task, she must read the concern on my face because she says, "You're not in trouble! I have some ideas for the store, that's all. I was coming in to chat about it. Do you have a minute?"

I nod and gesture her over to the fainting couch. Once we both get seated, I ask, "What's up?"

"Well, I know you've been doing well with the online store, but I want to do something more to revamp the brick and mortar. We hardly have any foot traffic these days."

"Yeah, but Halloween is just around the corner. That always brings an influx of customers, so I'm not too worried. We usually make most of our sales during October anyway," I say, leaning against the backrest.

Aunt Clarissa purses her wrinkled lips and leans forward, sending a waft of old cigarette smoke and amber my way. "Right! So, how do we get our October customers to want to come back the rest of the year?"

I wait a beat to see if she'll answer her own rhetorical question before asking, "Are you going to tell me, or do I have to guess?"

"Don't be petulant," she chides. She sits straighter and folds her hands together over her lap. "I know you've been hesitant to use your Gift in the past, but—"

"Nope," I say, cutting her off. I begin to stand, not wanting to finish this conversation.

"Wait! You haven't even heard me out yet."

I sit back down reluctantly and say, "Okay, fine."

Aunt Clarissa readjusts herself, excess jewelry jingling. "I know your... 'issue' with using your gift in such a way stems from the lack of anonymity. Now, I may not understand why you want to hide your Gift from the light,"—she sniffs in disgruntlement and continues—"but, what if we could ensure no one knew it was you? Maybe we could have you behind a curtain? Could be very mysterious."

"What, like the *Wizard of Oz*? You know I can't just summon someone from beyond anyway. There would be no way for me to do that authentically, and I'm not going to scam people." I fold my arms across my chest. This is a conversation we've had so many times. Well, okay, the whole curtain idea is new, but still.

"I know that, and I know you hold yourself to some ridiculous moral standard," I roll my eyes, but she barrels on. "But, I want you to try to summon someone. You've never allowed yourself to try because you don't want any more power than you already have," she says.

I purse my lips, annoyed at being read so easily. She's right that I've never tried to actively summon a spirit. Honestly, most of the time, I do my best not to seek out the dead. If they find me, I'll help, but I'm not going to go looking for Casper. It might be possible to summon a dead person, but I'm afraid of using that kind of power. For the most part, the spirits I've interacted with have been grateful for the help because they are the ones looking for me. What if I call on someone who doesn't want to be found?

"It could be dangerous," I say, which is honestly just a drop in the bucket of my concerns.

She waves that away with an elegant flick of her hand. "Pah. The dead hardly influence the living. It is no more dangerous than attracting butterflies to your flower box with aster."

"That's not true, and you know it. While the dead may not be as strong as the living, they can cause trouble when they want to. If we're going to talk about this, be honest with me. Why the sudden need for extra income?" I ask, knowing there must be something else going on.

She sighs dramatically and grabs one of my hands with her own. "Alright, dear. I'll be honest. You know I'm getting old and that I would like to fully retire soon. Do you remember my friend, Esther?" When I nod, she says, "Well, Esther moved to a fantastic little retirement community called Sunset Village down in Florida, and I want to join her."

I can't help the way my eyebrows shoot up to my hairline. "You? In a retirement community? Playing Bingo and riding golf carts?"

"That's ageist, darling," she sniffs. "Besides, bingo is quite fun when you're with the right people."

I shake my head incredulously. Never in my life did I think my larger-than-life aunt would want to do something as pedestrian as spending the last of her days in a retirement community. And besides, I'm not sure what this news has to do with the store or my Gift.

I take a moment to gather my thoughts before saying, "Other than checking to see if you've been switched with a body double, we have more to talk about. What does your retirement plan have to do with the store? Why are you so concerned with making more money?" Honestly, the store is mostly in my care, anyway. She hardly pays attention to the business side anymore. She likes to add in her opinion here and there, but for the most part, it's all on me. I thought we were doing okay financially, so I don't understand what all the fuss is about.

Her brows draw together, and for a moment, she genuinely looks her age, which is frightening in and of itself. "Mr. Beauhurst is upping the rent for this entire block of buildings, ours included. Even if I wasn't planning on going to a nice retirement community, we'd need to make more than we are now to stay afloat."

I sit back feeling more than a little stunned. The Veil has been both my home away from home, and my *actual* home. I quite literally took my first steps in here, tripping over the rug as I did it. I got my first set of keys to a place that was all my own here. I can't fathom losing it.

I look around at the artfully crafted chaos of the store and try to imagine it as a brightly lit, uniformly decorated supplement store. Or maybe it would become a new Starbucks and push Brewed Awakening out of business. I shudder. "How much more do we need to make a month?" I ask, immediately shifting into problem-solving mode.

She clears her throat and says, "Sunset Village costs about five thousand a month, and our rent is upping an extra three thousand per month."

I feel like I'm going to be sick. "We need eight thousand dollars extra a month? Almost an extra hundred thousand a *year?*"

"Don't go hyperventilating on me just yet. It's not quite so bad as that. I'm looking to sell my house, which should help quite a lot with the retirement home costs, not to mention there's an incentive program for new seniors moving to Sunset Village. Plus it's all inclusive, so if I plan appropriately, I only need about a thousand a month to support myself." While it doesn't seem like much, she hardly takes a salary as it is. She only takes enough to pay her bills, preferring to put whatever profits we make into the store and into my own pocket.

"So, we need an extra four thousand dollars a month?" I ask incredulously. Sure, it's less than eight thousand, but that's still a lot of zeros.

I appreciate that she hasn't tried to offer to sell me the business, considering there's no way I could afford that. Although I guess she probably already knows since she signs my checks. We've only managed to do as well as we have because I'm the only employee and am willing to work as needed without taking any overtime pay. I'd like to eventually buy the business

from her, I just need to save for another, oh, I don't know…
twenty years or so?

She nods. "Yes, exactly. It's either we come up with a plan
to make that extra four thousand, or we lose the brick-and-
mortar store and likely your apartment," she says with a wince.

"Why are you leaving? Why now?" I ask, blinking the gathering tears from my lashes. I know she can't control the raise in
rent, but does she have to compound that with her moving
away? She's always been a bit of a free spirit, going where the
wind takes her, but this move feels really out of left field. She is
getting older but even still, it's an odd choice. I never took her to
be a snowbird.

Her blue eyes soften at the sight of my tears, and she says,
"I know this probably seems sudden to you and that's my fault.
I haven't communicated with you enough. The truth is, I was
too prideful to admit that I need help occasionally at home. It's
also getting harder and harder to climb the stairs to my
bedroom. I… Well, I had a fall last month when I tried to go up
the stairs." I suck in a shocked gasp of air, and she pats my hand
placatingly. "I'm fine, obviously," she says as she waves over her
intact body. "But it scared me. So most nights I end up sleeping
on my couch, which isn't doing anything to help my back. I've
always been happy to live alone, but now I'm afraid it's getting
dangerous."

Despite the fact that I am surrounded by death, I've always
thought of Aunt Clarissa as immortal. Infallible. Unshakeable.
To hear her describe her increasing frailty is jarring, to say the
least.

"I could help you. I could move in with you and we could
rent out the apartment," I offer. I would hate to get rid of my

little place, but it would be worth it to keep Aunt Clarissa around. She's like a second mother to me.

She shakes her head vehemently. "No. I am not your responsibility. You already do so much more than I ask of you, let alone pay you for. I can't ask you to take care of me like I'm some invalid."

"First of all, you aren't asking. I'm offering. I love you and I would be honored to take care of you," I say, truthfully.

She smiles at me and pats my hand. "Even if that is true, Rae, I'm ready for a new adventure. Esther keeps telling me all about the gorgeous beach within walking distance of her cottage and all of the amenities. Plus, I have to admit it would be nice to be in a smaller space. They have housekeepers and grocery shoppers, so all your basic needs are met. Then, later, if I end up needing more care, they have people and programs in place to do that as well."

"You sound like a brochure," I say with a reluctant smile.

"I've read over their website a few times," she replies airily.

"This seems like something you really want to do." I study her face, noting the way she lights up as she thinks about her new adventure. Who am I to keep her from that? "How soon exactly are you planning on leaving?" I ask, even though I'm afraid of the answer.

"Sometime before March. Sunset Village is offering a special move-in price for the first six months of residency during the winter months. It's a relatively new place, so they're trying to attract more residents. I think they're banking on those who are sick of the cold and ready to move to a place where it's rarely under fifty degrees." I try not to balk at having less than six months to attempt to boost our income to account for everything. "Rent will increase in January, so we have the next few months to get a bit of a head start," she says.

I nod, the stress of it all making me feel like I'm viewing this whole tableau from above. "And you think offering a medium service will be enough to make up the difference?" I ask, getting us back on topic.

"Maybe not all of it, but it's a start. People would pay good money to communicate with a loved one."

"Taking money for it makes me feel... I don't know, Aunt Clarissa. Bad, I guess." Even though I don't view my ability as a "gift" (despite what my family calls it), it still seems like something I shouldn't charge people for. Helping others is sort of sacred to me. Asking compensation for that is something I'll have to think about.

"It's not like you'd be swindling them, dear. You can *actually* speak with the dead. But if that's not something you're interested in doing, then we need to come up with something else. And soon." She searches my face and says, "Unless, of course, you want me to sell The Veil. I would give you a portion of that sale to find a new place to live and keep you afloat for a few months."

My gaze snaps back to her and I reply, "No. You can't sell it. Not yet. Please, let me try to come up with something. I don't want to lose this place."

She nods and a relieved smile pulls at her cheeks. "It means more than you know that you care for The Veil as much as I do. I never want you to feel trapped, though. If you want out, darling, all you have to do is tell me."

I shake my head emphatically. "I don't. This place is everything to me. I know I don't embrace the whole medium thing, but I love The Veil. I love that we provide opportunities for people to spark their curiosity and introduce ritual into their daily lives. I love living above the store," I say, my voice cracking.

"Okay. Take a breath. I didn't want to upset you."

*Too late for that.*

I'm frustrated that she sprung this on me, but all the same, I'm not surprised. Aunt Clarissa does what she wants, and the rest of us can either get on board or get out of her way. So, I guess I better get on board before I lose it all.

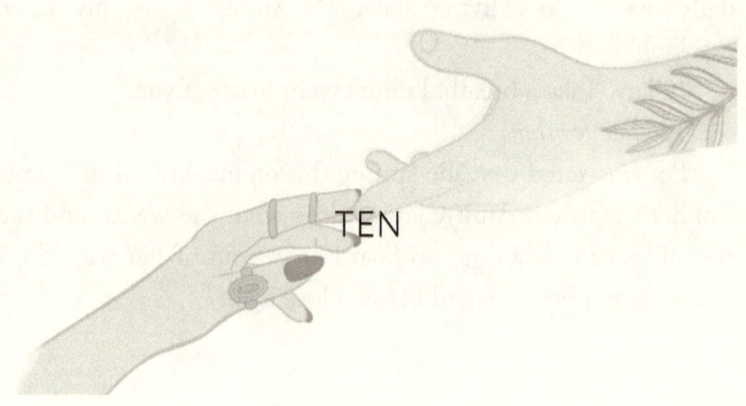

# TEN

AFTER MY TALK with Aunt Clarissa yesterday, I feel a pressing need to clear my head. I've been spiraling about it all day today. I need to come up with a plan quickly, or I might have to use my Gift.

Aunt Clarissa is right: I wouldn't be ripping people off. It's not like I would charge them the full price if I couldn't reach who they wanted. I shake my head, sending my long braid over my shoulder. I need to try to come up with something else first. I don't want to be the next *Long Island Medium.*

I throw my old trench coat on and lock up behind me. It's chilly enough to need a jacket, but not so cold that I need a hat and gloves. I decide to take a walk down to Beauhurst Park and around the manmade lake there. It has a nice walking path that I like to use to get my thoughts together. I'm not a huge fan of exercise in general, but taking a walk does wonders for my mental health. It's about two miles round trip from my apart-ment, so that gives me plenty of time to come up with a solution. I resolve that if I haven't come up with at least a couple of ideas by the time I make it back home, I'll think about Aunt Clarissa's option more seriously.

When I get to the park, there's only a few people milling about. I guess most of the Ravenwoodians are at home eating dinner. I shove my hands into my coat pockets to protect them from the cool air and start on the looping path that goes around the small lake.

If I were artistic, the park would make for a fantastic painting, especially now. The leaves on the trees are just starting to turn a rainbow of color. Mostly green, but the edges of the trees are a riot of reds and yellows. The low-hanging sun gilds everything it touches, and the only ripples on the calm surface of the lake are where the ducks drag small wakes behind them.

By the time I get to the halfway point around the lake, I still haven't come up with a better solution. I thought briefly of renting out the space for parties or something, but the witchy aesthetic of the interior would probably only attract people during the month of October. Which is kind of the thing we're trying to find a solution for.

We already sell a variety of supplies for anyone interested in spirituality or the occult, and even some basics for the average Joe who happens to wander into the store, so I don't know what else we could add that fits our niche. I think for a moment on the "potion" idea that the teen was asking after the other day, but that feels way too disingenuous for me.

I'm grumbling about retirement homes by the time I insert my key in the lock of my front door. I don't actually resent Aunt C for wanting to go. It does seem like a good fit for her, but damn—when it rains it pours.

I hang my coat on the rack by the front door and kick off my boots. In my socked feet, I walk to the couch and sit down with a huff. I cross my arms and lean back.

*I guess I can just... open up my senses and see what I can feel. If it gets to be too much, I can always pull back.*

Satisfied with that plan, I begin the process of slowing my breath and closing my eyes. I've done this in the past just to see if I could tug on someone I was already in contact with, but I've never just thrown out the net to see what I can catch. I reach out with an ever-expanding web, scanning with my mind's eye.

I'm a little scared of accidentally grabbing someone who would rather be left alone to really push myself. Like Dean. Apparently, *he* wants me to leave him alone. Well, lucky for him, I will. In fact, I'm so pissed off at the way he's treated me, that if I never hear from him again—

"Rae?" My eyes want to pop open at the intrusion, but I keep them screwed shut in disbelief.

*I know that voice. Oh, God. I know that voice. That can only mean...*

"Dean?" I ask, cracking my eyes open to see him standing in front of me. He's wearing a deep-navy suit with a crisp, white button-up shirt, undone at the collar. He looks the way he did on our date, but he's shimmering around the edges just so. And he's suddenly appeared in my living room. Unless this is a "living in the walls" situation, I think I just discovered why he never texted me back.

"Oh, fuck. You didn't ghost me! You're... Well, a ghost!" I blurt, jumping up.

"Ha-ha. I didn't ghost you, silly. Our date was literally yesterday. You can't miss me that much already, do you?" He gives me that same charming smile that made my heart race on our date, and while it would have worked on me weeks ago, now it just makes me nauseous. Because he doesn't know. He thinks I'm playing some silly prank on him.

*Oh, no. I'm going to be the one to have to tell him that he's dead.*

As he looks around my apartment, his smile melts off his face slowly, like an ice cream cone left in the sun for too long. "Wait... Where are we? And how did I get here? I just left work, right?" He looks down at himself, brushing his hands along his suit jacket as if to confirm his outfit is indeed work appropriate. "Where's my phone?" he asks, patting his pockets.

I wince. Yeah, he won't be finding that in the afterlife.

I gnaw on my lip, unsure of how to break the news to him. Of course, I've had to tell others that they were dead, but this is the first time I've had to do the same for someone I know. Someone I've kissed.

And *wow*, he's dead. And I don't even have time to process that information, let alone the surprising wave of grief. Because obviously, right after the one time I hit it off with someone, they have to give up the ghost. Really funny, Universe. Hilarious, actually.

But this isn't about me. Poor guy is about to have a rude awakening.

He continues patting his pockets and looks at me suspiciously. "Is this your place? Did you drug me? You know, you didn't have to do that to get me to come to your apartment, right? All you had to do was ask." He gives up on the search for his phone and crosses his arms. I can tell he's fighting to stay calm, but his mind is frantically trying to make sense of where he is and why.

He frowns at me. "Actually, after this little stunt, the

answer will probably be no," he says, backing away from me a step.

He must be very disoriented right now, and I would wager he hasn't been sentient since he died. Most people who die take a while to "come to" in this form. It's a traumatic thing for the soul to separate from the body. And I just yanked Dean to me without intending to. I wince, hoping I didn't disturb some vital part of the process that I'm not aware of.

"I didn't drug you, Dean. Our date was over three weeks ago now," I say slowly.

He shakes his head adamantly. "No, I swear. I *just* saw you, and then—Didn't I go home?" he asks himself, looking up at my ceiling as if to find some reasonable explanation among the cracking plaster.

"Look, it's September 27th and our date was on the 5th." I hold out my phone to show him the date on the lock screen.

His brows scrunch together violently. I consider blurting out the truth, but he's so confused, I think that would just freak him out more. I'm trying to slowly lead him to his new reality.

"That can't be right," he says, intending to grab my phone and pull it closer to him.

Only, he hasn't mastered anything about being a ghost yet, so his hand goes right through. He doesn't know he has to concentrate on the object and his hand to make contact. He's still operating like a live person who assumes that if they reach for an object, they'll be able to touch it. He shakes his head as if to clear it and reaches for my phone again, sending goosebumps along my arm as his hand passes through mine for a second time. "Okay, what the *fuck* is going on?" he asks, sounding close to panic.

Well, so much for easing him in. I sit down and gesture for

Dean to do the same. When he tries to sit, though, he passes straight through the couch and lands with an "Oomph" on the ground. Guess I should have seen that coming. Man, I'm really screwing this up.

Don't ask me why he didn't go straight through the floor. I know very little about ghost physics, but I can only assume it's something to do with his unconscious ability to control where he is. And while he definitely doesn't think he should go through couches, he *really* doesn't believe he can go through the floor.

"No, but actually *what the fuck?!*" he yells from his rumpled position on my floor. The air drops in temperature until I lock my jaw to keep my teeth from chattering. He sits up and scrambles away from my couch to the middle of my living area, passing through my coffee table while he does so. He stares up at me, panting hard.

"Okay, um... I'm so sorry to be the one to tell you this, and I'm clearly messing it up. But you've, um... passed on," I fumble out.

"What?"

"Like, you've gone over the rainbow bridge." I make a rainbow motion with my hands to punctuate.

"Isn't that for dogs?"

"Dead ones," I say, nodding.

"Are you calling me a dog?"

"What? No! I swear I'm usually better at this. I'm so sorry, but you're dead, Dean. You passed away sometime within the last three weeks," I say, biting my lip against the urge to make more euphemisms.

He shakes his head in disbelief. "No, that can't be right. I'm not dead. I'm right here," he says, pointing his thumb at his chest emphatically.

"*You* are, but your body's not," I try to explain, feeling once again like I'm royally screwing this all up. He runs his long fingers through his hair and even slaps himself on the cheek a little, then raises an eyebrow at me. "Okay well, explain why you couldn't grab my phone or sit on my couch then," I say, exasperated at his stubbornness.

He opens his mouth to argue, but snaps it shut and works his jaw a few times. "I... I don't know," he says finally.

"Look, I know this must be hard to come to terms with. I'm sorry you're learning this right now, and that I haven't done a better job at breaking the news to you. I swear I'm not usually so bad at this," I say quietly.

We sit in silence for a while, and I do my best to let him process. Hell, *I'm* trying to process that he's dead. I feel like an ass because I've been so mad at him for not messaging me back, but he's obviously had other things going on. I try not to let the wave of grief overtake me. I only knew him for a short period before he passed, but he was truly such a cool and special person. It feels like a punch in the gut to know that none of his family or friends will ever get to see him again. A light snuffed out before the candle was even halfway burned.

He looks at his hands, turning them this way and that, and for the first time, I wonder if ghosts see the shimmering too. "I'm really dead, aren't I?" he asks quietly. His gaze shifts to mine, and I can see the anguish and confusion written in his expression.

"You are," I say, matching his tone. Pure honesty is usually the best protocol in these situations.

His form flickers in and out rapidly, and I feel the room

drop a few degrees. Goosebumps texture my skin, and I rub my arms to keep warm. It takes a lot of energy to stay in a corporeal form, and he's what I've previously deemed as a baby ghost— new to the world of haunts and existential dread. So his battery is fairly small right now. I'll be surprised if he can stick around for more than a few more minutes. With that in mind, I say, "Look, you're probably feeling drained, so it's okay to let yourself go. You need to rest. I promise we can keep chatting when you're feeling up to it."

He stands and comes over to me. "How will I find you again?" he asks when I look up at him. He reaches out a hand as if to touch my cheek but stops at the last second. I feel the barest hint of energy crackling over my skin where his hand hovers. He drops it and flexes his hand by his side.

"You will," I say simply.

I've noticed that once a ghost finds me, it's easier to do so again. The hardest part is finding me for the first time. It's like stumbling upon a dinghy in the vast ocean. But once you've gotten to it, you can hook a safety line and wander as far as you want. You'll always be able to find your way back. With that reassurance, he flickers out, and I'm left reeling in the silence.

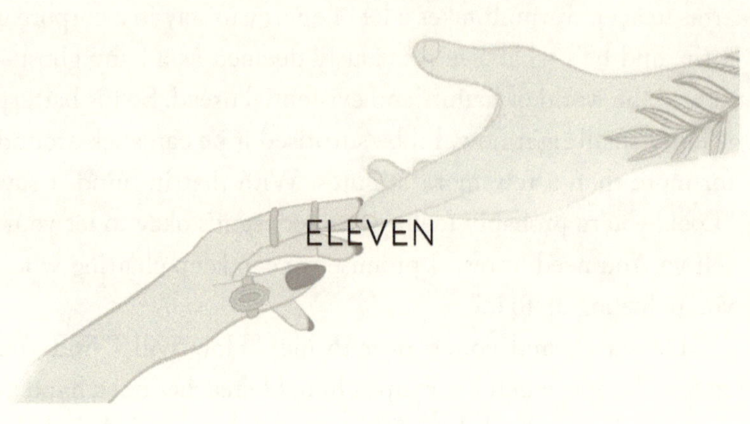

# ELEVEN

LATER THAT NIGHT, I'm shoving my feet into my favorite pair of Chelsea boots when I hear a *honk* outside. I blow out an annoyed breath because Wren is so impatient. She literally just texted me, "here," a minute ago. I grab my small crossbody bag off its hook by the door and head out, locking up behind me. As soon as Wren sees me reach the bottom of the stairs, she bleats her car horn again, making me jump out of my skin.

*Once an annoying little sister, always an annoying little sister.*

I dash grumpily through the rain to get to her car. Her dark maroon lips stretch into a wide grin when I plop myself unceremoniously into her passenger seat. "Gotcha," she says, beeping her horn one last time. I sigh and buckle myself in. I'm doing my best to hold it together, but I've only had a few hours since Dean blinked out. I'm feeling every emotion all at once. Horrible sadness that he's dead. Selfish relief that he didn't ghost me. Confusion and shock that he's gone. Determination to help him figure out why he's still here. And I'm trying to figure out how to shove all of that in a box so Wren doesn't sniff it out like the emotional bloodhound she is.

It's her turn to drive us to Mom and Dad's for family dinner; I always hate when she drives. Where I am overly cautious, she is overly daring. She loves to make a game of on-ramp chicken where she sees how many cars she can get past before finally merging onto the freeway. I loudly recount how many people I've seen who have died in car accidents while she blasts The Ramones and sings along without a care in the world.

Mom and Dad moved a couple of towns over after Wren moved out. They wanted to downsize and live closer to where Dad works. Their new place (it'll always be new to me, even if they moved over five years ago now) is located in a quaint little suburb where everyone has nice grass and large, established trees dominating their front yards.

Wren bumps onto their driveway and cuts the engine of her ancient Prius. I send a silent thank you to whoever's listening that we didn't die on the way here and restrain myself from kissing the ground. We scurry to the front door to get out of the drizzling rain. Wren barrels inside, protecting her freshly flat-ironed hair, and begins shedding her outer layers to deposit them on the coat hooks. I follow her inside and do the same, appreciating the warmth of our parents' home and the scent of freshly baked bread.

"What is with you tonight? You're more grumpy than me, and that's saying something," Wren says, eyeing me as we make our way down the hallway.

"I'll tell you later," I reply quietly before we round the corner into the kitchen. I didn't want to tell her about Dean before we got here, because then she wouldn't stop talking about it, and it would be an inquisition from my whole family. I'm still trying to process everything, and my well-meaning parents will ask more questions than I know how to answer. By the end of the night, we'd be trying to find his birth certificate online, and I'm not ready for all that.

"Are those my girls?" our dad asks, broad back turned to us as he oversees the stove. He looks over his shoulder, round cheeks ruddy from the heat of the stove.

"It sure is," Mom says, rounding the island to give us each a kiss on the cheek and a hug. When she hugs me, I can't help but squeeze a little harder than normal. I'm in need of some comfort after the week I've had. She takes my lead and gives me an extra-tight hug, pressing a kiss to my temple.

I have to steel myself against the tears that want to well up. Something about a hug from my mom just instantly makes it feel okay to cry. Being surrounded by her clean laundry and lavender scent takes me back to a time when I'd go running to her for comfort whenever I scraped my knee or failed a test. I get ahold of myself just in time, because when she pulls back, she gives me a questioning glance with eyes that look so much like mine and Wren's. The blue eyes, like the Gift, run in the family.

"Just missed you," I say in answer to her unasked question. Which isn't a total lie. She and my dad have been super busy, and it's been hard to find time to get together lately.

"I missed you, too, Bug," she says, squeezing my shoulder with her warm hand. "Come on, let's eat. Your dad made this roasted vegetable soup, and it is to *die* for with his homemade sourdough."

I immediately perk up because my dad's cooking is

legendary. He was the one to get creative when Wren declared she was a vegetarian, and he's come up with some truly delectable dishes over the years. We don't always make every meal vegetarian, but my parents try to make sure most of our shared meals are meat-free. When they're not, they always cook her something special on the side, so she doesn't leave hungry.

We gather at their round dining table, and my dad begins ladling out the soup into large bowls while my mom cuts thick slices of bread off the round loaf he must have made earlier today. Wren and my dad chat idly about the merits of carrots versus sweet potatoes in a vegetable soup, and I work to keep my expression neutral. Wren will bring up my weird mood to my parents if I make it too obvious that I'm struggling.

Luckily, after living with her for most of my life, I have some defenses I can pull out when I'm in need. She and I are close, but she doesn't need to be privy to my every thought and emotion. The way I protect myself from her prying senses isn't unlike your average grounding techniques. I work to be fully in this moment. I concentrate on the sweet and sour combination of the sourdough dipped in soup, the warmth of the air surrounding me, and the ambient sounds of my family enjoying a meal. As I do this, I feel myself relax, my shoulders coming away from my ears, and my heart rate slowing.

"So Bug, how's the store doing?" my dad asks, quirking a graying brow over the rim of his glasses. Well, there goes my calm. I look between my parents and realize they're oblivious to Aunt Clarissa's newest plan. It doesn't surprise me that she didn't bother to tell her sister, but it's frustrating that I have to be the one to tell my mom.

I take a bite of bread to stall for a second. After I wash it down with a sip of water, I realize I can't push it off any longer.

"Um, the store is good, I guess. Mr. Beauhurst is raising rent at the start of the year, so we'll need to come up with a lot of extra money to cover it."

My dad's brows furrow. "How much? Surely he can't be raising the rent that much, right?" he asks.

I push my soup around with my spoon and say, "No. I mean, yes, he is raising the rent a lot. But, it's not the only new expense. Aunt Clarissa wants to move into a retirement home."

"What?" my mom gasps.

"In Florida," I specify.

"Florida?" my parents ask together.

"What do you mean she's moving to Florida? We always made fun of those people," my mom says, sitting back and crossing her arms. While my mom and Aunt Clarissa have very different personalities, they look incredibly similar. My aunt has really leaned into the boho, free-spirit look, while my mom is most at home in a nice sweater and khakis. Their faces, though, are nearly identical, other than the ten years or so that separate them. My mom always jokes that looking into Aunt Clarissa's face is like looking into a mirror set a decade in the future.

"Yeah, I guess she's been having some trouble getting around her house, but was too proud to tell us that she needed help. Her friend moved down there a while ago and has sold her on it. I know it's surprising, but it sounds like it'll be a good thing for her, especially as she gets older. Anyway, she's going to need extra money every month to swing it. So The Veil has to bring in an extra four grand total." I blow out a breath, trying to calm the fresh spike of anxiety.

My mom shakes her head and gripes, "Just like 'Rissa to decide on something and make it everyone else's problem." She pinches the space between her brows and continues, "So is she expecting you to come up with a grand plan to pay for all of this?"

I feel the need to jump in and defend my aunt, who has given me so much, but I hold myself back. For all of Aunt Clarissa's greatness, she does have a tendency of going after whatever she wants and leaving the finer details to those around her. Even The Veil.

When she first founded the store, she got a business loan; but the payments were way too high for her to afford. After a couple of months of shirking the payments—in favor of going to festivals with her newly printed business card and wares in tow —my parents stepped in to save it. They became unofficial investors early on and helped supplement the payments for a good year or two before Aunt Clarissa was able to pay them fully on her own.

This newest development is one of many decisions that affect others just as much as herself. It's hard to be upset at her over it, though. She never means any harm, she just doesn't have any sort of foresight. It's exactly why, according to her, she never wanted a serious relationship or children of her own. She knows where she falls short and owns it.

At my mom's raised eyebrow, I realize I haven't answered her question yet. "Yeah. Yeah, it's pretty much up to me." I swallow down the bile that creeps up my throat at the thought.

My mom's lips thin, and she says, "You know, back when 'Rissa first opened the Veil, I had a premonition that the store would be good for our family. That's why your father and I helped her along at first. We knew that our investment would pay off later on. And I think that time is now."

"Seriously?" I ask with a maniacal giggle. "That's what

comes to you when you find out that the store is going to be short thousands of dollars a month, and your daughter, who never went to business school, is going to be responsible for bridging that gap?" I take a sip of water to stop the laugh. I think I'm cracking from the pressure of it all.

"Yes," my mom replies calmly. "I know you have a hard time believing in yourself, but I have a good feeling about this." When my mom says that, it's not just a pleasantry to make you feel better—she means it. Her foresight isn't exactly a clear image of the future, but she gets a general impression of what's to come. For example, she can't tell you the winning lotto numbers, but she can tell you if you're going to win or not.

"But how am I going to do it?" I ask in a small voice I barely recognize.

"You're going to figure this shit out because you never back down from a challenge," Wren interjects, nodding at me across the table.

"You've got this, Bug. And we're here to help if you need it," My dad says, reaching over to squeeze my shoulder affectionately.

"Thanks, Dad," I say with a smile.

"Of course. Have you come up with any ideas?" he asks, immediately putting on his business manager hat. He's managed a successful local chain of hardware stores for the last fifteen years. It makes me feel a little bad that I didn't think to call him because he loves it when I pick his brain for business advice, but I wanted to see if I could figure it out on my own first. Since I hope to buy The Veil from my aunt one day, I feel the need to do things on my own where I can. I don't want to rely on my dad for training wheels when I should be able to ride the damn bike myself.

"Well, you know the potion pulls for the mystery boxes online do pretty well. Aunt Clarissa also mentioned using my Gift—"

"She didn't," my mom interrupts. "Damn it, 'Rissa. She's always been so envious that she didn't get a Gift, but I think the universe knows she wouldn't have used it for good. Listen to me, Rae. You do not have to use your Gift for profit if you don't want to. There's nothing inherently wrong with doing so, but I know it's not something you've ever wanted to do. Whatever you decide is okay."

I nod and say, "I know. I don't mind helping people, but I also don't want to attach my face to it. Aunt Clarissa suggested a *Wizard of Oz* situation where I wouldn't have to be seen. I'm still thinking it through, though."

"Can you even reach out and contact specific people?" Wren asks, eyebrows drawn. She knows that I've never really attempted it because I don't particularly like being a medium. I usually only help people out of a sense of obligation because I'm the only one around who can.

I shrug a shoulder. "I don't know. I've never really tried." Dean immediately comes to mind, so I clarify, "I think it's possible, though." I don't want to lie to my family. Especially Wren, because she'll sense it.

"Well, that should be the first thing you figure out. Because that sort of determines the rest of it, doesn't it?" my dad says, scrubbing a hand over his salt and pepper hair.

I bounce my shoulders and say, "Yeah, I guess so. I just need a day to process everything. It's all coming at me too fast, and I feel like I'm barely able to tread water right now."

He reaches out his hand and sets it lightly on my shoulder. "Sounds like you need a little break. You've been burning the candle at both ends for months now. Take tomorrow off. Fully off. No social media, no store, no inventory, no looking for new products, nothing to do with The Veil."

I open my mouth to argue, but my mom speaks before I can get a word in. "He's right. I'd wager you haven't taken a full day off since you started there after high school. You're always doing something for the store. Take the day off. Sleep in. Allow yourself a chance to rest, and I bet your answer will come to you."

I mull it over for a minute before saying, "Fine. Tomorrow is a Sunday anyway. No one ever comes in."

"That's the spirit," Wren chips in. I roll my eyes at her pun and go back to eating my soup. I'm excited about taking a full day off, even if the thought sort of makes my skin crawl. It feels counterintuitive to take a break right now, just days before our busiest season. But Victoria Alderwood, psychic and mother extraordinaire, is very rarely one to be argued with.

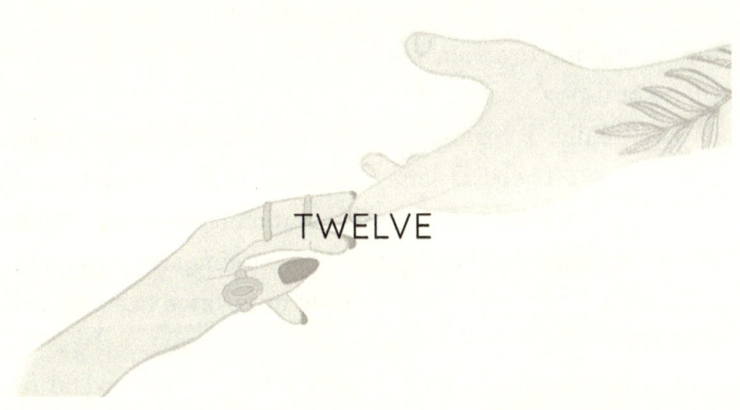

# TWELVE

I SLEPT IN. And by slept in, I mean I woke up at 7:30 A.M. instead of 7:00 A.M. I made my coffee, got dressed, and now I'm staring down my empty schedule with nothing planned for the rest of the day. I pat my thighs in a bored rhythm, literally having no clue what to do with myself for a work-free day. I never considered myself a workaholic, but wow, I guess I am one. Funny how that sort of thing just sneaks up on you.

With nothing else to do, I decide to grab my car keys and go for a drive. This time of year is stunning in Massachusetts.

I drive aimlessly for a while and find myself heading towards the Berkshires. There are a few trails I like to take when I want to be out in nature, but don't want to sweat. I pull off at the familiar turnout and hop out of my car, snagging my crossbody bag and water bottle on the way.

I crunch over fallen leaves to the trailhead and inhale the loamy scent of the mountains. Today is a gorgeous, blue-sky day; there's nothing better than walking through the forest with the sun shining through the changing leaves. I spend some time ambling along the trail, listening only to the sounds of my thighs swishing together, my feet crushing the leaves, and the trilling birdsong.

Eventually, I come to a small clearing that's an obvious resting point. There's a large fallen log to the side under the shade of a few evergreens. I take a seat on it and swig from my water bottle, relishing the quiet. The parking area was empty, so I figured I'd be alone, and my little introverted heart couldn't be happier.

I'm watching a chipmunk scamper up a tree several feet across the clearing when I notice something about it is... off. I'm concentrating so hard on the tiny creature that I can't help the squeak of surprise that escapes me when Dean pops into existence right where I was looking.

Dean tilts his head up at the sunshine-dappled trees and closes his eyes briefly, long eyelashes casting shadows on his cheekbones. He's the most beautiful thing out here, and I can't help but stay put and take him in. "I can't feel it," he murmurs, finally turning to me.

"The sun?" I ask.

"Yeah. Well I can't feel anything, to be honest. The rest of the world feels like I'm touching it through a thick blanket. Everything is blunted. I can't really smell or taste anything. I have the vague impression of feeling, and that's only if I concentrate."

"Being dead sucks," I say sympathetically.

He snorts a laugh and walks over, taking a seat on the mossy log beside me. I see we've mastered sitting. That's a good start.

"You could say that," he agrees. "I'm glad I was able to find you again."

I turn toward him, feeling goosebumps prickle over my leg where I accidentally brushed through his. "I knew you would."

He rubs the back of his neck. "So, you can see ghosts, huh?"

"Yep. And can you believe I was terrified of telling you on our date? I thought it would make you run for the hills."

"Honestly, I probably would have," he says with a laugh. "I told you I don't—didn't believe in all this. I guess seeing really is believing." He peers at the chipmunk, who stares straight at him from its perch in the tree.

"Well, I'm glad I didn't then. It was a great first date," I say, looking at him from the corner of my eye.

"It really was," he echoes, a small smile tugging at his lips. We sit in companionable silence for a bit, and then he asks, "What happened to me?"

"You don't remember?" I question. Sometimes ghosts recall what happened to them and sometimes they don't. It seems those who had a sudden death tend to have the most trouble remembering, or even realizing they're gone.

He shakes his head. "No. I remember leaving you at your apartment and driving home. Then, I watched some TV, went to bed, and woke up the next morning. I went to work like I told you I was going to. And then—nothing. I don't remember anything beyond turning my computer on at the start of the day."

"It's normal that you don't remember it. You'll get fragments here and there until you can piece it all together." I look at him and wait for him to meet my eyes before I ask, "Do you want me to look you up? It might help. I have my phone right here. We can find out together."

"You haven't done that yet?" he asks incredulously.

"No! It feels like a violation of privacy. I never Google the people who come to me for help unless they ask me to," I explain.

He purses his lush lips and says, "I guess, but you better believe I'd be Googling the shit out of anyone who suddenly appeared in my house."

"Well, we also have history," I reply, gesturing between us, "So that makes it more awkward. And, my Googling efforts were futile," I admit grudgingly.

He raises his eyebrows in acknowledgement and gestures to my bag.

"Okay, fine," I say, unzipping it to grab my phone. I swallow down the discomfort of Googling someone in front of them and type in his name. "What's your last name, and what town are you from?" I ask, realizing we still haven't exchanged that information. I shake my head a little at the thought because it's bizarre. I feel like I've known him forever, so to think we haven't dealt with the minutiae of last names seems ridiculous.

"Crawford. And I'm from Pittsfield." He shakes his head. "How have we never gotten there? I don't know yours either," he states, echoing my thoughts.

"Alderwood," I say with a smile, "And you already know where I'm from."

He returns my smile and says, "Okay Alderwood, let's do some digging." I feel my stomach flutter stupidly at the nickname and pack that feeling away to examine later. Crushing on a ghost is a bad idea and probably a conflict of interest. Whatever spark we shared was smothered the second Dean's heart stopped beating. Or at least, that's what I keep reminding myself.

I type his name and hometown into the search engine and find that other than a social media profile and a local article about one of the cases he won, there's only one other relevant article. It's titled "Local Lawyer Dean Crawford Found Dead in Home: What We Know." I figure that must be the one to read, so I click on it and wait for it to load. I'm lucky to even get cellphone service out here, but it's fairly slow.

"Do you want me to read it and give you the gist, or do you want to read it together?" I ask once the page loads, figuring he might not want to read about his own death.

"Together," he says, almost offended, "I'm a lawyer. I always need all the facts, even when they suck."

I nod and angle my phone towards him, trying to ignore the pleasant tingling up my spine when he sidles closer. We bend our heads and read together:

---

Local Lawyer, Dean Crawford (33), was found dead in his own home on Bradford Street on Monday, September 7. Authorities were called to the scene when Crawford's father, Jack Crawford, discovered his son's body. Authorities pronounced him dead at the scene.

Jack Crawford agreed to answer a few of our questions to get more eyes on his son's death and what he believes to be the mysterious circumstances around it. When asked why he was at his son's house, Jack Crawford stated, "Dean was supposed to be at work on Monday. When he didn't come in, that was an immediate cause for concern because he never misses a day, and definitely doesn't miss a day without calling in. I decided to check on him after work because I thought

that maybe he was sick or hurt... That's when I saw—
That's when I found him in the garage."

Jack Crawford let himself inside, spent time looking around the house, and when he couldn't find his son, he went to the garage to see if his car was gone. Crawford Sr. discovered Dean's body in the car in an apparent death by suicide. While the car had shut itself off after running out of gas, the garage smelled strongly of gasoline, and Dean Crawford appeared either unconscious or dead, according to Crawford Sr.

"I walked into the garage and was overwhelmed with the scent of gas. It was so strong it made my eyes water, and I had trouble breathing. I called 911 once I noticed Dean in the car. He looked like he was sleeping, but I knew. I just knew. He was already gone."

He attempted to pull Dean out in order to administer CPR as directed by the 911 operator. However, when he tried to move his son, he realized rigor mortis had already set in. "...That's when I walked outside and sat on the porch to wait for the ambulance," Crawford Sr. states.

The ambulance arrived at 5:31 PM, and as soon as the paramedics checked on Crawford, they called the local Pittsfield Police. Detective Samuel Gains gave the following statement regarding the incident: "We arrived on scene at approximately 5:56 PM and discovered Dean Crawford dead from apparent suicide by asphyxiation using vehicular exhaust. We determined that the time of death was at least twelve hours prior by the time we were on the scene."

While the local police have ruled Dean Crawford's

death a suicide, his father isn't so sure. According to him, "Dean would not have taken his own life. He never showed any signs of depression. There was no note, no prior signs of suicidal ideation, no reason for it. I'm not sure what happened, but to rule it a suicide is a serious miscarriage of justice."

Jack Crawford continues to seek any and all information regarding his son's death. If you or someone you know has any pertinent information, you are asked to call the tip line below. Pittsfield's chief of police, Fred Nostrum, could not be reached for comment.

---

When we get to the bottom of the article, I chew my lip and look at him, not sure what to say. Does he not know that he took his own life? He seemed so shocked at his death. Every spirit who got here by their own means is never surprised. They know. Even if they don't remember the finer details, they have an intrinsic understanding of why they're no longer among the land of the living.

Once he finishes reading, he sits straighter and looks me square in the eye. "I did not kill myself, Rae Alderwood. I didn't," he finishes emphatically.

"Are you sure?" I ask before I can stop myself. I can't help but think of the tired way he talked about his job. The pressure he was under. The way it seemed to be consuming his life.

He scoots away from me a little and says firmly, "Yes. I'm sure."

"Okay," I say back. Far be it from me to disagree with him when he's so adamant. My mind is scrambling, trying to find an explanation.

He puts a hand to his head and says, "Dammit. I think I'm at my limit for today. Rae, I need to figure out what happened to me. Will you help me?" His form flickers a bit, and he goes a little hazy around the edges.

"Yes," I say quickly, before he can disappear. "Find me when you can. We'll figure this out, Dean. I promise." He gives me a relieved look before he blinks out, and it's just me and the chipmunk again, staring at the now-empty space. I don't think I'm imagining the chipmunk's shock, and laugh a bit despite the pounding of my heart.

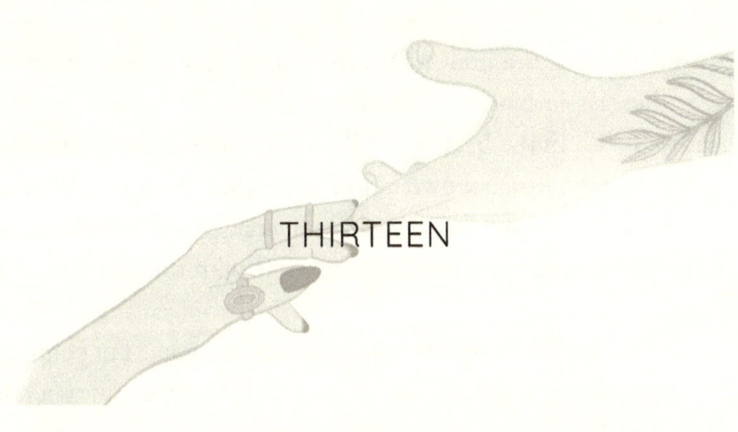

# THIRTEEN

WHEN I MAKE it back home, I sigh as I stare at the brick and glass storefront of The Veil. I'm no closer to coming up with a solution for the store, and now I'm playing Nancy Drew to help my ghostly friend figure out how he died.

It sounds awful, but I'm hoping to find out it was a random freak accident, like a heart attack or an aneurysm while his car was still running. At least that way, no one else is involved, and he can find some peace since it was out of his control. If someone did this to him... Well, that's a whole different ball game.

Not wanting to sit in my apartment alone with my thoughts, I decide to go for a walk to one of my favorite local diners. It's just up the road from me and serves the best patty melt around. The crinkle cut fries are the perfect pillowy softness with crunchy edges, and the soda is always crisp. My mouth waters at the thought, and I suddenly remember I haven't had anything besides coffee this morning. And that was before I drove off to connect with nature—and ghosts, apparently.

I pull open the door to Sarah's Diner and squeak my way over the classic black-and-white checkered floor to a maroon leather booth in the back. It's a little after one in the afternoon, so I missed the lunch crowd, and I appreciate the quiet. Within moments, a pimply faced, gangly teenage boy hands me a menu the size of my torso and walks off with the promise of a Coke.

I scan the menu briefly, already knowing what I'm going to order but wanting to look just in case. I close the menu when it turns out that I won't be branching out from my tried-and-true patty melt. I've ordered the same thing from Sarah's since I was a pimply faced teen myself.

While I wait for my order, I read a book on my phone, getting lost in a thriller with an unreliable narrator. There is just something so satisfying about getting absorbed in someone else's much bigger problems. Especially when you know that everything will be tied up in a neat little bow at the end, and you'll have all the answers you need. If only everything were so simple.

When my food gets dropped off, I devour a fry before it can cool down, cursing myself with a burned tongue for not having more patience.

"God, I really should have eaten more of those," Rebecca, the girl who died for sprouts, says, appearing suddenly across from me.

I scowl at her and hold up a subtle finger to silence her briefly. I pick up my phone, set it against my ear and say, "Mmhm, you should have. Now, can I please enjoy them before they go cold?"

She rolls her eyes at me and leans against the table, cupping her chin in her hand. "Aren't you supposed to help me?"

"I thought you didn't want me to look crazy?" I say, peering at her with a raised brow, gesturing vaguely to the public space around me.

Rebecca shrugs a toned shoulder. "I figured you had some sort of protocol for this sort of thing, and you're alone. Besides, who's going to do anything? The teenaged boy who hasn't stopped staring at your boobs? Please," she scoffs.

I purse my lips, deciding I'm not going to let her ruin my lunch. She can sit there and watch me eat, for all I care. I'm starving, and anyway, she's right. I *do* want to help her against my better judgment. Damned desire to be helpful. It's inconvenient sometimes. I heft the patty melt with one hand and ask, "Okay, so I'm guessing you need help figuring out why you're still here?" I take a giant bite and don't bother suppressing the moan of pleasure at the cheesy, oniony goodness.

"Do you two need a moment?" she snarks, snapping her fingers in my face.

Once I swallow my bite, I say, "Listen, I haven't eaten all day and I'm starved. I know you've probably already forgotten how annoying it is to be hungry, but it sucks, okay? So I'm going to eat and you're going to talk."

She sighs and nods. As I wait for her to tell me why she's back to bothering me, I realize that her lip gloss has made it to the afterlife. Typical—she looks like a model even in death. Meanwhile, I look like I got into a fight with that chipmunk.

I accidentally got lost on my way back to my car when I went off-trail to look at these huge mushrooms. They were farther away from the path than I thought, and it took me longer than I want to admit to find my way back. By the time I made it back to the entrance of the trail, I had anxiety sweats, had gotten a scratch on the cheek, and a branch stuck in my hair. I managed to get the branch out, but it left my hair looking like a rat's nest in its wake.

"Fine. Yes, I need your help," she says reluctantly. I raise my brow and make a "go on" gesture with my hand. "Well, I figured out why I'm still here." She clears her throat and sits up straighter, looking like she's never slouched a day in her life. "My fiancé is cheating on me."

"Cheating?" I ask, finally setting down my sandwich. She nods gravely, and I take a sip of my Coke. "I'm sorry. That must have been awful to find out... But what does that have to do with you sticking around?" I'm secretly hoping that she isn't holding him to their relationship postmortem.

"Before I died, I had a suspicion, but I could never confirm it. He always had an excuse for every weird behavior. Out late? He had a project that he needed to put in some overtime for. Smiling at his phone? Just saw a funny video. Starting to work out more? He cares about his health. He made me feel like I was going crazy." She scowls into the distance.

"So, how did you figure it out?" I ask, swiping my fry through ketchup before popping it in my mouth.

"I went back to our apartment after you and I talked last. He's already gotten rid of all of my things! He didn't even save a keepsake." She sits back and crosses her arms indignantly, her agitation causing a plunge in temperature. "Not even the nice watch I got him for our second anniversary. He probably pawned it!" she screeches.

"Okay, but maybe he's just grieving and having your things around makes him sad," I reason, shivering in the sudden cold.

"I would have thought the same thing, but I stayed long

enough to overhear a phone conversation with *Crystal.*" She spits the name like a curse. "Crystal was babbling on about their six-month anniversary. How special it was going to be, and that she bought some fancy new lingerie for the occasion. I died two months ago."

I wince. Yeah, the bastard definitely cheated. "But what does this have to do with you not moving on?"

"Well, obviously I want revenge," she deadpans with a raised brow.

I purse my lips and nod. "I get it, trust me. But I'm not really in the business of harming the living."

She glowers. "Again, what are you good for?"

"I resent that!" I say, wanting very much to throw something at her. Unfortunately, it would pass right through, so it would only serve to make me look like I was having a break down. I scowl instead and readjust my phone in my hand. "Rebecca, if you can't be polite, you're on your own."

She sighs through her nose and says, "I just want you to help me come up with a plan, okay? I know in my gut that this is why I'm still here." I frown because I'm sure she's right. She's here because she's seeking revenge. She wouldn't be the first vengeful spirit I've encountered, but she would be the first one I've helped. I usually stay away from them; I don't have the stomach for revenge.

"I don't want to be involved... But I might look the other way if you haunt him," I muse, pushing my nearly empty plate aside.

"What do you mean?"

"You know—" I wave my free arm around and groan theatrically. "Haunt him."

She scrunches her nose delicately, and I have a fleeting

thought about botox and the afterlife. "Is that something that actually happens?"

"You can make it happen. You just have to practice asserting your presence over objects and then you'll be well on your way to haunt your douchebag of a boyfriend." I flourish my hand to the side like a gameshow host.

"Fiancé," she corrects, ice frosting her words.

"Fiancé," I amend, taking a sip of soda. "Anyway. If you want to practice, you can come back to my place and work on it in a low-pressure environment."

"Your place?" Her lip curls. When she notices my scowl, she sighs and says, "Fine." Without another word, she blinks out, and I pretend to end a call on my phone.

*Goody.*

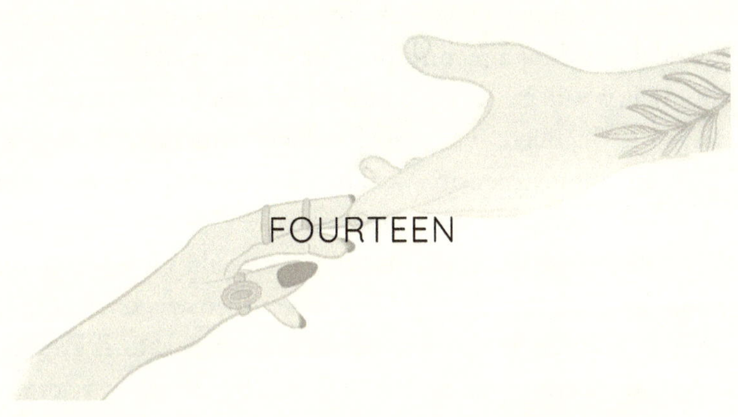

# FOURTEEN

AFTER SHOWERING OFF THE WOODS, I sit on my couch and get ready to binge-watch my newest reality TV obsession. I have a few hours left of my day off, and I intend to take full advantage by vegging out on the couch with some snacks and other people's dramatics.

I'm two episodes and a glass of wine deep into my Sunday night when the hairs on my arms stand up. The sigh that leaves my body should be studied. It feels at least three times my actual lung capacity. I look up to see the pull chain on my ceiling fan swaying ever so slightly and begin a slow clap. "Alright, Rebecca, look at you go," I say with mild approval.

She pops into existence, sapping some of the warmth from the air. She takes a dramatic bow in the middle of my living room. "Thank you very much," she says and stands.

"Pretty impressive considering we just talked about this less than five hours ago."

"I did tell you I was on my way to med school, right? I'm

nothing if not determined." In a blink, she's next to me on the couch and wrapping her arms around her knees. She looks like a model posed for a picture, her hair still scraped back into that bun that would be severe on someone else. But on her, it just serves to highlight her delicate bone structure. She's also changed into expensive looking loungewear. I see she's mastered altering her appearance already.

"Who knew being an over-achiever would serve you in the afterlife?" I ask rhetorically. I look over to see her concentrating on some knitting needles I've left on the coffee table. If I squint, I can see them vibrating the slightest bit. It really is pretty impressive that she's already able to move things.

I return my attention to my show, miffed that my favorite contestant has been kicked off the island and I missed it. I rewind the episode to the beginning and settle in, content to let Rebecca use the Force or whatever to move my knitting needles.

I'm just getting to the dramatic climax of the episode—someone had a drink thrown on them—when Rebecca asks, "What's that?" She's pointing to my desk where I have a ton of inventory set up for when I go live online for The Veil. I briefly explain about the shop and what I do, not wanting to be berated with her judgmental commentary.

To my surprise, she doesn't bat an eye or even make a snide comment. She seems genuinely curious and interested in the store. "So... You're a medium who runs an occult shop? Very on brand."

"Let's just hope I get to keep my job, because I really don't think my skills are suited for much else," I say, picking the emerald nail polish off my thumb nail.

She frowns at me. "Why would you lose your job? Didn't

you say your aunt owns it? Oh my god! You're embezzling aren't you?" She gasps dramatically and leans in closer, dark brown eyes sparking with curiosity.

"Sorry to be a disappointment, but no. Forget I said anything." I wave her away, attempting to go back to watching my show.

"You can't just say that and then not tell me. Come *on*! The afterlife is boring and you're literally the only person I can have a conversation with. Who am I going to tell?"

I think about the fact that she really can't talk to anyone else about this. And that she has a unique perspective considering she's a ghost. Even if she isn't exactly the warm and fuzzy type, it might be useful to talk it over with her. "You actually care?" I ask.

"Care? I mean, if it'll make you feel better, then sure. I care. I'm not in it for the drama of a stranger at all." When I scowl at her, she says, "Oh, come on. I haven't been able to scroll a social media app in forever. I miss hearing about other people's problems."

I sigh and relent. "Okay, fine. But one rude comment and I'm done." She mimes zipping her lips, so I continue. "We're going to be short a lot of money in the coming year. My aunt who owns the business is going to go to a nice retirement home and the landlord who owns this block is raising the rent. We do okay, but not so great that an extra four thousand a month wouldn't tank us. And because I'm the one in charge, I have to come up with a plan to make up the difference."

"That's a lot of pressure," she says, propping her chin on her hand.

"Yeah," I agree, annoyed at myself for bringing up the one thing I'm not supposed to be stressing about right now. "We're trying to figure out a way to make our surge of customers in October become returning customers the rest of the year."

"Do you have any ideas?" she asks.

"I mean, my aunt had one but I'm not sure about it." She gestures for me to continue. "She wants me to use my Gift to contact spirits on their living loved one's behalf."

"So... She wants you to get paid for something you already do?"

"I guess," I say with a shrug.

"Why would you be on the fence about that? It's like getting paid to sleep for normal people," she says. I dutifully ignore the implication that I'm *not* normal.

"Because I don't announce my abilities to the living. I'll help pretty much any spirit who comes to me in need, but I've never looked for a specific person and called them forward, let alone accepted money for it."

"Why not? I mean, I get that you help ghosts and whatever, but why not help the living too?" Rebecca asks, leaning back against the arm of the couch. I'm impressed by her ability to stick around for so long. Her overachieving nature obviously helps her in more ways than one.

I sigh and tilt my head back and forth, looking for a way to explain it. Finally, I settle on, "When I was younger, and much less discerning about who I shared information with, I told some close online friends about what I could do. There were a few different reactions. Either they were terrified of me and thought that I was a freak, they didn't believe me, or they wanted to exploit it and use me for their gain. I stopped being a person no matter what.

And don't even get me started on romantic relationships and how hard it is to date when you frequently talk to people no one else can see. I don't want to be known as the local ghost girl. And anyway, accepting money for something that feels almost like a duty seems wrong."

"I'm sorry you were shamed for something that was out of your control," she says, reaching out and setting her hand on my wrist. The static feeling of it isn't exactly unpleasant, but it does raise the hairs on my arm. She can't quite make contact, but there's an awareness over where she's touching.

Rebecca removes her hand and I watch as she rubs her fingertips together, absorbing the new sensation of touching someone this way. "But you know, if there was a way for you to do this anonymously, there's nothing wrong with taking money for it. Just because you feel it's an obligation doesn't mean you don't deserve to get paid for it. Think of people in the military. They're literally duty-bound to do their jobs, but they still get paid for them."

I've never thought of it that way. "Maybe you're right. But to be honest, I don't even know if I could do it—call someone out of the ether and draw them to me. Especially if I don't have a connection to them." I think of Dean and the fact that I popped him out of the in-between without trying, but we *definitely* have a connection. Speaking of which, I probably shouldn't be thinking of him too hard, lest he barge in unannounced.

"There's no harm in trying. It might be kind of fun to play the mysterious medium behind the curtain or whatever. It also would be cool to help people find closure," she points out.

"But what if I end up calling someone who doesn't want to be found?" I ask, thinking of the way she was so frustrated by me at first, even though she's the one who came looking for me.

"Then, they'll probably be annoyed and leave. So what? I

bet you most people would be happy to be connected to a loved one again. It's hard to explain what it's like over here, but it can be really difficult to find specific people or places. The only reason I easily found my old apartment is because I was killed so close to it. My place of death was like... A homing beacon. It's a lot of work to even stay here, but being around you makes it easier. It feels like you're charging me up or something. When I'm not focused in and concentrating on staying in one place, I just sort of disappear. I have some awareness of time passing, vague impressions of the world, but it feels like living in a dream with no clear borders. It's a relief to get pulled out of that. Or in my case, drag your ass out of it yourself." I can't help the laugh that bubbles up at that.

"Thanks for that. It makes me feel better about trying at least."

"No problem. But I thought you were supposed to be helping me," she jokes.

I snort and say, "Have at it," gesturing to my knitting needles that she abandoned. "You'll be on your way to scaring the shit out of... What's his name?"

"Kyle," she reluctantly offers.

I snort. "Fucking, *Kyle?* Oh, come on, Rebecca. You deserved better than a Kyle."

She heaves a long-suffering sigh. "I know. But I'm going to make him pay. And then I'm going to go rest in peace or whatever," she says with a delicate wrinkle of her nose.

"Sounds like you're really looking forward to your eternal rest," I quip.

"Might just torment my ex a little first," she says with a wicked grin. Suddenly I feel a teensie bit bad for Kyle.

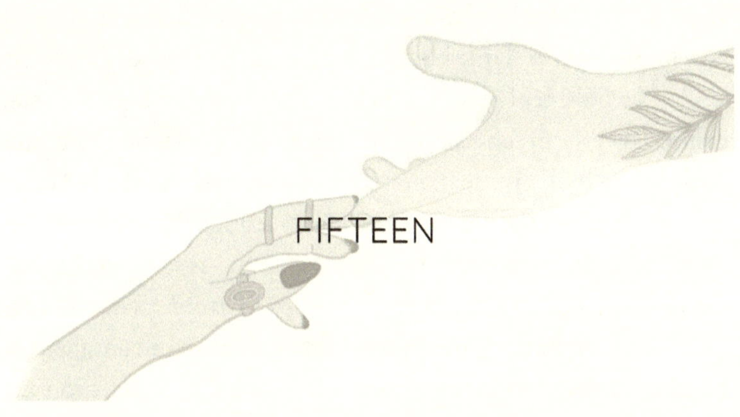

# FIFTEEN

A FEW DAYS LATER, I finally decide to give Aunt Clarissa's idea a try. I close the shop down for lunch and evaluate the space, trying to figure out where to install the "Medium's Meeting Room." I came up with the name last night. Anxiety had kept me awake most of the night anyway. Once the sun dusted the sky in periwinkle dawn, I gave up on sleep and got moving.

I skip my eyes over the library corner, chock full of books, the shelves holding all sorts of oddities from taxidermied bugs to rune stones. Then I scan the small antique section, filled with clothing, herbs, and crystals from local artisans. For the first time, I truly see just how stuffed to the brim this store is.

"Well, shit," I say aloud. I need a spot that can offer a bit of privacy.

My gaze catches on the smaller supply closet where we keep all the cleaning junk. I tilt my head and stride over to it, instinctively hopping over the curled edges of the antique rug at the center of the store. I pull open the door and assess the space. It's probably about six-feet deep and five-feet wide. It would be a little tight, but if I took out the shelves lining the walls, it would feel bigger. I flick on the overhead light and step inside, trying to envision the space fully cleaned out and outfitted to look mystical, matching the rest of the shop. "What are you doing in the closet?" Dean asks from behind me.

The only sign that he surprised me is a slight inhale through my nose. Other than that, I try to avoid giving him the satisfaction of making me jump. I don't want to encourage that; I've had a few too many ghosts make a habit of startling me. "I'm going to start helping people talk to their dead loved ones, but I want some anonymity. I was checking out the closet as a potential space for it," I explain, turning toward him, keeping my tone even.

"Are you going to wear a veil? That could be very sexy. Like one of those birdcage ones, but in black? Ohhh, or maybe a mask. Have you seen the masked dudes online? I bet there's a niche for masked women, too," he says, staring intently at the contours of my face as though he's going to place a custom order for me.

"Um, probably not," I say, marveling at the way his brain goes off in a million unexpected directions with the smallest push.

His shoulders sag with disappointment. "Oh."

I change the subject, hoping to point his attention away from sexy veils and masks. "You've been gone a while, Dean. How are you?"

"Have I?" he asks, twin lines of confusion forming between his immaculately groomed brows.

"Almost a week," I reply with a nod.

"Damn. Time flies when you're dead. Sorry, I needed rest, and then I was practicing staying in one place for a while. I got pretty good at it, so prepare to be sick of me," he says with a grin that makes my stomach feel funny. He steps closer until I can nearly count every eyelash and looks into my eyes before lowering his attention to my mouth.

*Stop it,* I chastise myself. Having a crush on a dead guy has heartbreak written all over it. It's difficult to leash the desire because I've kissed the man, and it was a damn good kiss. I really need to throw up some boundaries for my own sake.

"Look, Dean. I'm happy to help you, I am. I want you to move on and find peace. But I can't deal with the flirting, okay? It's confusing and makes my job harder." I take a step back so there's more space between us. Even though I can breathe normally again, I feel a little like I've just given up something precious.

"What's there to be confused about? I thought we had a good time," he says with a small pout of his plush mouth.

"We did. If we weren't in this scenario,"—I gesture between us—"I'm sure we would have gone on many more dates and gotten a dog or something eventually. But that's not our reality. So, no matter how much we liked each other, we have to keep things friendly. Anything else will just end up causing pain. There's only one way this ends, and that's you going to wherever spirits rest, and me here. Alone," I say, my voice scraping over the last word.

He searches my face and nods. "Okay. I'm sorry. I'll keep the flirting to a minimum." After an awkward beat, he clears his throat and says, "Why the new business venture?"

I'm grateful that he takes the lead in changing the subject.

I explain our upcoming money troubles again, feeling like

I'm reciting a script at this point. You'd think repeating it over and over would make it less anxiety-inducing, but no such luck. Once I'm done, he hums and asks, "So, this whole medium for hire thing, you're okay with it?"

I'm surprised at the question, because he's the first person who's asked me that. Not if I *could* do it, but if I wanted to. He's the first to understand the nuance between the two.

I surprise myself even more with my answer. "I am. I wasn't at first, but a new friend helped me see that just because I view it as a duty doesn't mean I don't deserve to get paid for it. I'm still not sold on attaching my face to it, but if I can remain anonymous, I think it might be nice to help people. There's also the hope that it would attract customers year-round, which would help with the money issue."

He nods thoughtfully. "I hate to ask this, seeing as how you're stressed over your job, but do you think you can still help me figure out what happened to me?" There's a vulnerability in his tone. A gentle crack in his voice over the question, and I'm slammed with grief and anger all over again.

When I talk with him like this, it's easy to forget that he's dead. It's easy to shove the heartbreak down and dwell in the pleasure of having him here, now. But I have to force myself to remember the reality of this situation again and again until it sticks. He's dead and in need of my help, so he can move on and be at peace. He deserves that.

"Yes. Of course I will." I look up into his eyes, and it's only then that I notice how close I've gotten—like a supplicant drawn to a deity. I take a small step back again, feeling his energy buzz along my body like a feather drawn down my spine.

He grins at the movement. "Where do we start?" I might be imagining it, but I swear his voice went a little husky.

I clear my own throat and say, "We should probably go to your house. Sometimes returning to the site of death helps jog a person's memory. Have you been back to your house yet?"

He shakes his head, saying quietly, "No. I haven't. It's been too... Difficult, I guess." He shrugs and runs a hand through his hair, clearly agitated at the thought.

"Would it help if we went together?" I ask, hoping that he has a spare key hidden somewhere. He nods again, so I say, "Alright. After I close the shop for the night, we'll go. You should probably rest until then. I know you say you've gotten good at hanging around, but it's better to conserve your energy so you don't blink out without wanting to."

"Off to get my beauty rest then," he says, pantomiming a giant yawn. "Will you yank me back into existence like you did the first time?" he asks, a slight smile tugging at the corner of his mouth.

I feel my cheeks heat. "Yes, but I'll try to be more gentle this time."

"Oh, don't do that on my account," he says with a wink before disappearing.

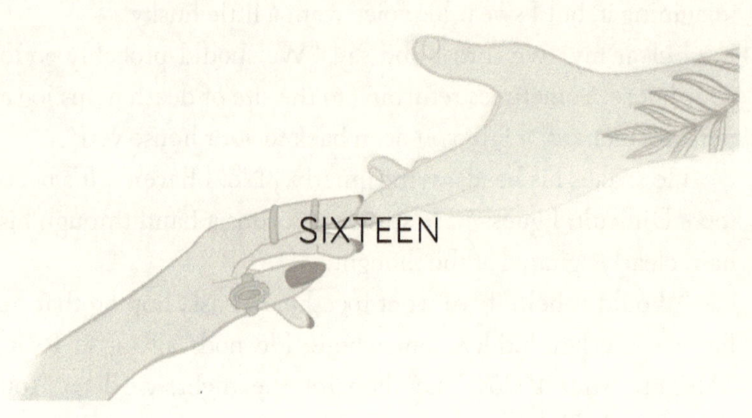

# SIXTEEN

"IT'S RIGHT UP HERE," Dean says, pointing to a beautiful, modern home with a long driveway, partially obscured by the encroaching forest. The clean edges of his house are a stark contrast to the nature bursting around it. His home looks like a giant built a sculpture out of concrete and glass, and then tossed it into a clearing. I knew Dean made good money, but *damn*; his place rivals the Cullen house with all its sleek lines and large windows looking out into the forest.

"Wow," I can't help but say as I pull into the driveway. I look around conspicuously. Thankfully, there's no neighbors to witness my tired little Toyota puttering into the driveway, practically screaming, "I don't belong here!" Or maybe I do... As the cleaning lady. Or dog walker.

"My dad may have convinced me to buy this place," Dean says with a wince. I look over to see embarrassment color his cheeks. "It was a surprisingly good deal because the person who started building it went bankrupt, so I got it from the bank and was able to add my own finishes."

"I think your version of a 'good deal' and my version of a 'good deal' are two completely different things," I say, mortified that he's been inside my little home, which looks like it could fit inside his living room. "My idea of a good deal is when my oat milk creamer is $4.50 instead of $5.00, or when my underwear comes five for $25. Not... *This*." I lean forward and peer up into the many black eyes of the house.

I'm not trying to shame him for his wealth. He should be proud that he earned so much before he even hit thirty-five. Dean can't help that he came from money any more than I can help that I didn't. It's just that this type of wealth is inconceivable to me. We weren't exactly poor growing up, but I have many memories of dinner decisions being weighed by what coupons were available that week. The only time we got to override the coupon rule was on our birthdays, and even then, we had a budget.

Money for me as an adult speaks the language of scrimping, saving, and even scavenging. So, this type of wealth is like a language I've never even heard before with an alphabet I can't decipher. We're not just in different social circles; we're in different stratospheres. And not just because he's currently a member of the dead-under-forty club.

"Earth to Alderwood," Dean says, snapping in my face. "You good in there, Rae?"

"Yeah, sorry," I gulp around the sudden dryness of my throat. "I guess I expected that you had money, but this is vacationing in Cape Cod for the summer in a private beach house, caviar for breakfast, retirement by fifty money." I turn my shell-shocked expression to him and notice that he's trying to fight back a smile.

"I guess I should have warned you? Sorry. It's just that there's no polite way to say, 'Hey, I make a lot of money, prepare to see my fancy house that I kind of hate,'" he says sarcastically. At my expression, he says, "See? Even saying that makes me seem like an ungrateful bastard. Which I'm not, but I had the privilege of not caring about money when I was alive. Buying something this... grandiose? It was my father's idea. He said it looked good to clients and gave the impression that I knew what I was doing. I was stupid and single, so I listened to him. Can we please not let this make it weird?" He turns puppy dog eyes to me and presses his hands together against his chest dramatically.

"Yeah, of course. I'm sorry. I didn't mean to make you uncomfortable. I'll shut up about your giant house now." I mime locking my mouth and tossing the key over my shoulder, which makes Dean smile, dimple popping.

"Caviar is disgusting, by the way. It tastes like you licked the bottom of the ocean and somehow came away with sea creature snot." He shivers at the memory of it.

"Thanks for painting such a vivid picture," I say, disgust screwing up my face. My car door opens with a creak, and I head up the immaculate driveway. He flits ahead of me, appearing in front of the huge, glass-paned door.

"The code to get in is 2452," he says, pointing to the keypad on the front door. "Or, at least it should be, as long as my parents haven't changed it."

I punch in the code on the keypad, relief washing over me when the deadbolt clicks open. "You don't have a security system, do you?" The afterthought strikes as I step inside the high-ceilinged foyer.

"I didn't end up installing one. It was one of those to-do items that I never got around to." He walks inside and goes to flick on the light switch. It's only when his hand passes uselessly through the wall does he seem to remember his predicament. He sighs and asks, "Would you mind?"

I press the switch, and am once again rendered speechless by his home. The sleek lines continue inside, but the interior is all warm wood, comfortable furniture, and plush rugs. Pictures flow up along the staircase to my right. They seem to be a mix of his family and friends, as well as some canvases painted by a very talented artist depicting various nature scenes.

I walk further into the home, Dean trailing behind. True to his word, he's used deep red as an accent throughout the house: on rugs, paintings, throw pillows, and blankets. As soon as I emerge into his large, cozy living room, I'm greeted with the biggest couch I've ever seen. "May I?" I practically beg, eyeing the couch.

"I'm not going to get any use out of it anymore, so be my guest," he says, smiling indulgently as I flop face-first onto his white, fluffy, cloud couch.

"*Ohmygodthisisthemostcomfortablecouchever,*" I mumble directly to the cushions. I also take a huge (hopefully secret) whiff of the couch that still smells of his expensive cologne and hair products. Ghosts don't have a scent, which in Dean's case is a shame because he used to smell *edible*.

Dean laughs and does his best to throw himself next to me, up by my head. The couch doesn't even shift, and despite the chill, his proximity makes me even more comfortable. I allow my eyes to drift shut for a moment and pretend that everything is fine and we aren't here on a mission to figure out why he died.

I feel a tingling sensation on my scalp and crack an eye to see that his hand is resting on top of my head, fingers moving ever so slightly in an attempt to card through my thick hair. My heart thuds irregularly at the dreamy look he's wearing, and I wish for what feels like the millionth time that things were different. I push myself up to sitting and smile at him a little. "Ready?" I ask gently, knowing it may be hard for him to see where he died.

He takes a steadying breath and nods. "Come on, let's get this over with." He stands and gestures for me to follow him again. We walk through his immaculately clean kitchen with its top-of-the-line appliances and through a door leading out to his garage.

I feel a chill roll through my entire body. At first glance, the garage is innocuous. There's a nice, black Mercedes sedan parked in the middle of the space, and on either side are the typical garage fare: yard tools, Christmas decor, snow shovels, and extra supplies for the house. On closer inspection, though, all outward ventilation has been sealed over with black trash bags and industrial grade duct tape.

I approach the car, drawn to it the way all people are drawn to places where awful things happened. I lean down, squinting through the driver's side window to see the car looking mostly harmless. Which is strange; it seems like I should be able to sense the horrible thing that happened here, but it's just a car.

I start to spin away, wanting to ask Dean about the day he died again, when something catches the light and attracts my eye to the driver's seat. I bend closer to the car, unwilling to lay my hand on the cool metal of the hood. Even if I can't see the horrible event that happened here, I don't want to touch the thing that took Dean's life.

Squinting through the window, I notice a small scrap of duct tape attached to the side of the seat. It would be easy to miss since it's nearly hidden by the center console, but the way the light catches it makes it stand out against the red leather interior.

"'Least it's a pretty car, right?" Dean says ruefully, mistaking my close inspection for interest in his car.

"Mm. Did you repair a tear in the leather recently?" I ask, eyes fixed on the small scrap of duct tape. "Or maybe pack some boxes?"

"No, why?" he asks, flickering closer.

I point to the duct tape in the car. "Because there's a tiny scrap of duct tape that matches the decorating in here. Maybe you were restrained?" I say, gesturing to the duct-taped ventilation, then back to the seat.

"I *was* murdered! Motherfucking-shit-*fuck!*" Dean exclaims, growing so agitated that the room temperature drops several degrees, and the snow shovel hanging on the wall near us starts vibrating. He wraps his fists into the silky strands of his hair and squeezes. He paces quickly, going back and forth faster than I can keep track of, taking the temperature of the room down quickly.

I clear my throat. "On the plus side, you can move things now, so that's pretty cool." I wave weakly towards the shovel that's picking up the pace, pounding hard against the cement wall. I wonder briefly how it hasn't fallen yet.

Dean abruptly stops pacing and tilts his head at the shovel, hair mussed. "Huh," he says, peering at the swaying tool that's losing steam and slowing its aggressive rhythm. I'm glad I was able to distract him from his end-of-life crisis, because I need him not to burn out now that we're getting somewhere. I turn around and start towards the rear passenger door behind the driver's side, curious if there's any more of that tape.

The door to the garage slams open behind me, and I spin with a gasp. My eyes widen when I see a gun pointed directly at me. In what feels like slow motion, I look up the barrel of the discreet handgun, over the fitted suit jacket, and land on a face that looks like Dean if he were thirty years older. "Shit," Dean and I say in unison.

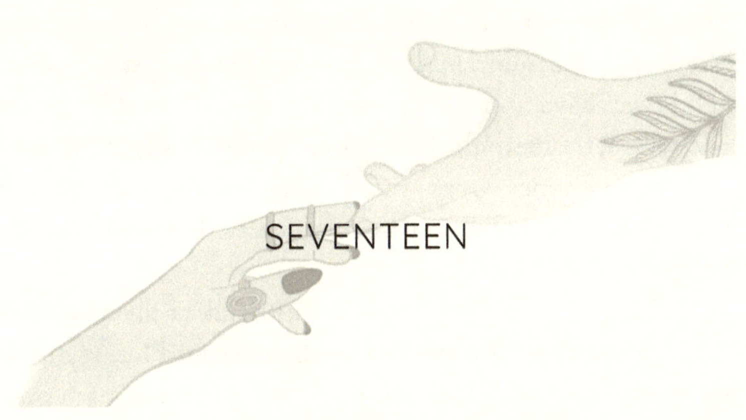

# SEVENTEEN

"DAD," Dean says, stepping in front of me. Sweetly, he thinks he'll be a shield, but he forgets that the bullet would pass right through him and end up buried in my gut.

"Who the fuck are you, and why are you in my son's house?" Dean's dad demands, not lowering the gun an inch. His finger rests on the side of the gun, but I have full faith that he could pull the trigger in an instant.

I raise my hands instinctively and say, "My name is Rae Alderwood." I swallow the bile rising in my throat and fight the urge to pass out.

*Great. Love learning that in fight, flight, fawn, or freeze, I'm a freezer. Or a passer-outer? Wonderful.*

"Tell him about me," Dean says tensely, not moving from his spot between his dad and I.

I shift my stare briefly from the *fucking* gun pointed at me, to Dean and shake my head minutely. The last thing I need is the cops called, along with a one-way ticket to a padded cell.

"And why, Rae Alderwood, are you in my son's house?" Mr. Dean's Dad murmurs cooly, clicking the safety off the gun, making me lightheaded with panic. "Did you have something to do with his death?" he all but whispers. It would be kind of sexy in a silver fox way, if I weren't one wrong move from finding out what it feels like to be intimately acquainted with a bullet in my belly.

"Um, I—" I stutter. "I was his girlfriend," I finally squeak out. Not exactly the truth, but truth adjacent. Plus, saying "I went on a date with him one time" will make me seem even more deranged.

Dean turns a very out-of-place, shit-eating grin my way. "Girlfriend, huh?"

"Will you shut up?" I say to him exasperatedly. And then my mouth all but seals itself shut when I realize what I've done. My face burns so hot that I fear my skin will melt off.

Awesome. We can now add "cracks under pressure" to my resumé.

Out of the blue, the name of Dean's dad comes back to me from the article I read—Jack. I'm glad my brain is focusing on the important things. Jack prowls forward, eyebrow quirking in a way that is so Dean, I soften to him a little even though he definitely still has a gun pointed at me. "What did you say?" he asks, baffled.

"I—Um," I stammer out.

"Tell. Him," Dean grits out. His pleading expression has me wavering. "I couldn't stand it if something happened to you because of me."

When he genuinely looks close to tears, I sigh and say, "Actually, I'm not Dean's girlfriend." At this point, I'm fully prepared to end up in a cell with no pointy things allowed by the end of the night.

"Explain," Jack demands, gun still trained directly on my furiously pounding heart.

"Okay. There's no easy way to say this, but um... I'm a medium," I break eye contact with the gun to study his confused face. "Like, I talk to ghosts?"

*Killing it, Rae.*

"Get out," Dean's dad says flatly, finally dropping the gun, apparently sensing I'm not a threat.

"No wait, I'm trying to figure out what happened to him. I know he didn't commit suicide," I rush out, lowering my hands.

"Tell him that I'm the one who broke the window growing up, but I cried so much that Luke took the fall because he wanted me to shut up. I didn't tell Dad the truth until my twenty-fifth birthday when I was sure he couldn't ground me," Dean says quickly, stare never leaving his dad.

I relay the message cautiously and watch as Jack's expression morphs from fury to awe to skepticism. "Tell me something else. Not something he could have told you on your date."

"You really think he'd tell me an embarrassing story on the first date?" I ask shakily.

Jack grimaces. "Knowing my son, yes. He'd think he was being charming. Go on," he says, clenching his jaw.

Dean rolls his eyes, thinks for a moment, and says, "He and mom almost got a divorce when they were remodeling their home in 2005, so they made us kids vote on the finishes so they couldn't be mad at each other. Oh, and I desperately wanted a red carpet in my room, but mom said no."

Jack listens closely as I recount what Dean said, face blanching in shock. "Dean?" he asks, looking around. "Is he here?" he questions me. I can see the war between wanting to believe me and wanting to call my bluff.

"Yes," I say, pointing to Dean's position in the room. "Move the shovel again," I tell Dean, knowing that for most, having a visible experience helps make things feel more real.

Dean focuses on the shovel intently and then pushes it with a finger. I watch as Jack's nostrils flare when it begins to sway. "Is that you, Dean?" Jack asks. Dean moves the shovel harder in answer, nearly taking it off the wall.

"If that's really you, make it stop moving," Jack commands, swallowing thickly. Dean puts out his hand, gripping the handle of the shovel so it stops swinging abruptly.

Jack's eyes close, a single tear trekking down his lined cheek. "Son," he murmurs brokenly. "I'm so sorry. I should have protected you. I should have come sooner. I should have known that you..." He's openly crying now, and I feel my eyes well up in response.

"Dad," Dean says, his voice ragged and breaking on the word. He flickers in and out for a moment before disappearing completely.

I take a slow breath, trying to reabsorb my unshed tears and say, "He's gone. Sorry, he has a hard time sticking around for long periods. I know it meant a lot to him to see you."

"Will he ever come back?" Dean's dad asks, vulnerability lightening his dark eyes and slumping his previously squared shoulders. He snags the deep-blue pocket square from his suit jacket and mops at his face as if he's trying to wipe away the crack in his hardened exterior.

"Yes, he will. It's very tiring to remain here. He just needs some rest, and then he'll be back. Maybe not tonight, though. It's hard to gauge how long it takes for them to recharge." I shuffle on my feet a little. "Look, I'm sorry to have scared you. Dean is determined to figure out what happened. That's what we were doing here. I'm not his girlfriend, but I did go on a date with him the weekend before he died. I just want to help him find peace. I may not have known him long, but I do know that he was a truly special person who had no business dying for at least the next forty to fifty years."

His lips straighten into a line, bowing his head, heavy with grief. He slides the gun into a concealed-carry holster at his hip and meets my gaze, his eyes slightly watery. "Thank you for helping him. Sorry about the, uh—" he clears his throat and gestures to his weapon.

"Well, to be fair, you did think I was an intruder," I offer with a tentative smile. He was probably also worried that I had some connection to Dean's death. My brows draw together and I say, "How did you know I was here? Dean said he didn't have a security system, and we didn't hear an alarm or anything."

"Ah. I had a new system installed shortly after the funeral. We couldn't bear to sell the house just yet, but it was also tough to be here. So we installed a state-of-the-art system that alerted my phone the second the front door code was entered. Silently," he adds with a raised brow and a small smile.

I nod my head. "That makes sense." We stand in awkward silence, the only sound the muted wind blowing through the trees outside.

"So. Dean brought you here to try to figure out what happened. Can you tell me what you know?" Jack asks, leading me back inside to the cloud couch. I sink into its heavenly cushions and wish this monstrosity could fit in my apartment. And that I had the extra thousands of dollars to purchase one just like it.

I pull a merlot-colored throw pillow over my lap and hug it, inhaling the subtle notes of Dean. "Sure, but honestly it's not much. So, the weekend before Dean died, he and I went on a date. It went pretty well, so I was surprised when I didn't hear from him for weeks afterward. Eventually, he found his way to me. Spirits have a way of doing that," I say, refusing to let him know that I was thinking about his son so hard, I yanked him out of the ether.

"Anyway, once Dean realized he was dead, we saw the article you were interviewed for. Dean is certain he didn't kill himself. He says all he remembers is getting into the office on Sunday morning. After that, it's a blank spot until he found me. We came here in the hopes that it would bring back more memories."

"And did it? Bring back his memory?" He shifts on the couch to face me, his posture so rigid I have a hard time envisioning him doing anything remotely relaxing. If he told me he slept standing straight up, I'd believe him.

I sigh. "No. Or at least, we didn't really get the chance to try."

He frowns, deepening the fine lines that bracket his mouth. "My fault," he says gruffly.

"You couldn't have known. And anyway, it's not a one-time thing. Eventually, Dean will be able to come back, and we can do our best to jog his memory again. We will figure out what happened to him, Jack," I vow.

He nods once, the gesture mechanical. I feel my face pull into something like both a grimace and a smile.

"So, a medium, huh? My son dated a *medium*?" he asks in disbelief.

"He didn't know until well... After." I look down at my lap.

"So you lied to him?" he asks icily.

"No! I just didn't tell him. It's not exactly first-date material. I'm not obligated to bare my soul to every person I go on a date with," I say defensively.

"I suppose I shouldn't criticize since your gift is giving us a chance at finding answers." He sighs and suddenly looks much older, having pulled back the curtain of grief once more. I can see it written plainly in the downturn of his full mouth and the drawn line of his eyebrows. "I would have never believed you if I hadn't seen him move that shovel myself."

"I figured as much. I gathered that you're one of those 'seeing is believing' folks." I shift on the couch and ask, "Can you tell me about the last time you saw Dean alive? I'm doing my best to piece it all together."

He nods, yanking the curtain closed over his vulnerable state once more, and says, "The last time I saw him was Sunday night. He had come in for a full workday that day. We had a large client, and it was all-hands-on-deck that week. He left the office a little after six at night, like he usually does if he's got a busy schedule. And then, I didn't see him again until—" He clears his throat, and I can see him adding extra bricks to the wall he's constructing around the hurt. "Until it was too late the next day."

"Did he do anything out of the ordinary? Talk to anyone new?" I ask, trying to keep him focused on the present and the purpose of this conversation.

Jack rubs the stubble on his chin and peers out the large window across from us. "No," he says finally. "He seemed completely normal. His usual self. He talked to the others in the office, but otherwise, I didn't see him talking to anyone else. We didn't have any clients in that day since it was a

Sunday, so it was just the six of us and our secretary, Courtney."

I hum in thought and shake my head. "I mean, Dean is adamant he didn't commit suicide, so someone other than him had to tape up all the ventilation. I'm sorry to ask this, but was an autopsy done?"

Jack nods slowly. "Yes, but they didn't find anything beyond that he died from chemical asphyxiation. My wife is angry with me for even looking at it. She wishes I would just throw it away and move on. She thinks that this... obsession is unhealthy. And that it's preventing me from moving on and healing." He grimaces as if he regrets how much he just shared with me. He doesn't strike me as the type to open up to many people, so I'm sure this whole conversation feels like a thousand tiny papercuts.

"I'm sorry. I can't imagine the toll of losing a child," I say, inclining my head.

"Thank you. This helps," he admits, gesturing between us. "If I can figure out what happened to him, I'll be able to move forward. Actually start healing and living again. I know it won't bring him back, but I need to know who murdered my son," he nearly growls.

My stomach drops at the word "murder." It's something I've been dancing around in my head because the thought of someone killing Dean was outrageous. But the more I learn about this whole situation, the more it seems like the only possibility. You don't accidentally tape up all the ventilation in your garage and then stomp on the gas until you die.

"The thing that I can't figure out is how someone would have been able to force him to cooperate. There were no signs of struggle, his car wasn't tampered with, just the ventilation in the garage, and there were no signs on his body indicating defensive wounds," Dean's dad says, as if he read my thoughts.

At the mention of the vents in the garage, I suddenly remember the duct tape in the car. I sit up straighter on an inhale and say, "Come with me."

I lead him back through the house and into the garage. The motion sensor light blinks on, and I point to the driver's seat. "I noticed a small scrap of duct tape there." I swallow around the lump in my throat as it's finally really hitting me that Dean didn't just die; someone hurt him. Someone played god and decided Dean's time was up.

Jack stoops so we're the same height and peers over my shoulder. I hear his quick intake of breath and a mumbled expletive. "I'm going to find a private investigator and see what can be found. I've held off until now out of respect for my wife, but I can't anymore. Something else is clearly going on here, and I want answers." His dark eyes, so like Dean's, laser in on that tiny scrap of tape, and I feel a chill roll down my spine. Jack Crawford is not a man you want to cross.

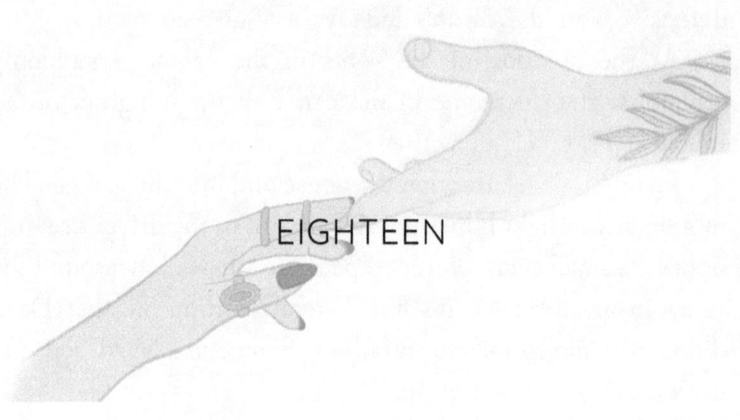

# EIGHTEEN

AFTER EXCHANGING numbers and agreeing to keep each other updated if we found anything else, we went our separate ways. Jack gave me permission to come back to Dean's house whenever I wanted and showed me how to disarm the security system. He also promised never to show up unannounced and armed again, which my racing heart appreciated.

It's been a few days since the night at Dean's, and I've spent most of my time after work setting up my little medium room, making it look all kinds of magical and cozy. I broke in my DIY hat and took down all the shelves and covered the ugly walls with swooping velvet fabric in different jewel tones. Then, I hung multiple strands of fairy lights beneath gauzy chiffon to diffuse the space with warm light. Finally, I put a heavy velvet curtain to separate my seating space from theirs. My side is fairly plain with a chair, a small fan, and a tall standing lamp. The customer's side is much bigger, with a cushioned stool to sit on as well as a small table and a vintage lamp.

The first week of October blew in with a new chill to the air. Our proximity to Salem means that we get a lot of the overflow from tourists checking out the local area. We've already seen a huge uptick in customers wandering in. My aunt and I even hired a temporary shop assistant to help out, and Aunt C now comes in daily to ring people up.

We're launching my service this weekend. I had put up a sign on the door at the beginning of the week reading, "Medium Coming Soon!" Every time I look at it, my stomach swoops.

"I'm so glad you're doing this, darling. You'll see. You're going to help so many people," Aunt Clarissa says, gliding out from the large supply room with an armful of moon water jars. She charged them under the last full moon, sealing them with twine and different colored wax. She plunks the jars on the counter and begins making room for them on the display shelf to the right of the cash register.

"I hope so. And I hope it helps us too," I say, walking over to the herb cabinet and straightening the sachets and bundles. I take a sprig of rosemary and put it under my nose, inhaling the calming scent.

"Something on your mind, darling?" Aunt Clarissa asks, nodding to the rosemary I'm clutching—and crushing.

I haven't told my family about Dean yet, including my sister. It's not completely unusual for me to keep my ghostly appointments to myself, because they happen so frequently. It would be like telling them every time I went to the grocery store. Most of the visits are fairly quick and resolve within a few days; Rebecca and Dean are the exception, not the rule. I haven't told them about Dean in particular because I'm still trying to wrap my mind around it. I've never been one to share what's going on when I'm in the thick of it. I'd rather wait until it's all resolved so I can gloss over the hard bits. I never want to worry anyone, especially my family.

I slowly nod my head, sticking the ruined sprig of rosemary in my jacket pocket. Even though it's out of character for me, I open up the tiniest bit and say, "Yeah, actually. The guy I went on a date with at the beginning of last month died."

Aunt Clarissa stops her organizing, turning to me as she says "Oh no. I'm so sorry."

I nod, gathering up courage to tell her the rest. "Well, um. He—he reappeared to me a while ago. I've been helping him. It's starting to look like he was murdered, but it was staged to look like a suicide."

She studies me for a moment, still processing before she says, "Oh. Well, that's... inconvenient."

"He needs to find out what happened to him before he's able to move on," I say, studying the scuffs and folds of my well-worn Chelsea boots rather than look at her.

"Oh, Rae. That is so much on your shoulders. Did you like him?" she asks gently, finally coming closer and rubbing my arm.

I inhale her familiar scent and say, "Yeah. Yeah, I did. I do. It was only one date, but I know it could have been more. We had this instant connection, and I felt so comfortable with him. He seems like a good guy. Even with him dead, we still have this intense chemistry. And now things are so confusing because I'm trying to help him, but I'm also kind of mourning him? It hurts to know that he's gone, but that he'll be *really* gone as soon as I help him," I say, surprised to find my cheeks wet with tears.

"And you feel conflicted because a part of you wishes to

keep him with you, even though your job is to help him move on," she states, rubbing soothing circles on my back.

I blink, stunned to realize that she's right. There has never been a spirit that I wanted to keep around. Sure, I've met plenty I liked, but the little bit of sadness at losing them was overshadowed by the peace I felt knowing they were somewhere better off. The satisfaction of a job well done. When Dean leaves, it will feel like losing him all over again. That's why I have to get a handle on these stupid feelings. If I allow myself to keep yearning for a man that's already slipped through my fingers, I'll only bring myself more pain.

"Yes," I admit. I brush the tears from my cheeks, irrationally angry at their presence.

"It's okay to feel this way, darling. You mustn't shut yourself off from these emotions, but rather let them flow through you. Acknowledge them, thank them for what they're teaching you about yourself, then let them pass. Even if this Dean was only a part of your life for a short while, his absence can still leave a major impact. We don't get to decide how our heart feels. The mind wants to rationalize what the heart already knows. He was—and is—special to you. That's okay. What you choose to do with that is up to you."

"What do you mean?" I ask with a sniffle.

"I mean, you can either keep him at arm's length, or you can enjoy the remaining time you have with him. It's going to hurt either way, darling. But ask yourself: What will leave me with the fewest regrets? Only you can decide that." She pats my back a final time, and places a kiss against my temple the way she's done my whole life.

She has this tendency of dropping intense bouts of wisdom and then breezing onto the next thing. I wonder if she ever takes her own advice. She's one of those people who can see others' situations so clearly, but has a distorted lens when it comes to her own life and decisions.

Still, I love her dearly. Even if she's *definitely* the cause of at least half my tension headaches since I began working here, I'm always grateful for her insight.

We say our goodbyes, and I lock up the store behind us. As I walk up the stairs to my apartment, shivering a little in the cool October night, her question rings in my ears.

*What will leave me with the fewest regrets?*

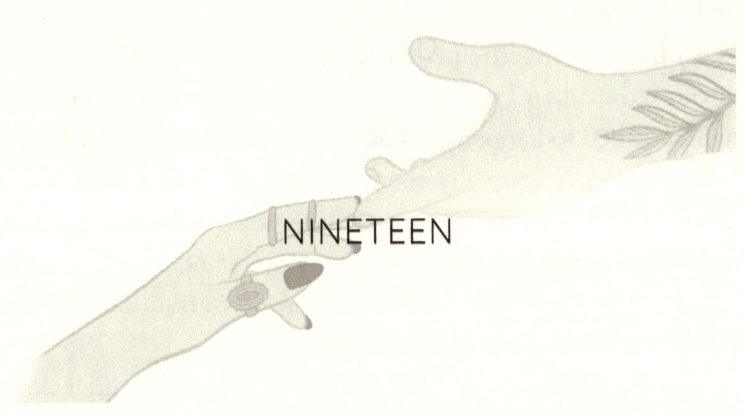

# NINETEEN

TELLING Aunt Clarissa first about Dean made me feel so guilty, I immediately FaceTimed Wren after. Even though I feel emotionally wrung out, it feels cathartic to finally release what's been on my mind. Talking to Aunt Clarissa gave me some clarity, but nothing beats talking to my sister; she knows me almost as well as she knows herself.

"I mean, Aunt C is right. You can't control the ending, but maybe you can enjoy the time you have with him," she says, focused on filing her thumbnail into a perfect point.

"I guess. It just seems like a way to cause more pain for both of us. I don't want to make things harder for him. It's supposed to be my job to make them easier." I sit back, tossing my knotted-up yarn away from me before I can do any more damage. At this point, I should just relegate my knitting needles as chopsticks. I'd probably get more use out of them.

"How do you know what he wants? Have you asked him, or did you just decide what was best for both of you and avoid the conflict of talking it out?" She stops filing her nail for a second to look at me with a lifted brow.

I have my mouth open, ready to argue that I talked to him about it, but then I remember how it actually went. I told him what needed to happen, and he agreed. We didn't really have a conversation. I snap my mouth closed so fast, I look like a Nutcracker chomping down on a hazelnut.

Wren purses her lips around a sly smile and says, "Thought so. So, why don't you have an actual conversation with him about it and see where you both land?"

I wrinkle my nose. "That sounds *vulnerable,* and I don't know if you know this about me, but I'd rather walk through town butt-naked in the dead of winter than be vulnerable with anyone but you. And even then, I only do it because I know you can tell if I'm lying or hiding things. Baring my soul with you is inevitable; vulnerability with anyone else is a choice I'd rather not make."

"But you're shutting yourself off from something potentially good to protect yourself from the possibility of bad. You approach life like a bad ending is inevitable. You've done it your whole life, Rae. I love you, but you need to do this for yourself. Shutting out high school mean girls is one thing, denying yourself time with someone who means something to you is another. You deserve to find happiness. Even if it's only a sliver of what could have been a lifetime. Isn't that all life is? Finding one pocket of happiness, relishing in it, then wading through the shit until you find the next one?"

"When did you get so wise?" I ask, tucking her words away for later so I can anxiety spiral over them from the comfort of my own bed.

Wren sighs and looks me in the eye. "I'm just sick of shying away from good things. And I'm sick of watching you do it, too. We've both been doing this in our own way for too long." She searches my face, and I see a rare softness playing across her features.

"Okay, I'll try it. Maybe. But only if you agree to work on it too. You hardly ever open up to me about anything. I want you to find some good in your life, too."

"Emotions," she says with a scowl, and then honest-to-god hisses. Like full on, alley cat protecting its dumpster territory, hisses. At my unamused look, she relaxes her face and says, "Okay. Sorry. It's hard to open up sometimes because I'm always bombarded with everyone else's emotions. And because we're so close, your emotions practically scream at me when I'm in the same room. You never make me feel like this, but I always want to address your needs first because they feel so... Pressing." She gives a half-hearted shrug.

"You've never told me that before," I say gently, feeling like the worst sister ever.

"I didn't want you to feel guilty about it, or like you couldn't come to me. It's not your fault." She takes a breath. "I'll try to share more with you, though. Promise." The corner of her mouth kicks up, and I feel like a weight has been lifted from me.

***

AFTER THE STORE CLOSES, I order new stock and add some finishing touches to my Medium's Meeting Room. When I can, I scour the internet for anything about Dean and how he died. I'm hoping the more I learn about it, the better I can be at directing Dean on where to go to trigger his memory.

The fact that there's no sign that he put up a fight is concerning. He's a large man. Well over six-feet tall and physically fit. There's just no way he would willingly allow someone to overpower him. It makes me think he was either drugged or knocked out in some way, although his body showed no visible bruising.

Pretty much every article I come across says the same thing: Dean went into the office for a full day on Sunday, didn't show on Monday. There wasn't any form of communication with his colleagues. Then, he was discovered by his father in his car, dead from seemingly self-inflicted carbon monoxide asphyxiation and hypoxia. It's the same information regurgitated over and over. If we want to learn anything new, Dean will have to get some of his memory back. Maybe we need to go to his office since it's the last place he was seen alive. Or back to his house?

"You rang?" his annoyingly smooth voice says from behind me. I sigh because I must have been thinking about him intensely for him to pop out of the ether like this. I was trying to allow him as much rest as possible before our next memory-seeking adventure.

I'm sitting on the fainting couch in the shop, using my phone for research. "Ah, you can't get enough of me, can you?" Dean asks, walking through the couch and sitting next to me. He leans in so close, every hair on the left side of my body stands at attention. I look at him and see that he's fixated on the article pulled up on my phone.

"Totally," I deadpan. "I love researching how my date died. It's *so* fun for me."

He snorts and throws an arm over the back of the couch. It reminds me, almost painfully, of our date where he pulled the same move. Only this time, his arm feels more like an awareness that makes my skin prickle. "Did you learn anything new? How long have I been out?" he asks.

"A few days, and no, not really. Are you doing okay? I'm sure it was intense to see your dad again." I turn, my knee passing through his.

He brings his hand up to rub his chin and nods. After a moment, he drops it back into his lap and says, "Yeah, it was. It was good, though. I never thought I'd be able to interact with him again. And I'm glad he didn't shoot you. Sorry about that, by the way. I probably should have anticipated that he would put in a security system since he was always hounding me to do it." Dean grimaces.

I nod good naturedly. "All part of the job. At least he believed me, eventually. I've gathered that you two have a complicated relationship, but he's more open-minded than most." It's true. Most people struggle to flip their beliefs on their heads—even if the evidence is clear as day in front of them.

Dean nods and says, "He didn't use to be. Growing up, my dad was a total hard-ass. He was never in the military, but he ran the house like a general, and each of us kids were treated like a product to be honed to perfection. It got better when I became an adult, but I think it's because I toed the party line. He and Adam have a rough relationship. If I had struck out on my own, it would have probably been the same for me."

Dean leans further against me like he can't help himself. My whole arm zings in a way that I know means he's passed through it. I don't say anything because I don't want him to feel self-conscious. Or move. Oddly, I find his presence more comforting than anything, even like this. I've never really initiated casual "physical" contact with a spirit before. It's always for a specific purpose or a means to an end.

I want so badly to lean my head against his shoulder like I did in Brewed Awakening. To smell his cologne and feel his warmth. To drink hot cocoa and taste it on his tongue later.

*"You deserve to find happiness. Even if it's only a sliver of what could have been a lifetime."*

"Hey, Dean?"

"Mm?" He stops his hand's slow perusal of the ends of my hair. I can feel the subtle shift of the strands and marvel at how good he's getting at influencing his environment.

"I'm sorry I shut you out the other day. I was trying to protect myself from hurting. But the truth is when you move on, it's going to hurt no matter what. Having you here now is amazing, but temporary. And to be honest, it was confusing to feel grief when I found out what happened to you, but also relieved that I still got to talk to you. Then there's all this... Stuff wrapped up with the whole medium thing. It's kind of my job, and I felt like it was somehow wrong to have any feelings for you outside of wanting to help you move on."

I try to think of another way to explain it to him, and land on, "Like a conflict of interest. If I want to have you around for myself, I might not do my job well. You deserve me at my full capacity. You deserve to move on." I gnaw on the inside of my lip, wondering if any of that made sense.

"What changed?" he asks.

"What do you mean?"

"You said you 'felt like it was wrong to have feelings,' but that was past tense. So, what changed?" He searches my face.

I smile a little. "I spoke to a very wise and scary woman

who pointed out that I made the decision for the both of us without talking to you first."

He starts moving his hand again, gently moving the ends of my hair until goosebumps populate along my spine. His brows draw together as he says, "I understand why you put up a boundary. It's confusing for me, too. I hope you know how excited I was after our date. There was this feeling of a puzzle piece clicking in place, or finally finding the perfect cheese to go with your favorite type of wine—"

I can't help the laugh that breaks free from my chest. "Wait, so am I the cheese in this metaphor?"

His dimple flashes in a lopsided smile. "Yeah, you are. My favorite Sartori BellaVitano Merlot cheese. Pairs well with a good red."

"I'll have to pick it up at the grocery store next time I go. Better make sure you're not saying that I stink or something."

Dean gasps theatrically. "I would never. Besides, I can't smell anything over here anyway. Or at least not much. I get some hints if I really concentrate, but everything is dulled. It's a delicious cheese, though. I'd eat a whole wedge in one sitting if it wouldn't wreak havoc on my digestive system. *God*, I miss cheese." He sighs wistfully.

"Well, I may not be a fancy, gut-destroying cheese, but I'm here for you," I say, relishing the way his smile widens.

I decide to experiment in the silence that follows because I can't help myself—and he's right there. I concentrate hard on my hand and lower it to his thigh, visualizing what it would feel like to touch him. As soon as I make contact, we both jump. "Holy shit! I felt that!" Dean bounces around in his seat like a kid hopped up on sugar. "Do it again," he commands. At my obvious hesitation, he begs, "Please?"

I bite my lower lip and catch him tracking the movement. I take a deep breath and look into his eyes again when they lift to meet mine. The hope and excitement there nearly cracks my heart wide open.

I reach out my fingertips, focusing on them as I skim my hand along his cheek. I marvel at the feeling of stubble and warmth. His breath hitches at the same time as mine, and he leans harder into my hand like a Golden Retriever begging for scratches.

His lips part on a sigh. "Yours is the first touch I've felt besides my own since I died. It feels so close to normal," he murmurs.

"I had no idea I could do this," I say quietly, mesmerized by the feel of his skin underneath my own again. His eyes open, and I'm suddenly very aware of how close we are, my entire body lighting up with the static of him. He looks at me openly, and for the first time, I notice the lighter specks in his irises. They remind me of redwood bark dappled with golden sunlight.

"Can I?" he asks, half a question, the rest communicated by his laser focus on my mouth. His tongue darts out to wet his plush lower lip.

"Fuck it," I whisper, already leaning in and fluttering my eyes closed. The end is going to hurt no matter what. May as well see if I can kiss him again while I can.

His lips press against mine, and I nearly groan from the light contact. He slowly increases the pressure, the brush of his nose on my cheek, the static of his hand in my hair, trying in vain to bring me closer. It's overwhelming. It's all-consuming. I want *more*.

I instinctively maneuver my way on top of him, and the

tingling of his body against mine is almost too much to bear. The moment I lose concentration, the spell is broken. I fall through him and barely manage to catch myself on the back of the couch. Dean flashes to the side so we aren't bisecting each other anymore.

I close my eyes against the burn I feel in my cheeks. I'm not sure why I'm embarrassed. Because I couldn't keep my composure? Because I almost said goodbye to my front teeth against the back of the couch? Because I have no clue what the fuck I'm doing, or what I hope to get out of this?

I'm suddenly aware of Dean's panting breaths next to me. He sounds like he just ran a marathon. It's only then that I notice how cold the room has gotten. I turn my head, still on my knees, and look at him. He's sitting on the couch facing me, fingertips of one hand pressed to his mouth.

He looks ravenous. And furious. I swallow.

"I really didn't know I could do *that*," I say, touching my own kiss-swollen lips, shifting to sit down next to him. His jaw flexes, angrily. "What's the matter?" I ask, worried he regrets the kiss.

"You're telling me I have to move on after that?" he asks, shaking his head. "Kissing you just now was so much more than it ever has been, dead or alive. Maybe it's because it's you, or maybe it's because, like this, all I can *feel* is you. All I can concentrate on is you. There's no other background noise. It's just... You. And I have to give that up later." He reaches out a hand, laying it possessively against my neck, thumb on my pulse point.

"You're getting good at that," I say, gesturing to his hand, searching for something neutral to say to bring me back down to earth.

"I have a lot of motivation to learn," he rumbles, pressing into my pulse point and pulling me toward him. I go willingly, because I am only human after all, and he rests his forehead against mine.

I have no idea what to say. My brain feels like mush, and all I can think about is kissing him again, feeling him again. Against me. On top of me. Underneath me. Inside of me.

That was the most intense kiss I've ever had even though it was over in seconds. But I'm supposed to help him move on from here. Help him leave me. My heart thuds heavily, as if it already knows it has to brace for another fissure.

"Hey," Dean says, using his hand to tilt my chin up. "Let's just take it one moment at a time. I can see your mind working overtime right now. This doesn't have to be complicated. We like each other, and we have a mutual goal. We can have both." When he says it, he sounds so sure.

"For how long?" Our mutual goal ends with him leaving me for good. But, he deserves to get there, wherever *there* is. I can't be selfish about this.

A shadow crosses over his face. "As long as it takes. Let's not think about the end yet. Let's worry about right now. I didn't do that enough in life, and I'll be damned if I make the same mistake in death."

I search his face, the lust taking a back burner to his sincerity. I think again about what Wren and Aunt Clarissa said. About deserving happiness, even if I know it has an expiration date. "Okay," I say, and lean in towards him like a magnet drawn to an opposing pole. Our lips brush for a moment, and I try not to think about how much this will hurt to lose.

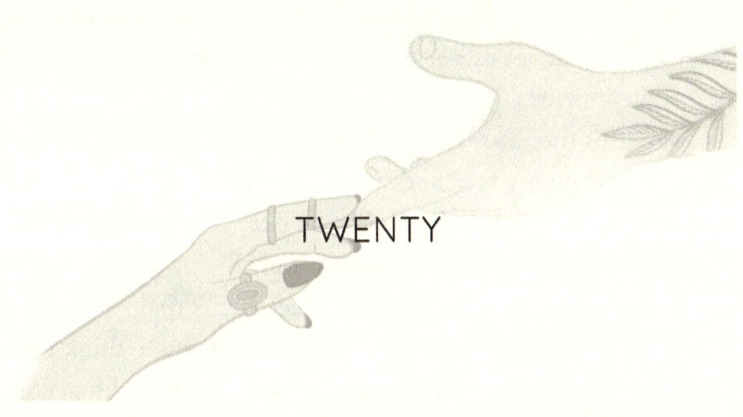

# TWENTY

"IS it possible for your stomach to actually eat itself from nerves?" I ask Wren, slipping one of her hoops into my earlobe. She brought them to the store for me, swearing they were good luck. The last time she wore them, she won twenty bucks off a scratcher a customer gave her as a tip. And the time before that, she was the thousandth customer at the bakery down the street and got a month's worth of free pastries.

She says her hoops will give me some good luck with my first few readings tonight. Wren can be sweet sometimes; it's just always buried beneath miles of sarcasm. The first appointment called and cancelled, so I have a little more time to get ready. Which, to be honest, feels lucky to me.

"I mean, have you ever heard of ulcers?" Wren asks, bringing me back to the present. I squint at my appearance in the dingy store bathroom mirror. I don't even know why I'm dressing up. No one is going to see me if all goes according to plan.

She comes behind me to adjust my hair. I'm fairly average height, and she's got a couple of inches on me, including the three to four inches of her platform boots, so her head is cut off in our tiny mirror.

She uses the razor-sharp points of her nails to rake my hair back away from my face and secures it with a gold barrette that matches her earrings. "It's going to be fine. No one will see you. Everyone tonight is a tourist anyway, right?"

I turn away from the mirror to face her. "Yeah, I think so. But what if no spirits come to me? They're going to think I'm a fraud." I pick at my already ragged cuticle, accidentally making it bleed a little.

Wren smacks my hand. "Stop that!" she chastises. She uses the hem of her black long-sleeve shirt to wipe the blood from my thumb. "If it doesn't work out, oh well. You and Aunt Clarissa will think of something else to boost the shop. You aren't a product, Rae."

I scrunch my nose doubtfully. "I kind of am."

Wren grumbles under her breath, and I'm fairly sure she's cursing me. "Okay, but you can always back out. I know you love this store, but it's all you've ever known. If this doesn't work out, it doesn't mean that you did anything wrong. And if you have to move on, you can. You'll be okay." She grips me firmly by the shoulders until I look at her.

I don't want to even think about what would happen if we don't make up the new monthly difference in profit. If I do, I'll run to the bathroom with anxiety guts and *definitely* won't be able to do any readings. At least, not with my dignity intact.

I pull the conversational emergency rip cord and blurt, "I kissed Dean."

"Huh?" she asks, dropping her hands from my shoulders

and blinking heavily. "Yeah, after your date. Why are you bringing this up now?"

"Not just after our date. Like, last night." I suck my lips in, watching her brain work to catch up with this out-of-left-field conversation.

"You can get freaky with ghosts now? Since when?"

"Uh, yesterday, I guess. I've never tried to touch another spirit, but it just sort of happened with him."

She raises an eyebrow and snorts. "Well, damn. I guess you did take my advice."

I feel my cheeks heat, and I press my cool palms against them. "No judgment," I demand.

She raises her hands in mock surrender and snickers. I can't help but laugh, too. "So what now?" she asks eventually.

The question immediately sobers me. "I mean, I don't know. We're not exactly staring down a future with picket fences and a puppy. I'm still going to help him move on, because he deserves to find peace. And I want to know what happened to him. He has a right to know, too. But, I guess in the meantime, we'll just do what we want. Enjoy a small sliver of happiness."

"Only you would start fucking the guy you're also Nancy Drewing for. Oh my god. You're Nancy *Doing* him!" She doubles over with laughter that sounds like a cat hacking up a furball. She's not one to laugh outright often, so the muscle is a little atrophied.

I scowl at her, forcing my lips to stay in a thin line. "I'm leaving now."

"Wait! I'm sorry," she wheezes. She reaches out a claw and snags my shirt, stopping me before I can storm out of the room. "I'm happy for you, really. Good for you."

I sigh and gently free my shirt from her grasp. "Thank you. And for the record, we aren't sleeping together. We just kissed."

"You aren't sleeping together *yet*. I mean, think of the possibilities! The man doesn't rely on gravity, Rae," she says gravely.

"Kissing was hard enough. The amount of focus it took was intense. And when I lost concentration, I sort of fell through him," I admit.

She purses her lips. "I mean, I'm guessing it's like a muscle. You had to work on every other part of your gift before it came naturally, too. Remember when you first started seeing spirits and thought you were going nuts because you only saw flashes of them? I know we were both young, but I have such a distinct memory of you whipping your head around and staring into the corner of the room. I could literally taste your fear."

"Wow, thanks for the memories," I say and cross my arms, not sure how this fits into my getting laid.

"Calm down, Patrick Stump." She gives me an eye roll so epic I can only see the whites of her eyes. "My point was, you eventually got better at it. Now you can see ghosts without even trying, as long as they want to be seen. I'm sure the physical stuff is like that too."

I shrug a shoulder. "Maybe."

"One way to find out," she says, grinning maniacally. "I knew my advice would work. You should really listen to me more often."

I huff a laugh and say, "Mmhm. You might want to think about that one time in sixth grade when you walked around with toilet paper coming out of the back of your pants all day until Emily Monroe finally told you. Give your head time to shrink, so you can fit through the door frame." I scramble out of the room at the murderous glint in her eye. I like Dean and all, but I'm not quite ready to join him in the afterlife.

I dart around the corner and into the storefront. Wren wouldn't claw my eyes out in front of other people... Right? I shiver and go hide behind Aunt Clarissa. She swats at me playfully. "You two. You realize you're both nearly in your thirties, right?"

"A sister's love is just as powerful as a sister's hate. One can't exist without the other, and I don't think that's something you ever grow out of. Look at you and mom," I say, gesturing vaguely to her.

She frowns at me. "What about me and your mother?"

"You two fight like cats and dogs!" I point out.

We still talk about Thanksgiving 2006. It was an epic fight. Mashed potatoes were involved, and we found them everywhere for weeks afterward. I bet the new homeowners will still find mummified globs of potato in my parents' old house.

The smoker's wrinkles around her lips deepen as she scowls even harder. "Well, maybe if your mother wasn't such an uptight—"

"Hey, Bug!" my mom greets, entering the store with a chime of the bell above the door. "'Rissa, how are you?" She ducks under the chandelier and meets us at the counter.

"Great, thank you, dear!" Aunt Clarissa squawks. She turns dagger eyes on me, and I'm not sure who I'm more afraid of in this moment: my aunt or my sister.

"Ready for this?" my mom asks, rubbing my arm reassuringly and searching my face for any apprehension. She reminds me of a general evaluating the war table, deciding if it's time to attack or hold the line. We had a long conversation on the phone yesterday, and she told me about a million and one times that I didn't have to do anything that made me uncomfortable. That, and that she would murder my aunt if she made me feel like I had to do this on her behalf.

"I am. I'm nervous, but excited too," I say, patting her hand.

I turn my head and catch the tail end of a smug 'I told you so' look crossing Aunt Clarissa's face. My eyes dart back to my mom, who looks like someone just took a dump in her high-fiber, low-sugar cereal.

I steer my mom away by the elbow and lead her out the door. "Here, you can hang out in my apartment until afterward. Remember, I don't want anyone to know it's me, so you can't be hanging around cheering me on like I'm playing high school volleyball."

"I resent that," she grumbles as we climb the stairs.

When we get to the landing, I unlock the door for her and usher her inside. "Make yourself at home, but that doesn't mean that you have to clean everything in sight," I say, flipping on the lamp by the door for her. "I'll send Wren up here, too, so maybe you won't feel the need to break out the Swiffer."

"And you know what? I resent that too," she says, hooking her bag on the coat rack. "I thought you liked my cleaning," she pouts.

"I do! But it makes me feel guilty that you don't relax. Just watch some TV or something."

"Relax? In this mess?" she asks, looking over my clean-adjacent home with a raised eyebrow. I can see her gaze catching on the dishes in my sink and the kitchen towel tossed on my island. She practically sprouts hives at my disheveled coffee table with last night's puzzle and my latest attempt at knitting strewn over it.

"Well, on that note," I quip, heading out the door. I marvel at the way my mom can make me feel eight years old again, shoving piles of dirty laundry under my bed and chucking stuffed animals in the closet to pass her random room inspections.

I head into the store and nearly collide with Wren. "Hey, Mom's upstairs and she's about to clean my whole place against my will. Can you go up there and make sure she doesn't find my vibrators in her cleaning frenzy?" I beg.

She snorts and says, "Yeah, sure. You owe me one." I nod in understanding, knowing she'll come to collect sooner rather than later. My sister has never been one to let an opportunity go to waste. She breezes out the door, and I heave a sigh of relief. One less thing to worry about.

I snag my water bottle from behind the counter, salute Aunt Clarissa, who is fussing over the store's sound system, and head to my Medium's Meeting Room. Aunt C will be the one to greet customers, explain how the reading will go, and then send them back to me. I duck under the heavy velvet curtain and switch on my lamp. I notice the bundle of herbs and flowers tucked into a small vintage vase on the table. Rosemary and lavender perfume the air in a calming balm, and I mentally thank Aunt Clarissa.

***

SNIFFLES RING out behind the curtain, and a wet cough, followed by a honking nose blow explodes through the small space.

*Get tissues for next time,* I scribble onto my notepad.

"Caleb? Are you doing alright?" I ask gently.

A huge wet snuffle. Then, a throat clears and, "Yeah. Yes. Sorry. I just never thought I'd talk to my grandma again."

The grandma in question, Eloise, smiles at me. She's been hovering somewhere between the curtain and ducking her head one way and then the other, depending on who's speaking. "Thank you, dear. I've been waiting to talk to that boy for a long time. He needed to hear it from me or else he wouldn't have listened."

I nod at her and ask, "Do you think you can move on now, Eloise?"

She sighs a bone-weary sigh and says, "Yes. My Paul has been waiting patiently for me. I'm ready to see him again." I nod to her, happy to hear she has someone waiting for her on the other side.

"Is she... Is she gone?" Caleb asks roughly.

"Not yet, but she's ready. Do you have any last things you want to say to her?"

"Just that—I love her and am glad she's going to be with Pop-Pop. And I'm sorry that I'm the thing that was holding her back."

Eloise makes a tsking noise against her teeth. "None of that now. I chose to stay. I could have gone, but I wasn't ready. That was my decision to make, and there's nothing he could have done to stop me. Tell him not to make my choice about himself. I raised him better than that," she harrumphs.

I relate what she said verbatim (I learned my lesson when she chastised me earlier for trying to soften some of her words).

Caleb rattles a sigh, and I can hear him shifting in his chair. "Alright, Grandma. I hear you. Thank you for waiting. You have no idea how much I needed to hear you say that."

Eloise raised Caleb from a young age. Her daughter got lost

within a drug addiction and made the choice to drop him off on Eloise's doorstep in the middle of an icy February night. Eloise was a mother to him in all but name, and only because she insisted he call her Grandma. At the end of her life, she battled heart disease and was eventually put on life support.

Caleb carried around the guilt of taking her off it for years, even though it was in her will to be removed from life support after a certain period. He didn't want to let her go, but felt like he had to. And once that decision was made, it couldn't be undone. It's been eating at him for a long time, but Eloise finally set him straight. She spent a long time during this visit lamenting the fact that he would rather have her unresponsive and miserable than not have her at all.

"I love you, Cay. You're going to be all right. Oh, and ask that girl out already. What's her name?" She snaps her fingers. "Cara? She's over the moon for you, you ninny. Stop dilly-dallying and grab happiness by the short and curlies while you can." I swallow my laugh and once again relay her message exactly.

Caleb lets out a strangled chuckle. "Noted. Thanks for—for everything, Gram. Love you. Tell Pop-Pop I said hello."

Eloise drifts to his side, whispers something I can't make out, and then flits back to me. "Thank you. We both needed this."

"Of course, Eloise. Rest easy," I say, watching as she shimmers and pops out of existence. I relish in the bath of comfort, smelling pine and coffee for just a moment after she disappears.

"Is she gone?" Caleb hiccups.

"Yeah, but I think she's going to like where she ends up," I say with a small smile.

The room warms in increments until I can finally stop

hiding my fingertips between my thighs for warmth. Eloise was sucking the energy out of here at an impressive rate. Caleb clears his throat a few times. "So, I won't be able to talk to her again?" he asks in a voice that makes me imagine him as a little boy with knobby knees, carrying around a prized teddy by the ear.

"No, sorry. Once they cross over, the connection to this world is severed. I don't know what's over there, but I know it's better than here."

He inhales noisily through his stuffy nose and says, "Okay, thank you. You have no idea what this meant to me." I hear shuffling and the rustling of fabric that tells me he's probably slipping a jacket back on. "Bye, Claire."

I had given a false name to protect my identity and thought Claire was cute, because, you know... Clairvoyant. Even though I'm the one who came up with it, it takes me a moment to respond because I forgot that that's me. "Oh, right. Yes—Bye now." I say, before dropping my head in my hands, grateful at least that he won't be able to see my mortified expression.

He was the final client of the night, and I feel wrung out. Emotionally and physically. My first one went okay, but the second one was a bust. The woman wanted me to contact her dead ex-husband, and when I explained that he wasn't coming through, she wouldn't leave it alone. I tried explaining that he was probably at peace if he wasn't picking up the proverbial phone. That only incensed her further, because apparently, the last thing she wanted that "gambling, no good, dough-for-brains asshole" to feel is peace. So that was fun.

It took my Aunt Clarissa threatening to call the police on the woman to get her out of my room.

Caleb and his grandmother were a welcome change of

pace, but I'm glad the night is over. Despite Delinda and her gambling ex-husband, I'm excited to do it again tomorrow. Facilitating a conversation between loved ones has always been one of the best parts of the job, but to do it in such a direct way was an even better experience. Mom's going to be so mad that Aunt Clarissa was right.

After the door chimes, I poke my head out of the room to make sure he's gone. Aunt Clarissa waves a wad of cash at me. "Look, doll! This is just your tip!" I take the money from her and count out well over a hundred dollars. *Damn.* "And he said he'd tell his friends about it!" I shove the wad of cash in my back pocket and do some mental math. Today, we brought in hundreds of dollars, and that was with one of the appointments storming out without pay. I feel something unclench in my chest. This might work out.

I smile tiredly, and reply "That's good, Aunt C. Really good. I'm going to go collapse on my bed now. See you tomorrow?"

"Tomorrow," she affirms, giving me an affectionate chuck under the chin.

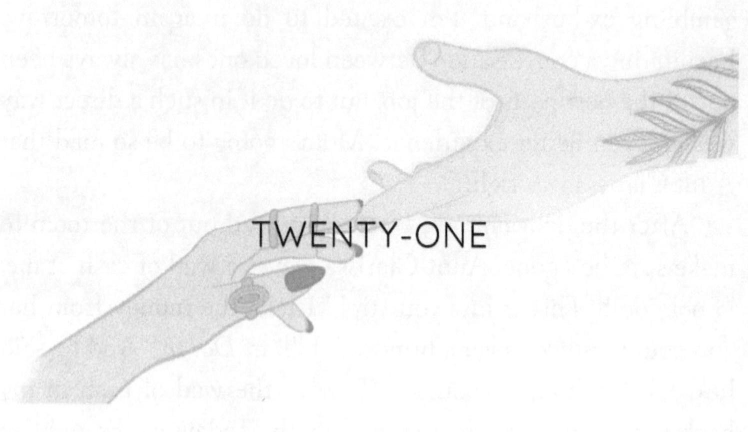

# TWENTY-ONE

THE MID-MORNING SUN streams in through Dean's giant windows. I let out a contented sigh, watching deer scamper by in the meadow out front. "This house might be an architectural monstrosity, but you sure do have a good view," I say.

"*Hey,*" Dean says. "This architectural monstrosity is my *home.*" He comes up next to me, crossing his arms defensively.

"That you admitted to hating," I say with a laugh.

Rather than argue my very valid point, Dean purses his lips in a pout I've already gotten to know so well. Today, he's sporting a casual t-shirt—something I've never seen him in—and sweats. He's definitely got the ghostly wardrobe change thing down. I've found that ghosts can change their appearance at will, so long as they can visualize the change well enough.

This outfit showcases the twisting botanical tattoo that fans over his right arm. Black monstera and fern leaves twist and writhe from his elbow over the muscular swell of his forearm and down to his wrist. It's deeply satisfying to finally see the full tattoo on display.

We decided to come here today on my morning off and see if Dean can jog his memory. Since we were interrupted last time, it's worth a shot to try again. I sent Jack a text earlier letting him know we'd be here, so he didn't need to bust in *Taken* style again. I promised to keep him updated on any new developments after the fact. I didn't ask him, but I think it must be emotionally draining for Dean to be around his dad, which makes it hard for him to focus.

"So, what's the plan?" Dean asks, rocking back on his heels. The man can't stand still, even in death.

"I think we should go through your typical routine. Walk me through it from the moment you open your eyes," I say, hoping that going through his routine will spark a new memory.

"You just want to get me in bed, don't you?" he teases.

I shake my head, focus hard on my hand, and give him a light shove against the swell of his shoulder. "Come on, Casanova. We have work to do, and we won't get any of it done if you keep being a shameless flirt."

"Because my masculine wiles will be too distracting?" he quips, booping my nose with a staticky tap.

"Masculine wiles? Is that a thing?"

"It is with me," he says, nodding sagely.

"Come on. Show me your bedroom," I reply, ignoring the way he bounces his eyebrows at me suggestively.

"Yes, ma'am," he says, winking at me. I *also* try to ignore the little molten pool that builds low in my abdomen at that.

He leads me up the stairs, pointing to the various picture frames, telling me the stories behind each one. Like I had suspected the last time I was here, most are of his family, but he has a few good ones of him and his friends.

My favorite is a wedding shot of him and his best friend, Marco. They stand side by side with their arms wrapped around each other's shoulders. Marco holds a reserved smile but there's a softness to him, and Dean looks incandescently happy for him. His smile is so wide that you can barely see his eyes, and his dimple is a deep slash in his cheek. I stare extra hard at the picture, hoping to commit it to memory.

He guides me down a wide hallway, our steps dampened by a deep, ox-blood colored rug. We walk through the last door on the right, and I pause for just a moment on the threshold. It swings open silently and reveals a bedroom that is so *Dean* it almost chokes me up. Something about this physical manifestation of him serves as an even more stark reminder that he'll never be alive in this space again. Light pours in from the floor-to-ceiling window on the opposite wall, spilling over everything inside and making it glow. The king-sized bed is unmade, but it's draped in nice sheets and a wine-colored duvet that looks so comfy, I want to cocoon myself in it.

I take a small step inside and sweep my gaze across the space. Above the deep mahogany dresser, two long shelves of records stripe the wall. The accompanying record player sits dormant on the dresser, looking like it's waiting for him to come home and play his favorite album.

More pictures and artwork surround the large mirror across from the bed, although these are a little less put together. Many of the photos look like they were quick snaps taken on a phone and then lovingly printed out later. There's one of him and his sister that looks a little blurred, like their laughter made his arm shake while he took the picture.

"Sorry I didn't get a chance to pick up," Dean says, squeezing the back of his neck, "I didn't think the next time I'd be here would involve being dead. Or having the girl I'm crushing on tagging along to help solve the whole, ya know, murder case. I definitely would have made sure I incinerated my gym clothes." He gestures with a wince to the pile of clothes directly next to the overflowing laundry basket in the corner of the room.

I follow him deeper into the room and laugh a little. "If you think a glass of water, an open book on the nightstand, and some dirty laundry are messy, you're never allowed to comment on what I consider clean," I say, pointing a finger in warning.

"Deal," he replies with a smirk, probably remembering the state of my place the last time he came over. I'm not *dirty*, but I am messy. My family used to call it "nesting" when I was growing up. I get all settled in one spot and surround myself with the book I'm reading, whatever hobby I'm fixated on, my laptop, a cozy blanket, and a snack or two. Then, I tend to have issues putting those things away. What's the point if I'm just going to use them again in a few hours—or the next day?

"So," he bounces on his toes. "What's next?"

"Well, I want you to pretend it's your normal workday. Lay in the bed for a second to start, then you're going to go through your whole morning routine and see if something brings up a memory."

"Are you going to join me?" he asks, eyes trailing over me appreciatively.

*As much as I'd like to...*

"I don't think that'll help with this whole exercise, considering I wasn't here that day."

"And what a damn shame that is. If I had known it would

be my last day alive, you wouldn't have left my bed," he rumbles, flitting closer to me. He traces a finger down my arm and grabs my hand with his. It's hard to distinguish if the buzzy feeling in my chest is run-of-the-mill butterflies or a result of his proximity.

"If only I had the foresight of my mother," I say ruefully.

"Your mom...?"

I smile quickly. "We'll get into my whole family history later. Come on, let's do this now while you still have the energy."

He sighs but lets his hand fall through mine on the way to the bed. I stand awkwardly near his dresser, not wanting to impose and screw up his memory retrieval, but hoping to provide silent support in case anything unpleasant surfaces.

He flops onto the bed—as much as one can flop as a ghost—and lies back against his pillow. He crooks an arm above his head, squirming around a bit. "So just, like, close my eyes?"

"Yeah. Just for a bit. Imagine your alarm is going off and take it from there."

"Beep, beep, beep! Hell—I mean work—is waiting!" Dean intones in a robot voice. I dig my teeth into my lower lip to stop my smile.

He sits up in bed, theatrically rubs his eyes, and stands, reaching high overhead in a languid stretch.

"You know this only works if you try to keep it as close to your actual routine as possible, right?" I ask with a shake of my head.

He drops his hands to his sides and walks past me toward the en-suite bathroom, muttering, "Spoilsport."

I trail behind but decide to stay in the bedroom in case he's really getting into his method acting by getting naked or something. I busy myself with taking a closer look at his record collection. He has an impressive array of albums. Everything from Bon Iver to Khalid. The Beatles to Nirvana. It's oddly endearing that he appreciates such a wide variety of music. He clearly finds joy in seeing so many different perspectives and must see a little of himself in each one, too.

"It's really weird to pretend to pee when I don't have those bodily functions anymore, Alderwood," he complains from the bathroom. I put the Hozier record back in its rightful place and chuckle under my breath.

"Well, we can move on to more exciting things now," I say, and for some odd reason, do weak jazz-hands. "What's next in the exciting routine of Dean Crawford?"

The hiss and squeak of a shower being turned on is surprising enough to intrigue me, so I cross into the room. I reason with myself that if he didn't want me in there, he would tell me. When I step into the large bathroom, Dean says, "Would you look at that," in wonderment, staring at his glass-paned shower. I nearly faint at the sight of the rainfall shower and luxurious hair products visible through the glass. The man even has a towel warmer right next to his shower door. I've foamed at the mouth over bathrooms like this in home decor magazines.

"Look at you touching stuff," I say happily, walking closer to his (thankfully or unthankfully, jury's still out) clothed body. "My god, that's a sexy shower," I find myself saying, trailing a finger down the glass, imagining how nice that rainfall would feel on my shoulders.

"Probably my favorite feature of the house," he says wistfully, watching the steam billowing out of the cracked-open door. "So, do I have to pretend to shower now?"

I tilt my head back and forth. "I mean, you can just stand in there for a bit, smell your fancy bath products, and then move along." It's only after I've said it that I remember he can hardly smell anything and feel like an insensitive dolt.

When he scans me with an amused tilt to his lips, I suddenly feel awkward at the thought of watching him shower, even if it would just be a pantomime version. I've only kissed the man *twice*. That doesn't give me enough leeway to leer at him in the shower. I think that requires at least third base.

I spin on my heel and decide to check out the paperback spread open on his nightstand. Anything to distract me from Dean, and bases, and the thought of him slick and smelling good while we race through them together. My nostrils flare at the faint scent of his products heated up by the water. Clean sandalwood, musk, and something deliciously spicy. I decide to breathe through my mouth to stop myself from joining him.

I pick up the book, careful not to lose his place, even though I doubt he'll pick it up again. The thought makes me briefly, sharply sad, so I set the book down again the way I found it without even so much as reading the back cover. I sit down heavily on his bed and decide to mindlessly scroll social media for a bit, if only to distract my brain from any contradictory sexy or sad thoughts.

The shower turns off, and Dean strides across the room, gliding toward what I presume is his walk-in closet. He's humming something almost recognizable, and it immediately puts me at ease. "This is the point where I pick a pretentious, but well-fitted suit and rue the day I decided to do a job where I couldn't wear a t-shirt to work," he calls from the depths of his closet. I laugh under my breath at that and shake my head, definitely *not* waiting with bated breath to see if he'll emerge wearing one of those sexy—er, well-fitted suits.

He flits out of the closet in a deep-navy suit tailored to fit him perfectly, and I nearly choke on my tongue. I want him to bend me over... something. Anything. A desk would be ideal, but I *am* sitting on a bed, so that seems like an appropriate option. Should I just roll over now and lift my hips? Will he get the hint?

"Are you going to have me for breakfast, Alderwood?" he teases, needlessly adjusting his already perfect cuffs.

"I think you're giving me a thing for suits, Crawford," I say nonchalantly. I stand from the bed, deciding that now's probably not the best time to try to figure out how to sleep with a ghost, considering we're supposed to be sleuthing. If I'm being honest, I'm kind of prolonging being back in the garage because it was awful to be in the place where he died. I'm not holding out hope that the whole routine song and dance will do anything significant for his memory until we get in there. But I'm selfishly enjoying this time with him.

"Good thing I have at least ten in my repertoire that I can conjure from memory," he says, suddenly in front of me and trailing a tingly finger down my cheek. I tilt my face up, fully in his thrall, and he leans down to brush a lingering kiss to my lips. I take a moment to revel in the feel of his plush, otherworldly lips on mine. I can't believe I can experience a kiss with him again. He gives me a final, playful peck and pulls away. "Sorry, you're hard to resist when you look at me like that."

"Like what?" I ask.

"Like you want me. Despite all this. You wear your want so clearly on your face, Rae. Right here," he murmurs, brushing his thumb over my lower lip, still tender from my biting it.

"Oh," I reply, coloring slightly at knowing my thoughts are so obvious on my face.

"I like it," he says, smiling his crooked, dimpled smile.

"What's next? Protein shake and a hundred push-ups?" I quip, trying desperately to move us forward and onto more even ground. He takes the hint, dropping his hand and backing up a little. I know I said I wanted to enjoy this little sliver of happiness, but every time he kisses me—touches me, even—I feel like I can't breathe.

These moments feel like cupping my hands around water, watching it trickle from between my fingers, no matter how hard I try to seal the gaps. I can't stop the ticking countdown in my head. How long will I have him? Have this? A couple of weeks? A month?

Every touch is better than the last, binding me to him atom by atom. When he leaves, he'll take a part of me with him. I need to minimize the coming hemorrhage.

"Please, on a Sunday when I'm forced to work? I eat a peanut butter-waffle sandwich, dunked in my coffee. And then I drag myself to the office and try not to think about all the other things I'd rather be doing."

"A peanut butter-waffle sandwich?" I ask, mildly disgusted.

He grins like the Cheshire Cat and says, "Well, since I can't eat it, you'll have to so I can get the sense memory." He disappears out of the room too fast for me to track, but I can hear him cackling all the way down the stairs.

*Stupid ghosts.*

# TWENTY-TWO

THE COOL METAL of the door handle feels foreboding under my hand, even though I know it's silly. This door is not threatening. It's a decidedly unthreatening door. What with the white paint and fancy modern handle. I've seen way more threatening doors in my day. Like pretty much any basement door. But it's what's behind the door that's sending preemptive chills down my spine.

"Why do you look more stressed about this than me?" Dean asks, nudging my shoulder with a finger.

"Maybe it's the disgusting coffee-soaked peanut butter waffle sitting in my gut," I grumble.

His eyebrows raise in mock outrage. "Um, excuse me, you know it was delicious."

I'll never admit it, but it was decent. Not something I'd ever do again on purpose, but if my waffle *happened* to drop in my coffee cup, I guess I wouldn't be that upset. "Delicious is a stretch."

"Whatever helps you sleep at night, Alderwood," he singsongs.

"Let's get this over with," I say, opening the door to the garage. This is the final stop in Dean's morning routine. He would usually get into his fancy car, select a playlist for his thirty-minute commute, and take off. Obviously we can't do most of that, but I'm hoping that being here will do something for his memory.

The automatic lights click on, and we're greeted with the same unsettling tableau as before: a seemingly normal garage. But when you look closer, you can see evidence of foul play. Dean appears in front of me and walks confidently towards the car. He flickers in and out as he gets closer to the driver's side door, betraying how nervous he actually is. I see him take a breath that he doesn't need, and then he's sitting in the car.

He wraps his hands around the steering wheel and closes his eyes. His brows furrow in deep concentration and he tilts his head back against the head rest. We wait like that for what feels like a small eternity, and then his eyes spring open.

He turns to me and chokes out, "Oh my god."

"What? What happened?" I ask, walking towards him. He emerges from the car, his frame glitching through the solid door. He paces in a tight circle in front of me, hands on top of his head in clear distress. The air drops a few degrees with his mood. "Can you fill me in?" I ask, getting more freaked out the longer he goes without saying anything.

I watch his jaw twitch in agitation. "Sorry, I'm just trying to calm down, because the last time I got worked up, it made me burn out. When that happens, it takes me a while to get back to you." I reach out my hand, focusing intently on it so I can grab his, and lace our fingers together. He gives my hand a squeeze.

"You alright?" I ask eventually.

"I will be. Can we get out of here though? I don't think I ever want to see the inside of this garage again," he responds with a shiver.

I nod and lead him by the hand back through the garage door and into his house. It's an odd feeling, because physically, I can only really sense his hand. So it's a lot like holding hands with Thing from *The Addams Family*. There's no sense of the rest of his body being tugged along behind me.

We land back in his living room, where my discarded coffee cup and plate sit on the coffee table. I'm not even sure yet what he saw in the garage, but I already wish we could go back in time to when I was giving him shit about his breakfast choices. He was so insistent that I eat his odd breakfast because of the "sense memory," even though I know he can't really smell anything anymore. I secretly suspect he just got some pleasure out of having a domestic moment with me.

We both sit on the couch and turn to face each other. I wait for him to speak, watching him look around the room as he tries to process whatever it was he remembered. I'm vaguely aware of the fact that this is the longest he's been able to be corporeal at one time.

I turn my attention to the view out the window again, watching as a mild breeze blows some of the bright orange and red leaves off the trees, creating something my mom used to call "nature confetti" when I was little.

Eventually, he clears his throat, dragging my eyes back to him. "I, um. Well—I saw the last few moments of my life. They were ultra-vivid, but also fragmented. Like watching the worst movie in 4K, but it keeps jumping around in time."

He adjusts in his seat restlessly. "I didn't see the whole day, just the end. Like, probably the last few minutes. I saw myself pull into the garage, and I felt weird. Bone-tired with a pounding headache. I remember thinking that I needed to look into blue-light blocking glasses," he scoffs and rubs his eyebrows in a show of frustration against his past self.

"Anyway, it was awful. I thought I was going to puke and pass out at the same time. I think I might have when I pulled into my garage...? I'm not sure. The next thing I can remember is waking up and feeling like I couldn't move. I remember trying to get out of the car, but it was like my body just wasn't working. It almost felt like I was being restrained. My vision was blurry, and all I could hear was the roar of my engine. It sounded so loud, I got scared that a dragon was on top of my house—" He breaks off into laughter which surprises me, considering we both know what's coming next; but it's contagious, and I find myself laughing as well at the absurdity of it all.

After a few moments, our laughter subsides. A shadow crosses his face. He reaches out to take my hand again. "Then what?" I ask gently.

"I felt even more tired. And I remember smelling gasoline. I drifted in and out for a while, and then finally... it was just darkness." He had been looking at our joined hands, but now he looks directly at me. "The next thing I remember is you. Suddenly I was in your apartment, more confused than I had ever been in my life. But also, weirdly happy that I was seeing you again, even though at first I was sure you'd drugged me or something." He smirks when I roll my eyes.

I absently drag my thumb over the back of his hand, drawing comfort from the feel of him here, even if he's not quite as solid as he used to be. "So, you remember coming home, feeling sick, passing out, and then waking up but unable to move. And then—"

"Lights out, curtains closed, the end," he says, running his free hand along the air as if listing a headline.

"When I saw you on Saturday, you were completely fine, right?"

He nods emphatically. "Yes. I was great. I ended the day with an extra pep in my step, even." He smiles crookedly at me, making me blush stupidly.

"Yeah, me too," I admit, looking away from him, unable to bear the tenderness in his expression. "So, you were fine the day before, your dad said you were fine the day of, but by the time you got home, you were feeling that out of it?" I ask. He nods, so I continue, "Do you remember if you stopped anywhere after work?"

"No, but I doubt I did. If I ever work—worked—on the weekends, I just wanted to get home. I wouldn't even stop for dinner; I'd eat a bowl of cereal or a PB&J halfway to comatose on the couch. Unless I stopped for gas or something, I'm sure I came straight home."

"Okay, we'll come back to that." It baffles me that he was so out of sorts by the end of a thirty-minute drive. Then I remember his words... "*Restrained.*"

"You said it felt like you were restrained?" When he nods, the flash of silver duct tape comes to mind, and my eyes widen. "Dean, I don't think you were alone when you died."

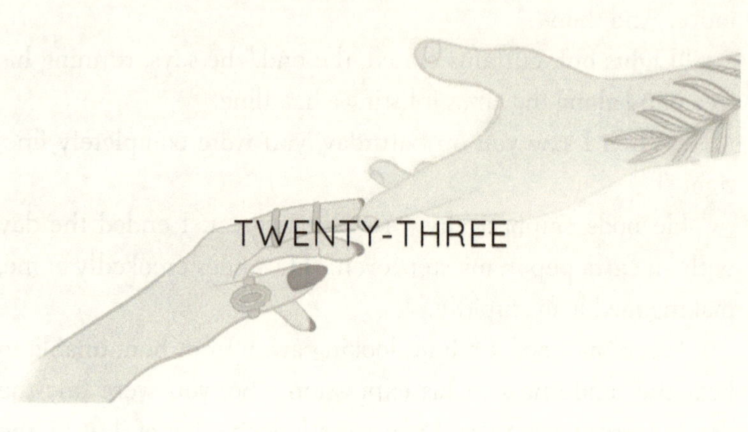

# TWENTY-THREE

"OH MY GOD, STOP," I beg, doubled over in laughter, tears streaming down my face. My cheeks are aching from laughing so hard.

Rebecca sits on my counter, a full smirk playing on her lips. She just finished telling me about how she drew bloodied lines in red lipstick on her ex's mirror while he was in the shower, like some B-list horror movie scene. She'd found a box of her valuables that Kyle had shoved in a corner of the closet, along with a couple of her lingerie sets (ugh). By the time he was done showering, she'd emptied the entire box and strewn the contents around the living room

He was so scared, he ran outside in only his towel, and then she locked the door behind him so he couldn't get back in. Kyle was outside, naked as the day he was born, with nothing but a too-small towel for three hours until his new girlfriend came home and let him back inside.

She looks down at her perfectly manicured hand with a

grin. "It was *fantastic.* Even better, when his girlfriend finally let him inside, she saw all of my stuff. She pestered him for over an hour, and he finally gave in and told her about me. It was positively decadent to watch him flounder."

"Please tell me she broke up with him," I say, fetching my half-empty bottle of rosé from the fridge and a clean coffee mug. I pour myself a healthy amount of wine and lean against the counter next to her.

She rolls her eyes at me. "Duh. He told her we 'sort of over-lapped.'" She snorts and carries on, "If you consider an engage-ment, 'sort of overlapping.'" Her mirth dies a slow death at that. "To be honest, I feel a little bad for her. She didn't know, and I've been messing with her too, because I kind of assumed she knew. She couldn't believe he asked her to moved in within weeks of me dying. It creeped her out on top of feeling betrayed. Now she's back to living with her mom in a one-bedroom apartment, nursing her own heartbreak."

"You know you did her a favor, right? Kyle was an asshole. He was bound to cheat again. Maybe scaring her wasn't the most moral move, but it served a better purpose in the end," I say, reaching out to touch her knee.

"What the hell?" she exclaims, jumping at my hand. "Since when can you do that little party trick?"

"Well, while you've been playing Amityville, I've been learning some new skills, too."

"Who have you been practicing on? Don't tell me you're cheating on me, too!" Rebecca exclaims in mock outrage.

So, I tell her the whole story. My stellar date with Dean. How his untimely demise is maybe (probably) a murder. The way I've been helping him and the tenuous ground we're walking on now. How we've kissed a few times, but I'm trying hard to keep my feelings at bay. It's cathartic to talk to someone who isn't related to me about this. It's odd to say, but I think Rebecca and I are friends. What is with me forming attachments to the dead lately?

"Wow," she breathes, shaking her head in disbelief.

"I know. We figured out he wasn't alone when he died. Someone must have come in, restrained him with what I'm guessing is the same duct tape that was used on the vents, and then cleaned it all off the car after he was gone. That way, it looked like a suicide."

"How's he doing with that information?" she asks sympathetically.

I tilt my head consideringly, remembering how he flickered in and out. He stuck around long enough to say that he needed time to process. He burned through his ghostly battery with the couple of hours we spent together, and then his heightened emotional state sapped the rest. Dean said he wanted to go before he was forced to, because apparently that makes it easier for him to come back sooner.

"He's doing alright. It's a lot to take in, but I think he's grateful that we're starting to get answers. He knew he didn't commit suicide, so we're trying to piece together what actually happened."

"Alderwood, are you never not thinking of me?" Dean's smooth voice teases from behind me. I fight a blush at being caught talking about him. I'm impressed with his ability to be back so soon after having to rest. He's definitely getting stronger. I turn to face him and offer an awkward little wave that I regret immediately.

"Ah, so you're the lover boy," Rebecca says, hopping off the counter and circling Dean the way one might circle a prized bull at auction.

"In the flesh," Dean responds, then scowls. "Or not. I guess. I'm not very fleshy at present." He allows his hand to drift through the lamp on my end table as if we might have forgotten that he's a spirit and needed a demonstration.

"*Ew,* I don't want to hear about your flesh," Rebecca says. "And on that note, let's just avoid the word 'flesh' from now on." I'm a little amazed at her ability to snark at someone she just met, but then I remember our first few interactions. I guess it's not that surprising after all.

Dean snorts good-naturedly and comes to greet me, reaching out to brush his hand against my cheek in a now-familiar gesture of affection. "Who's Sunshine and Rainbows over there?" he asks, tossing a thumb in her direction.

"That's Rebecca. My friend," I say, smiling a little at her when I see her expression warm a bit. From our few interactions, I gathered she didn't have many friends when she was alive. No time like the present to make friends, I suppose. Even if you're dead.

"I didn't know you kept other ghosts around," Dean says in a way that makes me think he actually might be a little jealous that he isn't my only recurring ghost. Not that I've ever had a room full of ghosts before, but I suppose there's a first time for everything.

"'Keep around' is probably the wrong term. She's living her own afterlife, but comes by occasionally when she needs someone to complain to," I say, giving her a teasing wink.

"Yes, I tend to prefer torturing men for fun in my spare time," Rebecca says gleefully.

He raises his eyebrows at that and I clarify, "Really, only one man. Her slimy ex that cheated on her."

Dean purses his lips in thought, and I try not to think about kissing him. It's unfair that he gets to look like that all the time. Rude, actually. Uncouth.

"You know what? I support it," he says looking down at me. "Once we find out who yanked me from the mortal coil, I wouldn't mind haunting his ass."

"Why are you so sure it's a man?" Rebecca asks, crossing her arms.

"Because statistically speaking, men commit the most murders," he says matter-of-factly.

"Or maybe women are just smarter at covering their tracks," Rebecca says, some how looking down her nose at Dean. An impressive feat considering she's shorter than me by a few inches, and shorter than him by around a foot.

Dean considers for a moment and says, "You could be right."

"Anyway," I interject, knowing that Rebecca can turn even an agreement into an argument if she's in the mood. She's the one who should have been a lawyer, if you ask me. "Do you guys want to watch a movie?"

It's Saturday night, and I spent the last half of my day talking to ghosts on behalf of paying customers—I'm tired. We're halfway through October and gearing up for our Night Before All Hallows Eve Ball. We do it every year; a time for customers to come hang out decked out in extravagant ball gowns and tuxes, enjoy themed hors d'oeuvres and cocktails, and bid on auction items. It's a huge money maker, drawing tourists and locals alike.

"What movie?" Rebecca asks skeptically.

"Um, only the most classic Halloween movie ever," I say. I turn on the TV and pull up a streaming service. "It's showtime!" I exclaim gleefully as I press play on *Beetlejuice*.

Rebecca frowns. "I've never seen this before."

Dean and I gasp in unison. "That's a crime against cinema," Dean says gravely. "You have to watch it at least once before you move on." He walks through the couch and then sits down, patting the spot next to him for me.

Since I can't discard the laws of physics, I walk *around* the couch. I snag a blanket, knowing being sandwiched between two ghosts will be cold, before sitting next to him. "Come on, it'll be fun," I call to Rebecca, like I'm attempting to domesticate the feral neighborhood raccoon. "Besides, if you hate it, you can just pop back into the ether or go devise a new way to torture Kyle," I argue.

She sighs a large sigh that probably would have made her lightheaded if she were alive. "Fine."

"I GUESS IT WAS OKAY," Rebecca says with a sniff when the credits roll. "You two are disgusting, though."

"What?" I ask, completely confused.

Her pointed glare is sharp enough to break skin. "I can sense your infatuation from here. It's like one of those horrid body sprays preteen boys choose to douse themselves in. I can't taste anything anymore, but I swear I can taste that."

I look at Dean. "Do you have more sensory input too?" I'm choosing to disregard *what* she was sensing, but this is the first time in my life I've had long, ongoing interactions with spirits.

He nods and says, "Yeah. I can feel the energy shift in a

room, especially if you're in it. I didn't think to assign them with emotions, but now that she says it, that's absolutely what it is. Huh." A slow smile spreads over his face, and it's like watching the sun come up over the mountains, painting everything in gold.

"Ack! See? Disgusting." Rebecca scowls, looking like someone just spat in her coffee.

"Just because you've been burned, doesn't mean others can't enjoy themselves," Dean says imperiously, not taking his eyes off me.

"Ugh. Okay, I'm gone." Rebecca says, standing from the couch so fast, I can't track the motion. "Thanks for the movie or whatever. See you soon," she says to me before disappearing from the room with a pop that covers my skin in goosebumps.

"What was she talking about?" I ask Dean, turning to face him on the couch.

He bites down on the corner of his smirk. "Well, dearest Rae Alderwood. Your desire for me is a force to be reckoned with. It bathes the room in a specific energy. It makes us feel what you're feeling."

My cheeks immediately flame. Oh, *god.* I never thought that I was projecting my emotions like that. "Is this something you notice with everyone?" I ask, trying to sound nonchalant.

He shakes his head. "No. Just you."

*Fantastic. So being a medium means I have even less privacy than I thought. Even when Wren isn't here, my inner feelings aren't safe.*

"Well, that's embarrassing." I bury my face in my hands, brain cruelly replaying every single time I've looked at Dean and felt my heart rate kick up.

"It's not. Rae, trust me, if you could sense how I felt, you'd see that I feel the same things," he says softly. "I'm not trying to invade your privacy. And if it helps, I didn't know what it was until now. I assumed that I was just feeling my own emotions."

I remove my hands from my face and sit back with a sigh. "It's okay. I know it's not your fault. My sister, Wren, can sense auras and emotions, so I'm used to it. She's my sister, though. She might ask questions, but my emotions won't scare her away. There's kind of nothing to lose, you know?" I say.

"Auras?" he asks dubiously.

"Oh, *now* you're going to be skeptical?" I say, sticking my hand through him and wiggling my fingers.

He glances down at my hand, making a humming sound. "Alright, fair point. But seriously? Auras?"

I nod, bringing my hand back to my lap. "Yep. She can sense the emotions and auras of everyone around her, and the more time you spend with her, the more in tune she is. So, being her sister..." I let the thought trail off, not wanting to sound like I'm not grateful to have her in my life or like her abilities are in any way her fault.

"It means that she can read you like a book." I smile a little and nod at his comparison, though it's more like she can sense and parse through my emotions as well as her own.

"That must have been hard growing up," he says with a mock shiver. "I can't imagine going through puberty and having someone else privy to my depraved, hormone-addled brain."

I laugh against my will. "Yeah, luckily for Wren, I wasn't exactly prom queen, so any lust I felt was alone at night in the safety and relative privacy of my bedroom," I say, picking at a loose thread in my sweats.

"Lust in the privacy of your own room, huh? Way to rub it in. My parents are well off, but I had to share a room with my older brother, Luke, until he left the house. Then I had one blissful year in my own bedroom. Jessica Alba and Ashley Graham were folded neatly under my mattress, free for me to drool over, amongst other things." Dean leans back and stretches with a feline grace that belies the frequent use of his home gym when he was alive.

I try my damndest not to think too hard about what other things he might have done under the cover of night with nothing but himself and his thoughts for company. Particularly in recent years, when he had a whole house at his disposal.

Dean groans low in his throat. "You're doing it again, Alderwood."

"Sorry," I say, not really sorry at all.

I'm suddenly aware that we're alone with no real objective —and he's *right there*. My heart gallops, but I try to distract myself by watching the movie previews playing one after another on the TV. I try to think of boils and scabs. Anything but the sexy specter to my right, who's looking at me like he wants to have me for breakfast, lunch, and dinner. I inhale a deep, calming breath, and can almost swear I smell his distinct brand of male deliciousness.

*Geez, am I ovulating or something?*

"You know, even when you're masking your thoughts, I can still taste the undercurrent of your desire. It's a physical weight on the room, Alderwood," he says, voice low. I look away, stubbornly trying to avoid the conversation he wants to have.

His demeanor changes, voice losing some of its rasp as he says, "I thought you were okay with taking this moment by moment and enjoying this while we can. If you're having second thoughts, tell me. Please. I never want to make you uncomfortable." He places a crackling hand on my shoulder until I look at him, eyes roving over his worried expression. I like his concern. I like that he puts me first.

"I am okay with it. I really am. I'm sorry if I'm being confusing. I told you when we went out on our date that it's been a long time since I've been with anyone. And, the truth is, even with my past relationships, they barely skimmed the surface before they ended. I'm not totally inexperienced physically, but... well, it's been a while. And it's never been like it is with you, dead or alive. Just kissing you alone is better than any sex I've ever had with another person. It's overwhelming." I swallow down the embarrassment of the admission and try to feel good about being brave. Even though I'm tensing for the inevitable pain of rejection.

I realize I'm still foolishly trying to protect my heart and to prevent myself from falling any harder for him. His humor, intelligence, and kindness, on top of the cologne-ad looks and physical chemistry we have, are all making it feel impossible. Even if he never touched me again, I'd still be devastated when he moves on. I don't want to tell him that, though. It feels like too much to admit. Too much to lay bare. The lust and physical attraction are fine, easy to dismiss. The deeper stuff, though? That needs to be guarded. Because at the end of the day, I have a job to do. I can't let my heart get in the way.

He nods. "I get it. It's a lot for me, too. I guess I just don't want to let any happiness pass me by, you know? 'Life is short' isn't just a saying; it's my experience. You make me happy, Rae. I want to soak up as much time with you as I can. While I'd love to touch you, if that isn't something you want or feel like you can handle, I get it." He gives me a tentative smile. His ability to be totally honest with me is refreshing. And it makes me feel guilty for guarding my own soft spots. But soon, he'll be gone and I'll be here—picking up the pieces.

I close my eyes against those thoughts, unwilling to follow my mind down that depressing spiral. When I open them again, he's looking at me. It's so tender and open, I could scream. Yell at him for baring his jelly-soft heart to me so easily. Doesn't he understand how much it hurts to give your heart to someone and have them toss it out with the trash? Hasn't he ever had it stomped on? It makes me irrationally angry that he's so trusting. The man was *murdered*, and he's still willing to hand me his heart on a silver platter. Meanwhile, mine's so far hidden, I don't even know if I can trust its' judgement anymore.

The longer I look at him, the more frustrated I become. The more I want to kiss his stupid plush mouth and feel his stupid gigantic hands on me.

His eyes darken, pupils blowing wide. He reaches out a thumb, brushing it delicately along the sensitive skin of my lower lip. I didn't even realize I was biting it until he gently frees it from the press of my teeth.

"Do you want me to touch you, Rae?" he asks my mouth, unable to move his focus from the motion of his thumb, sliding back and forth over my lip. Instead of answering, I open my mouth further and bite the pad of his thumb, before sucking the slight hurt away. "Fuck. Me," he breathes.

A slow smile spreads across my face. "Can I kiss you first?"

# TWENTY-FOUR

THE MAN positively launches at me, taking us both horizontal across the couch. I hardly have time to register the shock of his full body weight pressed against me, wedging me firmly into the cushions, before his mouth is on mine. All I can think about are tongues, and teeth, and gasping breaths.

He kisses me like a man possessed, and before I can think better of it, I'm right there with him. I feel like I'm losing my mind to this kiss and the way he brands me with the static of his lips.

My knees fall open, allowing him to press firmly between them. Dean's groan vibrates from his chest into mine. He rocks his hips against me and I greedily cant my pelvis into him, seeking as much friction as I can. I throw my head back against the arm of the couch, biting my lip against the moan that wants to fall from my lips. When I feel his warm, large hand at the hem of my shirt, I open my eyes to see a question in his.

"Take it off," I breathe, wanting as few barriers between us as possible. He sits back on his knees between my legs, trailing lightning down my thighs in the wake of his fingertips. In a movement indiscernible to my mortal eye, he's naked except for his merlot-colored boxer briefs. An affectionate laugh bubbles out of me, because of course even his underwear is red. He gives me a rakish smile and leans forward, getting my t-shirt off without my even having to sit up. Being able to defy the laws of physics sure does have its perks.

His pupils blow wide when he realizes I'm not wearing a bra. He looks at my sweatpants, running a finger along the waistband and asks, "Am I going to take these off of you and find that you have nothing underneath here as well?" He sounds almost angry at the thought. I lift my hips involuntarily and rub my lips together, because that is exactly what he's going to find. Shrugging a coy shoulder, I relax back against the couch, enjoying how flustered he is. For once, he's the one who's off-balance.

He focuses on his hand and—in a move I really should have seen coming—passes directly through the fabric of my sweats to press against my tender, aching flesh. His eyes flutter closed, and a faint redness stains his cheeks. He's slowly trailing two fingers around, exploring me delicately. All the while avoiding the one place I desperately want him to touch. His eyes open, and he makes a tsking sound against his teeth. "You made me sit through a full movie next to you, and you weren't wearing any underwear?"

I tilt my hips and nod, trying to get him to go where I want. "Ah, ah. Not so fast." He moves his hand back, running my slickness over the inside of my thigh, making me whimper with want. "Did it turn you on to think about it? These sexy thighs pressed together, knowing I'd do damn near anything to be between them? All the while I was right next to you, watching fucking *Beetlejuice* instead of touching you the way I've been dying to since we first met." His brows are a dark slash over his eyes, so frustrated with me.

*Yes.*

I was nearly drowning in it during the movie. Knowing my flimsy sweats were the only barrier between him and me. I hardly ever go underwear-less unless it's out of necessity, or neglecting to do my laundry. I have to say, I've never been more thankful for forgetting to throw a load in the wash than I am right now.

A tiny, distant part of me is embarrassed at the thought of Rebecca sensing my desire. She probably thinks I have some weird *Beetlejuice* kink. Oh well.

Dean trails his fingers back toward my center, but pauses just before he gets there. "Do you want this, Rae?" he asks huskily, rosy-cheeked and devastating.

"Y-yes," I hiss, because the moment the word leaves my mouth, he plunges his fingers into me, instantly finding that sensitive spot. I thrust my hips against him, making the heel of his hand put pressure on me where I need it most. The sight of his tattooed forearm flexing while he works his fingers inside of me is downright filthy.

"Fuck, yes. That's it. Look at you, so needy for me," he rumbles, looking almost pained.

*Oh my god.*

I did not know I was a dirty talk person, but wow it's working for me right now. My eyes close and I focus solely on chasing the pleasure that he's giving me. The combination of his hand and the slight zing that comes with it makes me climb higher, faster than ever before. A silent "Oh" leaves my mouth, everything in me spiraling tighter, until at last, with one solid thrust of his fingers and press of his palm, I shudder into a rippling pool of satisfaction.

I expect Dean to remove his hand, but he leaves it, gently pumping in time with the aftershocks of my release. Before the last wave can even finish crashing over me, his head is between my thighs, joining his hand. "Oh fuck," I curse looking down to see him, head half-buried in my sweats. The weird sight of him disappearing into my clothes is oddly a turn-on. I gasp when I feel his tongue, hot and flat against me, fingers picking up the pace again.

I open my legs as wide as they can go to give him even better access. He groans appreciatively, giving a firm suck that makes me lose my breath. His tongue darts out, continuing to ravage me.

*He might kill me this way. And I think I'm okay with that,* I think dazedly.

And then I can't think anymore, because all I can focus on is his mouth against me, his fingers working me. Every part of my body clenches again, my back bowing off the couch. I stay balanced on that precipice of shattering, getting wound tighter and tighter, until finally I break apart with his name on my lips. He continues lapping at me until I fully come down, and then he rewards me with a sweet, lingering kiss against my inner thigh. When my muscles stop quaking, he sits up, looking half-crazy with need.

"I can taste you," he says, eyes bright with a feverish pleasure. "My god, Rae. I can *taste* you. I don't even care that I'll never have cake again because I have you, right here. And you're better than any dessert." He licks his lips lasciviously, as if savoring me. I bite my lip, wanting to return the favor.

He must see my intent because a slow, wicked smile spreads across his face. "You want to be on your knees for me, baby?" I nod eagerly and reach for him. He stops me with his hand, holding my wrist firmly but gently. "Tell me. Tell me how much you want me." I search his face, finding a surprising amount of doubt there among the lust. It makes me want to be vulnerable too, even though it scares me.

Sex has always been a quiet activity for me, so this whole talking thing is new. I've never been vocal in bed before, always too shy to say what I wanted—but Dean makes me feel different. More confident. "I want to feel you everywhere. In my mouth, between my legs. I want to make you feel as good as you just made me feel," I say, pushing past my shyness.

He snaps his fingers, and his boxers are gone. I laugh at his theatrics, and he wiggles his brows at me. "Very convenient, isn't it?" he says, kneeling before me like some kind of spirit of Adonis.

I reach out and grasp the thick length of him, pumping my hand a few times until his eyes shut and his mouth opens on a broken groan. I spend time running my hand over him, learning every vein and ridge. Learning what makes him gasp and sigh. I lean forward and take him into my mouth, the crackling sensation a bit like holding a sip of carbonated soda on my tongue. "Oh, shit. Rae, I'm going to—" he breaks off, stuttering in and out of existence a few times. The bulb in my side table lamp pops, plunging the room into darkness.

I open my eyes to find that I'm alone again. I squint into the late-night gloom. I want to both laugh and cry that he felt so much pleasure, he lost his grip on this plane. I bury my face into the couch pillow and sigh, hoping he'll be back soon.

# TWENTY-FIVE

I SLOWLY COME to with the early morning light streaming in through my curtains. I pull my comforter over my shoulders, snuggling deeper into my bed, not wanting to face the day quite yet.

"I miss sleep," Dean murmurs from behind me.

I yawn and roll over to find him lounging with his back against the headboard, long legs crossed at the ankles. He's in comfy-looking plaid pajama pants and a black V-neck t-shirt. "How long have you been watching me sleep?"

"I've only been here an hour or so, I think. It's peaceful. You snore like a little mouse. Adorable."

I reach out and smack him on the thigh, earning myself a static-like shock to the palm. "For someone who's never seen *Twilight,* this is very Edward Cullen of you," I grumble.

"At least I'm not hundreds of years old and you're not a teenager," he retorts, sounding suspiciously like someone who *has* seen *Twilight.*

I tilt my head in acknowledgement, another yawn cracking my jaw. I scrounge around for my phone and light up the screen to see it's just after seven.

I groan, knowing I need to get out of bed and get going. I was planning on looking at our profits today to see how we're doing compared to previous years at this time. It's mid-October, so I know profits are higher than any other point during the year, but I'm curious if the last few weeks of medium-ing is making enough of a difference to stop us from coming up short. I should be able to compare this last month with the same time last year to see how much it's helping. I also have to do inventory, order more supplies, and finalize the donations for our Night Before All Hallows Eve Ball auction.

I slump out of bed and shuffle with my eyes half closed to my kitchen to prepare my French press for my morning vat of coffee. Dean appears next to me and leans against the counter, taking up way too much real estate in my small kitchen. "Why are you getting up? It's 7 A.M. on a Sunday."

"I have work to do," I say around yet another yawn.

"You know what working on a Sunday got me?" he asks, tilting his head. I give him a flat look, unamused by where this is going. "Dead."

*Yep, saw that one coming.*

"I've worked almost every day since I started at The Veil, Dean." I pour my boiling water into my French press, the aroma of coffee instantly filling the air. I can almost feel my eyes cracking open an extra centimeter.

"Well, that's just poor work-life balance, Alderwood," he says, appalled.

I scowl at him, not in the mood for a lecture so early in the morning. "Pot, meet kettle," I say, holding out my hand to shake.

He grabs it and pulls me in for a sweet kiss that immediately melts my grumpiness away. "Okay, fair point," he says, tugging me in closer for a hug. I rest my cheek against his chest, and feel his arms wrap tighter around me.

"Sorry about last night," he says into my hair. "I didn't mean to leave like that. It was so overwhelming at the end, though. I couldn't stop myself from vanishing."

"So you *did* finish. That's good to hear."

A surprised laugh makes his chest stutter against my cheek. "Yes, but it wasn't like anything I've ever experienced before. I don't even know if I can describe it to you. It was like every atom—or whatever I'm made of—burst apart and then reformed. It was like being high and having an out-of-body experience, despite the fact that I'm already literally out of body." He shakes his head. "I don't know. It was intense, but I didn't want to leave before we were finished."

I quirk my mouth to the side and disentangle myself from him so I can push the plunger down in my French press. "I think we were both finished," I say with a grin.

"I had so many more plans," he replies mournfully.

I bounce my eyebrows at him. "Practice tends to make these things better. Look at how good you're doing at staying here and touching stuff." I pour nearly the entirety of my small French press into a tall mug decorated with swirling patterns that remind me of the Milky Way.

He looks at me suggestively. "So, are you offering yourself up for practice?"

"Well, obviously. My job is to help you in whatever ways you need," I reply, stirring the cream and sugar into my coffee.

His eyes narrow. "Wait a minute. You've never helped another ghost like this, have you?"

I laugh before taking a sip of my coffee. "No. I didn't even know I could touch you, remember?"

His expression clears and turns haughty. "That's right. Only me," he says, standing up straighter.

I shake my head and wander over to the couch. "Speaking of my job to help you," I say, trying to distract the both of us from what we did last night before he derails my whole day. "We know you weren't alone when you died. Someone was waiting to get the jump on you. I think you were drugged, Dean. Nothing else explains the drowsiness you felt or that you didn't fight back at all."

He sits next to me on the couch, throwing his arm along the back of it. "But how? I didn't stop anywhere between home and work that I can remember."

I shake my head. "I'm not sure, but I think we need to go to your office to see if we can get you to remember anything. Let's go after I get some work done," I suggest before taking another sip of coffee, steeling myself for a long day.

---

I TURN off the ignition and lean forward, looking up at the large building that holds Dean's office. Crawford and Gaines Law Firm is at the top of five office pancakes stacked on top of each other in the behemoth building. "Remember, I can't talk to you when we walk through the lobby if people are here," I say, unbuckling my seatbelt.

"But *I* can talk to you. I wonder how many times I can

make you blush in public?" he asks rhetorically, looking at me with a devilish gleam.

"You know we're here for a very important reason, right? Ya know, to figure out who murdered you?"

"Exactly! How depressing. Why not spice up the murder mystery with a little dirty talk?" He rubs his hands together and waggles his eyebrows at me.

A lightbulb goes off in my brain. "You're scared," I state gently, reaching out to take his hand.

The taunting look he wore like a mask melts away, leaving a very vulnerable-looking Dean. "Of course I'm scared. Either some client was pissed enough to orchestrate my death, or even worse, someone I know did it. No matter what, figuring this out is going to suck."

"Yeah, it is. But I'm going to be here with you every step of the way," I say, squeezing his hand.

His lips quirk into a small smile, flashing his dimple. "Thank you," he says before flitting outside. "Let's get this over with," he calls from outside my door.

I take a calming breath and get out of my car. We parked across the street from the office since it's a Sunday and not very busy. Dean's hoping that not many people will be here. He thinks it should be quiet since that big case finished a couple of weeks ago.

We swung by Dean's house so I could get the keycard to the building. I also sent off a text to Jack letting him know we'd be poking around. He said he was in Boston watching a Patriots game with his other kids, otherwise he'd be here with us. I wonder if he's mentioned me to anyone else. Although I guess that would be a weird thing to try to explain.

*"Honey, I'm texting this woman who is thirty years younger*

*than me, but it's nothing weird, I swear. She's just a medium trying to figure out who murdered our son and may or may not be involved in a romantic relationship with him from beyond the grave. Pass the butter, please."*

Okay, so maybe Jack should keep this whole thing to himself. At least for now.

I use a passkey to get into the lobby, and we take the sleek elevator up to the top floor of the building. The door slides open on an empty hallway with large windows that look out on the street below. At the end of the hall is a door that opens with the keycard. The overhead lights flicker on automatically with the motion of the door opening.

I let out a breath at finding the law firm empty. We had come up with some story about my being Jack's new assistant sent to clean out Dean's office in case someone was there, but I'm a terrible liar and would rather slink around unnoticed.

"My office is right over there," Dean says, pointing to a small, glass-walled office situated between a few other identical-looking ones. We bypass the secretary's desk and walk past a few cubicles reserved for the paralegals. I use Dean's keycard one last time to get into his actual office.

When I push the door open, he's already sitting in his office chair, looking pensive. His decor is, you guessed it: a deep red color. He has a large, abstract painting on the right wall depicting black and white mountains against a burning red sky.

*Comforting.*

I doubt Jack allowed a cleaning person to come in here since Dean died. Everything is blanketed with a fine layer of dust, and there's still some debris in the small trash can next to his desk.

I come around the desk and am relieved to find that, at least from here, his office is a little less stark. He has multiple picture frames with his friends and family, including one digital one that scrolls through different, less-posed pictures. "Are you here for legal advice, Miss Alderwood? Have you gotten yourself in trouble?" Dean says, looking up at me from his seat with a mischievous glint.

I smirk and say, "No, I'm a good girl through and through. No law troubles for me."

"Are you sure? We have a special package for anyone who's been naughty." He raises his brows at me and I swat his shoulder, earning myself a static shock.

"Come on, let's sleuth away so we can get out of here. Large, empty buildings give me the heebie-jeebies."

Dean pouts. "You don't even want to hear the rest of my role-play script?"

"Not particularly."

"It's really good though. Very sexy."

"I'm sure... Wait, do you actually have a script?"

Dean sighs and says, "In the afterlife, I have much more free time than I know what to do with."

"So you spend your free time thinking up role-play scripts instead of wandering the Taj Mahal or the Pyramids?"

"Has that been an option this whole time?" he questions.

"I... honestly don't know. You could always try it. Visualize it on a map or something and see where you end up. I have a feeling that travel is much different for you."

He shakes his head. "No, thank you. I'd rather spend all my free time either with you or thinking up very sexy role play starring you."

"You'd rather picture me naked than see the Seven Wonders of the World up close?" I ask playfully.

"Some could say you're the eighth wonder," he replies with a toothy grin.

I roll my eyes. "Okay, come on, Romeo. Let's get this done and then maybe we can spend some time working on your next script."

"As long as it involves you bent over this desk, I'm down," he proposes with a smirk. I shake my head at him and try to think of anything other than getting bent over the damn desk. Because if I think about it too hard, we really won't make it out of here without me ending up with my jeans around my ankles.

*Sigh. Focus!*

"Okay. So. Walk me through your day at work. I'll sit here, so you can go about your tasks without distraction."

"You're always distracting, Alderwood," he says, standing from his desk and smoothing down his already perfect tie.

I smile, looking down at my phone to try and hide it.

"First things first, I need to go make coffee," he states. "And you need to come with me. Sense memory and all that. I need to actually go through the process of making the coffee, and I don't want it to go to waste. It's a Nespresso," he says gravely, as if that's supposed to mean something to me.

I shake my head in exasperation but comply. He's determined to have me along for the ride the whole way through. As much as I want to be hands-off to allow him to remember things, I also know he needs the support of having me close, even if he's unwilling to say it and would rather joke around or flirt to distract both of us.

I follow him out into the main office and down a walkway to the right. The whole place is eerily quiet; I get the same feeling I had in high school when I'd walk back to the student parking lot at night after putting the yearbook together. You know it's supposed to be bustling with noise and people, so when it's silent, the energy feels wrong. Lifeless. As if the whole building is holding its breath in wait.

I shake off the chill from being in here (mostly) alone, and we enter a decent-sized break room. I'm impressed with the stock of snacks and drinks on display. They have everything from healthy granola and fruit to Rice Krispies Treats and chips. It makes me soften a bit towards Jack. He cares about his employees, or at the very least doesn't want them going hungry.

Like the crown jewel, a giant coffee machine sits in the middle of the long countertop against the back wall. I swear there's even a spotlight shining on it. I scrutinize the ceiling above it and—yep, spotlight.

"So, you guys really like this thing, huh?" I ask skeptically.

"When you don't want to run out of the office every few hours for a decent cup of coffee, it's great. It doesn't top an actual pulled espresso, but it's a good substitute," he says, lovingly rubbing the machine like a long-lost pet. Or lover. I can't decide which I'd prefer at this point.

"Can you make a drink, or is that too much?" I ask, not wanting to mess up the machine.

"What's that? You want me to be your sexy barista?" he jokes, cupping his hand around his ear. I heave a long-suffering sigh and he says, "Yeah, I got you. I'm making my favorite, though. And there will be no complaints, capiché?"

"Deal," I agree with a salute. I sit at the circular table in the middle of the room and watch while Dean fiddles with the machine. I'm so impressed with how much control he has. I mean, just a couple weeks ago we couldn't hold a conversation for more than a few minutes without it exhausting him. And now the man is making me a cup of coffee.

He turns around with an artisanal ceramic mug in his hands—one of those fancy ones that you can tell has been hand thrown—and sets it gingerly in front of me. I breathe in and smell a rich caramel mingle with the deeper tones of dark roasted coffee. He gives me a smug look as he sits next to me. "I told you it was good."

"I haven't even tasted it yet," I scoff. He watches while I pick the mug up and bring it to my mouth. I take a small sip and laugh. Because, of course, it's blisteringly sweet. Dean would never have anything less.

"Told you," he says victoriously. I smile and shake my head at him because "good" isn't exactly the adjective I would have used. "Now obviously, I have to taste it," he says, leaning in until his face is only inches from mine. If I was confused before about what he meant, I'm not anymore. I know I'm supposed to be the responsible one and keep us on track, but one little kiss can't hurt, right?

*Right.*

So, when he leans in towards me, long lashes fluttering closed and his infuriating mouth ticked up in a smile, I meet him halfway. I open on a gasp when he cards his fingers through my hair, giving it a gentle tug. He sucks at my lower lip and dips his tongue into my mouth. "Delicious," he says lowly before coming back for more. He kisses me until I'm breathless and needy, gasping into his mouth.

I sit back with a sharp inhale. "I am not going to let you distract us from what we need to do here, Dean," I scold, although the sting is probably lessened by the whine in my voice.

"Worth a try," he says, leaning in to steal one final peck. What is it about him that makes me so feral? One kiss and I'm ready to strip naked and let him have his wicked way with me.

"Later, I promise," I say, reaching out to caress his cheek with my thumb. I can't stop touching him, no matter how hard I try.

He shakes himself like he's trying to recalibrate. "As long as you mean it," he says, laser-focused on my lips.

"I don't break my promises, Crawford," I say. "Now come on, what's next?"

# TWENTY-SIX

WE'RE NEARING the end of Dean's workday run through when he hits a roadblock. "Usually I start shutting down my computer and packing up my stuff, but this time, something happened. Something changed," he says, brows furrowing in concentration. He squints at the files on his computer that he was reading through. They're the same ones he would have been looking at the day he died. His eyes widen a fraction when he reads some more. "Oh my god."

"What?" I ask, standing from the surprisingly comfortable leather loveseat across from his desk. I stand so suddenly, I feel a little woozy. I shake my head to clear it and focus on Dean.

"That's what changed. I found something that would have helped my client win the case. It was an employee's family suing the factory she worked for, because they knowingly exposed her to hazardous health conditions. The poor woman ended up with lung cancer that metastasized to her liver. She died just a month after her diagnosis.

This report details all their internal testing and memos dating back at least ten years, showing Bushell Inc. knew about the dangers she was exposed to. Apparently, they were using pesticides inside the factory and would frequently spray them when workers were present. Their food products were free to absorb it as well. Basically, their reports say, 'Yeah it's bad for people, but worse for ants and roaches, so let's keep doing it,'" Dean says, shaking his head in disgust.

"That poor woman," I say sympathetically. I can't imagine how awful it must have been finding out that how you provide for yourself and your family is also what's going to kill you. I hope she moved on and is at peace now, at least.

"I know," he agrees. "I remember being excited at this finding because it was buried under layers and layers of bull-shit. It was in a folder titled 'tax returns 2008,' and it seemed only a handful of people at Bushell knew about it. I knew that this was the smoking gun we needed, so I practically ran to my dad's office to tell him."

He flits out of the room in a blink, and I scramble after him, trying to keep up. I catch the tail end of him melting through the door of his dad's corner office. He pushes it open for me from the inside, and I take a tentative step into the office. I don't want to encroach on Jack's privacy or step into any legal trou-ble. This has already been more "breaking and entering" than I've ever done, even if I do have the owner's permission. Breaking Jack's trust in general seems like a bad idea, especially when he's been so accommodating.

"So I came in here, showed him what I found," Dean mumbles to himself, sitting in the visitor's chair opposite where his dad would have sat. "And then... Then he called everyone in here to show them because, like I said, this was the big breakthrough we were looking for. It was getting late, like probably seven or eight at night, so we all decided to head out and start fresh the next day. My dad held me back after the others left his office and mentioned that this was a 'partner-level finding,' and that I should be proud..." he trails off, looking down at his lap.

He was so close to getting the promotion that he was fighting for, even if he wasn't sure he wanted it. It must be heartbreaking to realize just how close he was.

He audibly swallows and clears his throat, saying, "Then, I went back into my office to get my stuff together so I could get home."

He stands and guides me back to his office, walking at a much slower pace for my benefit. Just as we get to the threshold, he says, "Wait. No. I wanted to have a cup of coffee before I left."

"You drank coffee that late?" I ask. If I did that, I wouldn't sleep until dawn the next day. I can't believe he used to have more than one of those ridiculously sweet coffees every day. Just the single cup I drank was more than enough, and nausea is making my mouth water.

"Yeah, my caffeine tolerance was high, and I wanted to make sure I was awake enough on the drive home," he says absently, looking out toward the break room. "I went and got a to-go cup of coffee started and then came back to my office. I was trying to get out of here quickly because I was exhausted."

"Exhausted like how you felt at the end?" I ask, wondering if something had already happened by that point. I can feel a headache coming on, and absently rub at my temples.

*God, I feel awful. I really should have eaten something before we came here.*

He shakes his head. "No, just regular staring-at-a-computer-and-reading-legal-minutiae all day tired. I still felt normal." He rubs his jaw pensively, then guides me with a hand on the small of my back to the break room.

"So you grabbed your stuff and then came to get your coffee?" I clarify, committing it to memory so I can write it all down later and try to pin down a timeline. Normally, I wouldn't have an issue with remembering it, but everything feels fuzzy right now, and I could really use a nap, even though I drank that coffee.

He nods, entering the break room again. "Yeah, I came in here and got annoyed at the other senior associates for blocking my way. They wanted to celebrate because we had finally moved on from the purgatory of digging for information. Vanessa invited me to go with them to The Shamrock, a bar just down the street, but I declined. I just wanted to be home and texting you," he says with a small grin.

I smile a little at that. "So, who was going to go out?" I ask, trying to stay focused.

"It was all of the other senior associates. So, Vanessa, Blake, Maria, Richard, and Amari. They were all crowded in here with a couple paralegals as well. I said to have fun, and that I would see them tomorrow. Vanessa and Amari tried to talk me into going with them, but I wasn't budging. I had to sort of push through all of them to get to my coffee, which had already started to cool. I remember being annoyed about that. I didn't say anything, obviously, but I was frustrated that they wouldn't let me leave. Richard took pity on me and handed me a lid for my coffee, then distracted the others by asking which shooters they should take first. When they started debating between the Lucky Charms one and the Skittles one, I made my escape." He grimaces as if remembering one too many bad decisions.

"And then?" I nudge, trying to focus.

He shrugs and says, "I left. I grabbed my stuff and went home."

I try to hide my frustration, not wanting him to think it's about him. I just don't want this day to be a waste. I was so sure that if we came here, he'd remember something important. Some weirdo lurking around the office, or maybe someone accosting him on the way out. But nothing. Just a regular day at the office, minus the promotion talks and good research findings. So why did Dean wind up dead?

I walk back to his office, wanting to close his door and make sure we left things as they were. Plus, I'm ready to go home and get some sleep. I round the desk to turn off the computer and trip over a looped extension cord, put there solely for clumsy people like me to trip over. I catch myself on my hands and the room spins around me. My bag splats to the floor in the process and I sigh when everything inside scatters to the far corners of the room.

"You okay?" Dean asks.

"Yeah, I'm fine. You have some serious tripping hazards in here, though," I say, gesturing to the extension cord curling out into the walkway.

"Sorry. Consolidating all the wires and cords was on the list," he says, bending to help me pick up all my stuff. I'm halfway under the desk, hand closing around a rogue lip balm when Dean asks, "What's this?"

I straighten up and smack the back of my head on the underside of the desk, hard enough that my teeth click together. The headache that's been snaking its way through my skull tightens like a vise.

"Ow," I say grouchily, rubbing the sore spot and carefully maneuvering from under the desk.

Dean winces sympathetically. "Sorry. Again."

I scowl, my head still aching. "Why is your office full of booby traps?"

He twists his lips, failing to contain his smile at my expense. "You caught me. I set up totally normal office things like desks and cords disguised to be killing machines."

I blink at him, not appreciating his sarcasm. "What's what?" I ask, wanting to change the subject away from my clumsiness.

He looks at me confused for a second, and then says, "Oh, this." He holds up a little bottle of test strips and shakes them, making them rattle against the plastic tube.

"They test if your drink has been spiked with different date rape drugs," I say, grabbing them from his outstretched hand.

"Well, that's both convenient and sad," he says with a frown.

"The joys of being a woman of the world, my friend," I say, shoving them back in my bag. I scan the floor one more time to make sure I got everything, and find a stray, balled up gum wrapper. I grimace and scoop it up, chucking it in his little trash can. "Hey, wait a minute. Is that the coffee you drank?" I ask, pointing at a to-go coffee cup in the trash. It matches the ones I saw in the break room.

Dean nods. "Probably. Why? Are you mad I didn't recycle? I know I should have used one of the regular mugs, but I thought I might drink it on my way home, and—"

"Dean," I cut him off testily. I'm usually more patient, but right now I feel like I'm a second away from collapsing. "Listen, I'm not concerned about your recycling habits. Remember how

I told you that you might have been drugged? We should test the coffee with these if there's any left." I snag the test strips again and shake one out.

"Can't hurt."

He watches as I retrieve the cup from the trash and pop the lid off. Luckily, it's still about a quarter of the way full. I'm not even sure the test strips would work this far out from being dosed, but it's worth a shot. I grimace at the film of congealed milk, tipping the cup to the side to reveal a less-gross layer of old coffee. Using the underside of my long nail, I scoop out a little and drip it on the strip. Within seconds, the panel for the date rape drug, GHB, changes colors.

"Oh shit," we say together, watching as the strip further darkens.

"I'm the only one in the office who drinks those caramel Nespresso pods. Do you think the whole batch was dosed with it?" Dean asks. My stomach drops.

"Oh fuck," I say, the whole head-spinning, exhaustion thing suddenly making sense. "Dean, you drugged me."

"Huh?" And then it dawns on him. "Shit. The coffee!"

"The coffee," I agree, sitting down hard on his couch. I blink rapidly, trying to merge the two concerned Deans I'm seeing back into one. "I think I'm gonna take a little nap," I slur, lying back with a sigh. I close my eyes, drifting off quickly as the world goes dark.

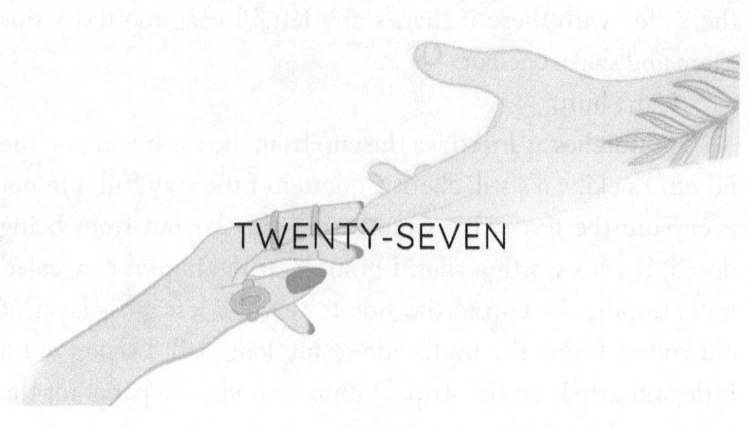

# TWENTY-SEVEN

"RAE, ARE YOU ALRIGHT?" a masculine voice asks from the velvet black. The gentle rocking makes me think I must be on a boat. Like the time my family and I took a sightseeing ferry from Salem. My parents were always adamant about being tourists in our home state, so most of our family vacations were centered around Massachusetts-themed outings.

I can practically hear my dad saying, "The history in our state is more than enough to explore for a lifetime and not get bored," while he animatedly points out all the landmarks from the boat. I sigh, grabbing Wren's hand to pull her toward the front of the boat where we can reenact *The Titanic*. Suddenly, the boat rocks harder, like way harder than a ferry in a Massachusetts harbor has any right to.

"Rae!" My eyes snap open and immediately squint to slits at the bright overhead lighting.

"Where am I?" I croak, my mouth and throat feeling like they've been stuffed with cotton balls.

"You're at Crawford and Gaines," the voice says again.

I work to open my eyes further, despite them being overly sensitive and dry. The face swimming before me looks like... "Dean?" I ask.

"It's Jack," he says, clearing his throat. He leans back, out of my space, but still hovers nearby.

I sit up at that, inhaling sharply. "Um. Hi," I say around my dry throat. What the hell am I doing here?

"Water?" I croak.

"Of course, here," Jack offers me a bottle of fancy water, and I chug almost half of it at once. "You okay?"

I wipe my mouth with the back of my hand. "I think so? I don't know."

"Did you mean to fall asleep here yesterday? You were really out. I was shaking you and calling your name for a while," Jack says, surveying me in concern.

"Yesterday? What time is it?" I ask, feeling my stomach drop. I scrub my eyes with the heels of my hands, belatedly remembering the mascara that's probably smudged beyond repair.

"It's a little after six in the morning," Jack says, sitting back on his haunches.

"What happened?" he asks, putting a friendly hand on my shoulder.

Then it hits me like bolts of lightning, zapping my brain with flashes of memory.

*Dean.*

*His office.*

*Coffee.*

My body starts to tremble, the panic hitting me like a truck. "I—I was drugged," I say around my chattering teeth.

"What?" Jack's voice is low and sharp, more demand than question.

"Is anyone else here?" I crane my neck to look out the glass wall of Dean's office. Speaking of which—

*Dean? Can you come back now? I'm kind of losing it.*

Dean pops into the room and I sigh in relief, immediately feeling a bit better than I did a second ago.

"No one else is here. I'm always the first in the office. What do you mean you were drugged?" Jack asks, drawing my attention back to him and away from Dean, who sits down next to me.

"Yesterday, Dean and I came here to see if we could jog his memory, like I told you. Part of that included drinking his coffee. For the sense memory, I guess," I say, shooting a glare at Dean, who admittedly looks pretty apologetic.

"Is he here?" Jack zeroes in on where I'm looking.

"Yeah, right here," I say, placing my hand on Dean's knee. It must look strange, like my hand is just hovering over thin air. Jack's gaze catches on my hand, and he must sense the placement of it because he looks at me with a raised brow. I remove my hand quickly and clear my throat. "Anyway, I had some of Dean's coffee and felt really out of it within twenty or thirty minutes of drinking it. I think someone spiked those coffee pods." I swallow down the rising nausea and take another sip of water to wash away the sick taste in my mouth.

"The caramel ones?" Jack clarifies. When I nod, Jack scowls toward the left of me, in an approximation of where Dean is. "Son, I told you those things would kill you one day. Too much sugar."

Dean grunts and says, "I don't think the sugar is what killed me, Dad."

I roll my lips together and say, "Actually Jack, we tested Dean's old coffee right before I passed out." I point to the to-go cup still sitting on Dean's desk with the small test strip right next to it. "It tested positive for GHB. I think that's why Dean didn't show any signs of struggling. He drank almost a full cup of coffee right before he left work that day. It lines up with when he was killed. By the time he got home, he was probably feeling extremely tired and out of it. He mentioned he was completely exhausted and disoriented right beforehand. So someone could have spiked his coffee and then waited for him at his home."

"Shit," Jack states, rubbing his mouth and cleanly shaven chin. "Are you okay to stand? I want to go check the rest of the pods, and you look like you need to eat something."

I nod and slowly stand up, both Jack and Dean immediately helping to steady me. "I'm good," I say, after the dizziness passes. Jack drops his hand, but Dean wraps a supportive arm around my shoulders, leaning in to press a kiss to the side of my head.

I follow Jack, only stumbling a little, to the break room, grateful that no one else is here yet. It would have been very difficult to explain being passed out on Dean's couch. Jack pulls out a chair for me and gestures firmly for me to sit down. I comply, mostly because I'm not in the mood for an argument. He hands me a muffin and a yogurt from the fridge.

Dean follows closely and squats next to me, laying a possessive hand over my thigh. While Jack inspects the box the coffee pods came in, Dean leans in and says, "I'm so sorry."

I whisper back, "It's okay. It's not like you're the one who roofied me. Or at least, not on purpose. Where did you go when I passed out?"

"I stayed with you as long as I could. Eventually, I couldn't hold on any longer, so I had to go before I was pulled back. But I didn't want to leave you." He looks so genuinely distraught that all my grumpiness melts away.

His thumb traces a distracting path on my inner thigh, making it hard to concentrate on what he's saying or to form a reply.

"I'm just glad no one else came into the office," I say loud enough for Jack to hear as well. I take a few small bites of the muffin, wanting to see how my stomach reacts before diving into the yogurt, even though mixed berry is my favorite.

"Me too," Jack grunts, inspecting one of the pods. "The seal on this one is different," he says, turning the pod over in his hand. "See here? It's a different color than the rest."

The other seals have darker, more industrial-looking aluminum, while the seal on the one Jack's holding is a silvery-white color and looks thinner. They almost look more like a sticker than an actual part of the pod. "Only the caramel ones have the new seal. Dean was the only one who drank them because everyone else thought it tasted too artificial. After Dean passed, one of the other associates even offered to throw them away so I wouldn't see the reminder. I wouldn't let him."

"Which explains why no one else has fallen over at work," I say. "So this was clearly targeted at Dean—I mean, obviously. But it had to be someone with that knowledge of him and access to this office."

"Most people who know Dean, even casually, know he had a sweet tooth. I mean, the man carried hard candies in his pocket like an old lady for god's sake," Jack says, sitting across from me. I snort a laugh so suddenly that it worsens the dull ache pounding through my skull.

"I resent being compared to an elderly woman," Dean retorts, with an indignant sniff. "But, even if most people know I have a sweet tooth, it's a jump to assume that I'd be the only one who liked caramel flavored coffee. It's a universally-liked flavor," he insists.

I relay what he said to Jack and add, "Dean's right. It had to be someone who knows his patterns and the rest of the office as well. They couldn't risk drugging multiple people. If we hadn't come back here, you wouldn't have known the pods had GHB. They were banking on the fact that no one else would drink them." I watch as Jack absorbs this, probably also realizing that this person has to be someone they all know and trust. "Jack, do you get the goods in the break room delivered through a service?"

He shakes his head slowly. "No, my wife is the unofficial office manager. She's in charge of keeping the break room stocked, among other things. And she definitely wouldn't have poisoned and killed our son. She's—she's not doing well." He says this last bit through gritted teeth, as if her pain is his to bear as well. He briefly closes his eyes.

"I'm so sorry to hear that," I say, brushing the crumbs from the muffin off my fingers and placing a hand over Dean's on my thigh.

"Thank you," Jack murmurs. He seems to shake the moment off and says, "I'm going to get this tested and start a paper trail of evidence against the bastard that did this to my son. It's going to be hard to stay under the radar in front of the others, but I have to assume it was one of ours."

He gets up to deposit the pod in a plastic sandwich baggie. "The P.I. I hired is digging into Dean's background right now, trying to figure out if he had any enemies that we didn't know about. So far, he's found nothing, but this might help narrow the search," Jack states, sticking the sandwich baggie in his pocket.

He turns to wash his hands at the sink, and I check the time on the clock above the window. "Damn. I have to get to work," I grumble, standing up when I see it's almost seven. "Just text me if you find anything else, okay?"

"I will, and you do the same if you two learn anything more," Jack replies from his position by the sink.

I nod, gathering my trash and throwing it out. I stick the yogurt back in the fridge for someone else to enjoy. The muffin was okay, but I'm still queasy.

Jack studies me like a concerned father. "Are you sure you should go to work today? Do you need to go to urgent care?"

"No. I doubt there's much they could do for me at this point. And to be honest, it would complicate things for us if I had to trace back where I got drugged. As far as work goes, I have to go, whether I want to or not. I'm the only one who can open." Aunt Clarissa hasn't been more than a cashier in years.

Jack frowns at me. "I don't like you working."

"Yeah, but I like to keep my lights on and my fridge stocked," I say with a sardonic smile. It's our busiest season; I can't afford to take a day off, even if I do feel like shit.

Jack shakes his head at me. "Okay, Rae. Take care."

# TWENTY-EIGHT

WITH THE NIGHT Before All Hallows Eve Ball coming up this Saturday, I have a lot to get done. Despite wanting to figure out who murdered my... Friend? With ghostly, orgasmic benefits? Whatever. The point is, I have very little time to do much of anything outside of preparing the store for the ball. I opened The Veil today after a quick "pits and bits" shower. Now I just have to hope Lenore, our seasonal hire, is up to the task of holding down the fort while I stop into all the other shops on Main Street and collect the donations for the silent auction.

One thing I love about this town is the way we all come together for each other. Each small, locally owned business on Main Street helps out when needed, and together, we collaborate on creating some of the most fun town festivals around.

Our Harvest Festival and Holiday Festivals are epic, but when I asked for auction items to help us boost sales at the last business owner's meeting, no one batted an eye. Every single person donated. Ravenwood rallies around its own.

I tear open a new box of shipping supplies and set them up in the stock room, wiping my brow free of sweat once I have them all sorted. Even though it's almost November, we're having an unseasonably warm day today. I'm still hungover from my little GHB latte, and the last thing I need is the sun's personal vendetta against me.

I dust my hands off on the seat of my jeans and head into the store. Lenore is already working, adding price tags to a few new clothing items we got in the other day. "Hey Lenore," I call. She swings her head my way, the decorative rings in her braids clacking musically as she raises a hand in a slow, fluid motion. Aunt C met Lenore at a yoga retreat she was teaching and insisted she would boost the vibration of the store. I take in Lenore's smooth, deep complexion and her wide eyes that are always at half-mast, as if she can't be bothered to open them all the way. She's too busy being Zen. I would love even a single crumb of her relaxed state of mind.

"Rae, hello. These crocheted cardigans are just darling. The woman who makes them has a fantastic Surya Virabhadrasana—Sun Warrior. So strong, she can stand there for hours. I don't know how that correlates to crocheting, but all forms of creation are intertwined, don't you think?"

I blink at her, the pounding headache drilling a hole through my skull not allowing me to partake in deep discussions about creativity and connectedness. "Um, yeah. One form of creativity usually lends itself to another," I say half-heartedly, not wanting to be rude. "But hey, do you think you have the store for an hour or so? I have to get the stuff for the auction." I throw a thumb over my shoulder towards the door.

She offers me a relaxed smile and nods. "Yes, I have it handled. Go about your business. And remember to drink some water. A hydrated body is a supple body," she says wisely. I made the mistake of telling her about my headache earlier today, and she offered me one too many turmeric chili remedies. I finally had to announce it had gone away on its own, even though it hadn't. My body and spicy food do not mix.

"Thank you," I say, grabbing my bag from behind the counter. She waves off my thanks and goes back to her task.

I make sure to put on my darkest pair of sunglasses and push my way out onto the bright street. Despite the near-black tint of the lenses, the sun still needles my retinas. I wince and hope that the ibuprofen I took earlier kicks in soon.

The street is nearly empty, which isn't surprising for a Monday morning, so I'm able to get to The Cracked Spine in just a few minutes. The used bookstore is my first stop because Carlos, the owner, offered to donate a special book to the auction. He wouldn't tell me much other than that it's a handwritten grimoire someone found in a local basement.

I open the door to his shop and am immediately overwhelmed with the smell of old books and furniture polish. Carlos likes the books to speak for themselves, so any decor is kept to a minimum. The store is a veritable labyrinth of bookshelves, stretching further back than you can see. His checkout desk sits at the front, with paths leading into the shelves veering off every which way. I'm sure it's a fire hazard; but hey, death by book is a great way to go in my opinion.

"Rae, hi!" Carlos greets me jovially from his desk. His round face and equally round glasses, coupled with his white, close-shaven beard, make him look like a Latin American Santa Claus. He has the demeanor to match, so I always enjoy talking with him.

"Hey, Carlos. How are the grandkids?" I ask. His only

daughter, Marisol, moved to New York around seven years ago with her husband to pursue the "big city nonsense," as Carlos likes to call it.

"Good, good. Maritza just won an award with her dance group, and Luis and Miguel are doing well in Kindergarten so far." Luis and Miguel are the surprise twins that Marisol and her husband had just a year after moving to New York. To say that their lives have been busy is an understatement.

"I'm glad to hear that everyone is doing well. So, can I see this book?" I ask eagerly. I love a good grimoire.

"Yes, yes. Follow me," Carlos says before rounding the desk and locking the front door. He flips the sign to "Closed," and then gestures for me to follow him deeper into the store.

We weave our way through the narrow aisles, the books looking almost like rows of teeth, as if we're being digested by some great, literary beast. When we get to his stock room, he yanks the door open and ushers me inside, clicking the light on in passing. A long wooden table takes up most of the real estate in the center of the room, and various books cover nearly the entire surface.

He turns to one of his floor-to-ceiling stocking shelves and reaches for a cardboard box. He brings it down, gently stacking a few other books and pushing them aside to make room on the table.

He carefully lifts out a book that's about the size of one of the Mirriam Webster Dictionaries I remember from every classroom growing up. But this book is no dictionary. The outside is made of a deep-mahogany, worn leather cover. It was bound by hand, the yellowed parchment pages sewn together with a thick cord. He hands it to me almost reverently, and I finger the symbol embossed on the front cover. It looks to be some sort of family seal, but I don't recognize it.

"May I?" I ask, fingers itching to flip open the cover.

"Of course," he replies, stepping closer to my side so we can both look through it.

I flip the cover open, and the spine gives a tired creak like old bones weary to be moving again.

*Leblanc Grimoire*

The name greets me in a fine script that is difficult to decipher with my modern eyes. "How did this find you, again?" I ask, gingerly flipping through the pages. It describes everything in painstakingly small script, from local fauna and herbal remedies to the cycles of the moon and planets. There are also several beautiful drawings and diagrams throughout.

"The Thompsons just moved into that gorgeous old home on the corner of Birch and Second Street. They found this under the floorboards in the basement when they did some remodeling. It was wrapped in linen and remarkably unharmed."

"Wow," I say, inspecting the page I'm on a little more closely. It's detailing how to open the veil between our world and the spirit world using ash from sacred trees.

*I wonder if it has anything else on spirits.*

"I think it will be the perfect addition to your auction, don't you? What better item for a mystical occult shop than a hundreds-of-years-old grimoire?" Carlos asks.

"I think it will be hard to top for sure. Thank you for donating it," I say, closing the book gently.

"Of course! Grimoires aren't typically what my customers

are after, so I'm happy to part with it to help a fellow Main Streeter out. Me and the wife will be there on Saturday. She's trying to talk me out of the silver sparkle bow tie, but I won't let her. It looks fantastic."

"I'm sure it does," I say warmly, wrapping the book in an old t-shirt I brought solely for this purpose. I tuck the book in my bag more carefully than if I were handling a newborn. "I'll see you and your fabulous bow tie there."

"You go on, I have to check a few books for mites and add them to the system back here," Carlos says, shooing me out of the stock room door. I wave to him in acknowledgment and make my way back through the claustrophobic stacks of books peering down on me from every angle.

I PULL open the door to Brewed Awakening, greeted by cool air and the decadent smell of baked goods and coffee. You'd think I'd be put off from coffee after yesterday, but I can't resist its siren song. And the owners of Brewed Awakening have agreed to donate a gift basket full of goodies, so we're calling this a business meeting.

"Hey Rae," Wren greets from behind the counter. She's in the middle of refilling the display case, tongs in one hand and a half-full tray of croissants in the other. Her perma-scowl is even scowl-ier than usual. I'm about to ask her what's wrong when Julian, the owner's son, swaggers out from the kitchen in back. He went to culinary school, and now he makes pastries for Brewed in the morning before going to work at Lune Doux, a French restaurant in town.

*Ah. That's what's wrong.* The two of them are like oil and water, and he loves getting under her skin.

"Rae, how's the prettiest girl in Ravenwood doing?" Julian asks, leaning close to Wren on the display case. I scoff because I know he's just trying to annoy her. His blue eyes dance with mirth, and he runs a hand through his unruly mop of curly, so-black-its-almost-blue hair.

"Great, thanks," I say flatly, not wanting to play his games. "Is your dad here? I talked with him on the phone a few days ago about donating a gift basket."

"You won't even acknowledge my compliment? I'm wounded, Rae, truly wounded," Julian says, touching the back of his hand to his forehead theatrically.

"Don't you have somewhere better to be, pest?" Wren spits in his direction.

"Why be anywhere else, when I can be here, in the presence of the two hottest sisters Ravenwood has ever seen?" Julian asks, a smirk tilting his mouth.

Wren looks like she's two seconds away from committing a felony, so I step a bit closer to catch her attention. "Hey Wren, can you make me a latte while I wait?" While I'm happy to help my sister bury a body, that would really disrupt my plans today.

"Fine. But no fancy shit," she grumbles, shoving the now-empty tray in Julian's hands before stalking off to the espresso machine.

"You know we charge more for the fancy shit, right?" Julian goads. "And you're supposed to be making us more money, not less. Since you work here, and all."

I purse my lips, watching as Wren's shoulders creep upward. I can practically see the steam coming out of her ears. I clear my throat and turn back to Julian to find him looking at Wren's back like an expectant puppy, waiting for his human to engage and throw the stick.

"Anyway. Can you get Robert for me? Please?" I tack on when it looks like he's about to shoot another verbal barb at my sister.

He sighs and nods, heading back through the swinging door of the kitchen. "So, I see you two are still at each other's throats," I say when he's gone.

"He's insufferable! Entitled! The worst!" Wren spews, steaming the milk for my latte in the most violent way possible. She grumbles more choice words to herself, finishing off my latte with practiced efficiency. The man who was waiting in line behind me wisely steps aside to give Wren a moment to chill out before placing his order.

"At least his parents are cool," I venture, trying to bring her back to happy, less-murdery thoughts.

"Yeah, his only redeeming quality isn't even him, it's—"

"Robert!" I greet, waving to the owner of Brewed Awakening. He's well over six-feet tall and has these piercing blue eyes that add to the whole silver fox ordeal. Rude how some men get prettier as they age. "Hi. Thanks again for doing this."

"Of course! My wife and I love your shop. She goes through journals like nobody's business, and your place is always her first stop to find a new one. Then she ends up leaving with a full bag of other stuff," he says with a laugh.

He hefts a giant, cellophane-wrapped gift basket stuffed full of different items onto the counter. It has various bags of whole bean coffee, two artisan mugs, a denim Brewed Awakening hat, multiple stickers, prepackaged snacks, and most importantly, a gift certificate giving the winner a month's supply of lattes. The whole thing is tied off with a chocolate-colored bow and a Brewed Awakening tag holding it all together.

I chuckle with him. "Yeah, The Veil is good for that. Walk in for a journal, walk out with that plus a tarot deck, a new sweater, and an antique."

He shifts the basket in his arms a bit and leans in conspiratorially, to say quietly, "So listen, I know the ghost talker who works for you guys is top secret, but do you think she'd be willing to do a private party? We'd pay her in cash and swear ourselves to secrecy."

I swallow around my suddenly dry throat and hope the panic doesn't show on my face when I reply, "No, sorry. She's pretty adamant about not revealing her identity to anyone." I shift my attention to Wren, who watches us closely.

Robert nods slowly, disappointment clear on his face. "Well, I thought I'd ask. My wife and I have heard nothing but good things about her. We're pretty sure our house is haunted, but it seems to be a benevolent spirit, which is why we've left it alone. We just wanted to try to help them out if they needed it."

"Feel free to make an appointment with her," I say cheerily, disguising how much I want to bolt away from this conversation.

He nods and hands me the basket. "Okay, maybe we'll try that. Anyway, here you go. I hope it's helpful and brings in a good chunk of change for you guys. We'll see you Saturday!"

"Thanks again! I'll be the one in red," I say, thoughts shifting to the blood-red evening gown Wren talked me into getting from the thrift store ages ago. She said it would be a crime to put it back after seeing it on me. I haven't had an occasion to wear it until now, so I'm going to take full advantage.

"Here's your latte," Wren says, sliding it across the counter to me.

My hands are full, and the gift basket is surprisingly heavy. "Um, I'll be right back. I'm going to go drop this off across the street."

"Here, let me carry it for you," Julian says, materializing from nowhere. Wren and I both squint at him, trying to gauge his angle. "What, can't I do something nice?" he asks, offended.

I shrug. "Fine. Less work for me. Thank you." I heft the basket into his arms and dig in my bag for my wallet, careful of the ancient book swaddled up and tucked to the side.

I pay for my coffee, say goodbye to Wren, and lead Julian across the street. We go inside The Veil, and I direct him to put the basket in the back room with the other auction items I've been rounding up.

"Hey, Rae? Mind if I take my fifteen now that you're back?" Lenore asks, wiggling a pack of smokes in her hand. I blink back my surprise—a yogi who smokes honest to god cigarettes. That's something I wasn't expecting.

"Sure, go for it. I've got it handled," I say with a smile. She smiles back, shakes out a fresh cigarette, and heads outside, rummaging in her bag for a lighter. I guess she and Aunt Clarissa have a few things in common.

I take a sip of the tasty (if not a little plain) latte and mentally run through my checklist again. I still have several stores to go to for auction items, I have three Medium appointments later this afternoon, I need to call back the DJ... Oh, and I should probably eat more than a stale office muffin. My stomach roils in protest at the thought.

Julian reemerges from the stock room and strolls towards me, nearly walking straight into the too-low chandelier. "Hey, Rae? Can I ask you something before I go?"

I nod, depositing my bag on the counter. "Sure."

"Why does your sister hate me?" he blurts, looking genuinely interested in my response.

I blink away my surprise. "Uh, well—Hate's a strong word," I say, gathering the heavy weight of my hair and lifting it off my neck. "Wren is who she is. She's mercurial and testy. Most of her attitude is all bluster. She holds people at a distance because it feels safer, I guess," I say, stopping myself from revealing more for fear of incurring Wren's wrath. "But you know, she'd probably be more relaxed around you if you stopped provoking her," I offer with a raised brow.

Julian smiles sheepishly, and I'm reminded of how hand-some he is. He's got the whole bad boy, devil may care attitude *and* a job that requires a lot of skill and precision. Hot. Too bad Wren would rather peel her own fingernails off and eat them for dessert than go on a date with him.

"I know you're right. It's just so easy to get her riled up. I should probably stop, though." He pauses, seeming to mull something over. "Or at least tone it down. She's been extra irri-table lately, and it's been hard to resist, but I'll do my best. The workplace is getting a little toxic," he says with a laugh.

"Good luck with that," I reply, shaking my head.

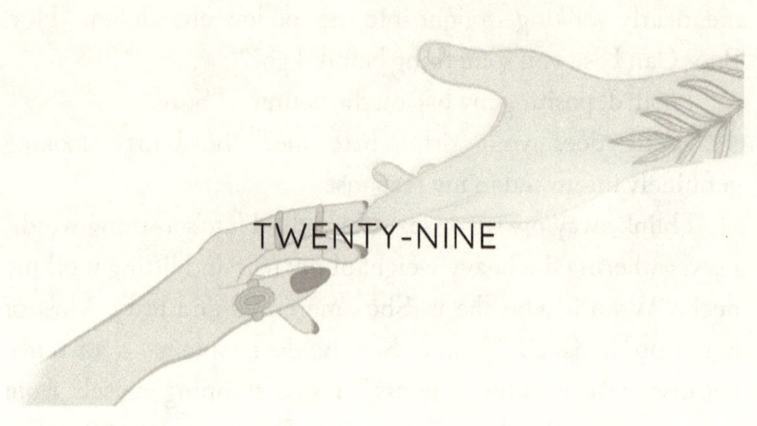

# TWENTY-NINE

I HUG the grimoire tighter to my body as I make my way up the stairs to my apartment. I feel a little like I'm stealing, but I'll bring it back… Probably. I want to see if there's anything in here that might be useful for me or my sister first.

It's late, going on nine at night, and I finally came to a stopping point for the day. We had a huge influx of customers the last few hours, meaning I had to eat bites of my award-winning dinner (peanut butter and jelly sandwich) between ringing people up. And then I had my Medium appointments (only one of which was successful). And *then* I had to restock our depleted items because I knew I wouldn't want to do it in the morning. Not to mention all the stressing and recalculating and spiraling I've been doing, trying to figure out if we'll have enough money to cover the raise in rent and Aunt Clarissa's grand retirement adventure.

By the time I keel over on the couch, I am bone weary, but still too keyed up to give into relaxation. I open up the grimoire, looking more closely at the first few pages to see if there's a table of contents. Unfortunately, the author didn't care to make the book navigable to anyone but themselves. So, I start flipping through carefully, scanning the first sentence or two on each page to see if anything catches my eye.

"What's that?" Dean asks from over my shoulder.

I suck in a startled breath and turn a scolding glare on him. "I know you don't have to knock anymore, but do you have to make a habit of appearing behind me?" I ask grumpily.

"Yes," he chirps, peppering my brow with kisses until I smooth it.

He walks through the couch and sits next to me, peering over my shoulder. "'So,' he asks again, 'what's that?'"

"Did you just refer to yourself in third person?" I ask.

"Mm. Trying something new. Too much?" he says, raising his brows at me. Today he's wearing a casual t-shirt and dark jeans, the botanical tattoo sleeve dancing enticingly down his arm.

"Maybe a little," I say with a laugh. "This is a grimoire. It's super old," I tell him, tilting the book so he can get a better look.

"Like, a spell book?" he clarifies.

"Yeah, sort of. It's the writer's collection of any and all magical knowledge, including spells. But even things like herbal remedies, dream journaling, and a witch's calendar can be kept in a grimoire. The Cracked Spine donated it for the silent auction," I explain.

"Are you trying to pick up a new hobby, Alderwood?" he teases.

"Not exactly, but I was just curious if there was anything useful for me or my sister in here. Anything about spirits or auras."

He purses his lips at me. "You do remember that you were drugged yesterday, had a full day of work today, and are in the process of solving my murder?"

"Yes...?" I reply, drawing out the word.

He grabs the book from me gently and sets it on the coffee table. "You deserve to rest a little. You have a lot going on. And I know you're going to be up early tomorrow to get back to work. Why don't you go take a hot shower and go to bed?"

"Are you trying to boss me around?" I grumble.

"I would never," he admonishes. "But I want you to take care of yourself, too. You're running yourself ragged. You deserve a break."

I sigh and nod, knowing he's right. In a blink, he's standing and holding his hand out to me, looking a little lust-crazed. "Oh, I see. This is a group activity," I quip.

"No funny business. I want to take care of you," he says, expression surprisingly tender despite the stoked heat in them.

I smile crookedly at him. "Okay, lead the way."

When we get to my small bathroom, he turns the shower on for me. Scalding hot, just the way I like it. "I wish you had a bathtub," he sighs.

"Me too," I say ruefully, thinking of the gorgeous jacuzzi tub in his en suite.

"This will do," he says, vanishing his clothes with a theatrical snap of his fingers.

"So, be honest: How much are you practicing that when I'm not around?"

"Oh, it's like, ninety percent of what I do when you're busy," he says mock-seriously.

"And the other ten percent?" I ask, keeping my eyes trained

on his face, even though they're practically begging to dip lower.

"I follow you around unseen in the ether because I can't stay away," he says, coming in closer to grab the hem of my long-sleeved t-shirt. He slowly brings it up overhead and tosses it in the small laundry basket in the corner.

"You do not," I state, feeling a blush creep over my whole body. The thought of him watching when I don't know is kind of hot. Maybe I've read a few too many dark romances, because that should be creepy, but it isn't. It's oddly sweet that he doesn't want to be away from me, even when he's "recharging" as we've come to call it. I thought I was sensing him when he wasn't there, but I had myself half-convinced it was just wishful thinking.

He's suddenly behind me, leaning in so his lips spark against my ear when he states, "I do. I watch you when I'm not with you because I can't stop myself. You're addicting." He unclips my bra dexterously and allows it to fall to the floor.

I can't help but watch my nipples tighten in the mirror, with a rosy-cheeked Dean looming over me from behind. He meets my gaze in the reflection, tilting his head like a predator evaluating its next prey. "You're the sexiest woman I've ever had the privilege of seeing. Touching," he says in my ear, reaching a large hand around to palm the heavy weight of my breast.

"I thought you said no funny business," I tease, watching his thumb make slow circles over me in the mirror.

"You're right, I did say that," he murmurs, removing his hand from my breast and letting it slide down to my waist, trailing goosebumps in its wake. I whimper in disappointment.

He encircles my waist with both arms and pulls me back into his hard chest, making static dance up and down my spine.

He slowly undoes the button on my jeans and pulls the zipper down. I feel like I'm having an out-of-body experience, watching him undress me this way in the mirror. I would normally see all the rolls or cellulite. The things that I wanted to change. But right now, with him treating me like a present he gets to unwrap, I feel like Aphrodite: powerful, and sensual, and wanted.

He bends down, taking my jeans with him, totally unencumbered by the wall behind him because he just passes right through. His control over his body in this form is truly amazing, and something I can think about in more detail later. Right now, I'm too busy trying to remember to breathe. Just when I think he'll stand, he hooks his fingers around the band of my underwear and strips them off in one fluid motion.

Dean presses a hand to my spine, forcing me to bend over and catch myself on the vanity, baring myself to him fully. "Hey, Rae?"

"Yeah?" I croak.

"I lied," Dean says simply. Before I can ask what he lied about, his hands slide to either side of my hips, pulling me open just that much more for him. I suck in a gasp when he leans in and tastes me. The gasp turns to a groan when his tongue starts to work along my center. With the angle, I can just make out his kneeling form behind me in the reflection. I've never been more happy that I can see ghosts in the mirror than I am right now.

Suddenly, he stands up, and I nearly sag into him in disappointment. "Why'd you stop?" I whine.

He gives me a knowing smirk in the mirror. "That was just the beginning. Come on, let me take care of you."

He guides me to the shower, and we both step inside under the stream of water. I sigh contentedly as the hot water runs over my body, despite the ache between my legs. I tip my head back and allow my hair to get saturated. "Turn around," Dean says, pumping a handful of my shampoo into his palm.

I comply and feel a totally different type of ecstasy as he works his blunt fingers over my scalp, massaging the product into my hair. I allow him to guide me back under the spray as he carefully rinses out the suds. He uses his fingers to comb through my hair, adding my sweet-smelling conditioner to it. "Is this the soap you use?" he asks in a low tone, picking up my lavender-scented goat milk bar soap.

I nod, and he sweeps my hair over my shoulder, exposing my back. He rubs the bar in efficient circles around my back and down my arms. He runs the soap over my legs before circling me and starting on my front. He's somehow managed to avoid every spot aching for his touch so far. I don't mind. Mostly. I'm enjoying the slow ascent, the way he draws out every step. Worshipping my body with touches that aren't exactly sexual, but make my heart race all the same.

He guides me under the spray of the shower, running his hands over me and wringing out my hair to rinse everything off. If I weren't so turned on, I'd be ready to fall asleep for the next nine hours. Someone playing with my hair is like a sedative for me. I've been known to doze off at the hair salon.

Dean shuts off the water, snags my towel from the rack, and wraps me up like a horny little burrito. The ache between my thighs is almost painful, but I don't want to push him to go any faster. I'm savoring this moment with him. It's so rare for someone else to take care of me that I'm inclined to let him. I wrap my hair in a towel and tilt my head at him. I love that we don't even have to talk. It's like we've done this a million times.

He leads me out of the bathroom and toward my bed, pushing me lightly onto my back, making the towel flop open on either side. He turns from me and evaluates my dresser. I'm about to ask him what he's looking for when his gaze catches on a bottle of my almond-scented body oil. "So this is why you smelled like a cookie," he says, retrieving it from its place among my other body care products. He smiles lazily at me, though his eyes betray his less-than-pure thoughts; they're nearly black with lust.

"What are you doing?" I ask, even though I'm pretty sure I know.

"Taking care of you," he says, drizzling the oil over my chest and middle. He glides his hands over my still-damp skin, rubbing the oil into it with all the care of a masseuse. Although a masseuse has never touched me quite like this. Or at all, if I'm being honest. Massages are a luxury I've never been able to bring myself to splurge on.

He continues to rub the oil onto my arms and legs, giving me a brief but decadent foot massage, before making his way up and cupping my breasts. His slick palms glide over them in circles until I'm practically delirious with how turned on I am. "What do you want now, Rae?" he asks from his kneeled position between my legs on the bed.

I reach forward, wrapping my hand around him and pump once. He pulls away, making me pout. "Use your words," he orders.

I falter, which feels silly considering I'm oiled up and splayed out in front of him. "I want you," I say quietly.

The corner of his mouth ticks up as he runs his hands over my breasts. He cocks his head to the side. "You want me to what?" he gravels.

I sigh in frustration. He knows what I want, but he's just being difficult. "I want you inside me," I finally burst out, unable to take the maddening emptiness between my legs anymore.

"You want me to fuck you, Rae?" he asks, wrapping a hand around himself and stroking a few times as though he can't resist. I nod vigorously in agreement. "Say it," he practically growls, though his eyes are still playful, letting me know that I'm as much in control as he is.

"Fuck me, please," I beg. The crude words fall from my mouth before I can second-guess myself.

Apparently, that's all he needed. "Gladly," he says, leaning down to kiss me while simultaneously coaxing my legs wider so he can press himself between them.

When he pushes inside, fully seating himself in a single slow thrust, I'm immediately overwhelmed in the best way. The faint prickle of electricity he gives off mixed with the heat and pressure of him is almost too much. I am aware of every square inch of skin he's touching, practically branded with him.

"Deep breaths," he coaches in my ear. I do as he says and slowly start to relax around him, allowing him the freedom to roll his hips into mine.

We both gasp at the sensation, and when he pauses to check on me, I reach up my hand to cup his jaw and make him look me in the eye. "Again," I demand, canting my hips to allow him a deeper angle. He obliges, easily finding a rhythm that has us both sighing with pleasure, gazes locked in a way that's almost more intimate than what's happening with our bodies.

I close my eyes, unable to take the way Dean is baring himself to me and the soft way he's looking at me. Unable to take the way it makes me want to do the same. I draw his face closer so I can kiss him, disguising my need to sever the connection between us before it gets too real.

I don't know what's happening to me. Maybe it's the way he took care of me multiple times, but I've never been someone who viewed sex as this be-all and end-all for a relationship. But now, as cheesy as it sounds, it feels cosmic. Like a key fitting into a lock. Utter rightness. And I'm terrified of it. What it means. How much I'll have to lose.

"You with me, love?" Dean asks after pulling his lips from mine, hips slowing until he's just barely rocking into me.

"Yes," I say, meeting his eye again.

"Good," he replies, before pulling out of me.

"Wha—" I start to ask. But then my jaw clicks shut because he's digging through my bedside drawer and pulling out my favorite vibrator. "How did you know?" I ask, my throat dry. And then I remember that he said he watches me.

He clicks it on, and I immediately snap my legs shut. I know if he puts that on me, I'll be done in seconds, and I want this to last. He makes a tsking noise and says, "None of that, love. Flip over for me." I hesitate for a moment before doing as I'm told, instinctively moving to my knees and arching my back as I press my chest down into the bed. "Beautiful," he says, suddenly behind me. I push my hips back when he doesn't move. "Needy thing, aren't we?" he asks before palming a cheek and squeezing.

I whimper in response. "Yes, I need you," I say, face half-buried in the mattress.

"Here?" he asks, dipping the tip of the vibrator inside.

"Yes," I breathe. He withdraws the vibrator and lines himself up, pushing into me slowly. He leans forward, draping his long body over mine, and reaches around with the vibrator until he finds a spot that makes me see stars. Heat immediately licks out from my center, and I have to concentrate on the swirling colors and patterns of my bedspread to stop from shattering.

His hips meet the back of my thighs in slow, deep thrusts that nearly bring tears to my eyes. "You take me so well," he murmurs in my ear, reaching his free hand forward to lace with mine, the other still between my legs. I can only moan in response, feeling myself spiral tighter and tighter. Finally, like a fishing line snapping, I unspool in waves, the vibrator he presses to me heightening the intensity.

His breath hitches, and he says, "I'm going to try to stay here with you, okay? But if I can't, know that I want to. More than anything." His muscles tense against me and he presses his forehead to my shoulder.

His thrusts become erratic until I feel him pulse inside me, the vibrator falling to the bed as he loses concentration. He seats himself deeply, gripping my hips tightly for purchase. He shudders and allows himself to lie on top of me. I can tell he's holding off some of his weight, but it's still the ultimate cuddle, our bodies pressed closely together. I smile into my comforter. "You stayed," I say, half-delirious.

"I stayed," he affirms, rolling off me and drawing me close, my back to his chest.

"So much for no funny business," I say with a snort, feeling slap-happy from all the oxytocin bouncing around my brain.

"Yeah, well. You're relaxed, aren't you?" he says, kissing the crown of my still-wet head. I snuggle deeper into him, holding him close like an oversized teddy bear. "Sleep, Rae," he says, caressing my side with his hand. I comply before I can voice the half-formulated argument brewing on my tongue.

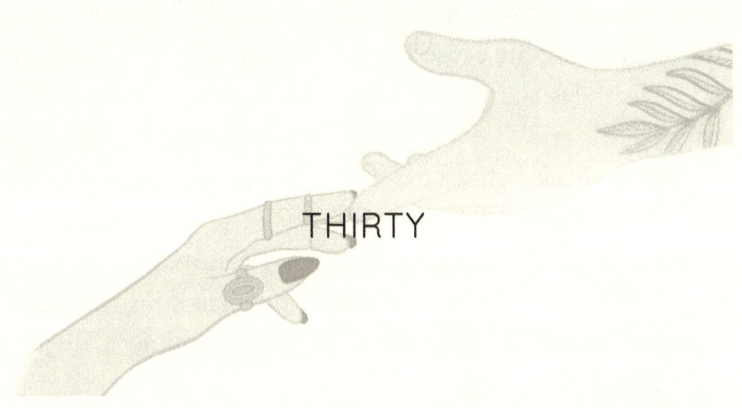

# THIRTY

WREN KICKS her combat-boot-clad feet up on my coffee table and sighs, closing her eyes. She just finished her closing shift at Brewed Awakening and didn't feel like making the drive home. This happens about once a month when her insomnia catches up with her.

I only have two days to go until the Night Before All Hallows Eve Ball and an overflowing to-do list to complete. I originally tried to get her to come up to my place without me, but she wouldn't hear it. "Ew no, you workaholic," were her exact words, actually. And then she proceeded to drag me out of the store, barely giving me enough time to lock up, and tossed a frozen vegetarian pizza into my toaster oven.

Now here we are, both so tired that neither of us has gotten up and pulled the pizza out of the still-dinging oven. I close my eyes, vowing that in just one more minute, I'll get up and pull the pizza out so it doesn't burn.

"Okay well, this is where I intervene," Dean says. I open

my eyes and look over the back of the couch to see him pulling the pizza out of the oven with his bare hands. "Can't have you dying in a house fire caused by an overcooked pizza. That's just sad." He slides the pie onto my countertop and turns off my toaster oven.

Wren wrinkles her nose and rubs the goosebumps on her arms. "Ugh. Ghost boy is here, isn't he?"

Dean snorts. "Ghost boy? I guess I can rock with that. It sounds like some sort of superhero." He places his fists on his hips and adopts a "Superman" stance, humming a theme I vaguely recognize.

"Okay, I knew you guys were still hanging out, what with the whole murder and everything, but does he have to be here now?" Wren asks, shooting daggers in his general direction.

"Geez, what's her deal?" Dean asks, dropping his fists and flitting across the room to sit in the chair.

"She's not a huge fan of ghosts," I explain. "She can read auras, and it's very unsettling to see an aura but not a person. It's like when you try to tune an old TV and get to a channel that doesn't have a good signal, so it's all broken up and fuzzy. Her mind tries to make the picture clearer, but it can't."

"Gives me a damn headache," Wren grumbles, standing and heading to the kitchen. I hear the *shing!* of her pulling my pizza cutter out and decide to risk her bad mood for a slice of pizza.

"Can you tell her I'm sorry?" Dean asks me. "I can go now. I just didn't want you to burn your pizza." He presses his mouth into a line. If I'm not mistaken, I would say that charismatic, people-person Dean is nervous about meeting my sister.

I relay what he said to her, and she sighs, cutting into the pizza with vigor. "I don't want you to leave, Ghost Boy. If you're banging my sister, I have to get used to you."

I choke on my spit and eke out, "Wren!"

Dean titters, shoulders shaking until it evolves into a full-blown laugh. I guess I should have seen this coming when I confided in her yesterday. I run my hand down my face to cover my smile. These two people of mine are ridiculous.

"What? Am I not allowed to talk about it? Is ghost sex taboo?" Wren asks, a mischievous smile curling her lips.

I sigh from deep in my weary bones. "We are not going to talk about sex with my—With Dean," I stumble out. I almost called him my boyfriend, but attaching labels is the last thing we need right now.

Wren senses the turn in my mood, so she hands me a plate with a couple of pieces of pizza. "Fine. Let's eat. Dean, you can stay, but don't get close to me, please. It makes everything go a little haywire in my brain."

"Got it," Dean says, settling further in the chair. I nod at Wren to let her know that Dean understands.

"So, you pulled out this pizza, huh?" Wren asks Dean, before taking a massive bite. She hardly chews before she continues, "That's weird, right?" She looks to me for confirmation, and I shrug. "Your ghosts usually don't have that much control. Like sure, they can move things sometimes, but to move around the world like a solid, flesh and bones person is unheard of."

I take a bite before I reply, "Yeah, it's a little odd. But I think Dean has more determination than most to stick around and get good at things. And maybe it's his frequent proximity to me. I know I'm like a homing beacon for spirits, so maybe I juice them up a bit too. It's not like I would know the effects, because most spirits only stick around for a week or so at most. He and Rebecca are my two longest-running visitors."

"How is Rebecca anyway?" Dean asks.

"She's doing okay, I think. It's been a while since she checked in, so maybe she finally moved on. It had to get old eventually, getting revenge on her ex. Even the most vengeful person has to get bored with that someday. Especially if you know you have something better waiting for you on the other side."

"Why aren't you getting revenge on people who've wronged you?" Wren asks, looking towards Dean. Despite the conversation, I'm grateful to her for the way she's trying to engage him, even though I know it makes her wildly uncomfortable.

Dean crosses his sweatpants-clad legs at the ankles in front of him. "I guess I'm not a very vengeful person. The only one I'd want to get revenge on is whoever killed me, but since we're still figuring that out, I'd rather hang out with Rae. She's much more interesting than anyone I've known before anyway."

I tell her what he said a bit sheepishly. I'm trying and failing to come up with a better way for them to communicate. As is, I don't mind being a translator, but it makes for stilted conversation. I guess writing would be good, but his handwriting is barely legible in this form anyway. Plus, it would be hard to concentrate on a conversation while he was using my hand the way Leo did. Just another problem to solve on my to-do list.

"Rae is amazing and the best person I know," Wren says, glaring in Dean's direction. "So if you ever hurt her, I will find a way to resurrect you so I can kill you again myself." Dean audibly swallows from across the room, which makes Wren grin menacingly. "Good. I can feel your fear. You should be afraid. But also, make her happy. Or else." She takes a massive bite of pizza, her scary-sister duties over.

Dean shivers and says, "Your sister is very intimidating."

I laugh. "Yes, she is."

---

AFTER WE FINISHED OUR DINNER, Dean decided to go check on his family. He wanted to give us a little alone time and figured it was time to see them. I appreciate that he wants to give us space and let me know he won't be watching.

"Wanna see something cool?" I ask Wren. She's hardly left her position on my couch other than to remove her shoes and toss them to the floor with a heavy thud.

Wren doesn't bother with a fully-formed verbal response, grunting a vague agreement instead. I pull open the deep bottom drawer in my desk and carefully extract the grimoire.

"What is *that*?" Wren asks, sitting up straighter to get a better look once I perch next to her. I swipe my hand over the cover gently and tilt the ancient book her way.

"It's a grimoire. Carlos at The Cracked Spine donated it for the auction."

"Did he donate it to get rid of a hundred-year curse?" Wren asks skeptically.

"No," I say and then frown. "Or at least, I hope not. I haven't felt particularly cursed." I shake my head after thinking about it some more. "Nah. Carlos is cool. He just thought a grimoire would be a good auction item for an occult and oddi-ties shop, and I can't say he missed the mark. Besides, I've skimmed through it, and it seems fairly tame. It's mostly herbal remedies and light magic rituals."

Wren looks slightly disappointed. She flops back and yawns so wide, her molars peek out. "So it's just a dusty old book about plants and like, protecting your energy?"

I hug the book to my chest as if it could be offended by her words. "You don't think it's cool? I thought we might find something useful in here for us."

Wren tilts her head back and forth and then nods in agreement. "Okay, worth a shot. Where's the section that'll help us?" She sits up again and leans forward.

"I haven't been able to go through the whole thing yet. I keep getting interrupted," I say, feeling a blush crawl up my cheeks as I remember the last interruption—Dean bending me over the vanity and kneeling behind me...

"Earth to Rae," Wren says, snapping her fingers in my face. "Also *ew*. Please stop thinking about what you're thinking about."

I clear my throat. "Anyway. I made it through about half the book. It takes a while because the writing is kind of hard to make out. I've been reading the first sentence or two on each page to see what they're about."

"Mm. Well, I'm gonna nap. Wake me if you find anything useful," Wren says, throwing herself to the side and curling up in a tiny ball. Within minutes, she's lightly snoring, clutching a throw pillow to her chest. Despite her insomnia, when her body wants to power off, it's an instant ordeal. She only gets like this when she's had long bouts of sleepless nights. Her body forces her to rest whether she wants to or not.

I sigh to myself. I'd hoped we would get a chance to catch up and that she'd be interested in helping me with the book. I should have known, though. Wren has never been interested in reading, and a grimoire is no exception.

I yank part of the throw blanket Wren is using toward myself and begin skimming the rest of the book. Eventually, I get to a section titled "Spirits and Communications," and feel like I might be getting somewhere. I scan excitedly through the pages, looking for anything that could be of use.

Disappointment washes over me in a wave when I get to the end of the short section. I hadn't found anything that I didn't already know. It's mostly about how you can communicate with the dead using different objects like divining rods and rune stones. I flip through nearly to the end of the book, skimming over different uses for animal bones and crystals, when I come across a section titled "Diary Entry." It's dated as September 12, 1820, so I finally have an idea of how old this book is.

I feel a little bad reading someone's diary, even if that someone is long dead. Although I guess for me, dead doesn't always mean gone. My curiosity gets the best of me, and I read through a very detailed account of this person going on a trip to visit an estranged aunt in Maryland. She's unmarried, so her older brother has to accompany her. After many mishaps, they finally get to Maryland and the grimoire owner discovers that her aunt practices the occult as well. She is baffled because her father was a preacher, so to have an aunt who practices was shocking. At first, she hides her affinity for the natural world. Apparently, plants sing to her in different resonances, essentially communicating with her.

*Ah, that explains all the plant talk.*

One midsummer day, her aunt found her coaxing a bush of blackberries to ripen and be sweeter, and instead of scolding her (or worse), her aunt revealed her own secrets. She could speak to the dead. Like me.

I start skimming faster, and find myself growing frustrated with the spidery, crowded print. This is the only account of an actual medium that I've ever read. I'm not saying everyone else who claims to be one is lying, but if you have a show on TLC, it's questionable at best.

Over the rest of the summer, her aunt reveals all sorts of family secrets. Her late husband had passed from some disease with a horrible fever. But that wasn't the end of the line for them. He came back to her as a spirit and stayed with her for decades.

*Decades?*

I try not to get too excited by the prospect, but I can't help the way my thoughts turn to Dean.

The aunt said she created a tether for her husband by doing what sounds like astral projection to me. The account isn't too detailed, which is frustrating, but I had no idea this was possible. But from what I can tell, the aunt astral projected into the ether and found a way to bind his soul to hers.

They lived quite happily, despite the fact that she was the only one who could see him. Suddenly, her aunt's isolation made sense. She was living her best life with the love of her life; and nothing, not even death, could separate them.

I sit back and blink my bleary eyes, suddenly feeling more conflicted than ever.

# THIRTY-ONE

WREN IS STILL SNORING on my couch while I lie in bed, staring at my ceiling hours later. I couldn't fall asleep even if someone knocked me over the head right now. Not when I know there might be a way I could keep Dean with me permanently. But is it wrong to want that? When he has the ability to move on and find peace?

The unselfish, helps-all-ghosts-in-need part of me says yes. It's wrong because he deserves to find that peace. The very selfish other part of me almost doesn't care. Because losing him would feel like a small death of my own. Like watching a part of me atrophy and disappear.

I've never felt this way before. He's taken possession of my heart and invaded my every thought. His humor and humanity. The way he achieves the goals he sets for himself. How much he cares for his family and friends. The way he decorates his home and office with pictures of those he loves, like he can't bear to be apart from them. The way he cares for me and makes me feel seen. How am I supposed to give that up?

*You don't have to,* says the selfish part of my brain. I groan and roll to my side, nearly jumping out of my skin when I come nose-to-nose with Dean.

"When did you get here?" I whisper.

"Just now. You were thinking about me extra hard," he says with a smirk. I roll my eyes and smile at him, unable to deny that he's right. "You don't seem happy, though. What's wrong?" he asks, searching my face.

"Nothing," I lie, not wanting to tell him about the tether. At least not until we solve his murder. I want him to know that he's free to move on first, and I don't want to add any confusion onto his plate. Or worse, make him question my willingness to help him. "Just tired and have a lot on my mind," I say truthfully.

I can't tell if he buys it, but he pulls me into him, pressing my nose to his throat so he can run his fingers through my hair. I don't fight my heavy lids, closing them while he finger-combs my long hair, gently untangling any knots. "Sleep, Rae," he whispers into the crown of my head, tucking me even closer.

---

I WAKE to the smell of coffee; *good* coffee. Which can only mean that Wren is still here, using the espresso machine she got me for Christmas a few years back. I never use it because my clumsy attempts at pulling shots don't compare to anything she could make blindfolded. I roll over and hear her talking to someone. I wonder if she's on the phone, but she hates phone calls, so I doubt it. Especially this early in the morning.

"So, anything new on the murder investigation front?" she asks, just as I round the corner of my partition into the living room and blink in surprise at the scene before me. Dean is sitting on the chair, a safe distance from Wren in the kitchen, but they seem to be... Talking?

"Are you guys talking?" I ask, voice rusty with sleep. I rub my eyes extra hard to see if I'm dreaming, but when they swim back into focus, there they are. Chatting, apparently.

"Yeah. We figured out a way to talk," Dean says at the same time Wren says, "Yup, I learned how to communicate with Ghost Boy."

I slump onto a barstool, tying my unruly bedhead into a haphazard knot on the top of my head. "How?" I ask her.

"Well, I can sense auras, and he has one, so I figured if I asked direct questions, he could answer me. He can't, like, describe a recipe to me in detail, but yes or no questions are pretty easy." She hands me a mug filled to the brim with what smells like a vanilla latte, topped off with a little latte art heart. Aww.

Wait...

"Is this a middle finger?" I ask, squinting at the mug.

Her face brightens. "Oh, good, I'm getting better at them. Trying to come up with more discreet ways to say 'fuck off' to my least favorite customers."

"Won't you get fired for that?"

"Nah, we always hand them their coffee with the lids on. It's just for me. Purely for my satisfaction alone, knowing that Brad the accountant gets to drink my large fuck you in his skinny vanilla, oatmilk latte, with whole milk foam, set to scalding temperatures." She scowls at the memory of picky

Brad, and I laugh into my latte, dispersing the foam middle finger.

"She was asking about my untimely demise. Have you told her you were drugged?" Dean asks, turning in his seat to look at me.

"No, I haven't," I answer, making a 'zip it' motion as inconspicuously as I can.

"Haven't what?" Wren asks.

"Nothing," I say, before taking a sip of my piping hot latte. Wren is very protective. I don't know what she'd do if she found out.

She scowls at me and folds her arms over her chest. "Tell me."

"No."

"Rae."

"No," I say, shaking my head.

"Has Dean ever heard about that time in eighth grade when you sh–"

"I was drugged!" I interject. Not wanting her to spill about the time I indeed shat myself. The stomach flu is no joke, and I caught a dodgeball in P.E. right against my stomach when it was already protesting. The kids called me "Dia-Rae-uh" for at least six months. Good times.

"What?" Wren says.

I clear my throat. "I was drugged. On accident. Okay, well, I guess it was a little on purpose, but it wasn't Dean's fault. He didn't know there were drugs in the coffee. He was just trying to be sweet—"

"Rae. Stop. Back up. What do you mean you were drugged? And what does this have to do with Dean?" Wren asks, placing a concerned hand on my shoulder.

I take a breath to gather my thoughts. "Okay. We went to his office last weekend to see if we could shake any more memories loose. When we were there, he made me a cup of coffee. He wanted me to try his favorite, so that's what he made me. Anyway, long story short, someone had put GHB into the type of coffee that Dean likes because no one else in his office drinks it, so it was a guarantee that he'd be the one to have it. I was unlucky enough to get one of the three pods left that had been tampered with."

"This was last weekend?" she clarifies.

I nod. "Yeah. I passed out on his couch and didn't wake up until the next day. I had to rush out so I could get to work and grab all those auction items. It was terrible. I had the worst headache all day."

Her scowl deepens. "The day when you came into Brewed Awakening to grab the gift basket? That day?" I nod, and she smacks my arm. "How could you not tell me that?"

I wince, more at being called out than the sting on my arm from Wren's assault. "Sorry, it just didn't seem like a great time to announce that. Especially since you were feeling particularly murderous with Julian."

"Who's Julian?" Dean asks.

"I can sense your question, ghost. He is the bane of my existence. The rotten ground from which nothing will grow. The drought, the plague, the blight that ruins everything," Wren says, getting surprisingly poetic.

"You seem to think about this guy a lot," Dean says with a smug grin.

Wren's eyes narrow to slits. I jump in to keep the fragile peace, "Anyway, yes. I was drugged, which heavily implies that Dean was drugged before he died."

"Are you okay?" she asks, expression softening.

"Yes, I'm surprisingly fine. I think I'm not freaking out because it was an accident more than anything. Although I probably won't be having caramel-flavored coffee anytime soon," I say, hoping to reassure her.

She nods and asks, "How long did it take to kick in?"

"I don't know, maybe thirty minutes?"

Wren turns to look in Dean's direction. "Did you only have the one cup of coffee that day?"

He looks up at the ceiling, brow furrowing as he tries to remember. "Ummm. No. I had at least two other cups of coffee," he says, looking at me.

I relay his answer and then ask him, "Do you always have a cup of coffee before you drive home?"

"I do, usually. Especially when we've been working a lot. Someone must have switched out the coffee pods later in the day." He looks at me and visibly swallows. It's looking more and more like this person is someone he knows.

"I'm going to call Jack," I state, pulling my phone out of my pocket.

---

"THANKS AGAIN FOR THE UPDATE, Rae. I'll call you when I have something," Jack says before hanging up. He agreed that it had to be someone in the office who drugged Dean (and me). So, he's going to look back at security footage from that day to see if someone slipped in to replace them without the secretary noticing. The security footage only shows the very entrance of the office, so he won't be able to make out the break room. At least it will narrow down who was there in the late afternoon before Dean drank his coffee.

"I have to get going. I need to go home and shower before my next shift. Please tell me important things, okay? Like being drugged, for instance," Wren says from the chair opposite my couch, eyebrow raised to the sky.

"Yes, Mom. I promise," I say, crossing my heart with my finger. I lean back against the couch and stretch my neck, feeling my impending thirtieth birthday creeping in with every creak and groan of my joints.

"You better," she states, standing and heading for the door.

Once she's gone, I sigh and say to Dean, "Well this sucks. It has to be a coworker unless someone snuck in."

Dean nods. "Yeah. And other than my dad and I, the only people in the office that day were our secretary, five senior associates, and two of our paralegals. Minus James, one of the paralegals, I've known each of them for years. I just can't fathom why any of them would do this. I considered them all friends for the most part. Marco, my best friend, ended up moving away with his wife a couple years back, so I really relied on my office friendships for socializing. I thought we were all close. I feel so betrayed and violated."

He pauses to look down at his hands and collect himself, and then continues, "And I doubt anyone would have snuck in. Courtney is like a guard dog, she takes her job very seriously. She doesn't let anything or anyone past her without her approval. She even insists on coming in and working the weekends that we all need to be there, too. The woman hardly takes a bathroom break."

I reach out and place a hand on his shoulder. He leans into

it and sort of falls into a hug, gathering me close so he can bury his face in my loose hair. "I'm sorry," I say quietly, not knowing what else to say or how I can fix this.

"Yeah, me too," he mumbles into my hair. I reach up and stroke the back of his neck, wishing there was a way to siphon some of his pain away.

# THIRTY-TWO

TODAY IS the day of the ball, and I have so much to do that my head is spinning. I feel like a cartoon character that just got hit with a frying pan, to-do list items circling my head instead of stars.

I shut the ancient vacuum off, bending to wind the cord up and put it away. The store, at least, is almost ready. I spent the whole morning with Lenore and my mom scrubbing every square inch of the place and ferrying most of the merchandise upstairs to my apartment, so it would be out of the way. We needed room for standing cocktail tables, the bar, the long silent-auction table, and the small dance floor in the back. I added long streamers to the chandelier so no one will hit their head on it. Lenore and Mom are even cordoning off a bit of the sidewalk out front, so people can spill out and get some air without having to be checked back in.

"Hey, Aunt C? Can you tell me if everything on the table looks right?" I call, repositioning the auction table items for the millionth time. The table is almost too long for the store, but it was necessary to hold all the donated goods. They're a bit crowded, and Aunt C has been unhappy every time I've re-arranged them. If she's got something to say again, she can fix it herself because if I don't move on, I'll scream. Moving the various gift baskets and local artists' work an eighth of an inch this way or that is not at the top of my priority list.

She glides across the floor, snuggled up in an oversized, chunky cable-knit sweater that she's probably had since the eighties. Her many bracelets tinkle on her bony wrist as she lifts her hand and rubs her mouth in a way that tells me she wishes she had a cigarette. She squints at the lineup and shakes her head.

I swallow down my rage and say, "Okay. Listen, I have a bunch of other stuff to do, so why don't you finish this up?" I clasp my hands behind my back, squeezing harder than neces-sary to work out the irritation.

She sighs dramatically. "Darling, you're the one with the knack for decorating. I couldn't possibly. It would feel like I was taking your job."

"I'm afraid I have to insist, Aunt C," I say through a smile that's probably more bared teeth than anything.

She throws up her hands in exasperation. "Fine, I suppose I have to do everything around here." She brushes past me and begins nudging things minutely until they're in the "perfect position."

I breathe deeply and count to ten, knowing this is coming from a place of insecurity more than anything. While she's always been content to let me run things, when it comes to big events like this for the store, she gets testy. She wants everything to go well and not disrupt the carefully curated image she's created for it.

I decide to clean up the tarot table that she has stashed in the store room. We've cleaned out a bunch in here, too. With a few choice lamps and a rug, it doesn't look half bad; as long as you don't pay too much attention to the dingy shelves and stained concrete floor.

I stack her tarot cards neatly in the center of the table, sighing as one jumps out and flutters to the floor. I squat down to fish it off the rug, flipping it over to get a peek at its face in the process. A cracked tower with lightning splitting it in half dominates the card.

*The Tower. Fantastic.*

I already know my life is changing drastically. Thanks, tarot. I flip the card over and place it delicately on top of the deck, lest another card decide to jump out. The rest of the room is in pretty good condition, so I think it's time for me to head out before getting any more unwanted premonitions.

Aunt C is still nudging items this way and that, so I creep past her before she can rope me into any more incessant positioning. "Rae, dear? What's this again?" Aunt C calls to me. My shoulders droop and I turn to her, ready to hear another lecture about how we need to take all the items off the table so we can rearrange the tablecloth. Again.

Instead, I find her holding the grimoire delicately, cover facing me. "Oh. That's from The Cracked Spine. It's a grimoire from the 1820s," I say, relieved.

"Did you look through it?" she asks while frowning down at the book curiously. "It could contain something useful for you or your sister."

I nod and amble closer. "Yeah, I went through it. To be honest, there wasn't much in the way of help for me, and basically nothing for Wren. The person who wrote it was able to communicate with plants, so most of the book is related to botany. There was a small journal section that talked about her aunt who could see spirits, but it was more narrative than informational. Something about a dead husband that she kept around." I shrug nonchalantly, trying to act like that information didn't tilt my world on its axis.

Her eyes narrow shrewdly as she scans me. "A husband she kept around in the afterlife, eh? And you don't think that's useful information for you and your dead boyfriend?" She raises a thin, white eyebrow.

"I don't see how that's important. I'm trying to help Dean move on. He deserves that."

"Does he not also deserve to have all his options presented to him? Is it really fair for you to keep that knowledge from him? You're making his choice for him when he doesn't even know there is one."

"I... Um. I don't even know how it works or if I could do it," I counter weakly. "The owner of the book said something about astral projection and soul tethers, but that seems way over my head."

This isn't something I want to be agonizing over today. I just want to get this ball and Halloween over with so I can take a much needed day off.

Aunt C harrumphs and thunks the book unceremoniously on the table. I wince, glad at least that I took some photos of the relevant pages. If she throws that thing around any harder, it'll probably crumble to dust. "All I'm saying is that you deserve happiness, and that boy of yours deserves to know that he has a choice."

"I'll think about it," I grumble noncommittally. We spend a moment awkwardly shuffling about, both finding seemingly random things to do. Straightening the cocktail napkins, rechecking the extension cord for the DJ, and whatever other menial tasks I can get my hands on. We never argue, so this is uncharted territory.

"You know I just want what's best for you, right?" Aunt C asks over her shoulder.

I sigh, nodding my head. "I know. I'm just frustrated because I'm also trying to figure out how to do my job without getting my feelings tangled up."

Aunt C chuckles and puts her hands on her slender hips. "Oh, darling. It's far too late for that, don't you think?"

My cheeks warm, and I decide against answering her.

"Go. I know you have plenty more to do today before you get all dolled up. I can hold down the fort here. Something's still not right with this table," she mumbles, rubbing a finger across her chin and staring at it like an artist might stare at a stubbornly blank canvas.

I make my escape before she can change her mind, scurrying past Lenore and my mother, who are setting up a few outdoor tables as well. I wave my goodbyes, calling over my shoulder that I'll be back soon. I round the building to the alleyway where my car is parked and hop in, ready to be alone for more than five minutes. My little introvert heart can't handle being around people all day. It's too draining. My battery definitely needs a listen-to-music-alone-in-the-car recharge.

I turn the key and listen to my car rumble to life, feeling more than ready to have this day behind me.

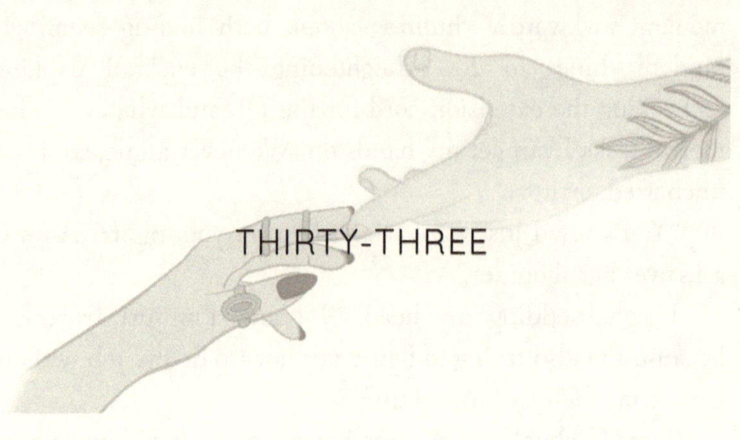

# THIRTY-THREE

I'M HUNCHED over in arguably one of the most unattractive positions, trying to shave the back of my knee in the shower. I always nick myself back there, but I've found contorting my body to bring my hand as close to parallel with the underside of my leg tends to avoid bloodshed. I press the razor to my skin and hear, "Is it wet in here or is it just me?" I gasp in shock, and the razor skids sideways, cutting through my skin like butter. I hiss at the nick and pull back the shower curtain a bit to glare at him.

"What? What happened?" Dean asks, the playful smirk falling.

I stick my leg out, a thin red stream running down my calf, and wiggle the razor in answer.

He winces and says, "Sorry. I thought this would be a sexy surprise. Not a bloody one."

I close the curtain again and stick my bleeding leg under the spray of the shower, grumbling, "It's alright. I know you weren't trying to get me to cut myself." Deciding that the back of my knee can be a forest for all I care, I hang my razor on the wall mount and begin rinsing the deep conditioning treatment out of my hair. At least it stopped bleeding already.

"How was your nap?" I ask, twisting my hair into a thick rope to wring the water out of it.

"Good. I'm noticing I don't have to spend as long there to recharge. I saw you last this morning, right?"

"Yeah," I say, turning off the shower. "That's nice. You can spend most of your time here, then. Has to be less boring." I swipe my towel off the hook next to the shower, pulling it through a crack in the curtain. I know he's seen everything, but I'm not quite ready for casual nudity. Which makes me wonder...

"Hey. When you said you watch me, even when I don't know you're there, does that mean you've, like... seen me naked when I didn't know it?"

Dean looks at me appalled. "No. I did not creep on you without your consent. Whenever it looked like you were going to get naked or, um—do something you wouldn't want company for, I would leave. Or at least go further away in your apartment." He hitches a thumb in the direction of my kitchen and living room.

"But you knew where my vibrator was," I point out.

He quirks a smile and nods. "Yeah, that's when I decided I should probably go find something else to entertain me."

I purse my lips and nod curtly in response, glad at least that he didn't stay to enjoy the show. Or... I don't know. Maybe I'm a little disappointed. But that sounds crazy, so let's go with relieved.

"Okay well, I need to get ready for tonight. So go find something else to do," I say, making a shooing motion towards the door. If he stays and I'm naked, I won't make it to the ball.

He leans in, feathering a staticky kiss against my brow, and *poof!* he's gone. Then, I get out my arch-nemesis: the blow dryer. I try to avoid using it whenever I can because I can't stand the noise or the way it makes me sweat. But today I'm planning on curling my hair in long, loose waves, so it's a necessity. I turn it on, grimly resolved to get the job done.

---

"MOTHERFUCKING *FUCK*," I grit out, arms contorted towards the middle of my back where the zipper on my dress is stuck. I scrabble my fingers closer, wishing that I had taken Aunt Clarissa up on her offer to join her for yoga on Saturdays. Angry sweat collects under my arms and between my thighs, and I'm about one second away from Hulking out of this dress and wearing sweats.

"Dean!" I call, mourning the big reveal moment I had been envisioning for weeks now. He's never seen me fully dressed up before, and I wanted to have it be this movie moment. Instead, he'll get me sweaty and half-zipped, with the zipper caught on my shape-wear.

He pops in front of me and does a double-take. "Wow, you look..."

"Haggard?" I supply, blowing a rogue tendril of hair out of my face.

"Gorgeous," he counters.

I can't help but roll my eyes. "You're being ridiculous. I'm not even done yet."

He steps closer, until the toes of his polished shoes nudge against my strappy heels. "Take the compliment," he murmurs before taking my chin in his hand and brushing a light kiss against my lips.

I drop my arms with a sigh, feeling the blood rush back to my aching biceps. "Can you please finish zipping me up? We've had a grave mechanical error."

He steps around me and zips my dress up in one swift motion, and then settles his hands on my shoulders. I look at the two of us in the mirror. With his perfectly tailored suit and my blood-red gown, we look ready to dash off into one of my fantasy romances. Although, his shirt could probably be more frilly. Piratey, even. But real-world Dean will more than do. "I very much like this dress," Dean says in my ear, thumbs gliding under the off-the-shoulder straps.

"Yeah? I was hoping so. You don't think it's too much?" I ask, suddenly feeling a little self-conscious under his intense focus.

I watch in the mirror as his eyes trace down the plunging cutout of the dress, which reveals the very tips of my sternum tattoo. A faint flush reddens his cheeks and the tips of his ears. "Dammit, Rae. I'm fucking flabbergasted. How am I supposed to have any coherent thoughts when you look like this?" His hands glide over my ample hips, and he shimmies me a little so the dress fans out. "Actually, yes. I do think it's too much."

My stomach sinks. "Oh," I say, feeling all kinds of disappointed. I lower my eyes, hoping he doesn't read the embarrassment in them.

"It's too much because how am I supposed to handle it if anyone stares at you for too long tonight? The most I can manage with anyone else is a little shovel shaking, but I'll want to scoop someone's eyes out if they look anywhere below your neck," he says and then frowns. "Nose, actually. I'll want to cause bodily harm to anyone who looks too long below your nose. Your lips are just too fucking perfect with that red lipstick." He places the pad of his thumb against my lower lip, and I bite it gently. He withdraws his hand with a groan.

"So it's too much because it makes you feel possessive?" I ask, eyebrow raised and butterflies pressing against the walls of my stomach.

He just grunts in answer, spinning me away from the mirror to face him. "Yes. But it also makes me want to show you off. You are always beautiful, but tonight you're extraordinary. I hope you have fun. I'll be around, attempting to ring the neck of anyone who gets too close or looks too hard," he says, eyes crinkling with mirth.

"Never in my life would I have thought I'd find the threat of violence hot, but here we are," I quip, dipping my finger in his dimple playfully.

"First time for everything," he replies. His face softens as he looks at me, running his thumb along my jaw. He kisses me chastely, at first. But when I suck in a breath and drag him closer, he follows my lead and nips at my lower lip until I open for him. Just when I'm about to give up on the ball altogether, he says, "Go. Do what you need to do. And then tonight I want to see what this dress looks like on the floor."

I breathe out a laugh at his line before turning to the mirror for one final check. I sigh when I see the state of my lipstick, heading for the bathroom to get a makeup wipe. I make quick work of the repair job, take one last look in the mirror, and swipe my phone off the counter. A glance at the time makes me hurry my steps. "Okay, time to go. Thanks for the assist," I say, blowing him a kiss.

"Anytime, Alderwood," he drolls, following me out the door.

*He wasn't joking about watching me tonight. Cool. No pressure.*

# THIRTY-FOUR

I DOWN THE last dregs of my champagne flute before walking to the auction table, eyes popping at some of the generous bids. The most popular by far was donated by a local cabin resort. It's an all-inclusive weekend stay in one of their treehouse cabins. If I had more money, I would have bid it all on that. A weekend in the trees with no one bothering me but room service and spa treatments sounds like a dream.

The dollar amounts listed under each auction item loosens the little knot in my chest. The silent auction still has thirty minutes before it closes, so those numbers might even rise a bit more before the end. This isn't a long-term solution, but it'll give us a little more breathing room.

I press a hand over my sternum and look at the crowd bedecked in evening gowns and suits, overwhelmed with gratitude that this town showed up for us. Everything has gone well tonight so far, but I don't want to think about it too hard in case I jinx it. Many of the local business owners have made an appearance, as well as a few tourists who were drawn to the glitz and glamour of the night. I worked hard on advertising this thing online, and I'm glad to see it paid off.

I pop my head in on Aunt C, making sure she's doing okay and not in need of anything. This is the most readings she's done back-to-back in a while, and I know they can be draining for her. Even though she doesn't have the Gift, she works hard on interpreting the tarot for her clients, trying to help them find meaning in them. Luckily, she seems to have a small pause in clients, so I can chat with her for a second.

"Hey, Aunt C. Need anything?" I ask, stepping further into the room and watching as she deftly shuffles the deck in her hands.

"I'm alright, darling. Thanks for checking in. Are you ready for your...ah, work?" she asks, stumbling a little over the words she's trying to avoid saying. We've managed to keep my little secret from the town so far, and I don't want an eavesdropper to be the reason everyone suddenly knows I'm a medium.

"Yeah. I think I'll be able to sneak in without much notice. Wren is still planning on being the guide, right?" We had planned for her to take Aunt C's place tonight in explaining how the medium thing works for my clients and leading them into my Medium Meeting Room. I circulated the party for a good hour or so because I'm sure people would have thought it strange if I hadn't shown up to the ball that I've worked so hard for. I'm just hoping no one will notice my little disappearing act.

"Yes, she's ready to go. She should be hovering outside your door as we speak," Aunt C replies, just as Yuri, the local florist, bustles in, long gown trailing behind her.

"Clarissa! It's been far too long since my last reading. I have a new question I want to focus on," Yuri says, hardly paying me any attention in her excitement. She sits down in the chair opposite my aunt, sets a handful of bills on the table, and launches into a detailed account of what she's seeking answers on. I laugh under my breath at the line of her questioning (something about pursuing two men and wondering which one she should go with), and leave them to it.

Outside the door in the short hallway, I briefly meet Dean's gaze and smile. He's been flitting about the party all evening and has been whispering the gossip he picks up in my ear like an old lady intent on sharing their prized intel at bingo. The little gossip monger has revealed that two of the tourists are cheating on their spouses with each other, someone else is close to losing their house because they have a gambling problem, and another person got caught sending nudes to a model from LA. I'll never be able to look Marcus, our local pharmacist, in the eye again.

I gesture with my chin to the door at the end of the hall that leads into the narrow alleyway. Dean follows me out, and I keep one foot hooked around the door so it doesn't lock me out.

"Listen, I'm about to do my readings, so don't pop in there and confuse things, okay? I think you would freak the other ghosts out," I say, glancing around to make sure no one is eaves-dropping.

He gives me a mock salute and says, "You got it, boss. I'm going to go follow that man in the pin-striped suit. I saw him slip off his wedding ring earlier."

"You know, I should probably be disturbed by how much you're enjoying this."

Dean smirks. "I'm a lawyer. I love gossip."

I laugh a little and head back inside, hoping to slip into my room without notice. I'm scanning the store for Wren, so I don't see the man who backs into me until it's too late. I bump into his broad back, knocking him off balance. "Shit!" he exclaims. He turns around, holding the front of his shirt out and away from his chest. Even in the dim lighting, I can see he spilled champagne all down the front of his dress shirt.

I look up to offer an apology when my mouth runs dry because *damn* this guy is attractive. Like, model or actor attractive. His chiseled jaw, perfect pout, and deep-set green eyes all press into a scowl, and it's only then I realize I'm gawking. "Sorry!" I squeak out. "I'm so sorry! I didn't see you, and just bam! Walked right into you. Please come with me so I can help you clean up. This is my party, so it's the least I can do," I babble.

"It's fine. Really. You just surprised me," he says, sultry voice wrapping around me like a velour blanket. He drinks me in and smiles appreciatively. I should be flattered or excited for the attention, but I find that I'm just not.

*He's not Dean.*

Which tells me just how much trouble I'm in if I have no interest in this very attractive, very alive man who likes what he sees.

"I insist. Let me at least get your shirt dry for you. Come with me to the bathroom. I think we have a blow dryer in there." He nods and follows me back through the crowd toward the hallway. I knock on the door, and when no one calls out, I push it open.

The door swishes shut behind us, and I bend at the waist to rifle through the vanity cabinet. I push past a mountain of toilet paper and cleaning supplies before my hand closes around the metal handle of our ancient blow dryer. I pull it out and plug it into the outlet by the sink.

I turn around and find that he's close behind me. Not quite in my personal bubble, but I could reach out and touch him if I wanted. I didn't think about how small this bathroom is, and with his well over six-foot frame, there's little room for much else.

"Okay, can you give me your shirt? I hope your undershirt didn't get soaked too," I say, holding my hand out.

"Would you mind holding my suit jacket?" he asks politely, shrugging out of it. I take it from him with a smile and surreptitiously step back, trying to gain even an inch more of distance between us, my butt bumping into the counter in the process.

He starts unbuttoning his shirt and I look skyward, feeling immensely awkward and regretting my insistence on helping. I narrow my eyes at the overhead fluorescent lighting, trying to think of anything but the man getting half-naked in front of me. When he holds the cream-colored shirt out to me, I switch his jacket for it. I turn my back, running the tap so I can rinse the champagne out first, grateful to have a task. I get the hair dryer going, and its loud screeching reverberates off the walls and drowns out the sounds of the party.

I turn my gaze away from the nearly dry shirt and look in the mirror, where I see the man has stripped out of his undershirt as well and has his jacket draped over his arm. The air shimmers behind him, and I stifle a sigh when Dean materializes looking furious.

I'm studiously ignoring Dean's glare, but he makes it much harder to do when he presses up behind me and whispers in my ear, "Why are you alone with a half-naked stranger? I was just with you five minutes ago."

"Sorry, this got wet too," the man says sheepishly, raising his voice to be heard over the hair dryer.

I give a tight-lipped smile when I shut off the hair dryer and reply, "No, it's my fault. I'm the reason you spilled your champagne in the first place. Almost done." I look at Dean in the mirror with raised eyebrows, hoping that answers his question.

I hand the man his dress shirt and get to work on the soft cotton undershirt in my hands. Luckily, this has a much smaller stain on it, his dress shirt having taken the brunt of the champagne splatter.

"I can't believe you got yourself in an enclosed space with a man you don't know. Willingly! Don't you know better than to trust strangers?" Dean lectures through gritted teeth, never looking away from the shirtless man.

I roll my eyes so hard it's mildly painful. The undershirt dries quickly, and I shut off the hair dryer, unplugging it and tossing it under the sink in one smooth motion.

I spin and hand the shirt to the man. "Here you go. Sorry again, but hopefully the last five minutes in our spa-like accommodations have made it up to you," I say, gesturing around the very small bathroom with its cracking purple paint and age-worn tile floors.

He smiles wryly, throwing his undershirt on in a fluid, practiced motion. "No problem. Any excuse to spend some time alone with a beautiful woman is fine in my book. Although if I'm shirtless, there's usually less laundry being done," he says with a chuckle.

"Hold on there, buddy," Dean says, stepping up to the man and getting in his face. Too bad he can't see Dean. He's putting on quite the alpha-male, squawking-territorial-rooster show.

My red-painted lips curl in a smile. "I'm sure. I'm taken, though, or at least have the whole 'it's complicated' thing going on."

He looks a little disappointed at that but finishes buttoning his shirt and slipping on his jacket. "Ah. No problem then. I had to shoot my shot or I'd have regretted it. Whoever has your attention is very lucky." With that, he sends me a wink and leaves, shutting the door lightly behind him.

"What a piece of work," Dean grouses, folding his arms over his chest.

I snort and ask, "Oh, are we looking in the mirror?"

"He was coming onto you!"

"Fairly respectfully, if I do say so. And I can handle myself. I know how to tell a man no. And when I did, he left. So, why are we throwing a fit again?" I lean back against the vanity again, crossing my arms in amusement.

Suddenly, he's directly in front of me and pressing me harder into the vanity. I have to throw my hands back to catch myself against the counter. "Because you're driving me insane in this dress, Rae. I'm using petty town gossip to distract myself, but every time I look at you, I fantasize about tearing this off of you." His fingertips spark along the seam of my bust, and I inhale sharply, annoyance forgotten.

"Why aren't we doing that again?" I ask, running a hand through his hair and giving it a playful tug.

"Because you have a job to do," he says, leaning in and pecking my nose before flitting to the other side of the small room.

"Rude," I say with a scowl.

He smiles, but it looks more devious than friendly. "Well, now we both get to have a one-track mind. See you out there, Alderwood," he says with a salute before fading through the wall.

I take a breath to steady myself and press my cool hands to

my cheeks, hoping to dull the flush a bit. A knock at the door startles me, and I push myself away from the vanity.

I walk past the woman dancing from foot to foot outside the door with a muttered apology and weave through the crowd toward my sister. She's waiting impatiently, arms crossed, a singular talon tapping quickly on her forearm. "There you are! I was about to send out a search party," she says reproachfully.

"Sorry, I got sidetracked. I was talking to Aunt C and then I accidentally spilled champagne on a male model, and then Dean got all jealous, which was frankly very hot..." I trail off when I notice her expression darken further. "Oookay, never mind. Let's get this show on the road." I give her a meek thumbs up and then, with a glance around to make sure no one is watching, I slip inside the Medium Meeting Room.

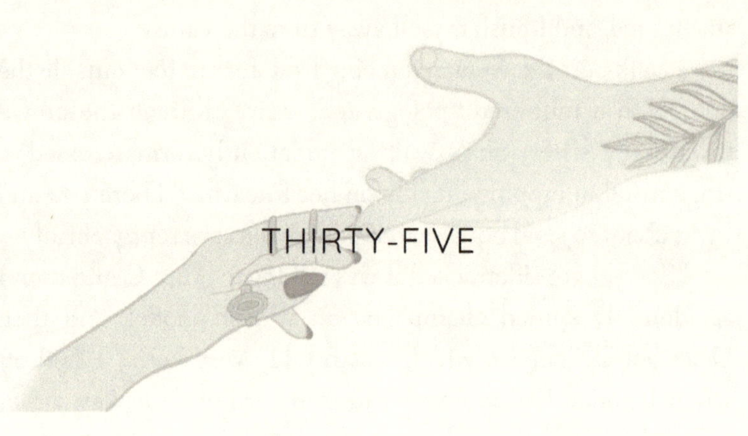

# THIRTY-FIVE

I WATCH as Mrs. O'Dell vanishes with a pop of light and smile a little to myself. Tonight has gone better than all of my past "medium meetings" combined. I've had three guests so far, and each has been able to make contact with the person they were trying to reach. No one has gotten angry. No one has had to sit in awkward silence while I call out into the in-between, trying to locate their loved one to no avail.

"Alright, Lilah, she's gone. She wanted me to tell you that she hopes she won't see you again for a very long time," I say through the curtain.

Lilah laughs a congested laugh and says, "Thank you for this, Claire. It means the world to me that I was able to speak to my mom one last time." I've gotten so used to being called Claire that I have to be careful not to look when someone calls out to another Claire on the street.

"I'm happy I could help. It seems you were her unfinished business, and now that you two have cleared the air, she's free to move on," I share, knowing that it will bring her a bit of peace. I hear a little broken inhale and tell her to take her time. This is why I typically leave fifteen minutes or so between appointments, but tonight we're on a tighter timeline.

Eventually, I hear her stand and she says one last goodbye before the door opens and a wave of noise from the party hits me. She shuts the door behind her, "The Monster Mash" dulled to a low hum once again.

I breathe a relieved sigh. Just with the readings and tips, I've already brought in over a thousand dollars. That alone will cover the cost of alcohol and the bartender for the night. And I still have two more to go.

Wren sends me a text letting me know the next person is outside. I gulp down the rest of my water bottle and reply, telling her to lead them in. When the typing bubbles on her side pop up afterward, I frown down at my phone. Wren is many things, but long-winded is rarely one of them.

> **WREN:**
>
> Heads up, your next client is Misha. I tried to talk him out of it, but I couldn't push too hard or else he would have been suspicious.

*Fuck.*

I've had a few people come in who I regularly speak to, but none that I would consider friends. Even still, I've been extra cautious and used a voice changing device to disguise my voice. It comes with a little microphone and speaker, so while it works in a pinch, it makes things a bit clunkier. But doing this for someone I talk to and joke with on a near-daily basis? Just thinking about Misha being on the other side of the curtain makes my heart pump double-time.

I try to force myself to relax once the door opens with a *whoosh*. It snicks shut, and the chair on the other side of the curtain creaks as Misha settles in.

I say, "Hello, please, make yourself comfortable. What's your name?" The voice I've chosen is an older woman's voice that I modify with a slight Boston accent, with elongated vowels and dropped r's.

"Hi, I'm Misha. It's nice to meet you." He pauses, looking for me to fill in my name.

"Claire," I say.

"Claire. I'm glad to meet you," his deep voice rumbles. A nervous sigh breaks through the silence of the room and he says, "Okay, I have to admit I'm scared shitless. Whether this works or not, I'm terrified."

I reply, "You don't have to do this now if you don't want to. I'm not going anywhere for the foreseeable future, so you can always come back another time."

He cracks his knuckles loudly and says, "No. I've been wanting to come see you for weeks, ever since I overheard Rae and Wren talked about you." I flinch a little at my real name. "I need to do this because if I don't, I'll always wonder..." He trails off, and I fidget in my seat, wanting to move this along so he can get out of here that much faster.

"Let's try then. Who are you attempting to contact? Can you tell me about them?" I ask.

Misha swallows audibly and begins to detail his uncle for me. "Ivan was a hard man in every sense of the word. I grew up without my mom, and my dad died when I was only six years old in a freak accident at work." He takes a breath and continues, "My uncle Ivan, my dad's brother, was the only living relative I had who was of age and had the ability to take me in, so he did. He wasn't happy to do it, but he did out of a sense of obligation. And, well—let's just say he let me know how much of a burden I was." He clears his throat.

I bow my head, tamping down the despair punching a whole in my gut on his behalf. I feel like I'm betraying him by not letting him know who I am. He's baring some of his most painful scars for me, and I'm not even telling him the basic truth of my identity.

"Anyway, sorry. You don't need the whole sordid backstory. I want to contact him. We had been doing a little better the last few years of his life. My moving out at seventeen really helped our relationship. But...We had a fight. A huge one, right before he died. He found out I was gay and just shut down. When I tried to get him to talk to me, we ended up blowing up at each other, airing out twenty years' worth of issues. It wasn't even about me coming out to him in the end. But I was so hurt and so angry that the last words I said to him were, 'I hope you rot in hell forever you huge fucking asshole.' And then he had a massive heart attack less than a week later. So. Yeah. If he's around, I want to tell him that I didn't mean it. I want to know that he's found peace."

My heart hurts for Misha. He's such a happy person, I never would have thought he dealt with so much darkness. I'm at a loss for what to say, but I eventually land on, "I'm so sorry that happened to you. You know, you don't have to make his afterlife easier if he couldn't accept who you were. You don't owe him that."

He chuckles softly. "I know that. I'm in my thirties now and am pretty happy with where life is and who I've become. My husband is the love of my life, and I like this town. It's just... The only regret I have is how I ended things with my uncle. He could have done better in a lot of areas, but he was still my only father figure for most of my life. I know he loved me, he just never knew how to show it. He and my dad weren't raised with that kind of love. If he patted my back, I knew that meant 'I love you.' He had the emotional range of an outdated refrigerator." We both laugh at that, although I keep mine silent.

"Anyway, I want to make peace with him. So, do you think you can find him?" he asks hopefully.

"I hope so. Let me try. Give me some time to reach out, and if he's here, I'll let you know. I'll be his voice, and I'll try to make the communication as seamless as possible," I explain.

When Misha agrees, I close my eyes and cast out my awareness, that inner net unfurling. I feel Dean just outside the room, flitting about. I nudge him affectionately with my awareness and then keep going. Looking for a specific person in the ether is like walking into a vast, dimly lit chamber, searching for a specific candle flame that flickers in its own unique way. Eventually, I find an essence that feels like Ivan. I reach out my hand and beckon him forward. I show him that his nephew is trying to make contact to entice him.

I gasp when he tugs away and race to keep up. I feel my eyelids flutter as I try to reason with him. None of this happens in words, more like my consciousness touching his. When he tries to pull away again, my anger gets the better of me. I can't believe he's unwilling to give his nephew just a little bit of peace—a few minutes of his time. Misha *deserves* that. So, I tug harder. And harder. Until we snap like a rubber band into the room. I slam back into my body so hard, the breath leaves my lungs.

"Everything okay over there?" Misha asks tentatively.

I fumble with the microphone and pant, "Yes, one moment." I look up... and up... and up at the imposing man towering over me. Ivan scowls down at me with a thunderous expression on his aged face. He's built like a brick wall, nearly as wide as he is tall, and if I didn't know he was mostly incorporeal, I'd be scared out of my mind right now.

"Why did you bring me here?" he seethes at me.

I swallow around my painfully dry throat and whisper, "He deserves some peace. It's the least you can do."

Ivan's face reddens. "The least I can do?" he hisses, "I've been stuck here because of that boy. He's the one who owes me. And now he's the one who coerced a damned witch to pull me from the ether. I hadn't moved on, but I found as much peace as I could. And now this?" He waves his massive arm around the space, and my arms pebble with goosebumps as the temperature drops swiftly. I bristle at being called a witch; first because it's untrue, and secondly because he says it derisively. We don't put up with that in these parts.

"Is—is he here?" Misha asks from the other side of the curtain, snapping my attention away from Ivan.

I turn my glare back on Ivan and say, "Yes."

"Uncle Ivan, I just wanted to say that I'm sorry. I never got the chance to apologize, and I just—I'm sorry for what I said. I know we didn't see eye to eye, but I never actually wanted any harm to come to you," Misha says quietly, voice wavering.

Ivan turns to face the curtain, but not before I catch the way his eyes soften the smallest amount. "What the hell is this for?" Before I can stop him, he reaches out and tugs hard. The velvet curtain that protected my identity falls to the ground with a heavy *fwump*.

I jump to my feet as Misha stares at me, face drained of

color. "Rae? What are you doing here? Where's Claire?" He looks behind me as if he's searching for a trap door, and my heart squeezes because his first thought isn't that I've deceived him, it's that the medium he was speaking to must have spirited herself away.

"I..." I don't know what to say, or how to fix this, so I word vomit the truth. "I'm Claire. Or, I guess Claire is me. I'm a medium. *The* medium," I feel the need to correct, holding up the microphone.

His expression shifts from confusion into disbelief, and then finally, anger. "So you just let me tell you all that shit, thinking you were someone else? You didn't stop and think, 'Hm, maybe I should stop him from spilling his guts because I know him and see him every single day?' Or at least that you should have told me who you were so I could decide for myself what I was willing to share?"

"I'm sorry, Misha. I wasn't trying to deceive you. I just... This is a part of my life that I don't share with anyone." I gesture weakly to the walls of the Medium Meeting Room and vaguely to Ivan, who has become a quiet bystander, watching us.

Misha crosses his arms and laughs sardonically. "Yeah. Well, I don't tell anyone about my childhood either, but here we are."

Frustration bubbles up inside me at being misunderstood and misjudged. I'm getting irritated that he thinks I did this just to hear his secrets. I understand why he's upset, but I wish he could give me the benefit of the doubt, considering he's known me forever. "I'm sorry, okay? I wasn't trying to have you spill all of your secrets, I'm just trying to help people!" I say, sharper than I intend. I toss the voice changer on the chair behind me.

"Yeah, this has been *so* helpful. Are you even really a medium?" he asks, standing from his seat.

"I am! I'm not lying about that," I say, looking to Ivan. "Your uncle is right there." I point to his uncle.

"I don't see anything," Misha says, staring hard at the spot where I pointed.

I grit my teeth and say, "Well, of course not. I'm the medium."

"Prove it," he demands.

"Fine," I say and turn to Ivan. "Tell me something only Misha would know," I demand.

He squints at me, heavy brow all but concealing his deep-set eyes. "No," he replies calmly.

"No?" I ask, my pitch going impossibly high.

"No, I think I'm good," Ivan affirms, a twisted little smirk pulling up one corner of his mouth.

"But then he won't believe me," I sputter.

Ivan shrugs, already starting to fade when he says, "Not my problem." And then he's gone.

I feel my mouth drop open in disbelief. "He left," I say to Misha, running my hands through my hair, probably doing irreparable damage to the carefully styled waves.

He opens the door with a bang before saying loudly, "Well, this was a nice show and everything, Rae. Very spooky and on-theme with the whole curtain falling, 'I see dead people' act. Happy Halloween."

He cuts his way through the crowd so fast, I lose track of him in an instant. I don't think, I just run after him. "Misha, wait!" I call, bursting through the door. But I can't even see him anymore. All I see is a dense forest of eyes staring back at me in astonishment.

I stand, frozen in horror. This is so similar to the recurring nightmare I've had, I find myself pinching the inside of my arm to make sure it's real. Unfortunately, this is a real-life horror show and not one I'll wake up from in a cold sweat anytime soon.

Wren grabs my arm but before she can ask anything, someone says, "Wait, Rae is the medium?" Murmurs and chatter spread through the room like an infection until my name becomes a stain on everyone's lips. People press in towards me on all sides, and my lungs struggle for air. People volley questions my way, but I can't hear anything over the loud buzzing in my ears.

All the blood leaves my extremities, and my fingertips start to tingle. "I—" I start, but can't finish. I don't even know what to say. I pull free of Wren's grasp and push forward until I make it outside into the brisk, late-October night. I pull the crisp air into my lungs as I step hurriedly around the building and stumble up the stairs to my apartment.

My heart feels like it's going to explode. I might be sick. My hand shakes as I try to put my key in the lock, and frustrated tears well along my lash line. At least, I tell myself they're from frustration and not the combo meal of remorse for upsetting a friend, anger that he revealed my secret to the town, and panic that my secret is no longer my own.

"Here, let me help," Dean offers, placing his hand over mine and guiding the key into the keyhole. I push the door open, and he follows me inside. I collapse on the couch, mortified that he's bearing witness to my sniffling, mascara running, snotty mess, but grateful he's here all the same. He sits next to me and puts an arm around my waist.

My phone buzzes with a text, and I check it with shaking hands.

WREN:

What happened? Are you okay??

Long story, but Misha found out it was me by accident and now he thinks I'm faking it. Everyone saw. Everyone knows.

It's going to be okay. Do you want me to come up there? Mom is asking, too.

No. Thank you, but I just want to be alone right now.

Talk tomorrow then, sis. I'll beat anyone's ass, just say the word.

I know. Love you

I put my phone down and collapse into Dean's chest, letting the tears go.

# THIRTY-SIX

I CALLED out of work today for the first time pretty much ever. I feel a little guilty because I know there's a lot of cleanup to do before the store opens for a half day, but I just do not have the energy. When I woke up this morning, my eyes were so puffy and irritated from all the crying I did last night, they felt like they'd been glued shut after being exfoliated with sandpaper.

Am I making a bigger deal out of this than I need to? Yes. Do I still feel like I was gutted in front of the whole town last night? Also, yes. All the stress I've been under compounded into an hours-long crying jag. I feel wrung out and hollow inside, and I need time to figure out what to do next.

Dean stayed with me the whole night, holding me against him while I went in and out of crying. Staying for that long drained him, so he decided to go recharge when he could tell I was okay enough for him to leave. I practically had to force him to go so he wouldn't burn out.

I've finally washed off last night's makeup, but you can take my ten-year-old sweats and holey t-shirt from my cold, dead hands. This is as good as it's getting today. I fully intend on wallowing until it's time to pass out candy to trick-or-treaters tonight.

I dig my hand into my popcorn bowl, stuffing my mouth full of the movie theater butter goodness. One of my favorite reality shows is on the final elimination episode, and I'm locked in. I'm so ready to lose myself in other people's drama for the day.

The last two couples are having an explosive argument, likely fueled by a lack of sleep and too much alcohol. The obscenities are coming out in a continuous stream, and all that's audible is one long *beeeeep*. Both gesticulate wildly, so I know it has to be juicy. What I wouldn't give for the raw, uncut footage.

My door opens behind me and I groan, hitting pause. "It was just getting good," I complain.

I look over my shoulder to see Wren stomping in, two large grocery bags dangling from her arms, both perilously close to bursting. She kicks the door shut behind her and tosses the bags on the counter. "It's never actually good. You know that, right?" She historically hates reality TV, although I don't believe her because she always watches it with me.

"You can't be mean to me today," I pout.

"Yes, I can. It's practically my duty as your sister to continue to treat you the way I always do." She haphazardly tosses things into the fridge, slams it shut, and then carries the rest of her haul over to me.

"I didn't even know you were coming today," I say, snatching the grocery bag from her hands and pawing through it like an animal.

"What? You thought I was just going to let you wallow in self-pity? When have I ever allowed that?"

"Well, there were these blissful twenty-two months before you were born..."

"Fuck off," she says with a laugh, pushing my shoulder and yanking the bag back from me.

"I'm not even allowed one full day of wallowing?" I ask when she hands me a bag of M&Ms to toss with the popcorn.

"It's been like eighteen hours. I'd say that's enough," she says, tweezing a piece of popcorn from the bowl with her long nails and popping it in her mouth. "Now, are you going to tell me what happened? All I know is that Misha ran out of there, nearly taking me out with the door, and then you followed him."

While we polish off the popcorn, I tell her all about Misha and Ivan, leaving out the more sensitive details from Misha's past. I tell my sister damn near everything, but other people's trauma is where I draw the line. Especially since she works with him almost every day.

"Well shit. Ivan is an asshole in life and death. I can't believe he left you hanging like that!" she exclaims, looking as though she'd like nothing more than to punch his ghostly face.

"I can. I could tell he really didn't want to come forward. But I was so mad on Misha's behalf that I kind of forced him. I should have known better. I let my anger get the best of me. Now I feel bad because Misha didn't get the closure he wanted, and he feels like I betrayed him. Not to mention he thinks I'm a fraud and exposed me to the whole community." I scrub my face with my hands, wishing I had a time machine so I could go back and stop myself from ever going in that room last night.

"Rae, I'm going to say this to you as gently as I can because

I love you," Wren says, surprising me by taking my hand in hers. "No one cares that you're the medium. No one. Are people surprised? Yeah, I'm sure they are because you've lived here your whole life and no one knew. But no one got their pitchfork. Sure, some people will probably treat you differently and that sucks, but the people who matter won't. The people who love you won't care, and they'll just think it's an extra interesting thing about you."

"But I didn't want anyone to know," I say, fighting the tears back. I'm so sick of crying.

"Listen, I've respected that you wanted to keep this part of your life private, but now that it's out there, I think you need to own it. You get to set your own boundaries around this. If people ask you about it, you can say no. This doesn't have to change anything for you unless you want it to," she says, squeezing my hand for emphasis.

I give her a trembling smile and squeeze her hand back. Sometimes I feel guilty about how much Wren takes care of me. I'm the older sister. I'm the one who is supposed to take care of her. Her personality has always demanded to be the one doing the protecting and the pep-talking, though. I can't pretend I'm not grateful for it, even if I do wish she didn't always have to be the one looking after me.

"Thank you for barging in here, even though I told you to leave me alone," I finally say, once I'm sure my voice won't break.

"Rae, that's practically the job of annoying little sisters. I'm always supposed to barge in," she retorts, squeezing my hand one last time and letting go.

We settle in and finish the episode. Wren complains the entire time about how unrealistic and overdramatic it all is, but

I can tell she's enjoying herself. Even when she tries to pretend she's scrolling on her phone, I can see her peek over the top of it and track the TV screen.

Wren, predictably, is more outraged by the outcome than I am. "How the *fuck* did Trevor and Stacia win? There's no way! She totally hates him. This 'love score' is bullshit." She sits back on the couch, arms crossed, glaring at the TV where Trevor and Stacia are frolicking in multicolored confetti.

"I thought you didn't like this show," I state, feeling myself smile genuinely for the first time all day,

"I don't!" she exclaims defensively.

"So, are you going to help me pass out candy tonight?" I ask to change the subject. If I push too much, Wren will never even look at another TV just to prove her point.

She crunches down on a piece of popcorn and says, "Duh. It's my favorite part."

"You're not wearing anything scary, are you?"

"It's not that bad," she says defensively. I sigh because Wren has a history of wearing terrifying costumes for the sole purpose of freaking out trick-or-treaters.

"I don't believe you," I say, raising my eyebrows at her devilish smirk.

---

"OH MY GOD," I groan.

"What?" Wren's muffled voice replies.

"How much did you pay for that abomination?"

"I really don't think that's important."

Wren struts out of my bathroom wearing a costume that I

can only describe as the result of a spider and a fly having a baby. A little, gross abomination baby.

An ababy if you will.

The mask, which covers her whole head, looks like a spider's head with six bulging green eyes and giant pincers. The sleek body glistens with exoskeleton-like plates. She's strapped iridescent wings to her back, and her hands end in pincer-like claws.

"How are you going to pass out candy like that?" I ask, gesturing to her claw-covered hands.

She walks over to one of the giant plastic cauldrons I've filled with candy, picks it up, and thrusts it toward me. "Any other questions? Wait, what are you supposed to be?" she asks, tilting her gross spider head in question.

I self-consciously adjust the fur-covered hood so it sits lower on my brow. "A wolf," I reply. I found the costume on a fashion resale website. It's comfortable and thankfully fits well (plus-sized costumes are unsurprisingly hard to find). It's a long-sleeved, gray dress with a furred hood and fur trimmed details on the hem. It goes just above my knees, so I paired it with black tights and boots, so I don't freeze. It's not the most inspired costume, but at least I won't be passing out candy with a side of trauma.

When I turn to gather up the extra candy, Wren exclaims, "Oh my god, you have a tail. This isn't like, some kind of furry thing, is it?"

I push her jokingly. "Shut up and help me take all this downstairs. It's almost dark."

We lumber downstairs, carting enough candy to give each child in Ravenwood a proper sugar high the way god intended. I'm a little nervous to hand out candy tonight, just twenty-four hours post medium reveal. But it's my favorite night of the year, and I know I'll regret it if I hole up in my apartment.

"Rae, how are you?" My dad asks, plowing into me as soon as we open the door. He gives me a suffocating and wonderful bear hug. It makes me feel like I'm seven years old again. And now I want to cry. I breathe deeply to hold it in, lest I mess up my cute, black-painted nose and exaggerated tear ducts.

"I'm okay. Still reeling a bit, but I'll get there," I reply, squeezing him back before he releases me. He's wearing a '70s disco costume made from shiny polyester and it's *way* too form-fitting for my tender eyes, so I keep my gaze at or above collarbone level.

"I can't believe that Misha would do something like that," my mom says, shaking her head and giving me a much more gentle hug. She's matching my dad with a '70s style romper, complete with white, knee-high go-go boots.

"I don't think he meant to reveal my secret," I say, looking to Wren, who's been friends with him for years. "I think he was just shocked and hurt to find out I was hiding my identity. He told me some pretty sensitive stuff about his past before the curtain came down, so I can understand why he felt a little betrayed, I guess. Even if that wasn't my goal."

Aunt Clarissa floats into the room, wearing a long, flapper-style dress with a dramatic ostrich feather sticking out from the headpiece pinned to her hair. "Darling! Such dreadful business last night. But! We made a bit over ten thousand dollars with the silent auction, tarot, and your medium meetings. Well, before that went up in flames."

I resist the urge to scream "I told you so" in Aunt C's face. I've been beating back my anger toward her for pushing me to do this. I know it's not her fault—I'm the one who ultimately decided to be a medium for hire. But it's hard not to blame her because she pushed so much. She was the one who told me everything would be fine.

I must make a face because she says, "Anyways! Ten grand! Yay us!" She claps, making her bracelets tinkle.

"Well, that's a start," I say, rubbing my brow. It's enough for a couple of months; we can squirrel it away and use it to help pay some of the bills.

"Okay! Let's set up this candy table," Wren says, her rubber claws making a dull clapping sound when she smacks them together. Her abilities also make her the best sort of social lubricant. She can sense the emotions of a room and work to shift them. I give her a grateful look and walk over to help her set up our trick-or-treat table.

All the businesses on Main Street set up tables full of candy and other goodies for trick-or-treaters. We all add our own spin on the extras, some catering more to the parents and older siblings taking the little ones around, while others focus completely on our pint-sized community members.

We set up just inside the door, filling the various cauldrons to the brim with sugary goodness. We have a few cauldrons dedicated to non-candy options for those who can't or don't want to partake, full of stickers, mini coloring books, some savory snacks, and one full of individual shots of different liqueurs for the over twenty-one crowd (that one is at the back of the table, and is only offered to parents/adults).

By the time we get it all organized, the excited squeals of children promised an abominable amount of candy echo down the street. Soon, we're visited by the first group of trick-or-treaters. We have a classic Ghost Face preteen, a princess Ariel who looks to be around eight, and a toddler dressed as a cat pawing through the offered goods.

Wren positively scares the shit out of them by sprinting across the room, from one darkened corner to the other, making a terrifying buzzy, clicking sound in her throat. She really commits to the bit, I'll give her that at least. A piercing scream, followed by loud crying from our tiniest trick-or-treater, makes Wren pull her mask off, sweaty hair plastered to her head. She slowly approaches the girl, holding out her mask.

"Sorry, I got a little carried away," she says sheepishly to both the girl and her parents. She bends down so she's eye level and exclaims, "Oh my goodness, are you a dog?"

The girl wipes her tears and says indignantly, "I'm a kitty-cat."

"Did you say a little crab?" Wren asks playfully, clicking her pincers together.

The girl cracks a smile, before bursting into a fit of giggles. "No! A kitty-cat."

"Oh, I see it now. Cool ears," Wren says, reaching out to bump one of the black ears with her claw. "Want some candy? I'll look the other way so you can get an extra big handful." She winks at the parents who look relieved they won't have to decide between forcing a cranky toddler to finish trick-or-treating or forcing an even crankier preteen to go home early.

Thankfully, Wren learned her lesson, so the rest of the night goes by without any tears. She waits to assess the age of the trick-or-treaters before jump-scaring them. To my shock, no one mentions the whole medium thing, but that might have more to do with me disappearing to the stock room anytime anyone looks a little too interested in speaking to me. By the time we've hit the bottom of our cauldrons, multiple refills included, the visitors have slowed to a trickle.

I go outside to sweep the discarded wrappers off the sidewalk in front of the store when movement across the street catches my attention. I look over and find Misha dressed as a baseball player doing the same thing I am. I raise my hand in a feeble wave and drop it quickly when he turns sharply to head back inside the coffee shop.

*I guess there's no more magical hot chocolate in my future.*

Which feels karmically unfair, considering we're heading into prime hot chocolate weather. I sigh, bringing the long-handled dustpan in front of me so I can sweep up my pile.

"Why the long face?" Dean asks from beside me. I turn to find him smirking at me in an honest-to-god pirate costume. Like, a good one. Like maybe Johnny Depp wore it on the set of *Pirates of the Caribbean.* He tips the brim of his tricorn hat at me like some anachronistic cowboy.

I lean closer and—*My god, he's wearing eyeliner.*

"How did you know I have a thing for pirates?" I ask instead of answering his question. I'm working very hard not to jump his bones in the middle of my quaint, small-town-America street. Thankfully, no one is out right now to bear witness to me fawning over what would look like the streetlamp behind Dean.

"The *Pirates of the Caribbean* franchise is your go-to comfort watch," he says casually, like it's no big deal that he knows and has catalogued this fact about me. It makes me stupidly emotional that he cares enough to have paid attention. "Okay well, go-to other than reality TV, I guess," he concedes. "Shit, should I have gone with a reality TV star costume? What would that even look like?" he wonders.

"No! No," I say again, quieter. "I like this... Very much," I say, running a finger along the slutty little V-neck that exposes his bare chest to me.

He clears his throat and blushes. "Well, your family is on the other side of that glass door, and while they can't see me, they can definitely see you."

"Right," I say, stepping back. "More on this later," I say, waving a finger over him. I look through the glass door to see Aunt Clarissa watching with a girlish gleam. I sigh. I'm not afforded any damn privacy in this town.

"Come on then," I say. "Time to meet the family." I turn to find that Dean has gone, well, ghostly. I snicker and lead him inside.

# THIRTY-SEVEN

"UM, Rae. What's your sister supposed to be?" Dean asks in my ear. We've just walked in to find my family milling about, eating the last few pieces of unwanted candy. Wren has yet to remove any part of her nightmare costume, choosing instead to lurk menacingly in the dim light.

"Some sort of spider-fly monstrosity," I whisper back.

"C-cool," he stutters, and I can sense a literal shiver running down his spine. I cough to hide my laugh.

"So, is the whole 'meet the parents' thing happening right now?" Wren asks, stalking closer. Aunt Clarissa looks over, interested.

"What are you talking about?" Dad asks Wren, looking around the room.

"Rae's ghost boyfriend," Wren says matter-of-factly. "Dean?" she clarifies as though they should know who she's talking about.

"Oh, is that Dean boy here now?" Aunt Clarissa asks, looking around.

I flush so hot, I feel feverish. I never exactly got around to telling Mom and Dad about Dean. It wasn't on purpose, I've just been so busy. And I didn't want to worry them. And, you know, all the other age-old excuses in the book.

"Rae, what is she talking about?" my mom asks, turning an inquisitive look my way.

"Um," I start. "I—well. It's complicated."

"Ouch," Dean says, looking wounded.

"Complicated, how?" Mom asks.

I clear my throat and try again, "Remember that guy I went on a date with a couple of months ago?" When both of my parents nod, I continue, "Well, he didn't actually ghost me. Or okay, he *kind of* did. But it wasn't on purpose! He died in this random way and we're pretty sure he was murdered? Then he appeared to me because of the whole, you know, medium thing..." I trail off.

"So, you've been seeing him... while he's a ghost? And he's here right now?" My dad tries to clarify.

"Yes to both? I mean, sort of. We haven't defined the relationship or anything!"

*Why is my voice getting so high? Why am I so defensive?*

"I would just like to take the time to point out now that I am totally fine with being your boyfriend," Dean says, patting my shoulder.

"Do we really need to worry about labels right now?" I ask him under my breath.

"Who's worried? I already know who I belong with," Dean says firmly.

I don't even have time to process this little side conversation before Wren peels off her gross mask and says, "Oh, and we should also mention that you're helping investigate his murder."

I shoot her a face-melting glare, but she's Wren, so she hardly flinches.

"What?" My parents ask at the same time.

"That is so dangerous!" My mom exclaims at the same time my dad says, "You should really let the police handle it, Bug."

I sigh and launch into a semi-detailed overview of the entire "investigation" so far, being sure to emphasize that the police had already brushed it off as a suicide and weren't looking into it. "So, now we're just waiting for something else to come up. Either for Dean to remember more, or for Jack's P.I. to uncover another lead."

My mom opens and closes her mouth before saying, "Hold on. Did you say you were *drugged?*"

I wince because I had sped past that part on purpose. "Yeah, but it wasn't a big deal!" I say brightly. "Anyway, Mom, Dad, meet Dean Crawford, my erm boyfriend," I finish weakly. I don't know how to feel about the title, but it's the closest thing to describe what he is to me.

They both paste on smiles that look like terribly done papier-mâché, all wonky and distorted. My dad shakes himself a little and looks to both sides of me. "Nice to meet you, son," he says.

"You as well, sir," Dean says, stepping forward a little as if to shake my dad's hand before realizing that that isn't a possibility. "Damn. I used to be way better at meeting the family. This whole being dead schtick is for the birds." He scowls.

I relay his niceties, leaving out the last comment for myself.

"So, everyone but us knew about this?" my mom asks, sounding for all the world like she might start crying.

I reach out and put a hand on her shoulder. "It wasn't on purpose, Mom. I just see Aunt Clarissa more often, and we got to talking. And Wren is Wren. Keeping anything from her is pointless. I'm sorry."

She smiles and seems to blink away the sadness of my not confiding in her. "It's alright, Bug. You're almost thirty. It's silly for me to think that you have to tell me everything."

"Maybe. But I should have told you about this," I say, threading an arm through Dean's.

She shrugs good-naturedly, and I can see the visions of grandchildren flashing and dying in her eyes. I was never sold on the kid thing, but now that the person I'm with physically *can't* have children, it's pretty much a done deal. She leans in to hug me, but pulls back in surprise.

"Did I just touch him?" she asks, astonished.

My head rears back in shock. "I don't know, did you?"

I look up to see Dean's wide eyes. "Try again. He's over here," I say to my mom, gesturing to my left side.

She tentatively reaches a hand out and pokes him in the chest. They both gasp, and my mom pulls her hand back like she's been shocked.

"How?" I ask, dumbfounded.

"You're probably acting as a conduit," Wren says around a glob of nougat. She studies the space between Dean and me, zeroing in on where we're touching. "Your connection to him is much stronger than any other spirit you've interacted with because you've spent a lot more time with him. And you two have an emotional connection. Or, maybe it's just all the *practice* you've been getting."

"Woah," Dean says. I agree.

We spend the next few minutes seeing if Dean can touch others, and if they can feel it. It only works if we're touching each other.

"Well I'll be damned," Aunt C says. "You're learning all kinds of new things."

I can tell from Dean's expression that he's starting to get drained, so I decide it's time for us to beg off. "And for my final trick, I'll go upstairs and get eight hours of sleep," I say with a bow.

Wren snorts and teases, "Yeah, right. Only if he lets you."

I send her another scathing glare. "Okay!" I exclaim, hoping to redirect my parents' attention away from that little comment. "Let's call it a night. It's getting late."

My mom gives me a shrewd look. "Fine. But we're going to have a family dinner soon, and you will bring Dean." It's not a question, but a demand.

"Deal," I say, offering her a smile. She pulls me in for a suffocating, but somehow still comforting, mom-hug.

I say bye to everyone else, flipping Wren off behind my mom's back for good measure. She draws her thumb across her throat in response, and I roll my eyes, tugging Dean outside.

"Your family is great. Really intense," Dean says as he follows me inside my apartment.

I laugh. "Yeah. Intense is one word for them."

"But they're good people. I can tell. They care about you."

"Luck isn't on my side for much, but I did win the family lottery," I say, pushing the hood off my head in the warmth of my living room.

"So," he says, stepping in front of me. "What are you supposed to be?"

"A wolf," I say indignantly, waving a hand at my black-painted nose.

"Ah. That explains the tail, then. I wondered, but was too afraid to ask," he says, eyes bright with mischief even though his face remains stoic.

I sigh and protest, "Okay, why does everyone jump to a furry thing? What does that say about me?"

"Hey, I don't judge! I can be into that if you want me to," he says, tilting his head coyly.

"Um, no. I don't judge either, but I think sex with a ghost is already strange enough for me," I state, shaking my head.

He just laughs, placing a hand against my neck and tilting my face up. His expression turns more sincere when he says, "I liked that you called me your boyfriend. That you even introduced me to your family."

I smile a little, feeling dazed in the thrall of his deep-brown eyes. "It's no big deal. I didn't know how else to explain us, and I wanted you to meet them before—Well. Before." I finish, not wanting to say the rest.

*Before you leave me here alone for the next fifty to sixty years.*

"Right. Yeah. The whole ticking clock thing," he says, stepping back. "And I guess you wouldn't want to tell your family that we're just having fun, right?" He nods his head, like it makes sense. Hearing him boil down whatever this is between us to just sex twists in my gut like a serrated knife.

I swallow, my throat suddenly tight. "Right, yeah," I echo with a nod.

"Because it would be dumb to want anything more when we can't have it," he says, more to himself than me.

I feel a twinge of unease, knowing I'm keeping a secret

from him... the possibility of more. But I want him to see what it feels like to have the option to move on before I bring it up. I want him to fully understand what he's giving up if he chooses to stay.

"Yeah," I finally answer, my body betraying me by stepping closer.

Dean searches my face, and whatever he reads there seems to give him the permission he needs. He steps into me, cupping my jaw reverently. "I can't pretend with you, Rae," he says, sounding almost angry with himself.

"What do you mean?"

"I can't pretend I don't want you, no matter how short a time I get to have you. I can't pretend I'm not so fucking angry at whoever is in charge for letting me meet you too late. I can't pretend that I'm not falling for you. I can't pretend I'm not terrified of losing you," he murmurs, pressing his forehead against mine.

`"I—" the words stick in my throat. I try to make more come out, to tell him that I feel the exact same way, but it feels like someone has wrapped a vise around my neck, cutting them off at the source.

"It's okay. You don't have to say anything. I'm the one with limited time, so I needed to tell you that. I don't want any more regrets."

I nod, taking the coward's way out that he presents me with. I tilt my head minutely, and he does the same, leaning down so he can brush his lips against mine. He takes control of the kiss, drawing me impossibly close until I'm completely engulfed by him. He's all I can taste. All I can feel.

Before I even realize it's happening, he has me seated on the couch, my legs bracketing his hips as he kneels before me.

He breaks the kiss and gives me a heated look that makes me squirm.

"So, I'm pretty sure this is one of your fantasies," he says, gesturing to his pirate costume with a raised brow. All I can do is nod along like an idiot, because I want him to get to the point and get back to kissing me. "I'm going to lose the hat, because I don't think it will allow for what I'm going to do," he says, snapping his fingers. The tricorn hat vanishes, and I pout. Now he looks more sexy-duke-that-got-lost-at-sea than pirate, but the eyeliner helps.

"Sorry, but I think it'll be worth it for the view," he states.

"The v—" I stutter as he flips the skirt of my dress over my stomach. He yanks down my underwear, grips me behind the knees, and tugs me to the edge of the couch. I step out of my underwear before he gets the idea to rip them off. He pushes on my sternum, coaxing me to lean back against the couch. He looks at me from his position on the floor, relishing in the anticipation of the moment. Then he leans in greedily, using his hands to spread my thighs as wide as they'll go to accommodate the breadth of his shoulders.

He was right. The view is definitely worth it.

# THIRTY-EIGHT

I WAKE UP NAKED, sheets thrown haphazardly over my back, hugging my pillow. My apartment is freezing because I forgot to turn the heat on last night.

"Rae," Dean coaxes. "Come on, baby. You have to get up now."

"Hmm?" I grunt, burying my face in my pillow and tugging my sheets higher up my back.

"Rae, I think I know who murdered me," he says flatly.

I sit bolt upright, spitting rogue hairs out of my mouth. I clutch the sheets to me more for warmth than for the sake of being precious about my boobs—the man has seen them plenty by this point. "What?" I croak, blinking the sleep from my eyes.

He sits on my bed, hands clasped in an attempt to tame his agitated energy. Looking at him right now is like looking at a fluorescent light on the fritz—buzzy and hard to focus on. "I've been going to check on my family once or twice a day, and I decided to pop in on my dad this morning. He wasn't home, so I followed him to the police station. Did I mention I can do that now? Track my family down? I can see them the same as you in the ether, but they're dimmer, harder to find. Anyway, that's beside the point." He gives his head a hard shake, as if trying to force himself to focus.

Dean continues, "I followed him to the police station and got the gist of why he was there. I guess my coworkers went out for drinks last night. The bar was pretty packed since it was Halloween. Vanessa saw Richard put something in some random girl's drink when she wasn't looking. She told my dad about it because she felt too nervous to approach Richard on her own.

My dad convinced Vanessa to call the police rather than confront him themselves. Long story short, the police got there just in time, because Richard saw my dad and Vanessa talking to the poor girl and was trying to bail. Amari caught wind of what was going on and stopped him from leaving. The cops apprehended him and had enough cause to search his person. Sure enough, he had GHB powder in his wallet."

"Oh shit," I breathe, dread punching a fist through my gut.

"Yeah." He runs a stressed hand through his hair.

"So, what now?" I ask.

"I don't know. It sounds like Richard posted bail this morning. He doesn't have any priors, so they're treating him with kid gloves. His dad used to be a detective there, so I'm sure that's helping smooth the way for him," Dean says angrily.

I bite my lip and then ask, "Why do you think he's the one who killed you? I get that it was the same drug, but it's a popular one for sexual assault."

Dean nods and says, "It is. And I hate to think how many women he's likely used it on to take advantage of them. He always wanted to go out to the bars, and he was usually the one to go home with a random woman. God, I should have paid more attention," Dean scrubs a hand over his mouth, lips turned down into a disgusted frown.

I reach out and place a hand on his knee. "You were not responsible for his actions. You didn't know."

He looks away and nods. "I know. I just feel so fucking awful for those women."

"Did you and he have a falling out?" I ask, trying to gently steer him back towards his own murder and away from any misplaced guilt.

"No, not really. I mean, I never would have considered us friends. He was too frat boy for my tastes. He hated that the law firm was owned by my dad. He always made snide little comments about me being a 'daddy's boy' and he'd drop little nepotism jabs here and there. But I brushed them off because I figured he was insecure, and I knew I was good at my job. My dad made it a point not to promote me unless I worked my ass off like everyone else."

"So wait, you think he killed you because of work?" I ask, my voice pitching up to screeching levels.

"I think so. I mean, my dad was making all these overt comments the night I was killed about me being promoted to partner because I found that damning evidence about the factory. Richard probably got so jealous that he killed me for it. And the worst part is that he got the promotion when I died, so his stupid plan worked," Dean says, anger and despair covering him like a thunderstorm blocking out the sun.

"Do you think they'll be able to pin him for it?" I ask, rubbing soothing circles with my thumb over his knee.

Dean shrugs a shoulder, but he's so tense it looks mechanical. "I don't know. My dad brought the lab results from my coffee to the police station. But they can't prove it was Richard since no one saw him do it, he's not in charge of restocking the snacks and drinks at the office, and it's been months. Not to mention they never found the drug in my system."

"You know, I need to talk to Jack. Because your death wasn't from a natural cause, they should have done drug testing when they autopsied you. I can't imagine that you were incapacitated in any other way since we literally found it in your coffee. Every article I read said that GHB testing is standard practice, so it definitely should have been there," I say, thinking about the various articles I read while researching everything I could about Dean's death that probably have me on some sort of list now.

Dean's brow furrows. "Fuck. Do you think Richard's dad could have had some connections to the coroner?"

"Maybe. If his dad was a police officer, I'm sure they would run into each other a lot," I say, rubbing the goosebumps from my arms. I can't believe how deep this goes.

"If they don't find something that sticks, he'll be able to get away with just a slap on the wrist. He might have to go to jail for a while for the drugs, but unless other people come forward, it would be hard to prove much of anything." Dean is visibly shaking with rage.

"Okay. Let's try to focus on what we can do and what we know. Do you think he's the one who actually killed you?" I ask.

"You mean is he the one who set up a *Dexter*-level kill room in my garage?" he asks. When I nod, he says, "I don't know." He pauses to think, dark brows furrowing. "I mean, he would have had to race me to get to my house. I saw that he was still at work, maybe ten minutes before I left."

A thought strikes me. "Didn't you say he went out to drinks with your coworkers that day? Something about a Leprechaun shot?"

"Lucky Charms shooter," Dean corrects absently, "And yeah. Unless he bailed out. We should call my dad and see if he remembers. He doesn't always go out with us, but he was in the mood to celebrate that night."

I get dressed in an old t-shirt and leggings, then give Jack a call.

"Hey, Rae. How'd you know?" Jack asks, his voice gravelly from his long night.

"Dean," I say simply.

"Ah. So, listen, I just left the police station. I'm guessing Dean told you why I was here?" I confirm, so he continues, "I don't want to talk about this on the phone. Do you and Dean want to come over tonight? We can have a family dinner, and it'll give us a chance to chat."

My heart warms at the term "family dinner." I smile a little and say, "I'd love to. Text me the address and time."

---

I KNOCK on the door of Dean's parents' gargantuan colonial-style home. Dog barking heralds the arrival of Jack as he swings the door open, putting a leg in front of the golden beast.

"That's Toast," Dean says, affection clear in his voice.

"Toast! Chill out," Jack grits, trying in vain to hold back the furry wiggle-butt.

"It's okay, I like dogs," I say, crouching down to be lovingly mauled by Toast's giant pink tongue. Once he's satisfied with his greeting, Toast fixes his attention behind me, and his whole body wiggles so violently, it looks like his tail will wag clean off his body. I stand to get out of his way before I get bulldozed.

"I think he's excited to see Dean," I say with a grin, watching as Toast trots around Dean, whining happily.

"Huh," Jack says, watching Toast. "He's been doing that little happy dance for the past few weeks, and we couldn't figure out why. Guess now we know." He smiles, brushing quickly at his eyes. "Anyway, please come in. Marielle will be thrilled to meet you."

"Uh, about that," I start in a low voice, "Does she know about me? About Dean and his current... Condition?" I ask.

Jack nods. "Yeah, she does. I broke down last night and told her everything. I don't know how much she believes me, but she knows." It's only then that I see the tired bags under his eyes. Must have been a long night of talking.

I swallow down my nerves, holding my hand over my stomach as if I can contain them there. Dean trails behind, and I try to take comfort in his presence. Meeting his mom would have been nerve-wracking under normal circumstances. The added weirdness of her son being dead *and* bringing his ghost with me in the middle of his murder investigation feel impossible. I'm fighting every instinct to bolt as we walk through their tastefully decorated home towards the kitchen.

"Mari, this is Rae Alderwood," Jack says as we enter a gigantic, modern kitchen with colonial-style touches.

Dean's mother is gorgeous. Her thick, dark hair falls to her shoulders, streaked through with strands of silvery gray. Her mouth has the same pouty quality as Dean, and I can see where he gets his amazing eyelashes from. If "aging gracefully" had a poster child, it would be Marielle Crawford. She wipes her hands down the front of her lemon-printed apron and extends a manicured hand my way.

"Rae, it's nice to meet you," she says in a way that I know means it's *not* nice to meet me.

I paste on what I hope is a warm smile and say, "You as well. It smells amazing in here, Mrs. Crawford." It's true. The smell of roasting chicken and root vegetables fills the room.

Her expression lightens a bit at my obvious flattery, but all she does is nod before going back to tend the stove.

"Sorry, she's overprotective of all of us. You'd think my dad is the scary one, but she definitely takes the cake," Dean says into my ear. If I weren't so nervous, I'd think it was cute that he feels the need to whisper into my ear even though I'm the only one who can hear him.

"So helpful," I mutter to him under my breath.

Dean's parents and I spend a while making awkward, stilted conversation. The tension between Jack and his wife is obvious, and her distaste for me almost poisons the mouthwatering smell of dinner cooking.

"Let's eat," Marielle says shortly, gesturing to the dining table. She's been nothing but polite, but she's doing it with old-money manners: razor sharp with an undercurrent of disdain.

We get seated, and I ask after Dean's siblings. When Jack mentioned a "family dinner," I assumed that meant the rest of the Crawford brood. Jack and Marielle exchange a telepathic, angry spat. Marielle finally turns to me, fork clutched so tight in her hand, her delicate knuckles look bloodless. "I—*we* decided that it would be better to have this meeting just between the three of us for now," she says, eyes squinting in an approximation of a smile.

I set down my fork and feel Dean squeeze my shoulders supportively behind me. "Look, Mrs. Crawford. I'm just going to address the Dean-shaped elephant in the room. I can't even begin to imagine how hard these last couple of months have been for you and your family. I know it might be hard to believe, but I truly care for your son—"

"Stop right there," she interrupts, palm upheld to ward off the rest of what I was going to say. "You don't *know* my son. This whole thing you have going with Jack is sick. You're preying on a grieving father. Maybe you went on a single date with Dean, but that doesn't give you the right to come into my home and speak about my son." Her face has gone completely white with rage.

"Now, Mari," Jack starts tiredly.

"No. Enough out of you, Jack. I thought I could do this, but I can't. I can't host this—this grifter." She pushes her chair back and stands ramrod straight.

This is the second time in two days that I've been called a liar, and I'm pretty much over it. I pat my mouth with the cloth napkin on my lap and stand too. "Okay, Dean. Time to put on a show," I say to him. He looks at me in question.

I lace our fingers together and step toward Marielle. "What are you doing?" she asks, shrinking back. I can't fight my eye roll.

*What, does she think I'm going to maim her?*

"Listen to me, Mrs. Crawford. Dean is here with us right now. He's going to touch your shoulder," I say, nodding to Dean.

He inhales and concentrates, brows furrowing together. I stay a good distance from her so she can't accuse me of faking it. He places his large hand on her entire shoulder, and her eyes go wide with surprise. She scans me, tracking where both of my hands are. Then, once she's satisfied that I'm not the one doing the touching, she looks across the table at Jack, who watches her with tears tracking down his cheeks.

"Dean?" she asks in a whisper, disbelief coloring her voice. He slowly raises his hand and presses it to her face in answer, his thumb gently swiping at the tear dripping from her jaw. She closes her eyes, chin trembling as she leans into his hand. His grip on my hand tightens as if he's trying to hold himself together through me.

She breathes out, and I watch her shoulders relax for what must be the first time since he's passed. Marielle finally opens her eyes and looks at me. "How?" she asks, voice breaking like a wave on the shores of her grief.

I smile a little and say, "I don't have an answer. I've always been able to see and communicate with the dead, but Dean has helped me develop my gift into something more."

Dean tries to give me a cocky smile, but the tears in his eyes ruin the effect.

"Can I see him?" Marielle asks thickly.

My heart sinks at the request because I wish I could make it happen for her. "No, I'm sorry. I've yet to find a way to do that. But hey, you never know. I had no clue I could do this until him, so maybe one day."

She nods, swiping at her eyes. Dean lets his hand drop, and Marielle fires off question after question for both of us while we get seated around the table again, digging into dinner. I answer in kind, and things only get a little awkward when she starts asking about the nature of our relationship.

"Well, we went on a date once when he was alive," I hedge. When she nods and gestures for me to go on, I say, "And we sort of, um, reconnected when he found me like this." Dean chortles, and I level a glare at him, cheeks flaming. "We've been getting to know each other while we work on his case."

Marielle is back to squinting at me distrustfully. "Do you care for my son?" she asks bluntly.

*Kill me now.*

"Yes," I say, resolve strengthening my voice, "Very much so. I will grieve the loss of his life for the rest of mine. But I have the chance to help him now. To figure out what happened to him so he can find peace." Dean places his hand on my knee under the table, the electric tingles sending goosebumps racing down my leg.

"And even with your special interest in him, you will help him move on? That's what Jack told me you do: help spirits move on," Marielle says, pushing a carrot through the sauce on her plate.

I swallow around the lump in my throat and nod. "Yes."

After that, we settle into more easy-going conversation. I talk about The Veil and what I do there, and Marielle tells me all about being a homemaker and how much she enjoyed raising her five kids. Jack interjects here and there to tell his own anecdotes, and I'm surprised at how easy it feels. A flash of a different life hits me; one where Dean is alive and well, and where he brings me to meet his family for normal, less murdery reasons.

The nostalgia for something that will never be is intense, and I find myself zoning out while Marielle tells me about the time Dean quit baseball in seventh grade and didn't bother to tell anyone. They all showed up to his game to find him munching on chips in the stands instead of pitching like he was supposed to. I laugh in the right places, but I just want to go home. This is quickly becoming too painful—this approximation of what should have been, and knowing this will probably come to an end.

I politely decline dessert, using an early morning at the shop tomorrow as an excuse to beg off quickly. Jack offers to walk me out and I let him, not wanting to discuss the more gruesome details of Dean's murder in front of his mom. Jack has told me before that Marielle is doing a little better, but any discussion of Dean's death sends her spiraling for days at a time. I'd rather not be responsible for that.

When we get to my car, I ask, "Can I see Dean's autopsy report?"

Jack stumbles and says, "Huh?"

"Sorry," I say, shaking my head at myself for not being a little more delicate. "I just want to look at the drug findings. It's hard to believe that he wouldn't have tested positive for GHB," I explain.

"Oh, sure," Jack says, pulling his phone out of his back pocket. He taps around a bit, then hands me his phone with a PDF of the toxicology report pulled up.

I wade through the medical report, looking for anything that references the drug. I suck in a breath when I see it mentioned, but deflate a little when the test result says, "negative." I squint at it and say, "Wait a minute... They tested for GHB using Dean's saliva. That's the least accurate way to test. It should have been a urine sample."

Dean and Jack both raise their eyebrows at me, so I feel the need to defend myself, "I did my research! Sue me." I hand Jack his phone so I can cross my arms.

"Not the best thing to say to a lawyer," Dean says with a chuckle.

Jack frowns down at his phone. "I'll talk to my P.I. about it. He's a retired detective, so I'm sure he would know more. It's definitely suspicious that they didn't use the more sensitive test."

"I'm scared this whole thing is bigger than just Richard's dad getting some favors thrown at him," I say, looking at Dean.

Jack sighs a bone-weary sigh. "Me too."

Dean nudges me and says, "Don't forget to ask about Richard."

I turn to Jack, leaning against the hood of my car. Twilight cloaks the sky in growing darkness, but with the bright flood-lights posted around Jack's house, it may as well be noon. "Dean has a question. So, obviously Richard is suspect number one, but didn't he go out with everyone the night Dean was murdered?"

Jack rubs his jaw and nods. "Yeah, he did. Everyone but Dean went out that night. I don't doubt that he's the one who drugged him, but it would have been nearly impossible to pull off the murder himself with the timeline we have."

I sigh and nod. "But listen, Richard had motive," I say, vaguely feeling like I've been handed the role of detective on daytime television.

"What do you mean?" Jack asks, focus sharpening on me.

"Dean mentioned that Richard made snide comments about nepotism. Apparently, a lot over the years. He said he always brushed it off, but that night you were talking about a promotion for Dean, so it's not too far off to assume that Richard might have wanted to..."

"Kill the competition?" Jack asks flatly.

I nod, hating that he's having to help me with this. No

parent should be put in the position of solving their child's murder.

We're silent for a while, and then I ask, "Jack? How are you so calm about this?"

He laughs, short and grating. "Calm? I'm anything but. I'm so angry, I can hardly think straight. But my wife and my children need me, so I can't go kill the fucker like I want to. Instead, I'm going to work with you, my P.I., and the police to get Richard and whoever he worked with put away and punished to the highest extent of the law. I can't believe I promoted that bastard. At least firing him gave me a little relief," he grumbles. He's balled his hands into angry fists, and he looks like he'd punch a hole straight through Richard's face if given the opportunity.

I reach out and place a hand on his shoulder. "I'm unbelievably angry, too. They took him from all of us. I know I didn't know him for very long, but he means so much to me," I break off, tears choking the rest.

"Time doesn't always dictate emotions, Rae. I know I don't look like a romantic, but I believe there's a person out there for everyone. That some people are meant to be. Maybe Dean is your person. You have every right to grieve and be angry, too. I'm just sorry you and Dean didn't get your time." He surprises me by pulling me in for a fatherly hug, squeezing me tight around the shoulders.

"I wish he could have grown old with you," Jack says into the crown of my hair. He presses a chaste kiss there and holds me while I fall apart. I feel Dean hug me from behind, and these two men hold me together while I let the grief for the life we could have had tear me apart at the seams.

# THIRTY-NINE

I'M WORKING ON AUTOPILOT, restocking the store. They gave Richard nothing more than a slap on the wrist, as expected. He's going to have to do community service, but he didn't even lose his license to practice law. Jack's P.I. confirmed our suspicion that Richard's father is woven deep into the underbelly of the county. Too many backs scratched and palms greased to let his precious son go to jail for intended sexual assault, let alone murder. And the worst part is, at this rate, we may truly never know how he got away with it.

Dean even followed him home and watched over his shoulder for days at a time, scouting through his house when he was gone. Richard's done nothing out of the ordinary, other than working out more than any person needs to and watching more porn than any pair of eyes can take. Clearly, his brush with the law scared him, because he's hardly left his house other than to go to the gym. Unless he plots another murder, we pretty much have our hands tied.

A tingle at the back of my mind catches my attention and makes me set down the armful of crystals I was arranging. My hair stands on end and I turn, grateful that we haven't opened yet. "Hello?" I call out, coaxing whoever it is forward. As they push closer, I realize their energy feels familiar. "Ivan, I know it's you, you can stop hiding," I say tiredly.

With a burst of energy that makes my ears pop, Ivan is suddenly looming in front of me.

I sigh. "You can stop with the dramatics. I've got too much going on right now. Would you like for me to help you move on, or did you just come to bother me?"

He scowls and says, "You made my nephew angry."

I laugh derisively. "Yeah, because you had no part in that."

"Hey, *I've* never lied to him," he states, thumbing his chest.

"Well, there are worse things than lying," I say, going back to stocking our crystal display. Obsidian and Tiger's Eye have been oddly popular lately. I arrange the crystals, taking pleasure in the menial task.

Ice-cold fingers wrap around my bicep and squeeze to the edge of pain, making me gasp. "Hey!" I exclaim, spinning around and shoving against his chest. He stumbles back, releasing me, eyes wide in shock. He doesn't seem to like that the playing field is more even than he thought.

In a blink, a familiar, muscular back is in front of me, anger radiating off of him in waves. "Next time you put your hands on her, you'll find yourself blasted so far into the black, you won't be able to find your way back here," Dean says through clenched teeth.

Ivan hacks a familiar smoker's laugh/cough and says, "Whatever you say. Listen, we were just having a conversation." He's using a calm tone of voice, trying to smooth over his unprovoked actions.

"Yeah?" Dean asks. "Well then, you won't mind if I'm here, right?"

Ivan raises his hands in surrender and says, "Not at all." He turns his bloodshot eyes to me. "I want to talk to my nephew again. You'll arrange that," he orders imperiously.

I fold my arms over my chest and chew on my lip in thought. I know Misha wants this closure. He deserves it, even if this jackass doesn't. "Okay. I'll try. I need to talk to him first. If he doesn't trust me, it won't do either of you any good. Give me some time and I'll call you if and when we're ready," I say reluctantly.

"And *don't* come anywhere near her until then," Dean practically growls.

Ivan looks like he's sucking on a sour lemon, but he nods once and then pops out of existence.

Before I can even process the movement, Dean is in front of me and dragging the V-neck of my oversized sweater down my arm, exposing it to the elbow. Red marks bloom over the pale skin on my upper bicep. Dean hisses in a breath and says darkly, "I'll kill him."

"He's already dead," I point out.

"I'll kill him again," Dean grits.

"So he can be double-dead?"

Dean mumbles something under his breath. Louder he says, "Why aren't you freaking out?" He traces his fingers lightly over the livid skin, making me shiver.

"Oh, I am. I'm very freaked out. No ghost has ever done that before. To be honest, I've never really interacted with an angry spirit. Sure, some of them have been assholes, but they've never really taken it out on me because they're so grateful that I'm trying to help them."

I cup his jaw. Just having him here is grounding. I don't know what I'll do when he's gone. He's quickly become my person. Losing him will be like losing a kidney, only more vital. Like losing my damned heart. The thought of revealing the tether is on the tip of my tongue. But I push the selfish impulse down. I will find a way to get him to peace. Even if it feels like stomping on my sad little heart.

He must feel the tremble in my body because he presses me close and says, "It's okay. I'm here."

I sigh into his chest, wondering how much longer that will be true.

"IS TODAY GHOST DAY OR SOMETHING?" I ask when Rebecca appears alongside me on my frigid walk around the park. I needed to clear my head after Ivan, and my lunch break was the only time I could get away. I already ate my soup, so now I'm meandering around the manmade lake. Snow dusts the ground, and it's yet to turn a dirty, grayish-brown like it usually does this early in the season. I try to soak it in, knowing that the forecast calls for rain in the next few days, which will turn this all into a gross slush.

"Why do you say that?" she asks, keeping pace with me.

I look around furtively, grateful that we're mostly alone. There are a few runners out, but they're all far enough away that they shouldn't overhear me talking to a ghost. "No reason, sorry. It's just been a long day," I reply, shoving my cold hands further in my pockets in search of warmth.

"Trouble in paradise," she asserts, nodding sagely. Before I can correct her, she asks, "Where is lover boy anyway?"

"He's off getting a little R and R," I tell her. I go on to explain the situation with Richard, and that Dean has been spending a lot of time watching him. Apparently, it's more draining than when he's with me, so he's needed more rest than usual.

"Ah," she says, tucking her hands into her own pockets. "So you guys think he's the killer?"

"At the very least, he's the one who instigated it and drugged Dean. Whether or not he actually got his hands dirty, I'm not sure. At this point, we might never know."

"Don't be surprised if something comes out that confirms his guilt," Rebecca says. "It sounds like he was dumb enough to use the same type of drug on that poor girl and get caught, so I'm sure something else will slip. And hopefully whatever comes out is too hard to brush off for those corrupt jerks down at the PD."

I sigh and say, "I hope so."

We walk for a while in silence, and then she stops me with a staticky hand on my shoulder. I look down at it surprised and turn to her. "Rae, I think it's time for me to move on," she says, looking up at me.

"What?" I ask stupidly. For some reason, I had taken her presence for granted, thinking that she would be around for a while. To be honest, I was beginning to wonder if she'd ever tire of haunting her ex. "What about Kyle? Who's going to make him miserable?"

She laughs a little. "I think he can manage that on his own. In fact, I know he can. He's burning his own life to the ground without any help from me." She looks out over the lake, face more serene than I've ever seen it. "I'm just ready to see what else is out there. I don't know how to explain it, but I feel like whatever was holding onto me here is letting go. And every time I slip into the ether, I get pulled a little farther away."

"Are you scared?" I ask.

She smiles at me and shakes her head. "No. Wherever it's leading feels like every positive emotion I've ever had. I swore I could taste my first birthday cake the other day. And then later, I felt warm sand under my feet and could hear the ocean. I just barely pulled myself back."

"Why did you do that?" I ask. It seems like it would be hard to let go of.

Her wistful expression sharpens into something more mocking, and she raises a dark eyebrow. "To say goodbye to you, dummy."

"Oh," I say with a laugh. And then more seriously, once it hits me. "Oh."

"Yeah," she says, squeezing my shoulder before dropping her hand. She clears her throat and says, "So, yeah. Bye, I guess."

"Bye, Rebecca. Thanks for being my friend, even with the whole *Beetlejuice* thing."

Her face twists in disgust. "Ugh, thanks for reminding me." I laugh and she says, "No, but seriously. Thank you for putting up with me and for helping me. You gave me a place to go when I felt lost. I wasn't as scared or alone."

I look up at the overcast sky, trying to keep the tears at bay. When I have control, I say, "Of course. It's what I do, and I was glad to be there for you."

"I'm still not sure what you even do with all this," she says, gesturing vaguely between us, "But I'm happy to have met you while I had the chance." Leave it to Rebecca to take something sweet and turn it into a jab.

I roll my eyes, saying, "Yeah, yeah. Whatever. Go wreak havoc in paradise." I jokingly shoo her away, even though my sinuses burn with unshed tears.

"Will do," she says with a smile. "Goodbye, Rae, see you over there some day. But not too soon, okay?" I nod, and she presses up on her tiptoes to kiss my cheek. I close my eyes and feel rather than see a flash of light and a flood of warmth. I could swear I smell the ocean. When I open my eyes, she's gone and the world is cold again.

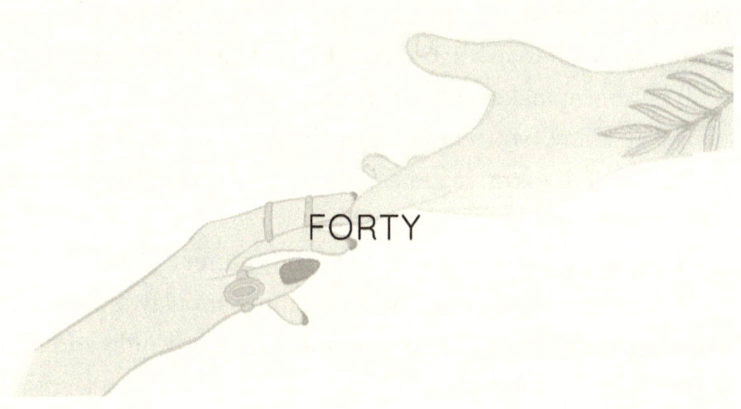

# FORTY

DEAN SETTLES NEXT to me while I curl up on his cloud couch. He insisted we come here to watch the latest *John Wick*. Apparently, my TV is too small to do the movie justice. I'm not much of an action movie person, but I'll watch Keanu Reeves in a suit any day. My drooling over him was so obvious in the first half of the movie that Dean got a little jealous.

"Really?" I had asked. "You're jealous of a celebrity when I have about a zero percent chance of ever seeing him in person?" I teased, poking him in the ribs when he started grumbling about it.

He looked at me and said, "Rae, I'm *dead*. You being with me should be impossible on pretty much every level, but here we are. I don't put anything past you. I fully believe that if you wanted him and put your mind to it, you could figure it out. If you want it to happen, it happens." I melted at that and resolved to stop undressing Keanu with my eyes—or at least be less obvious about it.

Now, he's watching me finish eating the Vietnamese takeout I had delivered. I polish off my Bahn Mi (sans jalapeños) while we chat about the store and whether or not we'll be able to make it once the rent increases.

"You know, you could move in here and rent out your apartment for extra income," Dean says casually, gesturing around him.

I almost choke on my sandwich and sputter, "What?"

"You could live here," he says more seriously, apparently warming to the idea. "Think about it. The rent would add a lot of extra income a month."

"You're missing the obvious," I state flatly. Oh, to be so casual with money that you can't fathom why someone won't just move into your gigantic house.

"Which is?"

"Dean. I love that you are so giving, but I could not afford a mortgage on this house. There's no fucking way. Didn't I mention I don't pay rent? Plus, I don't have much expendable income right now."

"It's paid for," he says, the tips of his ears going pink. When my mouth drops open, he elaborates, "I used the trust my grandpa left me, along with my savings. I didn't want to pay a mortgage, so I got a decent deal by paying cash." He shifts a little in his seat.

I open and close my mouth like a fish. I finally say, "So what, you'd just expect your parents to gift it to me since it's technically theirs now?"

"Or they could 'rent it' to you and just charge the property tax and utilities. And even then, I'll ask that the cash comes out of the money I left to them," he says.

"Dean, I can't. It's too much." I shake my head adamantly.

"Come on," he cajoles. "I never got the chance to spoil you while I was alive. Let me do it now that I'm dead."

"This is beyond spoiling," I say, dropping my head in my hands.

"Just think about it, okay?" he asks.

I sigh, and I can't believe I'm agreeing to this, but... "Okay. I'll think about it."

The grin that splits his face is positively giddy, and I feel myself smile in response. After I finish my dinner, he stands and holds out his hand to me. "Come with me? There's something I've been wanting to do with you for a while," he says with a tender look I can't resist.

I take his hand and he guides me upstairs to his room. He pushes open the door and clicks on the lights, which are set to a dim glow. "Ah. Does the thing you want to do happen to involve getting naked?" I ask, looking pointedly south.

His laugh is bold and sweet, and I want to be wrapped in it for the rest of my life. It's the most carefree I've heard him sound since he showed up in my living room, divested of his earthly body. "No. Well, that can happen later," he clarifies. He suddenly looks embarrassed when he mumbles, "I wanted to ask you to dance."

"To dance?" I ask, looking down at my sweats and oversized long-sleeve shirt.

"Yeah. But, we don't have to," he rushes out.

Before he can shut off the lights, I reach out a hand and grab his again. "Okay, let's dance," I say, not wanting him to feel embarrassed. I'd walk over hot coals for him if he asked nicely enough, so dancing is an easy yes. "I'm not much of a dancer, though," I warn.

He squeezes my hand before letting go so he can hunt for

the right album. "It's a good thing I can't break a toe in this form then," he teases, setting a record on his record player. He fiddles with it until "I, Carrion" by Hozier bathes the room in ethereal sound.

Dean reaches out to me and draws me close, placing my hand on his chest and the other around his neck. He covers my hand on his chest with his own, wrapping his other securely around my waist. I lean my head so my cheek presses over his heart and close my eyes as we sway. The music entwines around us, carrying my feet with it.

It's not perfect. I stumble once or twice, Dean disappearing his feet just in time to avoid getting a toe smushed. But we laugh it off and continue swaying, turning in a gentle circle.

He holds me against him like something precious, and I feel a tear slip down my cheek. I'm not even sure why I'm crying. Maybe it's the beauty of the song. Maybe it's the tenderness of the moment. Or maybe it's because whenever we have moments like this, it feels like I'm stealing a piece of him for myself. Like we're existing in borrowed time, and I know one day it will catch up to us.

Dean notices my tears and presses me extra close. "I know listening to Hozier borders on a religious experience, but I get the sense that you're not crying over Andrew," he murmurs in my hair.

"I'm just pre-missing you," I say into his chest.

He sighs, sending a wave of goosebumps from the crown of my head down my spine. "Yeah. Me too." We continue to sway, holding on to each other like this can last, but knowing it's more like holding on to sand cupped between our palms.

The song transitions to another on the album that I'm less familiar with, and Dean pulls back a little. Just enough so we can look each other in the eye. "Listen, I know I thought my unfinished business was solving my murder, but now I'm not so sure."

My brow furrows, and I ask, "What do you mean?"

He cups my jaw, tracing his thumb down the slope of my cheek tenderly. "You're my unfinished business, Rae. I can't leave this place knowing I'm leaving you behind."

The air whooshes out of me, and I close my eyes against the urge to tell him about the tether. "Dean, you can't stay here for me," I argue. "You deserve to go find peace. You deserve to find whatever's on the other side."

He shakes his head sadly. "I wouldn't know peace if I didn't have you. There would be no peace for me knowing I couldn't see you, be with you. Knowing that I *chose* to leave you."

"You don't know that," I say. "Rebecca just passed on, and right before she left, I could feel the other side for a moment. It was warm, Dean. And happy. If you went, you'd be okay. More than okay." My chin trembles with the strain of holding back a flood of tears.

"Do you not want me to stay?" he asks, his face suddenly guarded. "I'm sorry," he says, looking over my shoulder and clenching his jaw, "I should have asked before I assumed."

We stop swaying, and I say, "I want nothing more than to spend forever with you. I never want you to leave me."

"Then... What?" he asks, confused.

I swallow as something breaks in my chest. "Dean. I can't ask you to postpone eternity in paradise for me. I can't ask you to stay here in this fucked up world living a half-life when you can be somewhere better. You deserve that. You had your life ripped from you by a selfish asshole. I can't ask that you give me your eternity."

"You don't get it, do you?" Dean asks, pressing a hard kiss to my cheek, taking my tears between his lips. "*You* are my peace. I don't want any future that doesn't have you in it. I'm in love with you, Rae Alderwood. I'll gladly give up the cherubs and white fluffy clouds or whatever if it means I get to spend it with you."

My breath hitches, and I pull him in for a kiss, tasting the salt of my own tears. When we part, I say, "I love you, too."

He must see the hesitation on my face because he says, "Then what's wrong? What aren't you telling me? I can tell you've been holding something back for a while now, so what is it?" He raises one eyebrow. "You're not secretly married or something, are you?"

His expression lightens at my laugh. "No, definitely not," I say, thinking of Aunt C saying that he deserves to know his options and feel my resolve crumble. "When I was looking through that old grimoire, there was a journal entry," I say. And then I launch into the whole story, hardly pausing to catch my breath because I know if I do, I might chicken out.

"So, this tether. Does it hurt you in any way?" he asks afterwards.

I shake my head. "I don't know. I don't think so. It almost seems more like an energy exchange than anything. I think it's more a way to keep you here with me until I pass on, and then you go where I go."

"So, what's the downside? What's the big secret?"

"Um... That you would be stuck here until I died? And then even after that, I think you'd be stuck with me."

"Rae," he chastises with a scowl.

"What?" I ask, annoyed.

"That's not a downside. That's literally just a list of things I want to happen."

I search his face for any hesitation. Finding none, I venture, "Yeah?"

"Yes, Alderwood. Bind us together. I always knew I'd marry you," he says slyly, calling back to the conversation we had on our first date.

I hold my hands up, feeling my palms sweat. "Woah, woah. Who said anything about marriage?"

He snorts a laugh. "Uh, I'm pretty sure binding our souls together is much more serious than a piece of paper issued by the state of Massachusetts."

I tilt my head in consideration. "Okay, well I didn't see it that way until now. Listen, I want you to really think about this before we do it. Once it happens, I don't see how it can be undone. So let's wait until we fully solve your murder first, okay? I just want you to be sure."

Dean sighs and gathers me in close for a hug. "Okay, Alderwood. Whatever you need so you know I'm in this forever. No takesies backsies."

I laugh against his chest. "No takesies backsies?"

I feel him shake his head against my crown. "None."

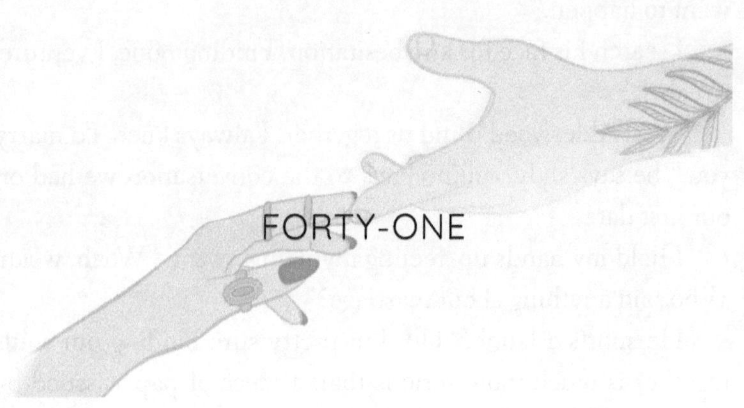

# FORTY-ONE

"OH MY GOD," I groan. I've never felt this relaxed before in my entire life. I sink further into Dean's giant jacuzzi tub, the steaming water cloaking me up to my neck. He convinced me to take a bath with him once we were done dancing. I didn't have it in me to argue with that, so here we are.

He's eyeing me from the other side of the tub, and somehow his gaze is both sweet and sinful. I close my eyes, savoring the languid lust brewing between us. "I'm glad you're enjoying this. Other than food, I miss this tub the most," he says wistfully, tracking a finger along the line of my shin.

I crack open my eyes when I feel his grip firm around my legs, massaging up my calves. I sigh into the simple pleasure of it. He applies deeper pressure as he works his way up to my thighs, digging into the muscle and finding knots I didn't even know existed. "Turn around," he asserts quietly.

I lift myself up and turn, draping my arms over the side of the tub, exposing my bare back to him. The air outside is cool, making me shiver while tendrils of steam float off my skin in languid coils. His hands slide up and around my back in lazy strokes, coaxing my muscles into relaxation and sending waves of heat between my legs. "Did I ever tell you how much I love this tattoo?" he asks, tracing a finger down my spine where the phases of the moon are laid out from just below my neck to my mid-back.

I smile sleepily against my crossed arms. "No, but I never told you how much I love your sleeve either, so I think we're even."

He glides his hands over my sides and around the front until he's cupping my breasts, lifting the heavy weight of them. I inhale slowly with pleasure when his fingers slide over my nipples, slippery with water and the aromatic oils we put in the bath. "Is this okay?" he asks, tracing a hand slowly down my stomach and between my legs.

"Yes," I breathe. He leans into me, using the pads of two fingers to trace decadent circles where I need him most.

I open my legs wider, and he nips my earlobe. "Look at you, riding my hand like a good girl." My eyes flutter at his filthy words, even while my cheeks burn. "Do you want me?" he asks, his hardness nudging my backside.

I lean forward in answer, bowing my back so he has a better angle. He grabs my hip with one hand and guides himself to my entrance with the other. He pauses, so I rock back into him, feeling him slip just barely inside. He tsks, pulling back. "You should know by now, Alderwood. I need your words."

"Yes, I want you inside of me," I pant. I can practically feel his smile as he seats himself fully. We both gasp as our thighs slide together. I rock my hips and meet him thrust for thrust, water sloshing against the sides of the tub in waves.

He wraps an arm around my waist and another over my chest, directing me to lean back with him until he's seated and I'm on his lap. He's managed to stay inside me the whole time, and the new position brings a deeper feeling of fullness. My eyes roll back as he positively surrounds me, guiding my hips the way he wants. His hands are everywhere—between my legs, over my breasts, possessively against the pulse point at my throat. I keep the motion going that has me forgetting the world outside this moment exists. He whispers praise in my ear and against my neck.

"I want you like this all the time for me," he bites out between clenched teeth. "Look at us," he says, chin on my shoulder, looking down at the blurry vision of us beneath the water. "Feel how good we are together," he demands, taking my hand and guiding it to where we're connected. It's too much. I feel everything inside me tighten. "You're mine, Rae Alderwood. For eternity."

He guides our hands to rub against where I'm the most sensitive, and before I can catch my breath, I shatter. It's so overwhelming, I let out a string of curses and praises, his name and the promise of forever on my lips over and over. His thrusts lose their rhythm, and then he speeds up until he shudders with his own release, water sloshing over the edge of the tub.

Eventually, I stand on shaky legs while he drains the tub and gets a towel off the heated rack for me. He wraps me in it, and I feel so exhausted suddenly, I could fall asleep standing up. Dean carefully squeezes my hair with a different towel, wringing the water out like he's watched me do.

He guides me to his bed, coaxing me to drop the towels and slip beneath the softest sheets I've ever laid on. I can barely keep my eyes open, so I don't. I close them and feel Dean wrap himself around me like a heavy, tingling vine, luring me into a deep sleep.

---

BUZZ. *Buzz.* I snuggle deeper into Dean's chest, chasing the dream I was having. I really need to be back on that ship. I was being called a wench, and I was very into it.

*Buzz. Buzz.* "Rae?"

"Ungh," I complain, screwing my eyes shut.

"You should probably get that. Whoever it is has called you like three times now," Dean says.

I sigh grumpily, reaching my bare arm out towards the nightstand where I threw my phone last night.

"Hullo?" I ask, putting the phone up to my ear before I even check who's calling.

"Rae?" Jack's voice blasts in my ear.

"Jack, hi." I sit up, taking the covers with me. "What's going on?" I ask. I pull my phone away from my ear to see it's just after 8 A.M on Saturday.

"Remember Amari? The other associate at my firm," he clarifies.

I put my phone on speaker for Dean's sake and say, "Yeah. Dean told me a little about him."

"Well, he just went to the police station last night. I guess Richard had gone to him back in July, asking if he wanted to help him kill Dean."

"What?" I all but shout.

"Yeah," Jack bites, the steel in his voice sharp enough to cut, "Amari laughed it off, so Richard pretended it was just a joke. About a week before Dean died, Richard brought it up to

Amari again. He said something along the lines of 'Wouldn't it be great if Dean were gone? Then we'd have a fair competition for partner.'"

Anger licks white hot flames up my spine. "Why didn't he come forward until now? It's been months!"

Jack sighs long and deep. I hear the clinking of a glass and the splash of what sounds like something being decanted. Jack takes a drink and replies, "I know. He thought Richard was joking. And when Dean was found dead, it looked like a suicide, so he brushed it off. It wasn't until Richard got caught with these drugs that Amari realized he was being serious. He saw that Richard is a shitty person, totally capable of heinous behavior, and his gut told him he needed to come forward."

"So, just to confirm, this guy passed the BAR, right? Like, your coworker says, 'OMG wouldn't it be so funny if he were dead?' And then he *winds up dead,* and you don't say anything?!" I screech.

"He probably didn't want to get in trouble, or be looked at as an accomplice," Jack states, his weariness clear over the line. "Oh, and I also spoke with my P.I. yesterday. He said the GHB finding in the autopsy was bogus. It definitely should have been a urine sample. But the county coroner has been in practice for decades, so it's unlikely they could or would do much to prove he intentionally botched the report."

I take Dean's hand in mine and squeeze. He's worrying me with his faraway look. "So, what now?" I ask.

"I just got off the phone with the detective. We're in luck because the one who got assigned to this case is a young guy who hopefully hasn't gotten the chance to get wrapped up in all the corruption. He's putting in an order for a search warrant for Richard's house and is going to try to get it pushed through today so Richard doesn't have a chance to hide anything."

I slowly exhale the breath that had been stuck in my chest. "Okay. I hope they find something."

"Me too. And listen, Rae, I know you aren't one to run your mouth, but keep this whole thing between us. No one knows Amari went to the police, and they want to keep it that way so they can hopefully surprise Richard. I called mostly so you can update my son, who I'm sure is within arm's reach as we speak," Jack says, amusement lightening his tone.

I feel my cheeks redden when Dean laughs a little, muscles bunching in his stomach in a very distracting manner. "You got it," I quip. "Keep me updated." We say our goodbyes and end the phone call.

I stand up and stretch, reaching my arms up above my head. Even with the rude wakeup, that's the best night of sleep I've gotten in a long time. Dean's eyes stay trained on my chest, and I snap my fingers to get his attention.

"What? You thought you could just be naked and sexy in front of me and I wouldn't look?" he asks incredulously.

"Well, I thought you were kind of used to it by now," I say, tossing my shirt from last night back over my head.

"I'll never be used to it, Alderwood. You will always be the best thing to look at in the room."

"Even when I'm old and saggy?" I ask. It's something I've thought about with the whole tether thing. He'll stay the same, but I'll age. One day, I'll look old enough to be his grandmother.

"Even then," he says, dimple peeking out. "A beautiful woman is a beautiful woman. Age is but a number. I'm ready for you to be whatever the female equivalent of a silver fox is for me."

"Silver vixen?" I supply.

Dean nods his head. "Yup." He chomps his teeth and winks.

"Well, we have at least a few years until then," I say.

"You're not even thirty," Dean counters with a scoff. "I think we have more than a few years."

"Whatever. I feel closer to sixty than twenty these days," I complain. "You're knocking years off my life."

"Maybe that's been my plan all along so I can have you over here sooner," he says, bouncing his eyebrows. I slip on my sweats and laugh.

"Well, lucky for you, I have something else going on today that takes years off my life," I say.

"What's that?" Dean asks, standing and suddenly clad in a casual t-shirt and jeans.

"It's the second Saturday of the month, which means it's time for a Main Street Business meeting," I say with a sigh. "I fucking hate public speaking. And it's worse now that my secret is out and everyone knows. They're all going to be looking at me." I shiver, hating the idea of it. If I could have chosen my Gift, invisibility would have been high on the list.

"Does it help to know that I will also be looking at you?" Dean asks, flitting in front of me.

I tilt my head side to side. "Maybe a little."

"Good," he says, leaning in to kiss me so thoroughly, I forget all about my social anxiety.

# FORTY-TWO

I CONVINCED Wren to go with me to the meeting, and despite her constant grumbling, I'm glad she did. It's been an odd feeling knowing that everyone knows I'm a medium, but nothing has come of it. People have been kind to me, but I could see the barely-restrained questions on their minds. Now when I walk among the cramped bookcases of The Cracked Spine, I feel too many eyes on me. Every time I turn to look at someone and meet their stare, they look away.

I feel like a social pariah in middle school again, and I want to crawl out of my skin.

Dean presses more firmly into my side, and Wren grits her teeth from the other. "The next person who looks our way is getting their eyes melon balled."

I sink further in my seat as Mr. Chase, the owner of Raven-wood Antiques, drones on and on about the upcoming Thanksgiving Day parade, various preparations we all need to make, the type of decor we should hang in our shop windows, etc. etc.

It's disconcerting to have my heart pounding like it wants to escape the cage of my chest and simultaneously be bored out of my mind.

Mr. Chase claps his hands heartily. "Okay! That's all I have for the Thanksgiving parade. Miss Alderwood, let's hear about your Night Before All Hallows Eve Ball." He gestures for me to come to the front of the semi-circle of chairs.

I stand on shaky legs, clutching my index cards tightly. Anytime one of us hosts an event, we're asked to debrief, especially when the others chip in like they did for our auction table. I lean back against the checkout desk and face the thirty or so people staring back at me.

I look past the first row of faces and concentrate on my sister and Dean, who both give me an obnoxious thumbs-up. I take a deep breath and begin reading from my notecards, detailing what went well and what could have been changed. I thank each business that provided us with a donation, and then I'm finally done.

My armpits are absolutely gushing sweat by the time I finish reading my last notecard. I give the audience a tight smile and turn to walk back to my seat. "Any questions?" Mr. Chase asks, holding a staying hand out to me. I stop in my tracks like a rabbit sensing a predator and turn a hesitant eye out to the crowd. My stomach bottoms out when half of the hands shoot up.

"Uh, yeah, Carlos?" I say, gesturing to the owner of The Cracked Spine.

He stands from his seat and says, "Is it true you're the medium who's been helping people the last few months?"

*And now the dam breaks.*

My eyes sting, but I will not cry.

"Um, yeah. I am," I say shortly. I hear a snort and find Misha sitting next to Julian in the back row of chairs.

"Have you always been able to see ghosts?" someone else asks from the crowd.

*Okay, time to wake up now! Am I naked?*

I tilt my head down to check. Nope, still clothed, so this must not be a nightmare. Great.

I swallow around the lump in my throat and nod. "Yes, my whole life."

"This isn't a scam, correct? We can't have false mysticism on Main Street. We're better than that," Mr. Chase says.

I clench my teeth. "No."

"Then why haven't you told anyone?" Sarah, the owner of the diner, asks skeptically, crossing her arms over her ample chest.

My anger kicks up from a simmer into a full boil. "Maybe because you all would think I was crazy?" I ask incredulously. "But you know what? I've *helped* some of you in this room talk to your grandmas and your fathers and your loved ones. I'm sorry if it feels like I deceived you, but I had a right to my privacy."

"She did help me talk to my gram," Declan, the owner of the frozen yogurt shop, pipes up. "She told me things only my gram would have known. And she was right about the jewelry hidden behind my grandparents' framed wedding picture. There's just no way Rae could have made that up on her own."

"Yeah, and I was able to feel the presence of my dad," the manager of the corner pharmacy says. "See? I get goosebumps just thinking about it," he states, holding his freckled arm up for everyone to look at. My heart warms the tiniest bit at these people jumping to my defense.

"I'm not scamming anyone," I reiterate. "And if I am unable to make contact, the person doesn't have to pay me a dime."

Mr. Chase can't seem to help himself though. "Miss Alderwood, if I may ask, why now? If this has been a skill you've had your whole life, why are you just now charging for it?" Mr. Chase asks.

I shift on my feet, but they already know we're struggling, so I say, "Because the store needed the extra income, okay? I thought I could help people and help The Veil. You all are aware of our financial situation." I cross my arms, further crumpling my index cards.

There. It feels good to finally own it. All of it. I see ghosts, and The Veil is struggling.

Mr. Chase nods amiably, completely unruffled by my prickly attitude.

"You aren't going to start doing ghost tours?" the pharmacy manager asks.

Despite myself, I laugh a bit. "No. Ghosts usually don't just hang around one place. And once they see me, they start haunting me. I only offer my services as a medium to people who need it. It's not a gimmick. I've been helping spirits and their loved ones my whole life."

I start to unclench my muscles when I see the crowd ahead of me nod amongst themselves. I can feel the metaphorical pitchforks lowering and thank whatever deity is listening that I wasn't born three hundred years ago. A rope around the neck doesn't sound like a good time.

"Anything else?" I ask tiredly. Multiple eager hands shoot up. "Anything else that's not about my seeing ghosts?" I clarify. Every single hand lowers, so I say, "You're welcome to come find me in the store if you have any more questions about this.

But this is my private life, not a public spectacle. So please respect that." I pause for a moment and then, sensing my freedom, speed walk out of the center of the semi-circle and head back to my chair.

"Proud of you," Wren says in my ear, her cinnamon-scented breath fanning over my face.

I nudge her shoulder with mine, and feel the tension slowly draining from my body. It's actually kind of nice having everyone know. At least I'll be less on edge when a spirit shows up in public now.

Mr. Chase takes center stage again, this time holding a clipboard with a thick sheaf of paper clipped to it. "Our last order of business tonight is this petition. As we all know, Mr. Beauhurst is raising rent on our entire block of buildings. While I believe an increase is fair to keep up with the market, the percentage at which he's raising rates is uncalled for. It will push many of our businesses out over time because very few of us can afford it. So, I created this petition to ask Mr. Beauhurst to lower the rate of increase to a more manageable level. Are there any questions?"

Everyone was nodding along while Mr. Chase spoke, and I feel a surge of gratitude that we aren't the only ones struggling and that maybe we can all band together and make a difference. Sarah raises her hand and says, "Where do I sign?"

The meeting wraps up quickly afterward, and soon enough, we're all helping to drag our chairs through the labyrinth of shelves toward the stock room. I brush shoulders with Misha in the cramped stock room and cringe away before he can look over his shoulder and see who he bumped into.

I walk hurriedly through the shelves, trying to get out of the store before Misha catches up with me. I know I told Ivan I would talk to Misha soon, but that doesn't have to mean today, right? I've had enough inquisition into my Gift for one day.

Just when I see Wren and Dean waiting for me by the door, I hear, "Rae! Wait up!" behind me.

My shoulders kiss my ears, and I turn slowly. Misha holds a hand to me with Julian right behind him. I sigh, letting my shoulders drop. It'll be just like ripping off a Band-Aid. Too bad I always leave mine on until they eventually peel off into a soggy beige heap on my shower floor.

"Walk with me?" Misha asks when they catch up.

"Sure. But Wren will have to come too." I gesture to the scowling gargoyle in question, looking like she's trying to ward off the evil that is Julian.

"Oh, that's fine. Wren and I will stay to chat for a bit, and then we'll catch up with you guys," Julian says, a much too pleased smile playing over his face. Then, he gently nudges me aside and practically skips toward Wren, whose scowl deepens so much it looks painful.

Misha and I laugh after him, and I feel my heart lighten a bit. I'm not great with conflict, and I always want to shrivel up when I know someone is mad at me.

"Fifty bucks says they're going to end up married with angry little babies," Misha says, looking after them.

I snort. "You're on. Never gonna happen."

We head down the shelves and pass Wren, who looks at me like I just made it to first place on her shit-list. Ah well, I've been there before. Julian is yammering on about various frosting piping tips and the merits of each one, talking so quickly, he barely seems to breathe. Misha leads me out into the brisk November air, Dean trailing far enough behind to give us privacy, but close enough that I know he's there.

We start walking down the street toward The Veil and Brewed Awakening, the cold air nipping at our noses. "So," I say when I can't take his silence anymore, kicking a stone out of the way with the toe of my boot. "What's up?"

I look up at Misha who studies me with a pensive expression screwing up his handsome face. "You really can see ghosts?" he finally asks.

I nod tiredly. "Yeah. I really can."

*Here we go again.*

"And I take it this is a secret you've been holding onto your whole life that you didn't want revealed any time soon?"

"Yup," I say shortly, feeling some of the anger return from the night of the ball.

Misha winces, scratching the back of his neck. "I'm sorry about that. I didn't mean to be the one to expose your secret. I'm usually pretty sensitive to that. It's no excuse, but I was doubly freaked out by finding out it was you all along, and I—I could tell Ivan was there. I didn't want to believe it, but I could feel him."

He's visibly shaken, so I reach out and wrap an arm around his waist. His arm drops over my shoulders, and I can feel the tension ebb out of him. I take a deep inhale and offer, "I'm sorry for lying. When you started telling me about your past, I should have stopped you. I felt stuck, and I just wanted to help you," I say quietly.

He squeezes my shoulders in a sort of hug and sighs. "No, I get it. I guess I should have figured that whoever was behind the curtain was potentially someone I knew. I wasn't thinking, and it wasn't fair of me to treat you like that when I found out. I was embarrassed, and I took it out on you."

I shake my head. "You have nothing to be embarrassed

about. Trauma should only be embarrassing for the people who caused it, not the people who suffered it. You were just a kid. You should have had a better adult in your corner. I thought it was honorable that you wanted to try to make amends with him, even though he doesn't deserve it."

"To be honest, it's more about me than him. I don't want to live out the rest of my life regretting what I said to him. I don't know. I heard someone say that forgiveness is more for you than for the person you're forgiving. I need that peace."

"Well, if you're up for it, we can try to find it for you," I offer. "Your uncle actually came back to talk to me. He wants to try to make amends, too." I gloss over the whole aggressive shoulder grab thing because it isn't Misha's fault, and I don't want him to carry any extra guilt.

"Yeah?"

I nod. "Yeah. The first time I made contact was a little rough because he didn't want to come through. And I kind of forced him," I say, ducking my head. "So that's why he was so resistant. This time should be smoother since he wants to come forward."

"Wow, I bet he was pissed. Uncle Ivan is an old mule; any time he's forced into something, he resists tenfold."

I clear my throat as we slow to a stop in front of The Veil. "Yeah, I got that impression. Do you want to meet after work tomorrow?"

"Sure. Your place?" He points up towards my apartment.

"Deal." I blow warm air into my cupped palms and then shove them deep in my pockets. "I'm glad we talked, Mish," I say quietly. I have very few friends, and the thought that I had lost one of them hurt more than I care to admit.

"Me too. And hey, now that I know your big dark secret,

maybe you can stop saying no to hanging out with me and Felix," he says with a raised brow.

I blush at being clocked so easily. Just as I'm opening my mouth to respond, a clawed hand grasps the back of my coat and spins me around. "You owe me your firstborn," Wren hisses in my ear.

"Sure," I reply easily, knowing I'll never have kids.

"No fair. Let me think of something you'll genuinely miss," she says, stomping her petite foot.

"What a nice night," Julian remarks, strolling up oh-so-casually.

Wren's eyes narrow so much, I wonder if she can even see. "You're polluting it with your pine-y vanilla stink," Wren complains.

Julian's smile slowly widens as he practically coos, "Vanilla and pine, huh?"

I do a double-take when I notice Wren blush so much, even her pierced ears turn red. "Shut up," she sputters. "I have to go feed my cat."

My brow furrows. "When did you get a cat?" I ask.

Her glare is so sharp, I find myself mentally cataloguing my body for injury. "Just yesterday. She's a stray."

"A feral cat, huh? Sounds like you two have a lot in common," Julian says amicably.

Wren just grunts and slinks away, rounding the corner to where she's parked her car behind mine.

I shake my head after her and meet Misha's eye. "Told you," he says with a smug smile.

"Told her what?" Julian asks suspiciously.

"Nothing," we respond together, grinning.

# FORTY-THREE

I CONCENTRATE ON DEAN, calling him forth from the ether. He was resting after a long day at the police station. He's been there for a while to get updates on Richard. The police didn't find much at his apartment, but they did seize his phone and computer. I'm worried that all of the sudden attention from the police will spook Richard and make him run.

Dean's presence wraps around me like a warm blanket before he's suddenly in front of me. I tilt my head and beckon him into the stockroom. There's only one customer wandering around the store for now, and he's deep in the books, so I think I'm safe to sneak off for a minute.

When I close the door, Dean crowds me against it and kisses me breathless. Eventually, the hazy reason for me calling him here floats to the front of my mind, and I gently push him back, breaking the kiss. "What? Is this not a booty call? Get it? Boo-ty call," Dean snickers and waves his arms like a cartoon ghost.

I laugh quietly so the tourist out there doesn't think I lost my marbles, and say, "No. I was just thinking that maybe you should watch Richard. What if he tries to run or something?"

Dean sighs. "Yeah, that's probably a better use of my time. I'll go watch him." Then he brightens a little. "At least they took his computer so I don't have to watch him... Ya know..." He makes an obscene gesture at his crotch, and I hold out a hand to stop him.

"Yep, I got it." I shiver. "Just keep an eye on him. Make sure he doesn't look like he's grabbing for his passport or anything."

"You got it, boss," Dean says with a mock salute. He leans in, pecking me on the lips once before he vanishes.

---

"ALRIGHT EVERYONE, that's the last order for the night. Thanks for watching!" I say, waving my hand in front of my phone camera. I have it set up so it's facing my desk with some fun purple lighting and mystical set pieces to add to the mood. I click off the live video and stand, stretching out my sore back. I sit like an overcooked shrimp for an hour and then wonder why I have upper back pain.

I'm glad that Misha isn't coming over until he finishes closing Brewed Awakening. It gave me a chance to do a live potion pull. It's been a while, and it always boosts sales for our online store. I spend the next twenty minutes packaging the orders from the live and stress cleaning my living room.

A knock at the door saves the dust bunnies under my couch. I sigh, getting to my feet and stowing my vacuum in my broom closet. I cross the room to my front door and open it to find Misha clutching two to-go cups.

"Is that your hot chocolate?" I ask hopefully.

He grins at me, dropping one of the cups into my grabby hands. "Yes. I figured you'd need your fix since you've been avoiding me," he says with a genuine grin.

I gesture him inside, taking a sip of the chocolatey deliciousness rather than responding to his comment. I take his cup too, giving him a chance to shed all his outer layers, and guide him into my living room.

"This place is very you," Misha remarks, looking around.

"A mess?" I ask with a laugh.

"No. Warm. Lots of wonderful things smushed together," he says happily as we sit on my couch. "A little spooky," he continues, gesturing to the taxidermied moths hanging in gilt frames on my walls.

I push his shoulder and bat my lashes at him playfully. "Are you flirting with me?"

"You know, Felix and I *have* been looking for a third," he deadpans.

I cackle and cover my flushed cheeks with my fingertips. "If I remember correctly, you once told me that I don't have the proper anatomy for that. And besides, I'm seeing someone who doesn't like to share." Now it's my turn to smirk at him.

He inhales sharply and leans in. "Tell me everything," he orders. And I do, relishing in his gasps of both horror and delight. "You saucy little minx," he says once I've brought him (mostly) up to speed. "Getting yourself a supernatural hottie. Some of us can only dream and write fan fiction about it." He sighs a beleaguered sigh.

"Yeah, he's pretty great," I say, feeling myself get all starry-eyed while I think about Dean.

Misha shakes his head at me good-naturedly.

After I drain the last dregs of my hot chocolate, I ask, "Okay, are you ready?"

He sits up straighter and nods. "Let's do this."

"Just a forewarning, your uncle is difficult. I know you know that, but let's just say it has continued into the afterlife," I warn.

He laughs humorlessly. "That doesn't surprise me. Let's get this over with." He takes my empty cup from me and sets them both on my coffee table.

I cast my awareness out and am unsurprised to find Ivan hovering nearby. I had a feeling he hadn't gone far since our last little run-in. I try not to let it give me the heebie-jeebies and call him forth.

He comes willingly, popping into existence with a violent burst of static that makes me flinch. "Finally," he grouses.

"Are you willing to cooperate this time?" I ask, watching as he struts to my chair and sits like a king upon a throne.

He grunts, looking like he's trying to work up either a belch or a fart, but his current state of being doesn't allow it. He looks disappointed by that fact.

"He's here, Misha," I say, gesturing to his uncle. Misha slowly turns to face him.

"Hi, Uncle Ivan. Long time, no see," he says, laughing awkwardly. Ivan scowls and crosses his arms. Misha looks to me for reassurance, and I nod. "So, I wanted to talk to you. I know the last conversation we had ended badly, and I wanted to make things right."

Ivan snorts derisively and says, "That's one way to put it. As I recall you called me an asshole and told me to go rot in hell."

I chew on my lip, reluctant to repeat what Ivan said. When

he turns his glare on me, I sigh and reiterate the gist of what he said, trying to take some of the sting out of the words.

Misha looks down at his lap, rubbing the goose bumps on his arms. "I know. I know I said that to you and then you were just gone," he pauses to look back towards the chair, "All I've wanted every day since is to have a chance to speak with you and tell you how sorry I am for what I said."

Ivan sits forward, elbows resting on his massive thighs. "Because of you, I couldn't move on. You became my unfinished business, whether I wanted it or not. Was everything I did for you not enough? You had to fuck up my death?"

I scowl at Ivan and say aloud, "I'm not repeating that because it's bullshit."

Misha turns a puzzled look my way, and Ivan stands, getting in my face in a blink. "You'll tell him what I said like a good little witch," he spits.

"Then be nicer. You're being a dick and I'm over it," I say, crossing my arms.

"I—it's okay," Misha says, reaching out and touching my arm, "He's allowed to be upset. I did say some awful things to him." I watch as he shrinks into a smaller, more vulnerable shell of himself. I see the scared little boy he used to be painted across the furrow of his brow and his tightly clenched fists.

"See? He knows he should be sorry," Ivan says, gesturing to Misha.

"What is your unfinished business, exactly?" I ask Ivan sharply. He gestures to Misha, and I say, "I know. But what exactly do you need to say to him? Listen to your gut." I glare at him until he looks away.

Ivan backs up a bit, stepping through my coffee table as he thinks. He looks down at his legs, which have disappeared through the table, and then says, "He needs to know that I never cared about the gay thing. I know I could be hard on him, but I was never angry about that." He crosses his arms uncomfortably.

I breathe out the breath that was held hostage in my chest and relay what he said to Misha.

"Then, why did you shut down after I told you?" Misha asks in a small voice. I take his warm hand in mine, hoping to give him an anchor point.

Ivan rakes his hand through his thinning gray hair. "I didn't know how to respond! I wasn't angry about it, but I also didn't know what you wanted from me. I fucked up just about everything as your parent. Every single thing. I didn't want to fuck this up too." Against my will, I feel a little empathy for Ivan taking root.

After I repeat what he said, Misha responds, "All you needed to say was that you were happy for me. That you accepted me. When you went silent, I couldn't help but think the worst."

"And see? I fucked it up anyway," Ivan says. For the first time, I start to consider that all his raging around is just a front. It's not an excuse for being an asshole, but it does offer an explanation. "Of course I still accepted you. I was just glad you told me. When you left at seventeen, I thought that was it for us." He stares off, eyes locked on my peeling wallpaper. "I'm sorry I didn't make the effort. I was the adult. I should have reached out. Instead, like a coward, I waited for you to do it. And once I finally had you back, I was too worried about messing things up again."

Misha listens, eyes getting a sheen to them as I convey Ivan's message. "I forgive you, Ivan."

"I forgive you, too, kid. I deserved to be called an asshole and told where I could stick it. I'm not proud of who I am, but I am proud of how you turned out despite all my best efforts," Ivan says with a self-deprecating snort. "All I want is for you to be happier than I was."

"He is," I say, squeezing Misha's hand. "He's such a great person, and he makes the best hot chocolate." Ivan smiles at that, and he suddenly looks decades younger.

I tell Misha what Ivan said, and he responds, "I wish we had more time. Until I met Felix, I was totally alone. I regretted what I said every day. I always worried that our fight contributed to your heart attack."

Ivan shakes his head. "You always did want to make everything your fault. No kid, my heart attack was courtesy of the bottom of too many bottles and an endless chain of cigarettes." He sighs, rubbing his fingers together as if he's searching for his next fix. "And before I go, I want you to know how much I love you. How much I respect you. And how glad I was to raise you, even if I did screw up a lot. I didn't tell you that enough when I was alive."

When I tell Misha what he said, he starts crying in earnest, the tears he was holding back flooding over his lashes. "I love you, too, Uncle Ivan. Thank you for coming back so we could talk."

I reach out to Ivan, and when he looks at my hand like it might bite him, I sigh. "Go on, if you're touching me, you can touch him. You both look like you could use a hug," I say. I hope this works with more than just Dean.

Ivan takes my hand, his large, calloused one swallowing mine. Misha and I stand, and Ivan pulls Misha in for a hug against his broad chest with his free arm. Misha's eyes widen and then scrunch closed as he hugs Ivan back, hard. After a while, Ivan gives Misha a few manly thumps on the back and then lets go.

He steps back, and focuses on something not even I can see. "I think it's time for me to go," he says distantly before disappearing in a shower of light.

I sigh, glad that death had finally made Ivan see a little more clearly and that today didn't end in a screaming match. "He's gone," I say quietly.

And then I hold Misha while he cries and tells me all the ways his uncle hurt him and healed him growing up. How Misha screamed and shouted in equal measure. How he left, and they finally found themselves on fragile ground. How much regret he's carried since their last fight. We even laugh at a memory of Ivan screaming at Misha's high school soccer coach for benching him. "To be honest, I was terrible at soccer, but it was nice to have him on my side anyway," Misha says with a small smile as he wipes a stray tear from his cheek.

I'm struck by how much I love this and how at ease I feel. The last couple of months, while I've been helping people communicate with the dead, there was always this undercurrent of fear. I was so scared I'd be found out. Now that it's out there, I feel that little piece of myself click into place. I've always helped the dead, but this is the first time I've felt like maybe I can help the living, too. Maybe I don't need to hide behind a curtain. Maybe I can just be me.

# FORTY-FOUR

IT'S BEEN a few days since Ivan moved on, and I'm badgering Wren into making me a fancy coffee at Brewed. She must be tired because she gives in, willing to add both toasted marshmallow *and* brown sugar to my latte in a for-here mug.

When she sets it down in front of me, I quirk a brow. "Wow, you're getting good at that," I say, gesturing to the foam middle finger gracing the top of my latte.

"Lots of practice lately," she replies casually. "Mish, I'm taking my ten," she calls over her shoulder to Misha, who is cleaning the bar. He waves in acknowledgement, and Wren sits next to me on the plush couch facing the floor-to-ceiling windows so we can people watch.

"What're you looking at?" she asks, peering over my shoulder at my laptop.

"I'm going over our profit and trying to see how this could work. If Aunt C would go to a retirement home closer to us, we'd probably be able to make it because they're cheaper around here, but she's dead set on this Florida place." I rub my neck where I feel a tension headache brewing.

"Have you talked to her about it?" Wren asks.

"Yeah. She's insisting. If we can't make it work, she's willing to sell the store. She's gotten a few offers that have been hard to refuse, but she's been hanging onto it for me." I take a sip of my latte, displacing the middle finger so it looks more blobby than crude.

Wren scowls. "That's bullshit, Rae. You've put a ton of work into that store, and helped it grow so much in the last five years. Aunt C is being really selfish."

I shrug and reply, "Maybe, but there's not much I can do to stop her. I don't have any rights to the store."

"Have you thought about getting a business loan? I know you were planning on buying it from her eventually."

"I have a decent amount saved up, but I couldn't afford to pay back a loan and keep the store afloat with the rent increase in January," I say with a tired sigh. Dean's proposition that I move into his house hits me, and I shake my head against the thought. There's no way I can do that.

"What did you just think about? You got all weird," she flutters her fingers around me, referring to my aura.

I close my eyes because I'm incapable of lying to her. When she jabs me in the ribs with a sharp fingernail, my eyes fly open and I glare at her. "Dean had an idea," I say slowly. She raises her eyebrows and gestures for me to continue. "He offered to have me move into his house so I can rent out my apartment. It would probably make up the difference in finances, especially if I scale up our online store, but there's no way I can do it, obviously."

"The giant house in the middle of a meadow?" she asks. I

nod. "The one you compared to the Cullens' house?" I nod again.

She flicks me on the arm. Hard. "Ow!" I exclaim, rubbing the sore spot. "What the hell?" I grumble. She doesn't usually resort to physical violence, so this is a fun new development.

"Why wouldn't you?" she asks incredulously.

"It's too much. His family would basically be giving it to me. And it's like, a cajillion-dollar home." I shift in my seat. "And anyway, he hasn't talked to them about it. It's technically theirs since he died. They might not even go for it."

"I think this is another example of you shutting down a good thing because you're scared," she replies. "If Dean told them this is what he wanted, I doubt they'd say no. Especially after everything you've told me about them."

I shake my head, taking a sip of my latte. "I don't know. I hate relying on other people for anything. It would feel like charity."

"Rae," Dean says, suddenly in front of us.

I start a little, and say oh-so-casually, "Hey, Dean, what's up?" I ask, trying to look like we weren't just talking about his proposition. Wren looks at him, eyebrows drawn tight together.

"He's trying to leave. You need to call the police now. Richard is going to run," Dean says, squatting so he's directly in front of me.

I sit up straighter. "Where is he going?"

Dean shakes his head, running an anxious hand through his hair. "I don't know. I followed him to the car, thinking he was just getting out of the house. But then I realized he had a whole bag packed, a cooler, and a few extra gallons of gas. When I left, he was headed north. I think he's going to Canada."

"Canada? Shit," I hiss. "Okay, I'm going to place an anonymous tip." Dean tells me the exact road Richard was on, and I call the police, hoping he was told not to leave the state. That way, they'll have reason to stop him.

After the dispatcher assures me they're sending a police officer after him, I thank her and hang up, palms sweaty. "She said they were sending someone after him," I tell Dean and Wren.

"Okay. I'm going to go track him down again, in case they don't catch him. The longer I'm away from his last location, the harder it will be for me to find him again since he's going somewhere unknown," Dean says, looking like he's about to break into a sprint.

"Keep me updated," I say, leaning in to accept the kiss he places on my forehead. He salutes and is gone in a blink.

"That fucking Richard guy definitely did it," Wren states, who has clearly been eaves dropping on my side of the conversation. "No one runs to another country if they're innocent."

"Hopefully they catch him," I say, hating that I just have to sit here and wait to see what happens. I text Jack, letting him know what's going on. He and I have been chatting back and forth the last few days as they scoured Richard's devices. They were unable to find anything damning (aside from a large, morally questionable porn collection). I know Jack is starting to lose hope.


Dean

I sit in the passenger seat, engaging in my favorite pastime as of late: berating Richard to his stupid face. He can't hear me anyway, so I may as well. It's the only fun I can have while I'm away from Rae.

I have a sinking suspicion that the dispatcher wasn't taking Rae seriously. They either didn't send someone or made it seem unimportant to whoever she did send. Hours have gone by without even passing a speed trap.

I try not to panic as day slips into night, and we pass the "Welcome to New Hampshire" sign. The state motto "Live free or die" really takes on a whole new meaning these days.

Richard readjusts in his seat for the fiftieth time, and I'm about to lose my mind if he does what I think he's going to do with that empty Gatorade bottle... Annnnnd yep. It's happening. The trickling sound is overly loud because he's the type of psychopath to drive in total silence.

I grimace, secretly hoping his knee-driving sucks and he rams his stupid Audi into the concrete divider. He is swerving a little, so it's not totally out of the realm of possibility. I perk up a little. He pops the cap back on to the world's worst flavor of Gatorade and chucks it out the window.

"Dude, seriously?" I gripe at him. Fucking litterers. It's not enough to have murdered me, you also have to try to murder the planet? I can't believe I was ever friendly with this guy.

Red and blue swirling lights light up the cab in a dizzying pattern, and I turn to look behind us. "Fuck," Richard shouts, voice breaking. The police siren sounds, and he immediately ducks like he can avoid being seen.

I kick back, letting my feet drift through the footwell, ready to enjoy the show.

*Finally.*

The car lurches forward, and I look toward Richard. "You are such a dumbass," I say, watching the speedometer climb towards eighty, then tick past it. He starts swerving around traffic, pushing the gas pedal down until we're eating up the roadway, going nearly a hundred miles per hour. Thankfully, there aren't a ton of people on the road at 8 P.M. on a Tuesday, so he probably won't kill anyone else.

"Pull over," the officer says over his loudspeaker. He's kept pace with us easily so far. Maybe Richard should have watched more *Need For Speed* and less *Barely Legal Busty Babes.*

*Now there's an image I'd gladly get lobotomized to remove.*

Richard refuses to pull over. He inches the speedometer forward a touch more, white knuckling his steering wheel as sweat pours down the sides of his face. Really glad I can't smell anymore; I'm sure the scent profile in this car is more barn animal than Armani right now.

"Pull over, now," the cop says through the loudspeaker, voice betraying his agitation.

Richard presses on, suddenly veering across three lanes of traffic and haphazardly taking an exit. I grab for the handhold on instinct before I remember I'm dead. Death has few perks, but at least I can't die again.

He swerves around the few other cars that are also taking the exit, laying on their horns as we shoot past.

I close my eyes against the rapidly approaching red light. Richard huffs a breath like he's prepping a deadlift and then yanks the steering wheel hard to the right, skidding into oncoming traffic. I crack my eyes open again once I'm sure I won't have to watch Richard get t-boned. We're flying through town, buildings flashing by in a blur, and I grudgingly have to wonder at his luck. How is it possible that he hasn't hit anyone yet?

He's taking seemingly random turns, trying to lose the cops chasing us.

Listen, I don't condone running from the cops. But I have

to say, as a passive bystander, it's actually kind of fun. Obviously, I want him to get caught, but it's always been a secret bucket list item of mine to take part in a police chase. Working behind a desk most of the day leaves a lot to be desired.

We're on the outskirts of town, flying down a country road, when the loudest *BANG! BANG!* I've ever heard nearly explodes my eardrums. Richard swerves, losing control of the car and bumping over the rocky shoulder of the road. His car comes to an aggressive stop, and he breathes heavily in the sudden silence, staring out at the large pasture of cows. They all have their heads swiveled toward us, eyes aglow in the headlights of the car, chewing the cud in their mouths. It's actually kind of creepy. Maybe the creepiest thing I've seen since I died. Something about their nearly identical expressionless faces turned our way makes me shiver.

Richard bangs his hand hard on the steering wheel. Almost instantly, the car is surrounded by state troopers and officers shouting at Richard to put his hands up.

He slowly lifts shaking hands in the air, chin trembling like a toddler. An officer approaches his door, gun drawn and trained on Richard. He throws the door open and says, "Unbuckle your seatbelt and get out of the car. I want to see both hands up."

"Yes, sir," Richard replies, nodding aggressively as if enthusiastic compliance can save him from the fact that he was leading the officers on a ten-minute car chase. I get out of the car to find that all of his tires have been popped, which explains the loud noise just before Richard lost control.

They handcuff him for evading the police, explaining that he was only going to get a littering ticket before he ran, but now the charges are likely to be much worse. Two officers were sort of joking around with him, but when a short female officer comes back with his I.D., they all take a cue from her serious expression. "Are you Richard Morganstern?" the officer asks.

Richard swallows thickly. "Yes, ma'am," he says.

"Mr. Morganstern, did you know you were under orders not to leave the state of Massachusetts?" the officer asks, setting his I.D. on the hood of his car. I lean in closer to get her name. Officer Rickman. She might just be my new favorite person.

Richard feigns confusion. "I was?"

"Yes. It says right here that you are currently under investigation for the murder of Dean Crawford. As such, you were told not to leave the state without approval."

Richard readjusts his shoulders, clearly uncomfortable with the handcuffs. "I'd like to speak with my lawyer," he states firmly.

"Sure. You can have him meet you down at the station. Although it might be a while since you're about nine hours from home," Officer Rickman says, thin lips pursed.

Richard nods as a different officer begins leading him by the arm to one of the police cars. Just before he gets shoved in the back of the cruiser, I watch his aggressively fake-tanned face blanche as a couple of officers begin going through his car. I smile slowly, knowing in my gut that they're going to find something.

I feel suddenly lightheaded and rub my forehead. When I look up, light from every color imaginable shines around me. I inhale deeply, smelling homemade cookies. Over the din of the police searching Richard's vehicle, I swear I hear a creek burbling over rocks. I'm overwhelmed with peace, feeling everything in me relax. I close my eyes against the beauty and rub a hand over my chest.

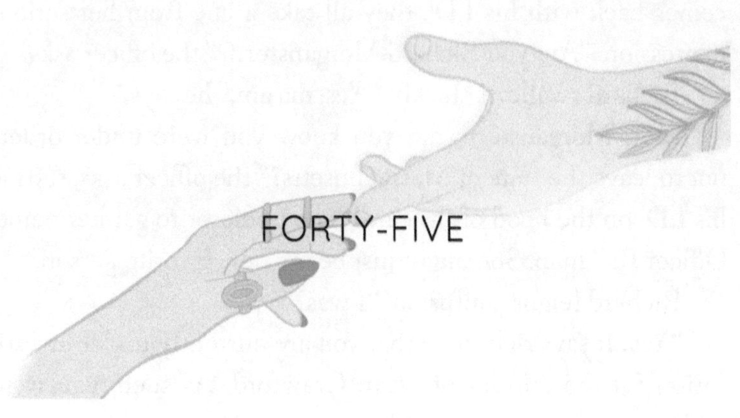

# FORTY-FIVE

WREN GRUMBLES UNDER HER BREATH, searching the dining table for the puzzle piece she needs. We're putting together a 1,000-piece jigsaw puzzle featuring a spooky bookstore, and she's working on the cash register with a black cat perched on top.

She insisted on doing this, saying my nervous energy was, and I quote, "the most aggressive shade of tangerine," she's ever seen. This is supposed to calm me down or distract me, or some other such nonsense. As if hearing Wren curse the family line of whoever invented puzzles is relaxing.

It's almost eleven at night, and Dean still hasn't checked in. Jack called me a couple of hours ago letting me know that Richard had been arrested in New Hampshire, but that he doesn't have any more details yet.

I click another puzzle piece in place, making steady progress on my corner. Our strategy when we do puzzles together is to start at opposite ends and meet in the middle. We used to build a lot of puzzles growing up. It was our Saturday morning activity, and our parents suggested this strategy so we would stop arguing over who does what. It worked, for the most part.

After Wren and I press the final piece down together (another remnant from childhood), I sit back, popping my aching neck.

"He's going to be back soon. You know that, right?" Wren asks, reaching her arms overhead in a stretch.

"I know. I'm not worried about Dean, really. Nothing can hurt him now. But what if he moved on?" I say with a sigh, thoughts racing.

She stands and shuffles into her kitchen to grab a glass of water. "Let's be honest, do you really think Dean would leave you without at least saying goodbye? That guy is so into you, it's almost sickening," she says after downing her glass.

"It's possible that he couldn't control it. Once he's completed his unfinished business, it's very hard to resist moving on. It goes against nature," I state, running my hands over the finished puzzle in front of me.

Wren grunts, knowing it's pointless to argue with me about this. She sits next to me, wrapping her surprisingly strong arm around my shoulders and engulfing me in her coffee and cinnamon scent. "Let's watch one of your dumb shows. It'll distract you," she states, reaching for her remote. She turns on the TV and easily navigates to one of my "dumb shows."

"Huh, that's odd. I didn't watch the third season over here with you," I say slyly when I notice the "already watched" banner across the previous season of *Love on the Slopes*, a reality TV show about ski resort workers who are always in and out of relationships or friendships with each other and their high-profile guests. Last season had a huge scandal because one of the leads started seeing a production assistant on the side. It was very messy and *very* entertaining. I don't blame Wren for watching it without me, although I will start giving her shit the next time she complains about it.

"So weird. I think my TV is possessed," she says quickly, clicking on the first episode of season four.

"I wonder if that blonde guy is going to be back on the show," I say, leaning forward as the upbeat, royalty-free music starts along with a recap montage of the last season.

"I don't think so. I haven't seen anything about him in any of the pre-season interviews," Wren says absently, smoothing her black throw blanket over her lap.

I bite my lip instead of shouting "Gotcha!" Wren would probably break her TV out of spite if I brought it up.

The episode is nearly over when Dean appears suddenly, grinning like a manic quokka. "They got him," he says simply before falling to the floor and splaying out like a starfish in front of Wren's TV.

I look down at Dean and ask hopefully, "They figured it out?" The relief at seeing him in front of me is nearly more than I can bare. My whole goal has been to help him move on, but I am so selfishly relieved that he hasn't yet. How much longer can I make this last?

Dean draws my attention back to him when he says, "Get this." He sits up faster than my eyes can process and continues, "He made it all the way to New Hampshire before he got pulled over. Okay, well, first there was a police chase—"

"What!?" I exclaim, jumping to my feet. Wren looks at me

curiously, and I promise to translate for her once I know the details.

Dean stands in front of me, warm-brown eyes crinkled with mirth. "I know! So he was originally going to get pulled over for littering. He threw a Gatorade bottle full of, well, *not* Gatorade out his window," he says with a grimace.

He grabs my hand, interlacing our fingers together absently and continues, "I think he knew that if he got pulled over, they would have seen that he wasn't supposed to leave the state, so he panicked." He goes on to explain all about the police chase, and he (oddly) has a lot to say about cows. I've always thought they were kind of cute, but he's insistent on how creepy they are.

"Why didn't you come once they arrested him?" I ask, not able to keep the accusatory tone out of my voice.

His smile ticks mischievously, and he says, "I wanted to watch him get booked. I also went back while they were searching the car and saw them find a burner phone under the passenger seat. They were getting a search warrant for the phone and laptop he brought with him. When they informed him, he immediately started sweating, so I feel pretty good about them finding something on there." I relay the gist of what he said to Wren while we all get comfortable on her sectional again.

"So now it's just more waiting," I say with a tired sigh.

"Hurry up and wait," Dean agrees.

"I say we should get some sleep," Wren says with a yawn. "Nothing interesting will happen until the morning anyway."

"I'm not sleeping on this couch," I say, standing up again. "I'll drive home. See you tomorrow." I have made the mistake of not going home only a few times. Wren has had this couch since she first moved out, and it was our parents' before that. I'm fairly sure I still have a spring-shaped indent on my back from the last time I slept over.

Wren states, "Suit yourself. Let me know what happens?"

"Of course," I reply, shrugging into my jacket.

---

DEAN and I are lying on our backs, moonlight playing across bared skin, fingers entwined atop messy sheets. I scan him, noting the slight glow his skin gives off, and heave a contented sigh. I never thought I'd find someone like him. Someone who feels like they're made just for me. Whose angles line up perfectly with mine, like we were designed with the other in mind. In a lot of ways, we're nothing alike, but I think that's what makes it feel so right. He's soft where I've been hardened, light where I feel heavy.

"What are you thinking about?" he asks, voice rumbling into the quiet of the night.

"You. Us, I guess," I say, tracing his hand with a gentle fingertip, committing the grooves and ridges to memory.

"Yeah?" he asks. I smile, thinking that this is the true magic of Dean. He never makes me feel like he's pushing me off some emotional cliff, but he somehow walks me right up to the edge without my noticing. Suddenly, I'm staring down at the vast canyon, and he's right there, ready to leap with me.

I swallow around the silly anxiety bubbling in my chest. "Yeah."

"Do you want to know what I was thinking?" He asks, capturing my hand and bringing it to his lips for a tingling kiss. I make a noise of assent, and he tugs me closer, so we're chest to chest and can look each other in the eye. "I was thinking that I need to expand my vocabulary."

I laugh a little. "Mm I don't know about that. You're already pretty verbose."

He feathers his fingertips along my side, and I laugh harder. "Hush," he admonishes. "I can't help that law school taught me big words."

"So why do you need a bigger vocabulary?" I ask, running a thumb across his ever-present five o'clock shadow.

His eyes soften. "Because I've been trying to figure out how to tell you how much I love you so that it makes sense to you. I can feel my tie to the world has been severed now that Richard is practically case closed. I felt the light, like what you were talking about with Rebecca. It smelled like my mom's homemade peanut butter cookies, and I almost followed it. But I don't want to go, Rae. I want to be here with you. I may not *have* to stay anymore, but I want to. I choose you in this lifetime and the next. Over and over, I'll choose you." My breath hitches in my chest, and he presses a finger to my lips. "I'm no Shakespeare, but give me a chance to tell you why this is the right thing?" he asks, searching my face.

I nod, blinking back tears, so he says, "Finding out you're dead is a fairly traumatic experience, you know. But the funny thing is, it hasn't felt that way. Even though we've been investigating my murder, it's just been... Fun. I haven't had fun in so long, Rae. My life was one monotonous day after another.

I felt like I *had* to be a lawyer, and I *had* to have all this fancy shit. I didn't even know what I wanted out of life other than that I wanted to make my dad proud. He's a good man, and I've always looked up to him. But I wasn't happy walking around in his shoes. Death might have been the best thing to happen to me."

"Are you nuts?" I ask, half-seriously.

He glares at me playfully. "No. Don't get me wrong—I'm furious that I died so young. But also, if I hadn't, I would have been promoted. And that would have been a kind of death too. I would have kept living an unhappy life full of expectation and working late nights.

In death, I got to get close to you in a way that would have been impossible if I had stayed alive. I got to fall for you. I got to see you like I've never seen another person. All the soft parts you try to hide, the way you help people even when it's hard. How driven you are. How much those around you love you. Death took down that barrier for us. I've never felt closer to another person. Being removed from the world gave me a clarity I didn't know I needed. A new meaning." He tucks an errant lock of hair behind my ear, letting his fingertips linger against the underside of my jaw.

"Oh?" I ask, gently prodding him to get to the point. Not that I'm impatiently waiting on his second declaration of love or anything.

Definitely not.

"You," he murmurs, tracing his finger along my cheek. "You're my new meaning, Rae. Every time I make you laugh, I feel an answering light turn on in my chest. Every time I kiss you, my heart feels like it's trying to beat outside of my ribs so you can hold it closer. Whenever you're in my arms, I feel at home. You're everything to me. You've carved a perfectly Rae-shaped hole in my heart, and it won't beat properly unless you're there, too."

"Technically, your heart doesn't beat anymore at all. Or at

least, the one buried six-feet down doesn't," I can't help but point out with a smile.

He laughs, and I ride the wave of his chest rising and falling, mesmerized by his dimple and the flash of white teeth in the moonlight. "Okay, I'll give you that one. But the point is, my *metaphorical* heart is yours if you'll have it," he says.

"Well, you already have mine, so it seems only fair," I reply, leaning down and pressing a kiss over his sternum.

"You sure? I don't share, Alderwood. We've already been over this. So if you're mine, that's it. It won't exactly be conventional." He has the audacity to look unsure.

I laugh. "What part of my life is conventional anyway? I run an oddities and occult shop with my crazy aunt. Every woman in my family has extra-sensory abilities. *And* I frequently commune with the dead. A white picket fence has never been part of the plan."

He tilts his head a little and asks, "So you don't want kids?"

I shudder. "No. They're great and all, but not for me. I'm about as maternal as a hamster."

"Don't they eat their babies?"

I bare my teeth. "Exactly."

"You're ridiculous," he says, flopping his head back on the pillow.

"I prefer the term: having a deep sense of self."

We lie in the specific, nearly complete quiet of two AM in a small town. My head rests on his chest, and my eyelids feel like they're slowly filling with lead, getting heavier and heavier by the second. "You know," I say sleepily. "I love you too. You make me feel seen and precious. No one's ever done that for me before."

"I know. I can sense your emotions, remember?" Dean says,

rubbing a soothing hand up my spine. I catch the edge of his smile before my eyes slide shut, and I burrow deeper in his chest, thinking about how nice this would be to have forever. That I might get to find out.

I grumble something drowsily about know-it-alls and slide under the tide of sleep that finally crashes over me.

# FORTY-SIX

MY EYES OPEN TO DISORIENTING, complete darkness. It presses in on me from all sides, caressing my skin like a lover saying hello after a long absence. I blink hard, trying to force my eyes to see through the infinite black.

How did I get here? I can tell I'm standing, but my senses are completely deprived otherwise. The space could be four-square-feet or have no borders. It's impossible to tell. I feel like prey waiting for a much larger predator to snatch me out of the dark.

I take a tentative step forward and am instantly even more disoriented. I have the sense that I've stepped over a vast distance. I hold my hand out in front of me and, for the first time, notice a faint glow coming off my skin, instantly distracting me.

*Oh, shit. Am I dead?*

I immediately start cataloguing my body, running my hands over my face, my arms. Everything feels intact, but something isn't right. I'm not supposed to be here. I'm struck with a sudden, breathtaking terror.

Spinning in a slow circle, I try to find something that sticks out—some way to judge where I am or where I'm supposed to go. My eyes ache from trying to focus on things that aren't there, so I close them. I breathe in deeply, the total absence of scent distracting me. I shake my head and concentrate, unfurling my extra sense slowly, the way you tentatively reach a hand out to test if a pan or dish is still hot.

It's only when I settle into my ever-expanding net do I realize I've been here before. Okay, well, not *here* here, but sort of. It's like going from a deep-sea fisherman to a deep-sea diver. Where before I would cast my line into the ocean, now I'm a part of the deep.

It takes no time at all for me to feel Dean. His presence immediately calms me. I reach out to him and find him suddenly in front of me, glowing faintly. "Rae? What are you doing here?" He asks, pulling me towards him.

I shrug and use my voice for what feels like the first time in a thousand years, "I don't know. I just sort of woke up here."

"Oh god, you're not dead, are you?" Dean asks, running his hands over me fretfully. "I'll be right back," he says, disappearing in a burst of light that somehow makes the ensuing dark seem even more complete.

I sigh, crossing my arms over my t-shirt-clad chest. I look down at it, noting the familiar hole along the cuff of the right sleeve.

*Huh, this is what I was wearing last night...*

Before I can follow that train of thought, I'm interrupted. "Okay, good news: You're not dead. Bad news, you may be in a coma?" Dean says, appearing with a pop in front of me again. "I just went back to your room. You just fell asleep like a second ago, but I felt you calling me here, so I came."

Suddenly, it all makes sense. "I'm astral projecting. This is the ether," I say with wonder.

"Woah, how'd you do that?" Dean asks.

I laugh giddily. "I have no clue!" I grab Dean's hand and force him to spin me in a circle. "Part of why I've been so hesitant about the tether is because I wasn't sure I could even get here. I've never done this before. The grimoire didn't exactly leave explicit instructions. I wonder if whatever is calling you to move on pulled me here by association as well."

"So we're doing it? The tether?" Dean asks, his whole heart audible in the tenor of his voice.

"If you still want to," I say, suddenly shy.

"Hmm, do I want to be tied to the love of my life for the rest of forever?" He taps his chin sarcastically before answering, "Of course I do, Alderwood. You're it for me." His tone softens like melted butter.

I feel my stupid little jelly heart wobble excitedly at the thought. "Okay. Forever sounds like a pretty good deal," I reply, the traitorous organ pounding against my ribs.

Dean reaches for me, and I go willingly. He pulls me close and touches his forehead to mine, arms cradling me familiarly. "So what now?" he asks, the faint glow of his skin making his smile that much more radiant.

"Give me a second," I murmur, closing my eyes and turning inward. The grimoire said something about a soul tether, so I swim deeper and deeper, looking for my effervescent center. The thing that makes me *me*. I'm vaguely aware of Dean still holding me, and my hand covering my heart of its own will.

All at once, it's in front of my mind's eye: the color of the moon with a shifting and whirling surface. I reach out and caress it with my senses, feeling a profound sense of love and awe.

With the hand of my mind's eye on what can only be called my soul, I see a rapid flash of my best moments. The things that make me who I am. Laughing with Wren when we wrapped our parents' whole bedroom in wrapping paper for Christmas one year. Even down to their toothbrushes. Being cradled in my mom's arms as an infant, feeling nothing but contentment. Sharing my dad's lap with my sister when we were young, while he read us *Winnie the Pooh*. Helping countless spirits cross over. Being given my favorite mug as a reminder. Making The Veil as successful as I can. Holding hands with Dean for the first time. Falling in love with Dean. Being willing to give him up, even though I knew it would crush me.

Then I see all the things that hurt, but there's the sense of watching them from a distance, so they don't sting as much. Scraped knees and hurt feelings as a child. Being called a freak and ostracized by my middle school friends. Turning away from anyone who wasn't family for fear of being turned away first. Distancing myself from the potential of love to protect myself. The fear of losing the store. The fear of being alone indefinitely. The fear that there is something fundamentally wrong with me that makes me unlovable.

I can't tell if I'm actually crying, but my eyes burn like I am. My soul takes me deeper, showing me and Dean from start to finish. That first date, chatting in Brewed Awakening with the sense that *this could be it*. The hurt when I thought he left me high and dry for no reason. The shock and grief when I realized what had happened. The determination to help him.

The ensuing months, holding each other up and being each

other's soft place to land. Falling for each other in the small moments we spent time together, making each other laugh. The tender moments where we shone light on our darkest parts. Curling around each other like two vines that learned that the other was the sunlight. Seeing each other the way no one else had.

I luxuriate in the feeling of loving and being loved by this man, caressing my soul in thanks for showing me the highlights. My fingers catch on what feels like a silken thread. I grip it instinctively and begin slowly pulling it out. My eyes flutter open at the ticklish sensation behind my sternum. I look down to see a silvery thread wrapped around my finger and thumb while I pull it out slowly.

"Holy shit," Dean gasps, taking a small step back to give me room. "Are you okay?" he asks, watching as I pull until the length of thread is as long as my arm.

"Yes. Come here," I say quietly, reverently. I take his hands in mine instinctively, bringing them together between our chests. I watch as the thread loops and winds its way around our clasped hands as if it has a mind of its own.

We watch as the luminescence of the thread begins to pulse, growing brighter and brighter until it flashes so bright it stings my eyes. I close them protectively, and when I open them again, the thread is gone. I watch as glowing lines creep up Dean's forearms, lighting up the intricate network of his veins. They push upwards towards his heart, where they finally coalesce. His whole chest glows so bright, I can see the outline of his ribcage like a reverse X-ray. He gasps, squeezing my hands and dropping to his knees.

"Dean?" I ask, panicked. His hands tremble in mine, and it's only then do I notice the static touch I've become so used to is gone. His skin just feels like skin, no layer of static charge to be found.

He breathes out hard. "I'm okay. Sorry, it just felt like my chest was on fire for a minute there. I'm good," he says breathlessly.

I come to my knees in front of him, the dark a soft cushion beneath me. I take him in my arms, hugging him tight, my eyes screwed shut against the onslaught of emotions. Out of curiosity, I release my senses and find that I can see a literal tether connecting him to me. A delicate, luminescent line between us.

I feel lightheaded with relief that I never have to let him go again.

"I can feel you here," he says gruffly, rubbing his knuckles over his sternum.

I place my hand over his and then put his other hand over my heart. "Me too," I say with a happy sigh.

"Forever?" he asks, mouth ticking up in a dimple-inducing smile.

"And even after," I reply.

And then I reach for him. Or he reaches for me. I can't be sure which because it happens at once, simultaneously. I revel in the feel of his skin on mine. The press of his lips against my own, my jaw, my collarbone. His hands sliding along my back under the t-shirt, and the hard press of him between my legs. He's everywhere. Everything. Both my undoing and the thing that sews me back together.

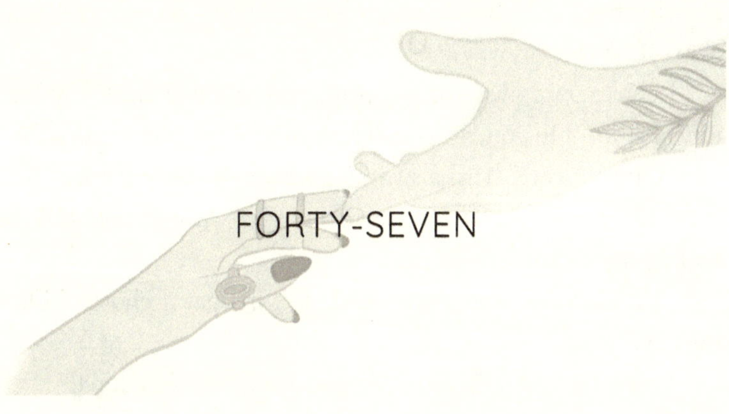

# FORTY-SEVEN

"SO, your souls banged and then you did?" Wren clarifies for Misha and Felix, shoving a soggy fry into her mouth.

"I mean, okay, I guess you can phrase it that way," I say indignantly, thinking it was actually much more profound than that, but that's unfortunately pretty much the gist of it.

"Cool." She nods agreeably and tucks her legs under her.

"I for one think that's the most romantic thing I've ever heard," Misha says, plopping on the other side of his dark gray sectional. This is the first time we've all hung out, but it definitely won't be the last. Misha acts as a natural shield between Wren and me, and I appreciate it too much to let him go now.

"Why don't you tether your soul to mine?" Felix asks grumpily, sitting close to Misha so they can share their bowl of popcorn.

"I'm afraid that's not in my skillset, my love," Misha replies with a laugh. "But hey, I did get you a very nice ring," he points out, tapping a nail on the gold band adorning Felix's ring finger.

Felix shrugs his slight shoulders amicably. "Yeah, okay." He rests his head on Misha's much larger bicep. "So, where is your ghost husband anyway?"

I choke on a piece of popcorn, and Wren pounds my back until I stop. "Oh god, don't call him that," I get out eventually.

"Ghost lover?" Misha supplies with a shit-eating grin.

I bury my face in one of their very nice throw pillows, feeling my entire face flame.

"I prefer the term ghost husband, if I get a choice," Dean says in my ear.

I turn my head a bit so I can glare at him. "You don't."

"Um, who is she talking to?" Felix asks Wren.

"Dean," Wren says tiredly. Now that we have this connection, it's easier for her to be around him. He's more visible to her, so it's less of a headache. My aura almost acts like glasses when she looks at him.

I sit up and take the handheld whiteboard and marker out of my bag at my feet and hand it to Dean. He begins writing, his neat, condensed script flying over the board.

"Woah," Misha and Felix exclaim together, watching the board hover and marker write seemingly on its own.

Dean flips it around: Hey guys, I'm Dean. Please do refer to me as Ghost Husband. Even if it annoys Rae. Actually, especially if it annoys her.

I push his shoulder while they all laugh. "Pest," I chide lightly while he uses the eraser on the marker cap to wipe the board. This was the best workaround for him to communicate with everyone else now that he's so strong. Before, he struggled with anything fine motor, so writing legibly on his own wasn't possible.

We tested it for the first time last week when we had a celebratory family dinner with his parents and siblings and their partners. Dean's murder has officially been solved. Richard had gone on the dark web to find a hitman, thinking that he'd be able to get away with it more easily. Richard drugged Dean at the office, and then the hitman, one Carver Bingham, lay in wait in Dean's garage. Apparently, Dean wasn't his first victim, but Richard was his first stupid client who didn't do enough to cover his tracks.

Bingham was attempting to extort Richard into taking the full blame because he was worried the investigation was getting too close to him. That's what ultimately spooked Richard into running in the first place. Bingham had sent him threatening messages, and Richard figured he'd take his chances over the border rather than stay a sitting duck for a historically lethal hitman. Now both men are behind bars with murder and conspiracy to commit murder charges, among others.

Good riddance.

All four of the male Crawford progenies look exactly like their dad, with threads of their mom woven in. It was like seeing Dean in different life stages if he had chosen different paths. It was a little awkward at first because Jack and Marielle hadn't told his siblings about me (understandably).

So, having to explain the whole complicated backstory and having Dean chime in with his handy whiteboard was interesting to say the least. By the end of the night, Dean was so quick with it, it was hardly noticeable that his contributions came in the form of an Expo marker and an increasingly grubby whiteboard.

They all talked over each other, shouting questions and jokes. I left the dinner with my head pounding but my heart full. By the end of the night, they folded me into the Crawford family like I'd always belonged. I can see why Dean loves them so much.

Dean is really excited that he doesn't have to give up his relationship with his family. It's not the same, but he can still be with them, too. When I told Jack and Marielle about the tether, Mari immediately began crying and thanking me. She wanted him to move on, but if that wasn't his choice, she was happy he could stick around in a more permanent way.

So, yeah. The whiteboard is great. Except when Dean used it to ask his parents to give me his house without my permission. That wasn't cool.

Jack grinned so widely, I thought his face would split in half at the suggestion. "Of course. Of course, you two should have the house," he had said. When I tried to argue, he folded his arms across his chest and said, "It's his house, Rae. If the man wants to move back in and have you there too, I'm not going to argue with him. You could say it's his dying wish."

"He's already dead!" I pointed out, not thrilled with being ganged up on.

"Exactly!" Mari wailed and promptly burst into tears, washing away any argument I had left. It's been a week, and I'm beginning to think the tears were a ploy. And yet, this weekend I'm set to move my stuff into Dean's place.

Mari and Jack refuse to let me pay for anything, even utilities. They were insistent that those would be paid from what Dean left them. They're demanding that I view it as a gift for helping solve Dean's murder. While I'll never admit it, I am so grateful they're strongarming me into it. I'll miss my apartment, but the money from renting it out should be enough to save the store. At least for a while.

"Earth to Rae," Wren says, waving her hand in front of my face.

"Sorry, I was just thinking about all the crap I have left to pack." Which isn't a complete lie; I have to pack my whole kitchen and bathroom still. I shudder at the thought of having to put together another box. There's a reason I haven't moved more than once in my adult life.

"Oh boohoo, you have to move into a big, giant, fabulous house," Misha says with an exaggerated pout, chucking a piece of popcorn at me.

Dean laughs next to me. "You make it sound like I'm kidnapping you," he says, prodding my side.

"Oh, it's entirely against my will," I deadpan to the room.

"Whatever. I'm moving in if my rent goes up again," Wren states, picking the piece of popcorn out of my hair and eating it like the heathen she is.

"I'm not sure the house has a basement, so you'd probably burn with all of the natural light," I quip.

"Oh look, a vampire joke, and it only took thirty minutes," Wren bites back.

"So, how about *Love on the Slopes*? It's supposed to be an extra-long episode tonight," Felix interjects.

I look at him gratefully and nod, snuggling into Dean's side. I don't often feel very lucky, but sitting here with these people around me makes me feel like I've stumbled into the best luck of my life.

# FORTY-EIGHT

## SIX MONTHS LATER

MY TOES WIGGLE into the sun-warmed sand, and I lounge back against my beach towel. This is the most skin I've exposed for public consumption since Alana Ruthen's sweet-sixteen pool party. I was invited as a joke and didn't find out until *after* my clothes came off. Good times.

The heated look in Dean's eye is enough to shake the decades-old embarrassment loose. "Stop looking at me like that," I say, pushing up my oversized sunglasses and peering at him in his low-slung board shorts.

"Like what?" he says to my cleavage.

"Like you're going to ravage me on this very public beach full of the elderly," I say, biting back a smile.

"I'm invisible. If you're quiet, I can taste you right here," he says, voice roughened.

A zing of heat shoots between my legs at the thought, but... "I don't think so. I'm not one for exhibitionism. Even less so when the viewers are my elderly aunt's neighbors." I chuck my swimsuit cover-up over my torso so he doesn't get any ideas, laughing at his despondent expression.

Aunt Clarissa has been an official resident of Sunset Village for one month, and predictably, she's causing chaos. Many of the nurses and community aids have already shared stories of Aunt C's antics. Good to see she's not letting old age stop her. Apparently, she leads an unsanctioned, nude sunrise yoga on Fridays. The other residents love it so much that management has agreed to look the other way.

Wren and her sun phobia are back with the rest of my family in Aunt C's cottage, catching a midday nap. I decided to sneak out and get some beach time by myself while I could. I love my family, but it's a really small cottage, and if I had to listen to Wren snore for one more second, I probably would have smothered her with the seahorse-print throw pillow I've been sleeping on at night.

"I miss being alone with you," he sighs.

"It's only been a couple of days," I reply, thankful that this stretch of beach is mostly empty, so I can chat with Dean easily. While I'm beyond hiding my Gift in Ravenwood, the rest of the world isn't ready to believe in ghosts yet.

"I'm having withdrawals," Dean groans, throwing himself back on the sand. One of my favorite things about Dean is that he dresses for the occasion, even though he's impervious to the weather changes, and that I'm the only one who sees him. My favorite are still his suits, which he thankfully keeps on a pretty constant rotation, just for me. Although, Dean in board shorts and nothing else is a close second.

"They do say absence makes the heart grow fonder," I say, lying on my side and facing him, using my arm as a pillow.

He copies me, lining up so we're face to face. "If I were any fonder of you, Alderwood, it would need to be a case study. It's already clinical. It's not normal to love everything about a person the way I love you," he says, smiling a little.

"You do not love everything about me. That's impossible," I counter, thinking about the way he piled all of my wet towels that I had left on the floor onto my side of the bed. We have very different definitions of "clean." Or the way I keep trying to "lose" money at his parents' house so I can pay them at least a little without them realizing it. I know I drive him at least a little crazy.

"I do. Even the imperfect stuff, or the things that make us different," he states, looking out at the horizon line where the deep blue of the ocean meets the candy blue of the sky. "I think I love those things even more, to be honest. It's a reminder that we chose each other, I guess. It's always felt easy with you, like breathing, but even when I want to trip you with your wet towel, it just feels fun. I even love the way you wake up grumpy every single morning, no matter how much sleep you get," he says with an affectionate laugh.

"Well, mornings are objectively the worst," I argue with a sniff.

He inclines his head in agreement, kicking his foot out so his leg is entwined with mine, and we lie in silence for a little while, soaking in the heat of the sand below us and the steady whoosh of the ocean ahead of us. It's amazing how much more Dean can experience now with the tether. When we're touching, he can fully feel the world around him. No more blanket of ether between him and the environment.

In moments like this, he makes it a point to maintain contact so he can feel the sun on his face again and the supportive hand of the earth beneath him. I knew he'd want to soak this in, so that was another reason to come out here alone. I get so happy watching him just be. His joy is the pitcher that fills my cup. And with someone like Dean, that pitcher is endless.

---

"RAE BABY! LOOK AT THAT TAN!" Aunt Clarissa exclaims from across the dinner table.

I peer down at my lobster-red chest. "I think you mean burn," I say with a laugh, touching the sore skin on my collarbone with a wince.

"And that's why I have beef with the sun," Wren states matter-of-factly, scooping some tofu taco filling into the tortillas on her plate.

"Right. Definitely not because you'd melt or anything," I say, nodding sagely.

"You'd better watch it, Rae, or you might wake up tomorrow without any eyelashes," she goads, making a snipping motion with her free hand.

"Well, that's an unsettling threat," Dean says from his place on my side. My family has lovingly (and a little ridiculously) given him a place setting, plate and all, to my right. They've accepted him with open arms, and Aunt C in particular is absolutely titillated by our relationship. She hasn't let me forget that she's the one who urged me on last year. I miss her most of the time, but I think the distance is for the best. She'd be at our house constantly otherwise.

"Girls," our mom and Aunt C chime, giving eerily similar looks of warning on their faces.

We both sigh and go back to being mostly polite, only

getting into a kicking fight under the table once when I casually brought up Julian to our parents. Their following inquisition was *so* entertaining. I'll have a bruise on my ankle tomorrow. Worth it.

Dad launches into a detailed description of his plans to manage a new store, and I listen raptly. I've been toying around with the idea of starting an honest-to-goodness medium business where I travel around to help people out. While it's a different idea than my dad's, he always has valuable insight.

I love The Veil, but lately I've been feeling the itch to start something on my own. My mom had mentioned seeing me in one of her dreams; I was on a plane, zipping from location to location. It made me want to find a new adventure.

That petition to lower the rent increase finally passed a couple of months ago. We all had to refuse to pay any increase for multiple months before Mr. Beauhurst gave in. I guess he figured he would lose money trying to find businesses to replace an entire street. Things are still tight, but it's given everyone a bit of breathing room.

Lenore has taken over a lot of my managerial duties, leaving me time to do my medium work around town most of the day. After that business owner's meeting, I started to have a trickle and then a flood of people looking for me to help them talk to their loved ones. Julian's parents were my first house call. His dad was right; their house was totally haunted. His great aunt had a lot to say about how they renovated her house.

It's been very fulfilling to help people and have them know it was me. Not having to hide behind a curtain and a false name is oddly rewarding. Sure, I've gotten some weird looks, and some of the mean girls from high school turned WASPs give me a wide berth at the grocery store these days, but that's okay. I'm not for everyone, and I like it that way.

For the first time in thirty years, I finally feel at peace with who I am. I don't feel the need to run from it anymore. And that's the greatest gift of all.

# EPILOGUE
## MANY, MANY YEARS LATER

WREN'S GNARLED, arthritic hand curls against my own, our papery skin whispering together as we hold on as tightly as we can. Labored breathing is the only audible sound in the room. The doctor turned off the ventilator a while ago, so the incessant beeping that had blended into the background for me is finally gone.

Death should be coming anytime now, but I'm not afraid. I've seen what's on the other side more than most. I know what awaits us all.

*Sort of.*

"I love you, you crazy old bat, you know that?" Wren's voice shakes with the admission. She's rarely sentimental, but she's gotten soft in her old age.

I soak in the feel of her hand in mine, and those familiar blue eyes lined with a roadmap of a life well-lived. Even though I know I'll love where I'm going, it'll never feel quite like this again.

I take a breath in that feels like trying to breathe underwater and whisper, "I know." Another painful breath in as the room starts to darken at the edges. "I love you, too. See you later." Two full sentences nearly deplete my energy reserve, but I have one more thing to say to my stubborn little sister who has always wanted to follow me everywhere and protect me from the world: "Take your time, though. Okay?"

I can feel myself slipping, every string holding me to this elderly, broken body snapping one by one. I wait for her agreement, holding tightly to the last few ties. When she nods, I release the last feeble breath in my lungs, allowing myself to fall into the enveloping dark.

"I'VE BEEN WAITING FOR YOU," Dean says, his ever-present smile pulling at his cheeks. He reaches his hand out to mine, and when I take it, light seeps around us. It fills the dark like a warm bath. With Dean by my side, I sink slowly into it, swearing I can taste hot chocolate on my tongue.

"You ready?" I ask Dean, taking a full, painless breath for the first time in months.

"Always," he replies, tugging me forward into the brilliant light of forever.

## A NOTE FROM THE AUTHOR

Hello again, dear reader! I hope you enjoyed Ghosted. If you did, please consider leaving a review. Like any indie author, word-of-mouth is one of the main ways I reach new readers. Every time you tell someone about my book or share a post online about it, you're helping more than you know!

I read all positive reviews because it gives me so much joy to know that my words took up a little real estate in your heart. I hope that Rae's self-discovery was something that you could relate to, or at least cheer on, and that her and Dean gave you all the warm and fuzzies—and a few laughs, too. They are my favorite couple so far, and it makes me sad to leave them here on the page.

If you would like to leave a review and you're on an e-reader, here's a link to do so. If you're reading this via paperback, please consider grabbing your phone or laptop and dropping a review on your favorite sites—Goodreads, StoryGraph, etc. As well as Amazon, if you're able. I am endlessly grateful to you for reading this book (presumably to the end) and for leaving a review. Thanks a bunch!

—Megan

# ACKNOWLEDGMENTS

Wow, how am I here writing acknowledgements again? As usual, I'm going to preface this by saying, "I'M BAD AT THIS," so if I get long-winded, forgive me.

First and foremost, I have to thank my husband for always encouraging me and supporting me while I write. You may never read my books, babe, but the fact that you listen to me while I bounce plot ideas off of you means so much. I hope one day I can have my books on audio so I can watch them make you blush in real time. Thanks for being the reason I can only write about supportive, wonderful men. I don't know any different, and that's all thanks to you.

I would be remiss if I didn't thank James, my best friend's husband for answering all of my questions regarding police work and procedure. While I'm sure I bent reality to fit my fictional world, I appreciate you being willing to answer my frequent questions and allowing me to pick your brain. You helped give this very fantastical story a dose of realism, so thank you!

I also have to thank my mom and my in-laws for watching the kids for me whenever I asked. You three are the reason I was able to get this story done as quickly as possible. Your support while I reach for my dreams means the world.

Next, I'd like to thank my friend, Kellie (@sisters_reading

on Instagram), for pushing me to write this book! If it weren't for your enthusiastic encouragement, Rae and Dean would have stayed a small snippet in *Like Home*. Thank you for always being one of my biggest hype-women.

I couldn't do these acknowledgments without thanking my wonderful friend and PA, Emily. Thank you for helping me manage all of the things so I can keep writing. You keep my head on straight and my deadlines on track, and for that, I will always be grateful!

To my editor and name twin, Megan Carver, thank you endlessly for making my words shine. Without you, this story would have endless comma issues and *so many* eyes looking around. You are a joy to work with, and I appreciate your humor and kindness just as much as your ability to raze a sentence to the ground and rebuild it.

For my beta readers, Cass, Sofi, Rebecca, Codi, Andrea, and Kellie, thank you so much for lending me your time and your brains. You all helped make Ghosted what it is, so thank you!

Lastly, thank you so much to YOU, my readers, for picking up this book and reading it all the way to the end. Thank you to all the people who shout about my books online, whether that's Instagram, or TikTok, or somewhere else. You guys are the reason I get to keep doing this, and why I get to have a blast while doing so. Forehead kisses for you. Mwah!

# ABOUT THE AUTHOR

Megan Bowen is an author of feel-good romance with complex characters and swoon-worthy moments. She prefers her stories with a lot of heart and a little heat. Megan lives in a small town with her high school sweetheart and two children.

Check out her website and sign up for her newsletter for all updates on future projects www.authormeganbowen.com